SAD PENINSULA

SAD PENINSULA

....

MARK SAMPSON

DUNDURN
TORONTO

Editor: Shannon Whibbs
Design: Jennifer Gallinger
Cover image: © neomistyle/iStock
Author photo by Ken Phipps
Cover design by Courtney Horner
Printer: Webcom

Library and Archives Canada Cataloguing in Publication

Sampson, Mark, 1975-, author
        Sad peninsula / Mark Sampson.

Issued in print and electronic formats.
ISBN 978-1-4597-0925-6 (pbk.).--ISBN 978-1-4597-0926-3 (pdf).-- ISBN 978-1-4597-0927-0 (epub)

I. Title.

PS8637.A53853S23 2014   C813'.6   C2013-908351-0   C2013-908352-9

1   2   3   4   5   18   17   16   15   14

 Conseil des Arts du Canada   Canada Council for the Arts Canada  ONTARIO ARTS COUNCIL
CONSEIL DES ARTS DE L'ONTARIO
an Ontario government agency
un organisme du gouvernement de l'Ontario

We acknowledge the support of the Canada Council for the Arts and the Ontario Arts Council for our publishing program. We also acknowledge the financial support of the Government of Canada through the Canada Book Fund and Livres Canada Books, and the Government of Ontario through the Ontario Book Publishing Tax Credit and the Ontario Media Development Corporation.

Visit us at
Dundurn.com | @dundurnpress | Facebook.com/dundurnpress | Pinterest.com/Dundurnpress

Dundurn	Gazelle Book Services Limited	Dundurn
3 Church Street, Suite 500	White Cross Mills	2250 Military Road
Toronto, Ontario, Canada	High Town, Lancaster, England	Tonawanda, NY
M5E 1M2	LA1 4XS	U.S.A. 14150

Dedicated to 2LT Gerald Arthur Moore

Author's Note

This is a work of fiction. Any rendering of actual people — living or dead — is coincidental or done strictly for the purposes of fiction. Astute readers may notice I have taken certain liberties with Korean naming conventions. Some may also know that Koreans measure their ages differently than we do here in the West; but I have transmuted those measurements into the Western standard so as not to confuse English-speaking readers.

"When you look into a Korean woman's eyes/ you want to stare/ at something far back/ dark,/ older even than the whole, sad peninsula."

— Tom Crawford, from the poem "Stones,"
published in *The Temple on Monday*

"A man's sexual aim ... is to convert a creature who is cool, dry, calm, articulate, independent, purposeful into a creature that is the opposite of these; to demonstrate to an animal which is pretending not to be an animal that it is an animal."

— Kingsley Amis, from
One Fat Englishman

PART 1

. . . .

SAME SAME, BUT DIFFERENT

CHAPTER 1

On an afternoon in August, Meiko lay on her mat straining to hear the sound of girls being raped all around her — and when she couldn't, convinced herself that she had finally died.

Meiko had been waiting to die for months now, for death to burst through the thin rug that covered her stall door and rescue her with the chivalry of an older brother. Death, she imagined, would not enter this cubicle like the soldiers did, day after day. Death would be tender. It would lift her softly into the air, float her like a piece of chaff on the wind, out and over the camp, above the burning hillsides of Manchuguo, and carry her away, as if on a river, to a place of incomparable silence.

But now, soundlessness had betrayed her. At this point in the day, the camp should have been full of the noise that she had come to refer to as The Arguments. That's what the soldiers' visits to the girls on the left and right of her always sounded like. Listening to them through the plywood walls of her cubicle, Meiko likened it to fierce arguing between a man and a woman. The Arguments would begin with harsh words from both parties, each trying to convince the other of something through shouting. But soon the man's voice would win over, growing louder and more intense. The girl's voice would try for a while to match that ferocity, to fight against whatever position the man was taking. But soon his grunts and his bellows drowned her out, growing impossibly loud in the small cubicle, crashing against its thin walls with the bluntness of a mallet. Soon Meiko could barely hear the girl's voice at all — just a whiff of pleading lost under the soldier's screams of aimless defiance. His hollers would build to some inevitable crescendo, rising and rising, and then at last peak with pride, a scream of triumphant conquest. And then, just as soon as it began, the noise would grind back down again, like a motor cut off. Next came silence that wasn't quite silent. Just the sound, barely audible, of the girl weeping to herself in shame, having lost yet another Argument. Scant moments to wallow in that disgrace before the gruff flap of her curtain, another soldier entering, another Argument beginning as the last one had.

Meiko sat up on her tatami mat. Oh, she was *not* dead. She could hear that familiar symphony inside her body, the wail of infection that started in her swollen genitals and burned all the way up to her sinuses. Thirsty, she reached for the jug of water sitting on the low table next to her mat, tucked its spout beneath her split lip. A mere tickle of water fell into her throat. Meiko cradled the empty vessel and stared blandly past the table to the paper box on the floor beyond it, wilted by the August heat and brimming with unopened condoms. She could see their familiar brand name gleaming in Japanese on the tinfoil — Assault No. 1. Next to the box was a ceramic dish the size of a shaving bowl full of cloudy grey water: the disinfectant that the soldiers were suppose to use after they had put on the Assault. But it had been months since the men had bothered with condoms or cleanser, and months since she had the strength to insist. Another box sat next to it, partially hidden under a blanket. It was stuffed with *Gyumpo* bills, the Japanese military currency, wrinkled and adorned with pictures of violent birds. Her tips from the more guilt-ridden soldiers.

Meiko couldn't handle the quiet any longer. She forced herself to her feet with one awkward thrust, and was nearly sucked back down by the rip tide of her fever. She picked up a faded orange shirt off her floor and put it on, pulling it down as far as it would go, to the middle of her bare thighs, which had scars and cigarette burns on them. One step and she was at her curtain; a second and she was outside of it, standing in the wooden hallway. Up one end and down the other, curtain after tattered curtain hung over cubicles exactly like hers. She spotted one of them rustle suddenly, down at the far end. A face peeped out, belonging to a girl named Hiromi. She stared at Meiko in terrified confusion. Meiko placed a finger to her split lip to keep the child silent. When she did, the girl vanished back behind her curtain, leaving Meiko to face whatever punishment awaited her for being in the hallway.

And that punishment could come at any moment, now that she was drifting up the mud-caked planks toward the common room. It would come as a scream from the camp manager. Or a soldier rushing over, followed by the quick flare of pain as the butt of a rifle cracked her in the jaw. But Meiko staggered into the common room to find it empty. *Empty*. In the months since the Japanese had moved them here from the last camp, she had never seen this room without people in it. The manager's podium stood like an abandoned sentry guarding the hallway. Resting behind its tall lip was the metal box of red tickets that the manager gave the soldiers after they coughed up their *Gyumpo* for the privilege of going into the hall and choosing a cubicle. Meiko moved deeper into the wide common room. On the dining tables in the middle, she found plates caked with half-finished rice balls, limp miso noodles, and jaundiced bits of cooked radish — remnants of a meal interrupted. She strolled over, brazen as a newcomer, and helped herself to the food, stuffing the stale, soggy chunks into her mouth with thrusts of her hand.

And that's when the unnatural heat of the room hit her. Despite the August temperatures, someone had lit the camp's charcoal furnace on the far side of the room for the first time since late spring; she looked over to see a shimmer of orange pulsing out of its iron cage. Meiko weaved over on unsteady legs to take a closer look, the heat intensifying the nearer she got. She stooped and looked through the grate, then grabbed the wrought-iron handle and pulled the door open. The thick cardboard-covered books had been stuffed in there haphazardly and were now curdling under the flames' snap and spittle. The ledgers. The manager's ledgers. The camp's history, the transactions that occurred and what the girls were owed, were vanishing into smoke.

A noise wafted over her then from the front entry beyond the stove. No mistaking it: the grind and rumble of army trucks. Meiko shuffled toward the opened doors. One stiff step after another and she was through the threshold and descending the stone blocks that led to the muddied ground. There in the courtyard, she waited for her eyes to adjust to the August sunshine. When they did, she saw dozens of Japanese soldiers, the anonymous faces that had visited her over and over in her stall, piling into army trucks at a pace that left her baffled. These men were not hopping into the back or onto the rails with the haste of warriors going into battle. They were instead climbing into the trucks languidly, their faces sunken and bodies limp with sadness. When each truck was full, it pulled away from the camp with no urgency beneath its wheels and joined the slow line of other trucks heading toward the Manchurian hills on the horizon. Men drifted past her with their packs and their helmets, but no one paid her any attention. It was like she had finally become the ghost that she had longed to be.

She turned to her left. There were two soldiers down at the far end of the building, sitting with their backs against the wall.

Nestled in the muddy grass between them was a portable radio, its antenna angled at the sky. Fearless now, Meiko sauntered toward them so she could hear what they were listening to. These hardened men, in their filthy fatigues and broken boots, were *weeping* like little boys, their eyes marinating in hot, uninhibited tears. There was Japanese crackling loudly out of the radio, a staccato voice speaking with authority. Meiko listened closely, muscled her way through the grammar, hunting for context, wanting to know who the speaker was. Her breath was yanked from her lungs when she finally figured it out.

Emperor Hirohito.

His Majesty spoke quickly, faster than she could entirely follow. But there was one word that he repeated, one word that hung like an ornament on this speech. And Meiko, much to her surprise, found herself translating that word into her native tongue, a language she had not dared to even dream in for so long. That Korean word was soft and playful compared to its Japanese equivalent. She let it bounce through her mind like a ball. *Pok'tan ... pok'tan ...*

A bomb. These men were weeping about a bomb. A big one.

She burst into laughter. She couldn't help it. And when she did the men startled, saw her standing over them, and blinked at her as if jarred from sleep. In that moment, Meiko knew her death was imminent, that one of them would yank out his side pistol and cut her down where she stood. But neither did. They just looked up at her, and, not caring who she was or *what* she was, pleaded with their wet frowns for an emotion that she could not fathom. These men, who had urinated on her, who had burned her legs with hot pokers, who had smeared their semen in her eyes, were begging Meiko for a small shred of sympathy.

She couldn't help it. She laughed all the harder.

CHAPTER 2

The pound and rush of alien traffic, long shiny streams of *Hyundai Hyundai Hyundai* racing through the blink and blare of this February Friday, and it took coming to Korea for me to realize that enduring friendships are built on a foundation of mutual envy. I am friends with Rob Cruise because part of me wants to be him. Let's get that straight, right off the bat. He and Justin Ford, my roommate, have been in this country for two years. Their existence here in Seoul seems like a neverending epilogue to tales already climaxed, lives back in Canada full of shut doors and embarrassing tragedies. I can relate to that.

The three of us stand upon the two words that will ensure I find my way home tonight — *Daechi Sa Guh Rhee*. "Commit to memory," they've told me, "in case we get separated. It means Daechi Intersection. Say it to a cabbie just like that — *Daechi Sa Guh Rhee* — and he'll take you right back here." This first week in, I've been thinking these men have adopted me, looking out for my safety in this city of 11 million people, but now I'm wondering if they're having fun at my expense. It's clear they've misled me about tonight's activities. They said "bar" and I heard "pub" (*hof* they call them here, just like in Germany) but these guys are obviously dolled up for something else and I'm dressed like a frump by comparison. We're not going to a pub, I've now learned. We're going to a club, a *dance* club. Thumping techno and bright spinning lights and boys with boners in their cargo pants — some of my least favourite things. Rob Cruise, who is wearing cargo pants below his winter jacket, has begun dancing already, standing at the *Sa Guh Rhee* with knees pumping like he needs to pee, cigarette making hurried trips to his lips. We'll hop in a cab as soon as Jon Hung shows up. Oh wait, there he is, descending the grimy stairs of a PC Room on the other side of the street.

"Look at the white boys standing on the corner!" he shouts as he crosses the intersection.

"Whatever you say, chink!" Rob smiles as he flicks his cigarette to the gutter.

Jon Hung is not a chink. He is a *kyopo* — dad's Korean, mom's American — and he possesses the Hawaiian good looks and designer clothes that scream to the world *I have half an MBA and will go get the other half just as soon as I'm done with this ridiculous antisabbatical.* Despite his heritage, he speaks less Korean than I do, and I've been in this country exactly eight days.

"You're going to have fun, so relax," he says to me, spotting my body language. "Is that what you're wearing?"

"Don't listen to him," Rob Cruise tells me. "The club we're going to, most girls won't care what you're *wearing*."

Justin, who says nothing, steps off the curb to hail us a taxi. One pulls up within seconds, winking out its dome light. The four of us pile in, Rob Cruise presuming shotgun, and then we're off, joining the long, shiny streams of *Hyundai Hyundai Hyundai*.

You don't so much see Seoul's neon as you taste it, like bright hard Christmas candy, reds and greens sprayed out across the city as if fired from a cannon. As our cab races northward toward the lugubrious Han River, I figure I'll never get used to this nonstop showcase of luminance. A landscape choked with discos and Starbucks outlets and soju tents on the sidewalks, with street-side barbecues and 7-Elevens that will let you drink beer on plastic furniture set up out front. As we settle in for the ride, Rob Cruise begins his complaining. He's been a flame thrower at the urinal for several weeks now. The nurses at the clinic near our school have started recognizing him when he walks in; the pharmacist doesn't even need to see the slip anymore to fetch him the right antibiotics.

"Dude, why don't you wear a fucking condom?" Jon Hung asks.

Rob laughs at this. "A lot of Korean girls don't like them. They got the whole rhythm method going on." Voguing his hands to show rhythm.

When I find it funny that he finds it funny, I don't recognize myself. I should be ashamed that his insouciance ignites a profound ache in me. Deflated, I lean back and try to look out the cab's window, but Justin's head blocks my view as he stares into the night.

Rob Cruise catches my sinking mood in the cabbie's mirror and twists around to face the backseat. This is where the envy is supposed to kick in, where he imbues the air of the cab with his raunchy wisdom. Is he really thirty-three years old? The guys have heard all this stuff before, but it doesn't matter because I'm the target. Rob begins telling me about life as a successful player, about how the best moments come when the serial seducer becomes the seduced. On those special nights, the girl he's with will seize the lead with needs that nearly scare him. He loses control of the situation, and that's his favourite part. Rob makes even the worries afterward, the insipient burn at the urinal that comes later, sound like an adventure unto itself. He details the inner rawness, the unwelcome discharge, the swelling that weighs on him like guilt.

"It sounds like the clap," I sniff.

"It's more than the clap," he replies, adjusting his groin. "It's like a fucking standing ovation!"

And we roar, loud enough to startle the Korean cabbie. Even Justin joins in, forsaking his stare out the window, laughing his deep bell-like laugh, perhaps forgetting for an instant that he once had a kid in Nova Scotia who died.

Our cab flies over a bridge crossing the Han, makes the turnoff, and then grinds to a near halt as we join the constipated line of other cabs oozing into Itaewon. Finally we make it to the strip, pay the cabbie, and get out. The street is an open-air party, a festival of boozy expat teachers, of Korean beauties, of U.S. army guys on the hunt for love and war. This is Itaewon, the foreign quarter, adjacent to Yongsan Garrison, the largest U.S. army base in the country. I will come to know this place as a hive of sexual hysteria with a neon glint of violence.

"It's this way," Rob says.

On the hike up the hill and through bewildering side streets I spot at least three *hofs* and nearly beg us to stop. But these men are on a mission — even Justin seems keen. We finally land in a lineup outside a two-storey club called Jokers Red, its sign a splay of cards and an evil clown face. The Korean girls lined up to get in are not dressed for February. They are shivering sticks in miniskirts and tube tops, more concerned with looking hot than being warm. Rob is nearly bursting. At the door, I'm burglarized for a cover charge, follow the men inside, and then get smacked with the *thumpthumpthump* and the epilepsy of strobe lights. It's then that I realize how far I have fallen: to be nearly thirty and spending Friday night in the sort of club I had zero interest in when I was nineteen. I need to be drunk.

So off we go to the bar. We take drinks up some stairs to a booth with expansive benches that overlook the rail surrounding the dance floor like a cattle pen. Despite the crowd and its accumulated body heat, this club is as chilly as a meat locker: drafts waft in from poorly insulated walls and windows. Rob and Jon rendezvous with some familiar faces just coming off the dance floor. A shivering stick hugs Jon Hung as he slinks out of his coat and tosses it into the booth. She must be one of his girl-friends. She's wearing knee-high bitch boots and a miniskirt that barely reaches her groin.

Soon Rob Cruise leads a migration to the dance floor; every-one but me. I tell them I'll "hold down the booth." I watch as they all congregate under the throbbing lights. Jon Hung moves like liquid, scoops into his miniskirted girlfriend as if she were a ball grounded deep into left field, leads her where he wants her, and then they grind into each other like turbines. Justin is a good dancer, too; his creepy stoicism complements rather than detracts from his moves. Of course, the star is Rob Cruise: the wind-chime swing of his hips defies his age, and, seemingly, grav-ity itself. Each sway proves he's got a profound sense of rhythm flowing through him. He's attracting moons to his orbit, girls curious and scantily clad. When he looks up to see me watch-ing him, he begins shuffling over to the beat of the music with a wolf-like grin, dances his way up the stairs, grabs my arms, and attempts to drag me into participation. I refuse. I know that down there I would be like the decrepit grandfather attempting the Macarena at a wedding. When he gives up, I scoot off to the bar to see if they sell Scotch.

Soon they're done dancing and return to the table. More people the guys know come in from the cold to join us — a few more girls wearing virtually nothing, and one of our cowork-ers, a kid fresh off a B.A., his baseball cap turned around backwards. Rob has brought a raven-haired stranger with him, a heavily made-up girl with bare shoulders peppered with gooseflesh and gleaming a cold sweat. In fact, it's obvious that all the girls are freezing. Their tight, inscrutable faces try to hide it, but their hands keep rubbing absently at their exposed triceps. The absurdity of it makes me wish I had thick duvet to throw over everyone.

Funny how even under the walloping techno we're still able to conduct halfway decent conversations. It's like our ears have adjusted to the noise in the same way that eyes adjust to darkness. Listening to Rob with the bare-shouldered girl, I'm once again awash in envy. His flirting is flawless; he's working over her defences and guiding her through convoluted hallways, all of which lead to his bed. He even incorporates my presence into his act. I'll come to learn that this is one of the chief ways Rob gets a girl to trust him, by lobbing huge, exaggerated compliments at his male friends. "See this guy?" he points at me, grinning. "He's *amazing*. Been in Korea — eight days. Already speaks lotsa lotsa Korean." He nods at me. "Go ahead, show her your Korean." I sip my Scotch without smiling, then rhyme off the handful of phrases I've picked up since the flight over — hello/goodbye, do you speak English, I would like a beer, may I make some change please?, etc. etc. I expect the girl to applaud with a frantic little clap of her hands. Instead, she nods once and turns back to Rob. In fact, none of the shivering sticks are paying me any attention, and frankly I don't blame them. I come off like what I am: a dumpy, balding, bearded orphan who has crash-landed on this peninsula. I might as well be part of the furniture.

Justin, who had bowed out briefly from a conversation, is suddenly laughing, a heavy drum beat, seemingly to himself. He has spotted something over the lip of the booth.

"Hey Rob, check out who's here," he says.

Rob twists to look and I look with him. Another Korean girl they know has just cleared the door and stepped into the club. She looks around briefly as if lost, as if she's not entirely sure she wants to be there. I notice that she's wearing a heavy winter coat that goes all the way to her knees.

"Ho-leee fuck!" Rob yells and begins waving madly in the air. "Hey, Jin! Jin! Come over here, would you?"

She turns to see our group in the booth, but then hesitates as if trying to gauge whether she wants to join us. She sighs, rolls her eyes, comes marching up the stairway, and arrives at our table, her face flushed from the cold.

"Look what the cat dragged in," Jon Hung clichés.

"Well, if it isn't my *waegookin* friends," she replies, using the Korean word for foreigner. "Friday night and you're *drinking*, surprise surprise."

"What are you doing here?" Rob asks, tucking an arm around the bare-shouldered girl.

"I came to hear the DJ. He played the Armada in Hongdae last weekend, but I missed him."

"Are you going to join us?"

"I suppose."

We all scrunch in to give her room to sit. Before she does, she opens her coat, but does not take it off. Underneath, she's wearing a white cashmere sweater and blue jeans.

"So I hardly recognized you without a cigarette in your mouth." Rob grins at her. "What, did you quit?" The other girls guffaw, as if what Rob has said tells them everything they need to know about this Jin character. Despite Korea's rapid assent into modernity, smoking among women is still considered verboten. Jin simply stares at him. "And you grew your hair long again, thank God," Rob goes on. "That bob you had was a disaster." She tilts her head and stares even deeper into him. He realizes

24

that he's probably jeopardizing her presence at the table, and he softens his tone. "So where you been, girl?"

"Working," she replies. "I see you're still cruising, Mr. Cruise." She turns then to the bare-shouldered girl and says with a sort of cheery, deadpan cattiness: "You know, he slept with nearly a *hundred* women last year — some of them *prostitutes*." The girl laughs loudly but uneasily. Within a minute she gets up to go to the bathroom, or so she says, but then disappears into the crowd's pulsating throngs. Rob keeps looking for her over the rail as our small talk chirps around his head, and when it becomes clear he's lost her, he turns back to the table to seethe at Jin.

"Why don't you take off your coat," he snipes at her.

"Because I'm fucking cold," she yells over the music. "You guys can ogle me later." I laugh at this, I can't help it, but nobody looks at me. "So who's going to buy me a drink?" she asks. As if by reflex, Jon, Justin, and the kid in the baseball cap all make intimations toward their wallets before stopping themselves as if they've been tricked. She just shakes her head. "Ugh. You *waegookins* are all the same." And scoots up fast, faster than I can make an offer to get her a drink, and heads to the bar on her own, her lengthy winter coat ballooning like a cape around her.

Aptly enough, the other Korean girls have yielded their place in the conversation to this Jin person: while they possess varying degrees of fluency, Jin's English is nearly flawless. It amazes me how even in a large group, it's always one or two people who become the focal point. Here it is Rob and Jin, riffing off each other with so much affectionate vitriol. He is a master of viciousness, of well-placed quips, but she is his equal — made more impressive by the fact that they aren't sparring in *her* native tongue. I drink silently; I have lost track of how many silent drinks I've had.

Because there are far more women at our table than men, we soon attract some unwanted guests: a handful of GIs, toting large mugs of beer, have suddenly invaded our space. These young guys are gruffly sociable in their crewcuts and muscles, but their intentions are obvious. "Do you mind if we join you?" the leader of the pack hollers. Without waiting for an answer, they pull up chairs seemingly out of nowhere and surround our booth. Conversations recalibrate yet again. The shivering sticks ask where the boys are from. The soldiers mention American-sounding towns in American states. Rob, Justin, and I — all from the Maritimes in Canada — grow uneasy. One of us will need to pick a minor fight.

"So tell me something," Justin wades in, "is it true what they say about American soldiers in Korea?"

"What's that?" asks one of the marines.

"That the only reason you're here is because you've had disciplinary problems in other postings? That it's a punishment to be here."

The leader just beams. "Hey man, we love Korea. We love the *women*." The miniskirted girls cover their mouths as they laugh. I catch Jin rolling her eyes and I feel a tingle beneath my skin.

Jon Hung pipes up next, mentioning that he's the only American in our group — born in Hawaii, raised in Seattle. "So tell me," he asks, "are we really going to war or what?"

The marines laugh again. It's true — their subliterate commander-in-chief will be launching an unprovoked invasion in another month or so. These boys contradict themselves by saying they'd love to get reassigned off this peninsula that hasn't seen real conflict in fifty years. The war would be their ticket to adventure.

"But it'll only be a three-month gig, man," one of them says. "Get rid of Saddam, root out al-Qaeda, then back home by summer."

"There's no al-Qaeda in Iraq," I point out, but assume my mumbles are smothered under the dance music.

"Yeah, man," another marine goes on, "we'll get in there and finish the job we started."

Rob Cruise, conspicuously quiet for several minutes, takes a long pull on his drink and says: "I served in the first Gulf War."

The table turns to face him. He takes another drink.

"Did you really?" Jon Hung asks.

"I did. Company C of the RCR, 1991. I took a break from university the year before and signed up. I was barely twenty." He says this directly at the lead marine, who looks like he would've still been in elementary school in 1991.

Jin tilts her head at Rob. "You never told me that." The way she says it — the gentle, almost caring tone, the slight hurt that he would keep such a thing from her — floods me with a knowledge that should've been obvious from the start. *Oh my God*, I think, *she was one of the one hundred*.

"So you've been over there?" the lead marine asks.

"Yep."

"So what do you think? We up for a good fight?"

Rob spits laughter at him. "What do I think? I think your D.O.D. has lost its fucking mind. First of all, Michael over here is right — al-Qaeda doesn't have any connections to Iraq. Second of all, you guys have no idea what kind of hornets' nest you're about to stir up."

The marine shrugs. "That's all part of the job, man. Army life's full of excitement and danger — you'd know that." He sips his own drink. "Of course, teaching ABCs to Korean kids must have its challenges, too."

Jin's laughter bounces off the table. Rob and the other guys need to say something to keep the balance in check, but they're struggling. I search for words that would get Jin's attention back, to return the ball to our court, or at least relieve this sudden tension.

I give up hope once the conversation becomes blatantly about sex. How could it not, with this kind of dynamic? The youngest-looking marine — maybe eighteen — kicks things off by lobbing a stereotype about Korean girls in bed, something about their aversion to oral sex. He meant for it to sound flirty and hilarious, but his joke sinks like a stone. It does, however, lead us to discuss other stereotypes — French lovers, American lovers, Canadian lovers. Jin, still in her coat, takes up the charge when we start imagining what kind of lovers certain people around the table would be. She deliberately skips over Rob as she does the rounds, but has a blast taking the piss out of Jon Hung ("You'd be such a businessman — you probably use a spread-sheet to keep track of your conquests") and Justin ("You would have silent orgasms") and one of the beefier marines ("Selfish brute — you have 'closet rapist' written all over you!") Then her gaze, for the first time, falls on me.

"And you?" she says, eyeing me up. It's only then that I become painfully aware that I had put on a cardigan before leaving the apartment. "You'd probably make love like an intellectual."

I catch the reference right away but allow the boys their laugh — after all, I do look like someone who'd make love like an intellectual.

"Kundera," I say as she attempts to move on.

She snaps back to look at me, her face sharp with surprise. "Excuse me?"

"Milan Kundera," I yell over the music. "That line about making love like an intellectual — you stole it from his novel *The Book of Laughter and Forgetting*."

She blinks at me. "You've read Kundera?" It doesn't come out as a question so much as a statement of intrigue.

"What the *hell* are they talking about?" asks one of the marines.

"Milan Kundera," I say simply.

"Who is she?" Rob Cruise asks.

"It's a he, idiot," Jin snips without looking at him. "He's only one of my favourite writers." She holds my gaze as if goading me to go on.

"I haven't read everything of his," I continue with a sigh. "*The Unbearable Lightness of Being*, of course."

"Of *course.*"

"And *The Book of Laughter and Forgetting*. Oh, and his new one, *Ignorance*, was one of the books I read on the flight over here. I didn't like it."

For the first time tonight, she stammers. "Well — well I've read Kundera in English, French, Chinese, *and* Korean."

Deliberately, I shrug with indifference. I turn to the lead marine and say: "Kundera knows a thing or two about unprovoked invasions. You should read him."

Rob Cruise is glowing at me; this is where I hold up my end of the mutual envy. It's as if he's passing me a torch, giving me permission to fan the flames of my sudden stardom. He also seems mildly stunned that I've trumped him and the other men at the table, that I've touched Jin in a way that they couldn't. "This is all too heady for me," he yells at everyone, giving me a wink. "What do you say we dance?" He gets up from the bench, anxious to lead us like Moses down to the dance floor. The soldiers don't hesitate; in the spirit of sexual rivalry, they rise en masse in time with Rob's movements, each trying to claim one of the shivering sticks as they too stand, adjusting miniskirts and straightening tube tops. Jin gets up, as well, trying very hard not to look at me. She finally, *finally* takes off her coat and tosses it onto the bench.

Oh my God.

She notices that I'm staring but haven't moved. "Are you coming?" she asks.

"I don't dance."

Her face flattens with disbelief. *What, you think this is about dancing?* The others can't quite believe that I'm holding my ground, that I'm about to squander what I've earned. Jin waits, maybe thinking that if she stares at me long enough with that face, I'll change my mind.

Rob Cruise stands watching at the top of the stairwell, growing impatient. "Jin, baby, let's go!"

She's waffling now — to leave and dance, or stay and talk? I refuse to give her an inch, and so she clucks her teeth at the air and races lithely to the stairs, her legs a rush of tendons and confidence. Rob has already begun descending, certain now that she'll follow him. Meanwhile, Jon Hung's girlfriend is pulling him to his feet. "Go on, baby, I'll be right there," he orders her. When she's gone, he comes over to me.

"What are you, *lost*?"

"I don't dance," I repeat.

He drains his drink and sets it noisily on the table. "Milan Kundera," he shakes his head in mock disgust. "You are in the wrong fucking place, my friend." He then motions to Justin, who is also still sitting. "Are you coming down?"

"No, I'll stay behind. Keep Captain Hopeless over here company."

Jon shakes his head at me again and then is gone. I slide over to the rail to watch them all on the dance floor. I find Jin right away. She stands out in the crowd not because of her cashmere and jeans but because her body in dance is an alluring twist and spiral to the mindless thump of music. GIs comes on to her, but she makes shoving them away look like just another of her moves. She looks up at me over the rail and holds my stare for a moment. At the end of a song, she hurries off the floor, trots up the stairs, and returns to the table to search for something in her coat. When she doesn't find it, she races back down again, without so much as a glance at me, to join Rob and Jon under the spinning lights. I look at Justin, who is also watching them, also drinking his drink, also keeping his sad mysteries below the surface. On the dance floor, Rob Cruise has abandoned Jin like a crossword puzzle he will never solve and has begun grinding into another girl. For an instant, we make eye contact. It's as if he holds my conscience in the same grip that he holds the girl. A stare that wants to liberate me from my principles. On a night other than this, he promises to seize my reticence and toss it with delight into Seoul's great fevered flow. He will teach me to take what I want here. And we will better friends for it, sharing the sort of bond that two men can have only after they've been intimate with the same woman.

CHAPTER 3

Through years that fell like rain to join the flow of the Han River, she would learn that the only thing that kept her alive was the value her mother had instilled in her, the value of knowledge. Her *umma* had taught her, as early as the girl was old enough to absorb it, that it was better to know things than to not know them. *Even* girls *need to know things*, her mother would say when tucking her in at night, whispering it so that the girl's father wouldn't hear. *Learn everything you can, my little crane. Even the hard things. Never be afraid of wisdom.* And whenever she uttered these words, her mother called the girl by her true name and never the one her Japanese teachers had given her.

In the years that fell like rain, the girl would learn just how much her mother had known about what was happening to their country, the fate that awaited the young girls in it, and learn that it was this knowledge that eventually pierced her mother's heart and killed her. These thoughts always brought the girl back to the Han River, its churning acceptance of the rain that fell like years. She would ponder that Korean word that shared the river's name, shared the name of their people, their language. *Han.* Which meant, among many other things, the long, constricting accumulation of a lifetime of sorrow.

. . . .

Despite her father's fussing, the girl was allowed to go to school. This was not what he wanted when he brought his family of six from their ancestral farm to the growing capital of Seoul. That was in 1934, a year after the girl's baby sister had been born. In the city, her father expected the boys, the two oldest, to study briefly before becoming labourers, and the girls, the two youngest, to stay home and help their mother in the small house that the Imperial government had allowed them. His plans were precarious at best, and the girl watched as her mother toppled them with a kind of quiet sedition, a restrained glee.

"She *is* going to study," her mother said one day in their dark kitchen, chopping vegetables for a stew.

"The hell she is," her father retaliated from the washtub, where he stood scrubbing the day's grease off his hands from his new job in a munitions factory. The girl watched them argue while spooning mashed rice into her baby's sister's mouth. "No daughter of mine will be caught in a school," she heard her father say.

"There's a small academy for girls near the police station. I found it on my way to market. I've already paid the tuition. I've already arranged it. She *is* going to study. Next year."

"*Aigo!* To what end?" her father snarled. "How will this help us? To have our daughter at a desk all day, learning to read and speak Japanese? How will this help *you*? You can barely keep up with your housework as it is. *Aigo!*"

"You don't know what the future will hold, my friend," the girl's mother said, dropping radishes into a dented pot of boiling water. "You can't say how it might help us to have at least one of our children properly educated."

"Must everything change?" her father sighed as he dried his hands and then collapsed into his flimsy wicker chair near the door. To the little girl's eyes, his now-clean hands looked weak and shrivelled as they fell limp in his lap, like two dead birds. He spoke almost to himself. "They have taken my fields, forced us to live in this city with less land than a dog. And now girls — *girls* — going to school. Must everything change?"

"Yes, it must," her mother replied, putting the lid on the pot and wiping radish juice off the knife with a rag. "I cannot watch her twenty-four hours a day. And I will not bear the thought of her wandering these streets unsupervised. I will not bear it." The girl watched as worry fell over her mother's face then, a shifting in the *han* that flowed through her. "She is going to school. She'll be safer there."

And the little girl felt that tickle in her mind, the ache for wisdom. "Safer from what?" she asked from the table. But to her surprise, her mother would not answer.

So here was the little girl in school, grappling with that ache, these questions, this sense of entitlement instilled deep within her. She perhaps learned more slowly than the other girls that some questions were okay to ask, questions like *when?* and *where?* and *how much?* — but others, like *why?*, were not. "Why" seemed off limits; "why" was a waste of time and reached for answers that existed beyond the outskirts of the teachers' patience. Questions like: Why can't I eat rice while sitting at my desk? Why must I ask before I can go to the bathroom? But also: Why do we stand each day at the beginning of class to sing the *Kimigayo*, the Japanese national anthem? Why is there a picture of Emperor Hirohito on the wall above the blackboard? Why must we bow to it several times when we finish singing? And why have you given me a Japanese name — *Meiko*? I hate this name. It sounds so babyish. This is not the name my mother calls me. It alarmed the girl how forcefully her teachers could quash those plaintive whys, cut them off before they were even all the way out of her mouth.

Despite these mysterious dead ends, the little girl did enjoy studying. Her first year was her favourite because they got to learn how to read and write *Hangul* — the Korean language that her family spoke in the privacy of their home. It enraptured Meiko to watch her tiny hand convert words and phrases into script, a multitude of tiny circles and tents and perpendicular dashes. Doing it correctly, getting full marks on her workbook, filled Meiko with greedy pride. And yet, in Grade Two, things inexplicably changed. All of a sudden, the girls were not *allowed* to write or even speak Korean. If one of them was caught doing so, the teacher would make her stand in the corner under the picture of Hirohito and hold a metal pail heavy with pebbles over her head. "You're not babies anymore," the teacher would tell the rest of the class while the offending girl, head down, struggled in the corner to keep the pail upright. "It's time to leave your childish habits behind."

So every class became in some way about Japan. The girls learned to read and write its language. In geography class, they memorized Japan's islands and major cities. They learned about the bodies of water surrounding the nation, including the one that led to its colony of Korea, the very colony they lived on, but the geography for which they were taught nothing. By Grade Four, the girls began learning Japanese history. They were told of how Japan had generously taken over the "administration" of the Korean peninsula in 1910 with the idea of leading its illiterate peasants toward an overdue modernization. This, they were taught, was part of an even grander initiative that Japan, in its infinite graciousness, had taken upon itself throughout the wider region, a program called "the Co-prosperity Sphere in Asia." This involved Japan overseeing the administration of less-evolved nations all around the Pacific Rim (the teacher pointed to these countries on her map), to insulate and expand the Oriental way of life in the face of growing influences from the West. The teacher spoke as if this were her nation's greatest accomplishment, its gift to the world. Meiko raised a hand. If the Co-prosperity Sphere was so great, then why had all-out war erupted between Japan and China the previous year? (Meiko had, after all, overheard her parents arguing about it: the conflict had increased her father's hours at the munitions plant and also threw into doubt the future of Meiko's two older brothers.) The young teacher, usually a tight drum of calm, grew instantly enraged by these questions. She stomped over and began screaming into Meiko's face in a flurry of Japanese that came too fast to follow. She then struck Meiko around the head with her pointing stick, dragged her by the collar of her dress to the corner, filled the pail with a double helping of pebbles and made her hold it over her shoulders for the remainder of the class.

Despite these cruelties, Meiko could not deny how much she enjoyed being smart. She loved to pore over a text, to memorize fascinating facts and fill out answers in her workbook, even if they were all in Japanese. The knowledge she gained gave her an advantage over the children in her neighbourhood who did not get to go to school: she could read the growing number of Japanese street signs and understand the stories that appeared in the free newspapers on every corner. If she and her friends were playing outside and were approached by the *Kempeitai*, the Japanese military police, Meiko could speak to the officers in stilted but serviceable Japanese. The police often accused them of being spies, which struck Meiko as silly. "No," she would tell them, "we're just little kids playing innocent games. No spies here."

But the more Meiko studied, the more it infuriated her father. Sometimes he came home at night to find her on the floor, her papers spread in a halo around her textbook. He'd march over to grab a fistful of them at random and head toward the kitchen stove. Meiko would chase after him in tears, upset that he had disrupted the careful system of memorization that she had set up for herself. He would fend her off with one hand while stuffing her papers into the stove with the other. When finished, he'd turn to her and yell, "Girls who study become foxes! Why don't you get a job, you slut?"

Getting jobs was exactly what had happened with her two older brothers that year, 1938, when they were fifteen and thirteen respectively. As planned, the boys dropped out of school after acquiring a bare minimum of education. They took jobs as delivery boys for a local Japanese restaurant. Their total combined income was less than half of what their father made at the plant, but the family was desperate for money and the boys were forced to work every day. It was also that year that the plant announced a pay cut for all Korean workers despite the growing war in China. This left Meiko's father in a constant state of fury. He would explode at the children over the simplest of trifles, like if they raised their rice bowls a fraction of an inch off the table while eating. Whenever these outbursts happened, Meiko and the boys would mutter at each other in Japanese about their father's bizarre behaviour. This would send him into another long rant about how the Japanese had infiltrated every aspect of their household, to the point where children could mock a father in a language he did not understand.

Meanwhile at school, Meiko's teachers had begun grooming the girls to join a new organization that Japan had introduced, called the *Jungshindae* — Voluntarily Committing Body Corp for Labor. The teachers said that this was the highest calling for every girl in the Empire, to give her body and spirit over to Emperor Hirohito and his many worthy causes. In a few years, they would be called up into good-paying jobs as teachers and nurses and entertainers, contributing whatever they could to

Japan's military success in the region. Meiko rushed home to explain the *Jungshindae* to her mother, expecting her to share in Meiko's excitement. Instead, her mother exploded into anger and broke a rice bowl on the lip of her washing tub. "Don't listen to them!" she shouted. "They will not *have* you. Do you hear me? I will pull you out of that school and lock you in the cellar before I let them own you!"

But every day Meiko would come home praising some new aspect of the *Jungshindae*. When her baby sister, who was now six years old, heard these things she began wanting to go to school herself, but her mother would not allow it. "Why does *she* get study and I don't?" the youngest daughter asked. "I wish to learn things, too."

"Girls who read books become sluts!" their father belched by rote from his wicker chair.

Her mother squatted down to be eye level with the girl. "You will stay home with me, little one. We can't afford to have two girls in school. I will teach you things here."

Meiko watched this with a shake of her head. "Umma, you should let her study. Our teachers have promised us good-pay-ing jobs with the *Jungshindae*. In a few years, we'll be able to support both you and father."

Her mother's eyes filled with an emotion Meiko could not understand. "Don't listen to them," she wept. "My wise little crane, do *not* listen to them. And you are to come straight home after school — every day. Do not linger on the streets with your friends. Do you hear me?"

The girls could not know what their mother knew, nor could their father. It took being a housewife, going to markets every day, talking to other women, to learn what she had come to know: that young girls in their teens had begun disappearing from the neigh-bourhood. It became a common sight to see a mother, not much older than Meiko's, splayed out on the curb outside her house in anguish, her fists pounding her face as she screamed incoherently at the sky. The only words that Meiko's mother could make out were, "My daughter! My daughter! Mydaughtermydaughtermydaughter! Theyhavetakenmydaughterawayfromme!"

In early 1941, the boys both received draft notices from the *Teishintai* — the Japanese Volunteer Corps for Men. The government was mobilizing the entire country for war and this included conscripting Korean boys as young as fifteen into the Imperial army. When the draft notices arrived, Meiko's mother burst into wails and collapsed onto the floor in front of her washtub. Within a couple of weeks, the boys were sent to the city of Daegu for six weeks of basic training before getting shipped off to the battlefields of Southeast Asia. Meiko's mother was inconsolable. Her husband lamely brought up the boys' lost income in his first attempt to comfort her, as if this were partly the source of her grief. "Are you insane!" she wept as she shoved his arms away. "Don't you realize that your sons are as good as dead? *As good as dead!* Their lives mean nothing to the Japanese. They will put them right up … up on … on the front lines …" Meiko and her baby sister watched as their mother choked on this knowledge as if it were poison. Over days and weeks, Meiko's father would try different ways to comfort his wife, and grew frustrated at his inability to do so. This precipitated even more arguments between them. Their fights raged for hours in the evenings, growing so intense that Meiko and her sister had to hide away from them in the small bedroom they shared.

It was on a morning during the height of these battles that Meiko, now thirteen years old, discovered the sticky marks of blood that had arrived overnight in her underpants. She found them while dressing for school. She did have an inkling about these blood marks, suspecting that they were not uncommon for a woman. She sometimes found faint droplets of crimson left behind in the squat toilet if she used the bathroom immediately after her mother. But still, Meiko convinced herself that this blood was a dire omen of illness, and to share this news would only add to her mother's stress. She found a rag to place between her legs before dressing and hoped the bleeding would go away. Yet the discharge got worse the next day and worse still the day after, until Meiko had to discreetly drag her mother into the bathroom, close the door and show her what was happening.

At first, a blush of pride swept over her *umma*. "Oh my wise little crane, this just means you are becoming a woman," she said, taking the girl's face into her hands. "I should have mentioned something to you long before this." She went on to explain how the girl should expect a number of days' bleeding each month, and when it came she was to place a special kind of cloth in her underpants to catch the flow. But no sooner had her mother finished this instruction than a shadow darkened her face, as if a delayed reaction, an ominous and barely spoken secret, began sinking through her like a stone through water. "My sweet child," she said, and began weeping. "We must figure out … what we're going to *do* about this …"

Do about what? Meiko thought. *About the blood? Or about me becoming a woman?*

Meiko soon became the focal point of her parents' arguments. Her father was adamant that she now leave school to get a job. The plant had yet again cut his wages, and even with the boys off at war he still struggled to feed his wife and two remaining children. "She could become a cleaner or errand girl," he said. "Or she could use her Japanese to work in an office somewhere. That would bring in some money."

"Absolutely not," her mother said. "We must find a match-maker and get her a husband. Now that she is a woman." Meiko's mother knew that other families were rushing their teenaged daughters into a *chungmae* — an arranged marriage. Girls not much older than Meiko were getting paired up with neighbour-hood widowers who were often twice or three times their age. Meiko's father scoffed. "Marriage? So soon? She's only thirteen. Besides, who in this neighbourhood could afford an acceptable dowry for a girl with seven years of schooling and good Japanese?"

On a day during the peak of this bickering, Meiko spoke up for herself. "I don't want a *chungmae*, and I don't want a job right now," she blurted from her ring of homework on the floor, inter-rupting her parents in mid fight. She climbed to her feet to face them. "I want to stay in school until I'm eighteen and then join the *Jungshindae*. To support you and father. And then, when the war is over, I want to find a *yonae*." They both stopped to stare at her, nearly burst into laughter at Meiko's use of that word: *yonae*, a love match.

"You naive fool," her father spat at her.

"My little crane, this is not practical," her mother said. "You don't understand what is happening to our country. We must find you a husband right away. You shouldn't —"

"Mother, it's you who placed me in school. It's you who always said it's important to learn everything you can. Why has the blood between my legs suddenly changed that?"

Her father took two large steps across their wooden floor and struck Meiko hard on the face. She fell in a heap amidst her homework. He stood over her, trembling in rage. "What did my ancestors ever do to burden me with this life?" he quaked. "To live in a house full of *vulgar whores*? Am I not the head of this family?" He looked at his wife, at Meiko, at Meiko's sister who was watching the fight from her bedroom door, her eyes filling with silent tears. "We're all going to starve," he said, then walked over to grab a jacket off the hook by the door. "Don't blame me. We're all going to starve." And then he was gone outside, into a street vandalized with Japanese signs he could not read.

Meiko remained in school mostly by default because her parents refused to agree on what to do with her. School seemed to be the safest place to be, even if every class simply groomed the girls to serve the Japanese empire. By Grade Nine, Meiko and her classmates had flowered into silent and hardworking servants of the Emperor, skilled at music and storytelling, experts at keeping their faces pleasantly devoid of emotion. They came to class with their hair tied into the long, twisted braids that were the Korean symbol of chastity, and their developing bodies were covered in the unflattering tent of *hanbok*, the traditional Korean dress.

One day, their teacher announced they were having a special guest to class. She welcomed him in and told the girls he was a well-respected Japanese businessman. He took his place in front of the blackboard, his masculinity so foreign in the room. To Meiko's eyes, he didn't *look* like a businessman; he looked like an army sergeant. The teacher made some more introductions and then turned the class over to him.

"How many of you have older brothers?" the man began. Several girls, including Meiko, raised their hands. "And how many of those brothers have been shipped off to fight for the Emperor?" None of the hands went down. "And how many of you have fathers who work in factories or on construction sites, barely making enough to feed whatever remains of your families?" Most hands stayed in the air, including Meiko's. The man nodded as if he knew all along what the answers would be. "Well, I am here today to offer you all an opportunity. An opportunity to provide for your families in a way that your men cannot." He told them that Japan was prepared to offer each girl a year-long job in a new textile factory in the Japanese city of Shimonoseki. The government would cover everything: their transportation to and from Japan, their accommodations while there, their meals and clothes and entertainment. And the jobs themselves would be some of the highest-paying in the Empire. "You'll most likely make more money than your fathers, and you'll be able to send those earnings home each month to help out your families. There will also be extra pay for those willing to work extra hours."

The girls were too frightened and excited to raise a single question. Meiko thought: *Why us? Why not just send our fathers?* But kept her "why" questions to herself.

"Go home tonight and discuss it with your parents," the man said. "It's a big decision. You'll be away from your families for a year. But the journey will not be too arduous: Just a train ride south to Pusan and then a ferry across the Sea of Japan to Shimonoseki. If this sounds like something you're interested in, come to the Tanghu train station two Sundays from now, in the morning, and we'll provide you with more information. You won't have to make any decisions then. But we can at least tell you more about this and begin filling out the necessary paper-work should you decide to say yes."

For the next few days, Meiko could not keep Shimonoseki out of her thoughts. Walking the streets of her neighbourhood with the early January snow falling, she kept pondering what it would be like to live and work there and become the main provider for her family. Was this not what she had been training herself for all these years? It was a Korean girl's duty to be silent, respectful, and hardworking. She knew she had probably failed at the first two, but at least she was capable of hard work. Her studies had proven that. She could go away and make enough money to put an end to her parents' bickering.

She came home one afternoon about a week later to find her father home alone, sitting in his wicker chair by the door. His presence in the house startled her; he should have been at work. "Father, are you okay?" she asked, hanging her wool shawl on its hook. He raised his left hand to show her what had happened: streaking across his blackened knuckles was a dark paste of half-clotted blood. "I got careless with one of the machines," he told her. "They sent me home to let this heal." Meiko hurried to her mother's washtub to fetch a clean rag. She brought the soaked cloth over, knelt in front of him and began washing away the oil and grit seeping into the wound. "There there," she said with the gentleness of a nurse, "let me look after that for you. Here, turn your hand this way. There. Let me wash that ..." She sensed him staring down at the top of her head as she worked on him, and that was when she caught the odour of *soju* on his breath. It filled her nostrils each time he exhaled. *Ah, so you didn't come straight home after your accident*, she thought. Meiko would not look up at him as she washed his hand; she would not look up at him even when he cupped his other hand, also filthy but unmarred, to the side of her head and allowed his fingers to crawl up into her virginal braids. She froze. "My daughter," he said. "I feel like I fail you every day. Do you know that?"

"Father, don't say such things," she swallowed.

He leaned back against the wall, the wicker chair creaking beneath his weight. "Did you find a job today?" he slurred. She resumed cleaning without looking up. He let out a laugh that was tinged with frustration. "Of course you didn't. Because you're just a girl. Your mother's right. You need to be in school for a couple more years and we'll arrange a *chungmae*. Then you'll become some other man's problem." When he laughed, his grip on her skull grew tighter, as if he wanted to grind her head into the floor, or somewhere else.

"Father," she said, "if I am ever offered a job, do you think I should take it?"

He looked down at her with his dark eyes and drew her closer to his lap. He leaned over her until his face was nearly crushed into hers. "I no longer care," he whispered, his words as poisonous as his breath. "Whatever happens to you, I don't care. As long as you become another man's problem before these devils kill me."

Outside, they could hear Meiko's sister hurrying up the stone walkway to their house, her mother's voice hollering behind her. Meiko and her father quickly released their grip on one another. She was just standing up and straightening her dress as her sister burst through the door, her mother appearing a moment later. She looked at the two of them over her canvas sack of vegetables. "What are you doing here?" she asked, and for an instant Meiko thought she had been speaking to her.

You don't have to make any decisions today. That's what the man said. You can just come and get more information about the job in Shimonoseki. That's all.

When Meiko arrived at the Tanghu train station, she found about forty girls standing in a line that snaked up to a long table manned by what were clearly Japanese soldiers. She recognized only a few girls from her class, standing up further in the line. They were dressed as she was — in full *hanbok* and braids, looking to make a strong impression on these potential employers. But the other girls here were clearly not from their academy or any other. They looked as if they had been shipped in from villages outside of the city. They wore ragged, rural-looking dresses, and their hair was matted against their heads as if they spent the previous night sleeping awkwardly on a train. She also noticed that they did not seem to speak Japanese very well. A soldier was moving up and down the line asking random questions, and when one of the rural girls attempted to reply in Korean he screamed in her face and then struck her. Meiko swallowed and looked around, trying to figure out a way to slip from the line she had entered without getting noticed. But it was impossible: the soldiers were watching to make sure each girl made her way to the table, answered their questions, and then moved off to the side.

When Meiko arrived at the table, the Japanese man sitting there made only brief eye contact before hovering his pen over the large ledger in front of him.

"Name," he ordered.

"Meiko Teshiako," she answered.

"Year of birth?"

"1928."

He then asked for her parents' names, their address, the name of her academy, and how she had come to learn about the day's recruitment.

"Recruitment, sorry?" she asked. "No, I'm here only to get more information."

"Any sexually transmitted diseases?" the man asked.

Meiko flinched, stared at him while he waited for her answer. "I ... I don't even know what those words mean," she replied.

He gave the smallest smile, then motioned to the side. "Okay, go stand over there with the others. We're done."

"But I don't —"

He looked past her and screamed at the next girl in line. "Please move forward! You're next. Keep the line moving please."

Meiko floated over in a daze to join the group of girls who had cleared the table and were now huddled under a metal awning by the railway tracks. She spotted one of her classmates, Huriko, standing with her chin buried in her chest, tears pouring over her face. "Huriko, what's going on?" she tried to whisper to her. As soon as she did, a Japanese soldier stomped over and yelled in Meiko's face. "No talking! Stand still and don't talk, *Chosunjin!*" The word he spat at her, *Chosunjin*, was a racial epithet for Koreans, bastardizing the true name of their nation, *Chosun*. His use of it froze Meiko where she stood.

Once all the girls had taken their place under the awning, they had to wait several minutes in silence while the soldiers processed the names in the ledger and typed up small passports for each girl. When one passport was completed, a soldier would call out the girl's name and then hand her the slip of folded paper. When Meiko stepped forward to receive hers, the young Japanese soldier handing them out leered at her. There was no kindness in his grin. "You're very beautiful, *Chosunjin*. Look at you — like a little porcelain doll. You will do very well where you are going." And Meiko thought, stupidly, *What does beauty have to do with working in a factory?*

When all the girls had received their passports, the soldiers herded them across the station platform and told them to board the waiting train. The girls were no longer making attempts at silence: they were crying, calling out for their mothers, pleading with the Japanese to let them go. Some tried to run, but soldiers chased them down and threw them gruffly back into the line that flowed into the open train carts. Meiko was squeezed through the door and pushed deep inside, nearly tripping on her *hanbok* in the swell of bodies. Soon she was pressed up against the far window. All the windows were covered by a canvas blanket tied loosely down with twine to hide the view outside. Once all the girls had squeezed in, the soldiers pulled the rattling metal door shut and locked it with an iron clunk. For a few seconds, there was an absurd silence as the girls stood stunned in the darkness. Along the cart's walls, squares of sunlight peeped around the blankets covering the windows. Soon the girls broke out with more weeping, with more calls to their mothers. "I don't want to go to Shimonoseki," someone yelled in panic. "I'm not ready … I just wanted *information* …"

There was an abrupt jolt beneath their feet as the train began to move. The girls closest to the door began pulling at it uselessly, whimpering "No! No!" as they realized there was no way to get it open. The shift and steer of the moving train squeezed them all to the right, crushing Meiko where stood against the blanketed window. The crying grew louder, but Meiko found she could not summon the breath to join in. She moved her fingers to the edge of the blanket at her shoulder and pulled it back to reveal the moving landscape outside the window. She watched as the structures of the train station and then the city itself thinned out and faded away, replaced by a spare and rural landscape. She looked up to see the sun hover in the cold January sky. Its position above them filled Meiko with a sudden, frightening wisdom. As the train picked up speed, Meiko beseeched the sun to shift its place in the sky. When it didn't, her realization rose up like vomit and suddenly she *could* find the breath to speak, the breath to scream.

"We're moving north!" she yelled out. "Do you hear me? We're moving north! They're not taking us to Pusan. They're not taking us to Shimonoseki. Do you hear me? They're taking us north!"

But her knowledge seemed lost in the cacophony of weeping. And Meiko realized too late that this had been her mother's worst fear all along — this, a train packed with ignorant, terrified girls, and heading in the wrong direction.

CHAPTER 4

I stand at my whiteboard, glossy Basic 5 storybook in one hand, green marker in the other, uncapped and ready for business. This is me, pretending to know what I'm doing. My tiny classroom is packed — fifteen Korean students aged eight to eleven. Fourteen of them sit at their miniature desks, each one littered with storybook, homework book, grammar book, and pencil case. The fifteenth student, a troublemaker named "David," stands facing the corner of the room, his back to the class, head arched downward in shame. This is his punishment from ten minutes ago when I caught him speaking, for the third time tonight, a quick burst of Korean to one of his buddies. The Canadian flag I've taped to my wall hangs just above his head.

"Get the ball," I read to the class.

"Get the ball," the class echoes.

"Now Billy has the ball," I chant.

"Now Billy has the ball."

"MichaelTeeee-chore!" David weeps from the corner, as if I've forgotten he's there. I look over at his slouched frame and hesitate before speaking, allowing him to stew a moment longer in my feigned authority. "Okay, David, you can sit down." He skulks shamefaced back to his desk.

We begin working through the storybook as if it's Henry James. I get the kids to read lines aloud, correcting their pronunciation as they go, then begin to ask leading questions about what is happening in this soccer game, and they recite back exactly what I want to hear, exactly what the storybook says. I'm obligated to stay standing and write these insights on my whiteboard, lest the school's director (Ms. Kim — confirmed Asian spinster, a hostile little touch-me-not) looks through my classroom-door window, fixes me in her angry little crosshairs, and confronts me at the end of the night for Not Following the Curriculum. Time is winding down, so I get the kids to close their books so I can hand out their nightly quiz. For the next five minutes, they will hunch over the test with great purpose, filling in blanks with nouns and verbs left out of the exact sentences we've just read. I take a slow walk up the aisle to inspect the kids' progress, hoping my presence will hurry them along. Soon I have all the tests in my hand and with a few seconds to spare — which doesn't feel right. I'm forgetting something.

"MichaelTeacher, homework?" asks "Jenny," one of the older girls. They always seem to be named Jenny.

"Oh shit," I mutter aloud, and the kids all gasp in horror. I hustle to my whiteboard and begin frantically jotting down workbook page numbers and grammar exercises, reciting them aloud for the kids as I do. Meanwhile, the class bombards Jenny with a Korean phrase, which I'm sure if I could translate would say, *You stupid bitch, he nearly forgot!*

"No Korean, please!" I shout with my back to them, still scribbling furiously. Then the bell does chime, an annoying rendition of "Mary Had a Little Lamb," and the kids burst from their chairs and pile toward the door. Some go gliding out on their Heelys— rollerskate wheels built right into the heels of their sneakers. I finish getting all the homework down and turn around. "Did you get that?" I yell. But I'm nearly alone, except for the last couple of kids squeezing into the noisy hallway, looking back over their book bags at me with a sense of vague pity.

. . . .

I am not a teacher by trade. You don't have to be to work here. Anybody with a university degree, in anything, can come to Korea and teach English in this *hagwon* system. Korean parents believe in education, as best as they understand it, and this involves sending their children to as many of these after-school academies as they can afford. Kids go to public school from 8:30 until 3:00, but after that they move through a long parade of extracurricular learning — math academy, science academy, English academy, taekwondo academy — that stretches well into the evening. ABC English Planet is one of the more reputable *hagwons* in this neighbourhood of Daechi: we boast a regimented curriculum, reading-writing-grammar-conversation, and a staff of native-speaking teachers from around the West. And I am now one of them.

How things got this far — with me falling into the chair at my desk to watch the next class of exhausted students pour in to my room — is a tale of minor tragedy, of personal failures and squandered opportunities. Many of my coworkers here are like the guy in the baseball cap from the club — in their early twenties, recent graduates with relatively useless university degrees, spilling out of planes at the mudflats of Incheon with unfathomable student debt and a misguided sense of adventure. By contrast: I am nearly thirty years old and with a fairly practical degree under my belt: journalism. Up until the spring of 2002 I had a career as a reporter for the Lifestyles section of *The Halifax Daily News*. For a long time, I treated that background like a godsend, the one clear way out of my chaotic family situation and into a life that would prove stable, reliable. And, for a while, it was.

Of course, my ex-fiancée Cora would tell you that I was *never* a good journalist, and I would have to agree with her. I was probably two years in to the job at the *Daily News* before I realized that I lacked the one quality essential to being a good reporter: extroversion. I could research the hell out of any topic, learn all there was to know about occupational health and safety, Black History Month, municipal budgeting, Goth fashion — but to actually pick up the phone and call a stranger or go knock on someone's door filled me with a gumbo of paralysis. It was only through Cora's positive influence that I forced myself to do the sort of harassing essential to my career. She and I met at J-school and she was, even from the first semester, already a journalist's journalist. She got on with CBC Radio at the same time that I started at the paper, and she was always pressing me to get out there, get out on the streets of Halifax and "Talk to People." It was probably her nagging that kept me from getting fired in those tough early years. So when she eventually left me for one of her radio colleagues, some French fucker named Denis (pronounced *Din-ee*, never Dennis) and transferred with him to CBC in Montreal, I had a sense that I was doomed in more ways than one.

But I'm getting ahead of myself. The story of how I ended up slinging English like hamburgers in South Korea does not begin with Cora leaving me for another man, nor with the crippling introversion that eventually got me fired from the *Daily News*. No, the story starts much farther back than that.

I never knew my father. He died of a rare blood cancer when I was two and my sister Heidi was eight. What I know of him is based on the pedigree he left for me and on the photographs of him that my mother kept framed around the house, like totems to his memory. He was involved in Nova Scotia politics and worked as a speechwriter in the later years of the Robert

Stanfield government. There was a photo of Dad that stood out in my childhood above all others, a picture that Mom kept on one of the crowded bookshelves in the living room. It had Stanfield in the foreground, mid-speech at a bouquet of microphones, fist raised and finger extended, and my dad in the background, arms folded loose across his chest and face full of a mirth that said *I got him to say that.* There were many who believed that, given time and proper mentoring, Dad would become Stanfield's heir apparent and lead the Nova Scotia Conservatives throughout the eighties and nineties.

It was not meant to be. The cancer that arrived in the fall of 1975 took less than six weeks to kill him, or so I was told. There were generous obituaries in the papers and letters written to our family from MLAs on both sides of the aisle. My mother stored these in a shoebox she kept under her bed, and would take them out and reread them whenever she felt her grief was fading to unacceptable levels.

My mother, as winsome and as wise as she could often be, had a weakness for the drink even as a young woman, and, faced with the unfair, inexcusable death of the man she'd been infatuated with since high school, descended into an alcoholism that Heidi and I could only watch with a kind of perplexed horror. The rattle of empty beer bottles stacked in sagging cases in the kitchen, the chime of hidden gin and rum bottles that sounded each time we opened a linen closet, became the white noise of my childhood. Mom insisted that my father was worthy of such mourning. (I even got a sense of his reputation when, sixteen years after his death, I arrived at journalism school to discover that some of the older profs had known him, and thus anticipated great things from me.) And to imply that Mom needed to let go of her sense of injustice was the highest sin you could commit against her. I cannot tell you how many friendships she ruined in a drunken rage because someone had dared to suggest that she Move on with Her Life.

The truth is, Mom was unstable even before my father died; his death was merely the green light that her deepest-held insecurities had been waiting for. I will give Mom her due: I believe she was touched by genius. She could recite entire passages of Robert Browning from memory; she knew, down to the minutest physiological detail, the difference between a gecko and a salamander; she followed Ronald Reagan's atrocities in Nicaragua with rabid condemnation. But she couldn't find a way to channel all this undigested knowledge into the stability that our family needed so badly. And when, in 1984, seventeen-year-old Heidi fled our house after a marathon screaming session with her, never to return, my mother went off the rails completely. After that, the beer bottles disappeared. After that, she drank exclusively hard liquor. She drank it every day. And she drank it straight.

And Heidi? Oh, what can I tell you about Heidi. She has remained her mother's daughter, only more so. In the last nineteen years, my big sister has left a half-dozen half-finished university degrees in her wake. She has slept on streets. She has hitchhiked across Canada. She has been a Wiccan, a vegan, a skinhead, a tattoo artist, an eco-terrorist, and through most of it, a single mother herself. As far as I know, she lives somewhere in British Columbia with her teenaged daughter, where she makes a not-very-good living selling her unimaginative folk art at farmers' markets on the weekend. I have not seen Heidi since Mom's funeral.

My mother died while I was in the middle of my journalism degree; I had not yet turned twenty-one. Funny, how hard it is to stop resenting somebody when you assume they'll always be there. Thinking of her death reminds me of a line from Nora Zeale Hurston, something about what a waste it is when our mourning outlives our grief — and I think it doubly shameful that my mom failed to outlive either of hers. When she was gone, I refused to put the label of *orphan* on myself, even though that's what I was. I think Cora's presence in my life, then my girlfriend, soon to be my fiancée, had a lot to do with that. As long as she was by my side, I knew I was not alone. It took burying my mother for me to realize what it feels like to be in love.

And for a few years there, we got on with it. Graduated with good grades, got J-jobs right away, got engaged. You could find Cora traipsing the streets of Halifax on the hunt for the perfect sound bite, her jet-black hair pulled tight against her scalp. Meanwhile, I worked at the *Daily News* offices on the outskirts of town — researching topics, crafting sentences, interviewing people by phone when I had to. The Lifestyles section suited me because I could get away without asking tough questions if I didn't want to. In the evenings, we'd reconvene in our small apartment on Shirley Street where we'd drink red wine and listen to Miles Davis, and Cora would lightly chide me about whatever risks I chose not to take that day. I believed, like a fool, that she not only tolerated my pathological shyness, but celebrated it as a part of who I was. Life was good. I felt like I had broken through a wall.

But then Denis-never-Dennis arrived in our lives and shut the whole show down. What a vertiginous feeling it is to watch the woman you love fall in love with somebody else. Denis-never-Dennis started out as just The New Guy at Work, described one night to me while we were doing the dishes. Soon Cora began referring to him as My Friend Denis. I wasn't all that suspicious at first: the fact that he was ten years her senior provided me with a false sense of security, rather than a harbinger of the Nick Hornby-esque angst that I would experience later. Then came days when she'd mention that the two of them had spent a sunny lunch hour eating French fries together from Bud the

Spud on the ledge outside the public library. She'd do so in pass-ing, a peripheral detail to whatever she was talking about — as if I wouldn't notice her subliminal subterfuge and call her on it. Then came the Friday nights where I'd come home and wait sev-eral hours alone in the apartment until Cora eventually arrived, obviously tipsy, and she'd say "Oh sorry, Denis and I just grabbed a glass of wine or two after work at the Argyle."

Even when she started spending less and less time at home, she denied it. Even when the sex dried up, she denied it. I fig-ure my relationship with Cora ended a full two months before I realized it. When she was ready to move out, she taped the small, pathetic engagement ring I had given her, all that I could afford, to a note left for me on the kitchen table. It read simply: *I'm sorry, Michael. I truly am. But there is something in you that lacks*.

And then sent her girlfriends over to get her stuff.

Was I enraged? Of course. Did that rage express itself through some vehicular vandalism in the CBC parking lot? Possibly. But more to the point: I was now ready to accept the labels I had been denying myself for years: orphan, rudderless, alone in the world.

In fact, with Cora gone I was free to descend into the char-latanism that I knew rested at the heart of my character. It began manifesting itself through my job, with me growing less fastidious about capturing accurate quotes from the people I interviewed. *It* sounds *close enough to what they said*, I would tell myself. Then I was making up entire quotes from interviews: they still came off like something my sources *should have said*, and I convinced myself that it was okay, that I could get away with such behaviour, because after all this was the Lifestyle sec-tion, with so little at stake.

I knew my negligence had taken a sharp turn when I found myself creating entire sources out of thin air. The topics of the stories were (at that point) still genuine, but when I couldn't bother finding someone to say what I wanted, I made them up. By this point, I was addicted to the rush of not getting caught, day after day. And soon enough, I was in for a pound: I eventually fabricated entire stories — topic, news angle, sources, quotes, even the occasional post-publication letter to the editor from a fictitious interviewee.

I consider it a scathing indictment on modern journalism that my dalliances could go on for *four years* before I got busted. Like a serial killer or corporate criminal, I grew arrogant and reckless. The "story" that did me in involved a book club comprised of immigrant housewives from the Palestinian territories who read novels exclusively by Jewish writers as an act of cultural understanding. It wasn't the story's questionable premise that sent the red flags unfurling. It wasn't even a single sentence within the story. It was a passing clause within a sentence, sandwiched between em-dashes and mentioning an organization that did not and could not exist — The Jewish Consortium for the Annihilation of Arab History — that finally raised the eyebrow of my managing editor and sent her digging. And digging. And digging.

The unearthing of (most of) my ruses took no time at all. Needless to say, the *Daily News*'s competition had a field day when they became public. The *Herald* ran several days' worth of articles about my misdeeds and subsequent termination, column inches that went on and on, needlessly. (They even mentioned my father, his noble reputation and work with the province, a *tsk-tsk* sort of reference.) The *Canadian Press* picked up the story and ran it nationwide. I know the girl who wrote it — we had a one-night stand my first year at J-school before I started dating Cora.

I was, of course, done for. Let me remind you that this was the spring of 2002 and Google was just achieving critical mass. Plug "Michael Barrett" in a search engine and you'll need to click through several pages of results before you find a link that *doesn't* include the words "disgraced journalist." So I took some time off to recalibrate. But before I knew it, "some" turned to "a lot": spring became summer and summer became fall. Meanwhile I had student loans I was still paying off from ten years earlier; the banks would not give me relief. I was now taking cash out on my MasterCard to pay for essentials like rent and vodka. It was almost fun to be in this kind of free fall into hopelessness. Nobody would give me a job. The few friends I had weren't speaking to me. I was drinking all day long. And watching month after month as I spiralled toward personal and financial Armageddon.

Cut to a foggy afternoon: I was on the waterfront drinking alone in the Nautical Pub when I ran into an acquaintance from my university days. Over dinner, he told me how he had gone on to do an expensive MFA and then paid off the student debt he incurred by teaching in South Korea. Had arrived in Seoul $35,000 in the red, but after three years of teaching returned to Canada $15,000 in the black. Said I could do the same. "But I don't have a teaching degree," I told him.

"Neither do I," he replied. "You don't need one. I wouldn't even call what you do over there teaching. You just stand up in front of a bunch of Asian kids for eight hours a day and Be White, Be Western." We parted company with him giving me the address for an online job board.

So I checked it out. And I applied for something. And I got a job offer right away. During the brief, perfunctory phone interview, Ms. Kim didn't even question why my seven-year tenure at *The Daily News* had come to an abrupt end. Nor did she ask what I'd been doing with myself in the eight months since. All she needed was for me to Fed-Ex a package containing my valid passport, notarized confirmation of my university degree, and a photograph, a headshot of myself — which, I later learned, was to confirm that I was in fact white. It would take her a couple of weeks to process my E-1 visa. After she did, she confirmed my salary — 1.9 million won a month, virtually tax-free — and that upon my arrival I would move into a free apartment, albeit with a roommate. "His name is Justin," she informed me. "He is from Nova Scotia, like you." She could have added *He is also emotionally damaged, like you*, if she had known.

As my departure grew imminent, I gave notice on my apartment, sold off whatever shabby furniture I hadn't hawked yet, cancelled my phone. But it didn't feel like a new beginning, a chance for a fresh start. Not at all. Even before I stepped on Korean soil, I knew the truth about what I was doing. People don't go to Asia to *find* themselves. They go there, for better or for worse, to run *away* from whatever they *have been*. And all I could hope for was to butt up against something, anything, to fill in the craters that resided within me.

It's the photos of Justin's kid that always get me. He has a collage of them tacked to the wooden headboard in his bedroom; I see them every time I go in there. This is what Justin *has been* — a father to a son who died in 2000. His name was Cody. Nearly six years old when he was killed in a freak accident while the family was vacationing in Gros Morne National Park in Newfoundland. The photos on the headboard show the little guy in various states of little-guy animation. They overlook Justin as he sleeps.

It's early on a Saturday afternoon and I'm just getting mobile. Freshly showered, I towel down the remnants of my hair and try to shake off my soju hangover from the night before. A crew of us had gone out after work for *kalbi*, Korean-style barbecue, and the liquor had been flowing; Justin and I didn't get home until nearly dawn. Let me describe what I mean by *home*, this shoebox that ABC English Planet has provided. Imagine the smallest apartment you've ever seen and cut in half. It has the Korean-style floor heating, called *ondol*, a plastic simulacrum of hardwood that you never walk on with your shoes; you must leave your footwear in the small, sunken entryway by the door. Our kitchen is just a countertop with propane hotplate sitting below a row of cupboards, and with a small fridge to the right. We have no kitchen table. The living room is a leather couch parked in the centre of the apartment facing a tiny TV in the corner. We get a few English channels — CNN International and the Armed Forces Network. There are two bedrooms to this apartment. Justin's is much bigger than mine. The benefits of seniority.

After I've dried off and dressed, I knock on Justin's door and enter when he calls me. I find him on his bed reading a paperback. The photos of Cody hover all around his head.

"What did you say we should do today?" I ask him. "You mentioned it last night but I can't remember."

He laughs his deep laugh. "Wow, you really were drunk." He sets his book aside. "Scrabble at the COEX."

"Right. Scrabble at the COEX." This had been our plan, to take Justin's Scrabble board and play a game in the food court of the COEX shopping mall. He and Rob Cruise had done this once before, with humorous results — it had caused a growing and enthusiastic crowd of Korean passersby to stop and watch them. Koreans are generally fascinated by English, even if they don't speak it; most know that access to English means access to power. Scrabble is especially captivating, since there can be no equivalent of it with their own alphabet. My students are always begging to play the game in class, but Ms. Kim frowns upon it.

Justin gets up and digs the Scrabble board out from under a pile of clothes. It's an early version of the game — the maroon box is sagging and held together with an elastic band. "We'll probably only have time for one game," he says. "I have my private at four o'clock."

"Fair enough," I reply. By private, he means a private tutoring session, not exactly the most legal of activities in this country. In theory, you can be deported if you're caught teaching English outside of the regular channels. But of course we all do it — the extra money is too good to pass up.

He stuffs the board and a dictionary into his backpack and then we head out the door. The COEX is a twenty-minute walk from our apartment, and by the time we get there, our hangovers have turned to hunger. We order a couple of bibimbap in the food court. As we set up the Scrabble board, I notice a few curious stares from other patrons, but that's all.

While we eat and play, Justin tells me more about the private he'll be teaching later in the afternoon. She's a twelve-year-old named (of course!) "Jenny," a former student at ABC English Planet whose parents pulled her out after they realized how preposterous the curriculum was. But Jenny loved Justin's demeanour and teaching style, and so her mother approached him discreetly to ask if he could teach her privately on weekends at their home near Dogok Station. The family is loaded — Justin makes 160,000 won for four hours of work. Jenny's dad is an executive with a big Korean company, putting in ninety hours a week, and Justin hardly ever sees him during the tutoring sessions. ("Hell, Jenny's *mom* hardly ever sees him.") Still, Justin has found kinship with both parents — they're only in their mid-thirties, just a couple years older than he is.

"It's like they've adopted me," he says, putting DIAL on the board. "They feed me; they buy me gifts; they help me with my Korean. And of the dozen sessions I've done, only about five have taken place in their apartment. The rest of time, Jenny's Mom —"

"What's her name?"

"Sunkyoung — she doesn't have an English name. The rest of the time Sunkyoung says 'Let's take Jenny to a museum today' or 'let's take Jenny to an English movie.' She's so adamant that we get out and do things together. The three of us."

"And you go?" I say, adding ET to TOIL for a triple word score.

"Of course I go," he replies. "It doesn't feel like work at all. It feels," and he lowers his eyes, ostensibly to add my score, "it feels like being part of a family."

As our game progresses a few passing Koreans throw us a glance. One nosy woman stops to inspect our board and points at the word RASCAL. "What means?" she asks. "A very bad man," Justin deadpans. She covers her mouth as she titters and walks off. A few minutes later, an older gentleman approaches our table with an awkward smile. Does he attempt his own comment about the Scrabble board? No. Instead he points at my face, then points at his own and rubs his chin jealously.

"I like-uh your beard-uh," he blurts out, but then scurries off, embarrassed.

I turn to Justin. "He liked my beard."

He nods. "It's an enviable beard. Korean men can't grow one like that. They just get the Fu Man Chu thing going on."

"I like your beard, too," I hear someone say over my left shoulder. I turn in the swivel chair and am surprised to see the girl I met at Jokers Red a few weeks ago. Jin. The girl in the long coat and cashmere. Jin. Rob Cruise's clandestine conquest. She stands holding a tray of food and wearing a black business suit, smart and well-tailored. It takes me a second to believe it's her. Justin clears his throat.

Before I can even shove out a hello, she marches over to our table. "Why are you playing this silly game in a food court?"

Justin and I look at each other as if we've forgotten. "I guess it's our way of offering free English lessons," he jokes. "Do you want one?"

"My English is fine, thank you very much." She seats herself next to me.

"Funny we've run into you here," I say.

"I work in COEX Tower. I'm on my lunch break, *finally*."

"You work Saturdays?"

"Of course. Most Koreans do. You ESL teachers have it easy — most of you get Saturdays off." She hasn't taken her eyes off the board. "So can you explain how this game works?"

We talk her through it as we play, elucidating on what the coloured areas mean and how to place the high-point letters on them strategically. She nods with growing comprehension and restrained delight. I'm very aware of her proximity to me, the way she leans across my arm to cast her curiosity over the board. I want to ensure that I win this game in front of her. I clinch the deal when I place my last letter, an *X*, on a triple-letter score with it buttressed by an *A* and an *E* for a total of fifty points.

Jin lets out a little laugh and claps. "Wow, all that with one letter?" She turns to me. "You're good at scoring points with very little."

Justin chuckles at this, perhaps thinking of our night at Jokers Red. "Well, that's the game," he says, getting up. "I have to go if I'm going to make my private on time. Do you mind taking the board back with you?"

"Sure," I say. I almost expect Jin to leave, too, but instead she scoots over with her tray to take Justin's seat after he's gone. I notice she's eating a hamburger and fries. When I start gathering up the slates, she stops me. "Hey, aren't *we* going to play?"

"All right."

I set up another game and offer her the bag to draw her seven letters; I feel her hand muscling around in my palm to dig them out. She places them gingerly on her slate and then stares at them with great concentration, as if they might contain a plot. We sit for a long while in focused silence. For the first few rounds, Jin can only play three-letter words — DOG and WIG and TOE — but does so with great deliberation. With each hefty strategizing thought, her bottom lip sticks out, hangs there between the two streaks of her black hair framing her face. She munches on her lunch and doesn't look up from the board.

"So what do you do in COEX Tower?" I ask.

"I work for a clothing exporter. I do sales and marketing. In fact, I'm supposed to be in Beijing on business, but all this SARS nonsense made my employer keep me home." She proudly puts her first four-letter word on the board, BENT, doing so with both hands, the letters pinched in her fingers. She goes on to explain how her fluency in four languages results in regular trips abroad — Shanghai and Paris and London. I learn a few other things as she rambles: Though twenty-seven and professionally successful, she still lives at home with her parents — the norm for young unmarried Korean women.

I try not to cream her too badly, but when the game ends I have twice her score. She checks the time on her cellphone. "Ugh. I should get back to my office," she moans.

"Okay."

"It was nice seeing you again, Michael."

"Thanks."

She hesitates, looks at me as if I've forgotten something. Forgotten my manners somehow, or to ask another question. Whatever it is, I don't say or do it. She gets up curtly and leaves. I begin putting the tiles in the bag and packing up the slates. When I look up again, Jin has come stomping back to hover over the table.

"Hi there," I say.

"So what, *you don't ask out girls*?"

My mouth falls open a little. "I, I beg your pardon?"

"Oh *come on*, Michael." She begins rhyming things off on her fingers. "I engage you about Kundera at the club; I ask you to dance; I write my handphone number on a piece of paper to give you, except you never ask for it before you leave; then today I tell you I like your beard, and stay behind to play Scrabble. What's your problem? You would think by now you'd ask me to go on a date with you."

My problem? My problem is you slept with Rob Cruise. My problem is I'm a fucking mess. "Jin, will you go on a date with me?"

She lowers her head. "No. You're not my type." I feel as if I've fallen through the floor to land on the floor below. "That was a joke," she says, looking up. I laugh weakly. "Look, tell me something," she goes on. "Did Rob Cruise take you back to Itaewon since the night we met?"

"Yes."

"And did he take you to Hongdae yet?"

"He has."

"And let me guess — you guys always go for *kalbi* at that dumpy restaurant near your apartments and drink soju until you can't stand up straight."

"We were there last night."

"*Ugh.* So predictable! You need to see the *real* Korea, Michael." She takes out a pen and piece of paper from her purse and writes on it. "Meet me here, at Anguk Station. It's near the top of the Orange Line on the subway. Tomorrow at two o'clock. Exit 3. Don't be late." She taps the paper before sliding it across the table at me. "And there's my handphone number."

Then she hurries off before I can say anything else.

. . . .

She was one of Rob's conquests. She was. But she is not the same as the rest. She isn't. She is … what?

The next day I dress in my least frumpy clothes and concern myself with remembering what Jin had said: two o'clock at Exit 3, or three o'clock at Exit 2? I'm certain I know the answer, but to be safe I arrive at Anguk Station by two and bring a book along in case I'm wrong or she's late.

She is not late. She pushes her way through the turnstiles, a purse over her shoulder, and hustles over when she spots me leaning against the wall of the marble foyer with my book. Grabs me by the wrist without greeting. "Come here, Michael, I want to show you something," she says.

She pulls me back to the turnstiles and nods at a Korean couple who have come through and are now stopped to gawk at a shop window full of Korean bells and masks and other knickknackery. The man and woman are, alarmingly, dressed in identical clothes — baby blue golf shirts with bright yellow collars, beige pants, and spotless white sneakers — and they're gaping at the objects in the window with a hand in each other's back pocket.

"Honeymooners." Jin rolls her eyes. "So obnoxious. We have this silly tradition in Korea to dress in the same clothes as your spouse when you're on your honeymoon. It's supposed to be romantic but I think it looks ridiculous. Don't you agree?"

"They do look a bit foolish."

"Ugh. I'm embarrassed by how sentimental my country can be sometimes." She looks at me with a flip of her hair. "What do Canadians do on their honeymoon?"

"I have no idea," I answer honestly.

We ascend out of the subway stop and onto the sidewalk. We take a left onto a wide, long cobblestone street that's been closed off to weekend traffic and turned into a massive market-place for Korean artwork and crafts. "This is Insadong," Jin tells me with relish as we stroll. "It's the heart of cultural Seoul and my absolute favourite neighbourhood. This is the kind of place Rob Cruise and those guys would never take you." I cringe at the sound of his name, but she's right: there is an air of ancient artistry here that Rob would have little interest in. I notice the numerous alleys that stray off from the main drag of Insadong, alleys that look as though they suck you back to the Korea of five hundred years ago. We come across kiosks in the middle of the street selling jewellery and calligraphy brushes and rows of pottery. Jin speaks to each of the proprietors with clicks of Korean as she inspects their wares.

She's so authoritative; I wonder how on earth someone like this could fall for one of Rob Cruise's lines. While she's busy, I look off to the side and see a crowd of people amassed in front of a large food stall with a man dressed entirely in white standing in its window. "What's going on over there?" I ask and she turns to look. "Oh, Michael, you must see this." She takes my arm and leads me over to join the crowd. We watch as the man in white raises up a large, thick roll of what looks like dough and begins spinning it wildly in his hands, playing it like an accordion.

"It's almost hypnotizing," I say. "What's he making?"

"Pumpkin candy," she exclaims. "Here, come with me."

We push our way up to the front where chunks of the white candy are sitting on a sample tray. Jin hands me a piece and I place it in my mouth. The candy is hard and chewy, like taffy. It is sweet, with a mild, pleasant pumpkin flavour.

"It's good, yes?"

"Very good."

"I'm going to buy a box to take home to my father," she says. "He's addicted to this stuff."

Her purchase comes in a small cardboard box quarter-folded at the top. She tucks it into her purse and we walk on.

"So what does your father do for a living?" I ask.

"He's a project manager for Samsung," she replies. "It's about as glamorous as it sounds. Typical Korean businessman, he works *all the time* — about ninety hours a week. I hardly ever see him."

I think of Justin and the father of his private, Jenny. "And your mother?" I ask. "What does she do?"

Jin snorts. "What does *she* do?" She flashes her fingers in derisive quote marks. "She's a 'homemaker.' What to say — we are a traditional Korean family. My mother cooks and cleans and does the laundry, goes shopping for hours at a time, has lunch with her girlfriends just so she can *gossip* about me. Plus: she is always buying the latest household appliances and having unwholesome relationships with them."

"Really?"

"Don't laugh. I suspect she talks to the washing machine when we're not there."

"You're making fun of your *umma*," I chuckle.

"I *am* making fun of her. I probably shouldn't. She's the reason I speak four languages. When I was kid, she would — what do you say in English? — *micromanage* my education. Made sure I was in all the best *hagwons* and forced me to study very hard. I guess I owe her that." She turns to me. "So what do your parents do?"

"My parents are dead."

"Oh," she says, lips forming a gentle little O of surprise. "Michael, you're an orphan?"

"I am. I've been once since I was twenty."

"You're an *orphan*." She nods, as if this explains so much about me.

We move along the cobblestone street, taking in Insadong's atmosphere, until we come across a hole-in-the-wall shop that catches my interest. In its dark window there's a display of old Asian coinage and paper money, ancient books, and tobacco paraphernalia. We go in and are greeted by an elderly Korean woman, an *a'jumah*. I bow a hello in her language, then take a respectful stroll through her shop. I leaf through a wooden box full of old South Korean money from just after the war. I pick up a bill inside a plastic sleeve and show Jin the ancient bearded face on it.

"King Sejong," I say.

Jin smiles. "Yes. He created the Korean alphabet many hundreds of years ago. How do you know King Sejong?"

"My students talk about him sometimes — especially when arguing with me about why Korean is so much easier to learn than English."

She moves on, begins browsing through a row of crumbling old books, and soon lets out a little yelp of delight. "Oh, see this one?" she says, pulling out a tome with a deteriorating green cover. "This is a very famous Chinese text, a collection of ancient folk tales. I read this in reprint when I was first learning Mandarin, but this looks like the original."

She opens it carefully to show me the Chinese characters inside. They look daunting in their complexity, tracing down each page in intimidating columns. "You can actually read this?" I ask.

"Of course." She shrugs. "I learned Mandarin before I learned English. The way the world is going, Michael, you may have to learn it one day."

"Either that or Arabic."

I grab another decrepit book out of the row at random, peel it open, and see an entirely different alphabet scorched onto its pages. "Can you read this one?" I joke.

She leans in to look and her face darkens instantly. "No. That's Japanese." Her voice is like a stone falling through water. She sets her book back and slides past me, moves in so close that I can practically smell her shampoo. "I refuse to learn Japanese," she whispers, as if she doesn't want the *a'jumah* at the counter to hear.

We decide to get something to eat. I suggest the Korean diner next to the Starbucks at the end of Insadong Row, but Jin just scoffs. "That's for *tourists*," she says. "Follow me."

She leads me down one of the ancient alleys that branch off from the main drag, an alley that seems to narrow, cartoonishly, the farther we go. We arrive at a traditional Korean restaurant — pagoda roof and low walls — and enter to find the inner decor done entirely in cedar. There is traditional Korean music coming from the sound system, the melodic squeal of a *gayageum* that reminds me of weeping. The hostess seats us in a booth. I pick up one of the menus but frown when I see no English translation. The waitress comes. She's about the same age as Jin, and just as pretty. They chat in Korean, nodding several times at the menu and a few times at me. After the waitress has collected the menus and left, Jin says: "I went ahead and ordered food and drinks for us. I hope you don't mind."

"Not at all."

The waitress returns a few minutes later to set a large clay bowl with a ladle and two cups at our table. Inside the bowl is a milky white liquid, but it's not milk: the smell of alcohol coming off it is strong. Jin thanks the waitress, then takes the ladle and transports some of the creamy liquid into the cups.

"This is *dong dong ju*," she says, "a popular Korean beverage. Michael, it's very potent so you should drink it slowly."

"Hey, I can hold my liquor," I say, lifting the cup and smelling its contents. "I come from a long line of alcoholics." I take a full pull of the *dong dong ju* and something magical happens: I'm buzzing the instant it hits my stomach.

"You like it?" Jin asks, taking a girly, tentative sip from her own cup.

"Very much," I reply. I take another generous pull, and then another. Pleasant summer campfires begin burning behind my eyes.

We chat for a bit and I try with questionable success to pace myself. Before long the waitress arrives with our food, a sizzling stone plate covered in what Jin informs me is *pa'jun* — Korean green onion pancake. It comes with little ceramic dishes of sesame oil for dipping. Jin chats with the waitress while she sets up a small armada of side dishes around our table, kimchi and bean sprouts and some kind of scrambled-egg concoction carved into a square. The two of them nod a few more times in my direction. When the waitress leaves, Jin throws me a tight little smile.

"She thinks you're handsome."

"Do *you* think I'm handsome?" I, or possibly the *dong dong ju*, ask in return.

She wrinkles her nose. "Maybe a little."

"Do you think Rob Cruise is handsome?" I venture, realizing that he's still preying on my mind.

"Ugh. Rob Cruise is *not* handsome. But he is —" and here she mulls around for the right idiom, "he is *larger than life*. Every Korean girl he meets thinks so. I certainly did."

"So I've heard."

Miraculously, she does not take offence. "Do you really want to talk about me and Rob?"

"We don't have to." But then find myself asking: "Are you two still friends?"

"I don't know," she huffs. "He can be so cruel, but you know, in a hilarious way. This one time, he accused me of being *kong'ju'byung*."

"What's that?"

"Oh, it's very hard to translate directly into English, but it means, like, a high-maintenance princess. That I suffer from the *disease* of being a high-maintenance princess!"

I laugh because this is exactly the kind of Korean phrase that Rob would insist he learn.

Jin thinks I'm laughing at her. "I am not *kong'ju'bong!*" she whines, slapping the table with her palm. "I am very, how you say, *down to earth*."

"Hey, I believe you." I grab the ladle and refill my cup.

"Anyway. Rob Cruise was a mistake. Try not to think about him."

"I won't if you won't."

A silence falls between us as we work our way through the *pa'jun*. It's impossible to hide from Jin how useless I am with chopsticks; they fumble around my plate like paralyzed limbs. Without prompting, the waitress passes by to set a fork discreetly next to my plate.

"So tell me — what is the deal with your roommate, Justin, anyway," Jin says. "He's even more reserved than you are. What's *his* story?"

"Justin's stories are his stories," I reply. "I'll leave him to tell them."

Jin refills her own cup and blinks at me a little. "Okay, so tell me your stories, Michael," she says. "Why did you come to Korea?"

I have my stock answers prepared to unleash on her, the same answers I give anyone, Korean or *waegookin*, who asks:

half-truths about lingering student loans needing to be paid off, the desire to see another part of the world and experience a different culture, blah, blah, blah. But the impatient tilt of Jin's head tells me she's heard it all before and won't buy it. I'm feeling loose and fuzzy-headed, not at all like myself, and, consequently, embrace the truth.

"I got fired from my job in Canada."

"Oh? Really?"

"Yes. In fact, you could say I got fired from my *career* in Canada." I could leave it at that, sufficiently mysterious, but I find words coming out that I'd rather keep in a box. There is something in the angle of Jin's chin, in her freakily beautiful double eyelids, in the restaurant's shadowy light falling on her hair, which welcomes full disclosure from me. So I tell her every- thing — or almost everything. I at least have the good sense not to mention my ex-fiancée; this *is* a first date, after all. But I tell Jin about my father the politico and about my mother the lush. I tell her about my journalism in Halifax, such as it was, and how, orphaned and rudderless, I drifted into disgraceful acts of forgery and fiction. Soon I've gotten up some steam and tell her about getting caught and how my dishonourable deeds were broadcasted across Canada. I was fired and with no hope of find- ing other work in my field. I needed money and a *break from myself*, so I came to teach ESL to Korean kids, which has proven more palatable than suicide, which I also considered.

"I'm very ashamed," I tell her, finishing off my cup and looking into the pot to find all the *dong dong ju* gone. "I'm very ashamed of what I did."

Jin looks as if she might touch my hand lovingly, but doesn't. "Michael, don't be ridiculous. You're in Korea." Then she pauses. "You have no idea what real shame is."

"What do you mean?"

But she shakes it off. There's more there, I can tell, but she won't say what it is; unlike me, she has control of her tongue. "Look, I've met many ESL teachers," she says, "and sure, I've had relations with more than a few of them. But one thing I've noticed is that they've all come to my country because they're running away from something in theirs. Maybe not as big as *your* something, but they're running just the same. Except, *they* never admit it." I think of Justin and Rob, the little bits of themselves they've shared with me. "You're different than that," she says. "You're *better* than that." She leans in. "Tell you what. Whatever you did before we met is none of my business, and I promise not to judge you for it. And whatever I did before we met is none of *your* business, and you promise not to judge me for it. Deal?"

"Deal," I reply.

"Good." She settles back again and flags down the waitress to order us, me, a pitcher of water.

Out on the street, away from Insadong, we're standing in that awkward, absurd silence that comes at the end of a first date, where I feel the full weight and obligation of my gender crash down around my shoulders.

"You're not taking the subway?" I ask, stalling.

"No. I have to go to a family event not far from here, so I'll take a taxi." Her face goes grim. "Ugh. My mother will not be pleased that I'm half drunk on *dong dong ju*."

"Half drunk," I snicker.

"Anyway, this was fun," Jin says. "I want to see you again, Michael."

"Okay." So I lean in to do the unbearable, to take that one brave step. Big mistake. She pulls back from me at a forty-five degree angle as if forced by the wind. For the first and only time, her face looks ugly to me — all flat and slanty, muscles pulled back as if by wild dogs, and full of cultural indignation. It says, *What are you* doing?

I fall back and she falls forward. "Call me," she says, patting my shoulder.

I stand there as she disappears into a cab, disappears into the city. And I hate myself for the thoughts that plague me then. I blame the drink. *What the fuck, Jin. It was just a kiss. What the fuck. You bloody well slept with Rob Cruise the first night you met him.*

CHAPTER 5

North. An incredulous direction. Above Seoul, above Panmunjom, above Pyongyang itself — did the earth not drop off and vanish if you went farther, become a place that existed strictly in textbooks, in rumours? The thin black thread of the rail track weaved through the unwelcoming white of winter, the train hurrying from the cold stasis of Chosun and into the hot oven of war. Chugging toward the place that Meiko knew only from textbooks and newspaper articles, declaring the glory of battle, of empire. A place someone, somewhere had named Manchuguo.

Manchuria. Northeastern China.

They stopped at a small station nestled in the mountains not far from the border and the girls were unloaded and allowed to eat. They sat outdoors in the frigid wind on wooden tables, huddled over plates of pale, wet rice and hard radish, shovelling the food into their mouths with their fingers. The Japanese soldiers orbited them like leering moons, their rifles slung on shoulders, long bayonets pointing at the sky. The girls were not permitted to finish before they were forced to their feet again and returned to the train platform. There they were separated into groups, pulled apart from friends by stern soldiers and ordered to wait in silence. One train arrived and a group disappeared into it, leaving the others to stand weeping and confused in its wake. Another train and another set of girls gone. And then another.

Meiko's group was the last to leave; they stepped onto a smaller train, just a few carts long, which began moving the moment the doors closed behind them. Meiko felt her stomach hollow as the heavy thump of track lines beneath their feet went on, hour after hour.

Two days later, they arrived at another, smaller station on an icy mudflat near a large marsh. The girls were unloaded, fed, and then made to line up at a loading dock. A large army truck with a canvas roof came rattling in and backed up to where the girls stood, and they were ordered to load boxes into the back. Unlike the other girls, who appeared more or less illiterate, Meiko could read most of the Japanese words on the boxes' wooden lids. She saw boxes for ammunition, for dry goods, for medical supplies. There was one Japanese word she didn't know stamped on smaller, lighter crates. *Saku*, it said. Something like *sack* or *bag*. Small sacks.

Once all the boxes were loaded, the girls were ordered to get in the back with them. As Meiko waited her turn to climb on board, she spotted a small wooden sign dangling on the side near the front of the truck. Her eyes strained to read the words. At the top, they said:

WAR MATERIALS

and below that:

ESSENTIAL

As she was shoved up into the truck and found a box to sit on among the other girls, she thought vaguely to herself: *Essential. They have labelled us all essential, like the ammunition.*

. . . .

What is this huge house nestled in the mountains, this bright red mansion? It was someone's home at one point — perhaps an aristocratic Chinese family lived here before the property was confiscated for Japanese purposes. As Meiko was unloaded from the truck with the others, she looked around and imagined this courtyard a peaceful place for wealthy children to run and play, to read under a tree or explore the copse that surrounded the property. Now it was a place of menacing line-ups: lines of trucks pulling in with supplies; lines of trucks pulling out with soldiers ready for battle; lines for food and water; and lines leading inside the house.

The girls were forced into their own line to stand outside a large green tent set up at the courtyard's edge. This was the camp's makeshift hospital. The girls were led inside the flap one at a time, grasping their identification papers in terror. Meiko noticed that the girls didn't come back out the front again, but were instead led out the back and toward one of the wings of the house, their skin flustered red and chins crushed into their breastbones. When it was her turn to enter the tent, Meiko swung in under the flap to find an army doctor and a Japanese soldier waiting for her, the latter ordering to see her passport and papers. He gave them a cursory glance and then told her to sit up on the examination bench. The doctor came over, tilted her head back, examined each of her eyes, stuck a tongue depressor in her mouth.

"What is this place?" she asked when he began checking her braids for signs of lice.

"You speak Japanese," the doctor said, then turned to the soldier. "This one speaks Japanese. That should make things go faster."

The doctor ordered Meiko to lie on her back on the bench. He came around the other side and she thought he was going to examine her feet. "Take off your underpants," he ordered. She sat up quickly. "What? Sir, I couldn't. What are you asking me? No man has ever —"

The soldier was over to her in a second, grabbed a handful of her braids, pulled her head back and placed the intrusive weight of his knife at her throat. "You will learn quickly, *Chosunjin*, to do what you're told here!" he barked. She looked up at the doctor who stood between her legs, waiting. She panted under the weight of the knife, stared at the doctor with a fury she refused to hide. He huffed impatiently and forced his hands into her dress, bunched it up, then yanked down her underpants and spread her legs apart. Meiko screamed as she rested her head back against the bench, and the soldier's knife followed her down. The doctor's fingers were stiff and impersonal as they moved her labia around and around. He looked up at the soldier. "She's intact," he said. Then: "And beautiful. You should check out the clit on this one."

The knife left her throat as the soldier came to look. They each grabbed one of her knees to keep her legs apart so they could stare at her loins, and then the doctor began batting at the small nub of flesh atop her opening. When she felt her nipples stiffen, Meiko let out another scream of shame and lashed out without thinking. Her heel slammed into the doctor, a short horse's kick right to his hipbone, and he took a step backwards. The soldier's knife was up in a breath, and he moved to stab it like a peg into the slit between Meiko's legs. "Oh, just leave her!" the doctor said with his hand raised, half-laughing under the pain, and the soldier stopped. "She's got some spirit, but she's a virgin. Leave her."

The soldier lowered the knife, but then grabbed Meiko by the back of the knee and threw her off the bench and onto the floor like a sack of peppers. As she scrambled around on her knees, he kicked her in the rump towards the tent's back door. "You exit that way, *Chosunjin*," he spat at her as she pulled her underpants up. Then he turned to the doctor. "I'll get the next girl."

So this was how it worked. You got your own small room in the house — a stall really — and some nice clothes and make up and some musky perfume to spray on yourself. They gave you a tatami mat to sleep on and a box for collecting the tickets that the men brought in to give you. Each morning you would bring these tickets to the house manager, who wrote the quantity down next to your name in a ledger to keep track of your pay for providing services to the soldiers. But what services? What is this place? It was a question Meiko had kept asking herself all through the afternoon and into that first evening. "This is a place of comfort," the manager had told her, told all the new girls. "You are here as a gift from Emperor Hirohito; your job is to give our warriors comfort." But what did that mean? *If we're here to entertain these men, shouldn't there be instruments in our rooms — a beautiful* gayageum *to rest on our laps, to send our fingers fluttering across like birds? Am I to sing, to dance, to tell the men adorable little stories that help them forget the horrors of the battlefield? What do they mean by comfort?* The girls who had already been there when they arrived, who knew, offered no answer — they moved through the hallways of the house with their heads down. In her room, Meiko saw nothing with which to comfort the men. Besides the ticket box and tatami mat, there was a small wooden crate of the *saku* she had seen on the truck. She opened it to find mysterious squares of tinfoil inside with the words Assault No. 1 stamped on them. Next to the box, there was small ceramic bowl full of cloudy water, heavy with the scent of disinfectant.

Meiko lay on her mat waiting all evening, listening to the sounds of men being comforted in the rooms down the hall from hers. What wretched noises! They sounded like they were in such delirious pain, that the girls were injuring them somehow. Wait, that wasn't quite right: there were mutual screams, men and girls, reciprocal anguish, though the girls' tears seem to go on for several seconds after the soldiers had let out their last, tortured bellow. If it was all so unpleasant, then why were the soldiers lined up the hall, awaiting a go at it? They were yelling *hayaku! hayaku!* — hurry up, hurry up! It's my turn. Hurry up and finish. It's my turn.

Night came and a strange, errant peace fell over the house. There were still sounds of comfort coming from the rooms but the hallway seemed less busy, less crowded. Meiko was nearly asleep on her tatami mat when the curtain to her stall opened abruptly. She perked up in an instant and scuttled back against the wooden wall to see a man, a Japanese officer, standing at her threshold. He was short and corpulent but full of authority, his eyes sharp and small.

"Hello, my little one," he said. She could not bear to talk. Tears were already forming below her eyes. "Do you speak Japanese?" he asked. She nodded hurriedly. He smiled, tossed the little red ticket he came in with into her box, a minor formality, then glanced down to make sure it was the only one in there. "Don't be afraid. There's no point to being afraid. What is your name?"

Again, that silly temptation to summon the Korean name her parents had given her, but she shook it off. "Meiko," she replied.

"Meiko," the officer repeated. "What a pretty name for a pretty little girl. How old are you?"

"Fifteen."

The officer let out a slow, happy breath and took a step forward.

"Sir, are you here for comfort?" Meiko stammered.

The officer blurted a chuckle at her. "Oh, Meiko, very much so, yes."

"And how am I to comfort you?"

"By doing exactly as I say. Do you understand?"

Meiko could not bring herself to nod. She looked at the floor, and when she looked up again she saw the officer already undoing the front of his trousers and pulling away his loin cloth. His man muscle fell out, a thick, short cord, and he took it in his hand and began stroking it to life. Her eyes widened in horror.

"See this?" he moaned softly. "Watch me, Meiko. Watch me. Don't turn away." He petted himself slowly and the meat in his hand grew longer and stiffer. "Now come here. Come here, little one."

She was too terrified to disobey. She took one reluctant step that brought her close enough for him to take her by the wrist and pull her all the way over. "Now you do it. Here." And he put her hand on him. "Now you do it. You do it." She ran her hand up and down him clumsily, her face streaking tears.

The officer leaned into her and began bunching up her dress in his hand, pulling it up by her hips. "Oh, you have such beautiful legs, Meiko. Look at that. Look at that." He stared at her legs for a long time while she stroked him. Then he turned up at her with eyes glossy with pleasure. "Now put me in your mouth."

She thought she heard wrong, got his Japanese wrong.

"Meiko, here, put me in your mouth." He forced her to her knees, took his meat back from her and pressed it toward her face. He slapped her chin with it, a heavy thump that left what felt like a cobweb behind. "Stroke me with your mouth. Come on — comfort me."

"No," she blurted out, finally. "No!"

"Meiko, take it. Take it in your mouth."

"No!"

He thrust his hips against her head, mashed the tip of his meat between her lips. Without thinking, she seized it in her teeth and bit down. The officer let out a howl and ripped himself away from her. "She bit me!" he screamed. "Fucking bitch!" and he drove his knee as hard as he could into her sternum. She yelped. Crumbled onto the floor in front of him, a deep bow.

"She fucking bit me!" he screamed again, pulling up his trousers and hustling from the stall. He was gone for only a moment, not long enough for Meiko to regain her breath or find a way to escape. When he came back, he was holding an iron poker he had yanked from the charcoal stove in the main room, its tip glowing an angry orange. The house manager was racing up behind him, pleading "Give me that! Would you give me that? What the hell are you doing?" He shoved the manager away and then knocked Meiko onto her back with one expert stomp into her clavicles. Even before her head hit the mat, the officer was climbing aboard her, pinning her legs down with his knees. Hiking her dress up with one hand, he dragged the hot poker across the narrow shelf of her shin with the other. She filled the room with a scream that seemed to originate from every cell of her body. The manager reached over the officer and stole the poker from him. "Would you give me that! You're going to start a fire in here!" The officer turned himself around and forced Meiko's legs up and apart, draping the back of her knees over his shoulders before fumbling with his trousers again. "Put on a sack!" the manager yelled, reaching into the wooden box by the tatami mat and tossing him one of the tinfoil squares. "Put on a sack, would you. Follow the rules!" Meiko fought him even as she watched him liberate the little ring of rubber from its tinfoil square and roll it down over himself. When he leaned with all of his weight into her, she felt the room slip backwards, slide away as if the house was collapsing down into the earth. It felt like every gram of the officer's bulk had poured into her, filling her insides with a horrible, tearing weight. He shoved her knees all the way forward until they were squashed into her eyebrows. Began pumping at her with wild, canine thrusts. Meiko grew vaguely aware that the house manager had left the room once this act began, confident the officer could do no damage to the house itself. Meiko closed her eyes and let her mind flutter away. She thought of cranes lifting off into the sky from a vast body of water, taking their wisdom with them. What had her mother always called her? *My wise little crane.*

This was a wisdom she did not want.

The officer screamed into her ear and stopped his thrusting, just held himself there and melted away like wax off a candle. His breath was a wheeze that smelled vaguely of oysters. He pulled out of her and slipped off the condom with one motion of his hand. Threw the limp, soggy sack, stained red on the outside and bloated with a milky white on the inside, at Meiko's face.

"Stupid *Chosunjin!*" he said, pulling his loin cloth back up. "You ruined your first time. Let that scar on your shin be a lesson to you!"

So this was how it really worked. This was what they meant by comfort. At least there were rules you were supposed to follow — chief among them to insist that the men put on the *saku* before they took comfort from you, and to cleanse yourself with the antiseptic liquid in your little ceramic bowl after each man had finished. There were also rules about time. Mornings to mid afternoons were for enlisted soldiers, mere boys, really; late afternoons and early evenings were for the noncommissioned officers; and the nights were for officers. Everyone was on a strict schedule so that they would never cross paths and interfere with someone of a higher rank. The enlisted boys did not stay long — they would enter your stall with a quick little snap of your curtain, climb aboard you and pump away until they let out that little scream of triumph, perhaps urged on by the yells of *hayaku! hayaku!* from the hallway. The officers were, by contrast, far worse. They were allowed to stay longer, sometimes all night, and asked for the most awful, humiliating things.

Another rule was that you were not to speak Korean at any time. This meant the girls ate in silence at meals, huddled over their plates of bland rice balls and miso soup, silent because most of them couldn't speak Japanese, couldn't even speak enough Japanese to find out if the girl sitting next to her spoke Japanese. *What a clever way to keep us from conspiring*, Meiko thought. Of course, some girls forgot or couldn't help themselves, blurting out a brief Korean phrase while at the table or lugging boxes of supplies to the trucks lined up in the courtyard. It enraged the soldiers to hear Korean because most of them didn't understand a word of it and assumed that the girls were planning an escape. Speaking a single Korean sentence could result in a ten-minute beating.

One afternoon a couple of weeks after her arrival, Meiko was at the lunch table admiring a ferocious little bruise that an officer had left on her ankle, when one of the older girls came over and said in fluent Japanese: "They will lose interest in you soon enough, you know."

Meiko gaped at the girl who had spoken at her. She looked about twenty years old, but it was hard to tell: her hair was matted against her head and her eyes had gone yellow from some form of disease.

"The officers, I mean," the girl went on. "They've a taste for the virgins — or at least the virginal. You have that look for now, but don't worry — you'll lose it eventually." She half smiled then, revealing a mouth full of missing teeth. "Before long you'll start to look like me and they'll leave you alone. Leave you for the common soldiers."

Meiko said nothing.

The girl glanced down then at the bruise on Meiko's ankle, and above it at the weeping blister across her shin where the first officer had burned her with the poker. "The other girls have been murmuring about you," she said. "Did you really bite a corporal on the penis your first night here?"

Meiko nodded solemnly.

The girl looked like she wanted to chuckle, but held it in. "You shouldn't resist them so much. They'll kill you if they think you're too difficult to handle. If you want to live, then you should follow the rules and accept what they want from you. If you want to live, then just do what needs to be done. Make sure they wear the sack, make sure you clean yourself, give your tickets to the manager on time, and don't make a fuss — about anything. If you want to live, be a ghost. Be anonymous."

Meiko licked her lips. "Do I want to live? Should I want to live?"

The girl did chuckle then. "My name is Natsuki," she said. "That's not my real name, of course. What's yours? What's your not-real name?"

"Meiko."

Natsuki placed a hand on the back of Meiko's neck and leaned in close. Whispered low, so the house wouldn't hear. "You bit a corporal on the penis, Meiko. Trust me — you want to live."

Natsuki proved to be an expert at anonymity, at being the sweet silent flesh that the men expected to find on the other side of a stall curtain. Her background was similar to Meiko's: she had attended a private school for girls in Pyongyang before being taken away, and she was fluent in Japanese. She took it upon herself to teach Meiko how to be just another nameless spectre living in the house, as opposed to a girl with a reputation for defiance. "I consider it my obligation, as your *unni*," she said. So strange, Meiko thought, to hear Natsuki speak even a single word of Korean. *Unni*: an older sister, but here meant as a female friend who is older than you are. "Firstly, you cannot blame the soldiers for their tantrums. They see all this as a simple transaction. They give money to the manager, the manager gives them their ticket, they give the ticket to you, you give them service. Refuse to service them, or refuse to service them in the way they wish, and they feel cheated and perfectly within their right to go berserk on you. So don't refuse them." Be pliant, she said. Eat quietly. Don't ask questions. Don't breathe loudly. Don't even let them see you go to the bathroom. Achieving anonymity made respecting your own role easier. That meant collecting your tickets and guarding them against thievery, and making sure that the house manager accurately recorded your day's take in the big ledgers. Meiko noticed that Natsuki always pushed her way to the front of the line to have her tickets counted, standing over the podium and staring at the manager's hand to make sure he wrote the numbers down correctly. "The ledgers are *everything*," Natsuki told her. "It's how we and our families will be paid when this ordeal is over. Endure whatever the soldiers want of you, Meiko — no matter how disgusting or violent — but make sure you're paid. If the house sees these acts as nothing more than simple transactions, then treat them as such. But make sure you're paid."

But Meiko couldn't endure. Defying the men just came too naturally to her. This *wasn't* a place of simple transactions. It was a battleground. Any number of things would enrage the soldiers, and trying to guess what wouldn't was a fool's errand. Even the sight of her monthly bleeding would make them ferocious, accusing her of deliberate poor timing. How could she not fight them, when nothing was off-limits, when every crevice of her body was open for exploration? And despite Natsuki's promise, the senior officers were not losing interest in her; they continued to spend the night in her stall. They wanted to bury themselves deep in her folds, clutch her to their fat chests, violate her body in the most horrendous ways. Even insisting that the soldiers follow the most basic rule of the house — wear a sack — grew more difficult as the weeks and months went on. Before long, of the forty-odd men who raped her each day, a full third of them didn't put on a condom.

And so. Each scar on Meiko's legs came to represent a moment of resistance against the men, a trophy she had earned for herself. It was her legs that aroused the soldiers' passions the most — but they were also what the men took out their frustrations on when she refused them certain acts. They "loved" her legs; the soldiers would rub their crotches into her calf, run their fat tongues along her ankles, suck her toes, tell her how the shape of her knees reminded them of their mothers. Yet if Meiko defied the men in any way, it was her legs that they would lash out against. They would burn her thighs with their cigarettes, stomp on her shins, pierce the flesh of her calves with their knives. To her, it seemed like such a Japanese thing to do — to vandalize that which they found beautiful.

It was around April that Meiko first spotted the sesame seed-like bumps cropping up on the lips of her *poji*. They were bright white, oily, and burned with an insatiable itch. No matter how often Meiko scrubbed the disinfectant from her little ceramic bowl into herself, the bumps would not go away. She knew what awaited during their monthly doctor's examination if she couldn't get them to subside. The girls were well aware of the army doctor's dreaded "606" injection, used on them to combat diseases that the men passed around. Natsuki had somehow learned the clinical names for this treatment — Salvarsan, arsphenamine — but to the girls, it was known simply as 606, or sometimes "the rat poison."

In the line outside the doctor's tent, Meiko held Natsuki's hand in a state of dull panic. "The first time is always the worst," Natasuki told her. "The first time for *everything* around here is the worst," Meiko replied. When it was finally her turn, she pried herself away from Natsuki's grasp, entered the tent, climbed onto the examination table, and laid back as she was ordered. There were fresh cuts and burns on her legs, but, as usual, the doctor paid them no attention; he was concerned only with whether she was carrying a disease that she could pass on to the soldiers. He shoved her legs apart and looked at the curtains of her genitals. Stuck his fingers inside her, jerked them vigorously, gave her clitoris a thumbing on the way out.

"You need the injection," he said, throwing her legs shut again. Meiko began to weep as she sat up. She stared at the tent wall, unable to watch him prepare the enormous syringe.

"You really should wear the *saku*," the doctor said, tapping at air bubbles. "That is, after all, what they're there for." *We don't wear the* saku, *the men do*, she thought, but didn't bother pointing it out. The doctor rolled up Meiko's sleeve and pulled her arm taut. "This will hurt immensely," he said, and jabbed the needle into the flesh just below her shoulder. Instantly it felt as if her arm had been severed at the point where the needle went in. Meiko screamed at the tent walls, felt nausea erupt in her stomach, and her bowels twist like hoses. The doctor lifted her gruffly off the table and thrust her toward the tent's back door. She staggered outside into the cool spring air, fell forward, and vomited onto the grass. Doing so didn't quell her nausea; in fact, her retches only stirred up the arsenic racing through her blood until her whole body became a water skin of poison, a battle between what the soldiers had infected her with and what the doctor had given to cure it.

And on it went. Convulsing chills. Vice-like stomach cramps. Vomiting and diarrhea, involuntary evictions from opposite ends of her body. And Natsuki, sitting next to her on the grass, unbothered by the stench and mess and willing to hold her hand through it.

"You should go," Meiko said faintly, spitting out chunks of vomit that had gathered around her gums. "Your afternoon off. Should find something better to do than this."

"Foolish girl," Natsuki said. "I'm your *unni*. I'll stay with you for as long as I'm allowed."

And she did. Kept Meiko company through the dry heaves and debilitating shivers, the dribbles from her anus. Stayed until the sun touched the western horizon.

"It's time," Natsuki said morosely. "I have to go get raped now."

"Okay. You go get raped. I'll talk to you later."

A nearby soldier caught the nonchalance in their Japanese and came over to grab Natsuki by the arm. "Back to your stall, *Chosunjin!*" he barked, throwing her toward the house. "Go earn some money for your family." Then he looked down at Meiko, at the vile paddies of sick that orbited her. "Ugh. Why don't you wear the sack, you slut?"

The 606 did its job. Soon the manager began allowing soldiers to line up outside Meiko's stall once again. A cruel irony: the 606 had left her too enervated to fight with the men about putting on a sack, and many more than usual enjoyed her without one. She became like a latrine for the boys, only instead of relieving their bladders they relieved their lust – fully into her. The line ups were getting longer. The soldiers' hollers of *hayaku! hayaku!* were a constant chorus in the hallway. Anxious men watched from the threshold of her stall with the curtain pulled back, their faces like moons floating in her doorway as one of their comrades did his business with her. As soon as he finished, the next soldier entered, practically climbing over his friend to get at Meiko, sometimes rolling on a *saku*, sometimes not. Her genitals had now swollen into some mutant fruit, stone-hard and leathery.

Spring turned to summer and summer into fall. Something was happening beyond their stalls, out on the battlefield — a growing sense of hopelessness among the platoons as defeat loomed over their heads. The manager became less fastidious about making the men adhere to the rules: stopped bothering to keep the intoxicated boys out of the hallway, allowed a few soldiers to slip into the lines with the non-commissioned officers in the evenings. The war was practically lost, they said. We're all going to die tomorrow, they said. So why not enjoy these fleeting pleasures while we can? One day, Meiko peeped outside her curtain to see a girl getting raped in the hall: she was down on all fours with a fat, oily soldier pumping away behind her with other soldiers cheering him on and the manager making tacit requests to take it back to a stall. When the soldier finished, he pulled up his loin cloth, grabbed the weeping girl by her throat and dragged her outside. No one ever saw that girl again.

Meiko was awoken in the middle of the night by a boom that shook the house. Instant voices of panic, of men and girls, above and around her, and the sudden shuffling of feet, of racing bodies through the hall. She sat up on her mat. Another boom, and a wave of muddy earth slapped the side of the house. Meiko screamed, grabbed for her clothes. Her curtain snapped and there was the manager. "Out, now! Out of the house now!" The hallway was full of smoke. Meiko raced into the plumes and fell in line with the herd of other girls thumping up the planks while soldiers weaved among them in a dash to the doors. Out into the courtyard and Meiko saw the night sky glow a fiery orange. Shells whined over their heads and ripped into the ground. "Trucks! Get into the trucks!" someone was screaming. Meiko found Natsuki, nearly crushed into her. "What's happening?" she screamed at her *unni*, but then an explosion blew through the centre of the house behind her, sending wood splinters into the air like a cloud of startled bats.

"Truck!" Natsuki bellowed over the noise. "Find a truck. Find a *truck*."

They did, at the edge of the courtyard. Hustled aboard with other girls, found wooden crates to sit on under the canvas top. When the truck was full, it tore out from the grounds and sped toward the dirt road leading down the hill. Meiko looked to see other trucks lining up behind theirs, each full of girls and soldiers. A hard whistle and then the vehicle directly behind theirs sank under an eruption of flames, a mad bang that seemed to suck the very air out of her mouth. Meiko buried her face in her arms and screamed. Felt Natsuki's face on the back of her neck.

By dawn, everything was silent except for the rattle of the truck beneath them. Meiko awoke to look at the other frightened girls sitting on their crates. Some were holding one other, others were alone in their terror. Meiko turned to see Natsuki staring at her.

"What happened?" she asked.

"We're moving houses," Natsuki replied. "I'm surprised we lasted this long. I've moved four times since becoming a comfort girl." Her face grew serious. "That was the worst of the moves. By far."

Four days south and they arrived at their new comfort station. Not a house this time but just a camp of wooden structures cobbled together in the dip of a valley. A scorched forest of bare, ashen trees lay just east of it, offering no protection from whatever lay beyond. *Much worse than the house*, Meiko thought as the girls were unloaded from the trucks. *No "comfort" here at all.*

The girls lined up in front of the hospital tent for their examinations. Natsuki stood behind Meiko and held her hand while they waited their turn. Why was the line moving so slowly? Meiko thought. It didn't make sense: There were fewer girls now than before, and yet each one seemed to take her sweet time inside the tent. At one point, an officer came by and bullied his way inside to yell at the doctor for taking so long; the girls could hear their curt argument echoing off the canvas from where they stood.

When it was finally Meiko's turn to step through the flap, she found the doctor standing in the pale light, his face soft and unsmiling and yet somehow kind. "Please come in," he said. "Do you speak Japanese? What is your name? Come in. Please, come. Don't be afraid." He was an older man, maybe in his forties. His uniform was neat and well-pressed. He took Meiko's hand and helped her up as if she were a lady climbing into a carriage. And then he surprised her by asking permission — *permission* — to look between her legs. Meiko laid back and spread herself for him by rote, not trusting this kindness. But the doctor's fingers were warm and gentle on her. She could sense his eyes fall on the scars of his legs, could feel him wanting to ask about them. But he didn't. When he finished his examination, he sighed and helped her back up. "I'm sorry, my child," he said. "But you need the injection."

So in went the 606, the blinding pain and the flush of poison that seeped right into her organs. The doctor told her to go next door to a shack of cots that he had set up for sick girls like her, a quiet place where she could recover. Meiko left the tent under a cloud of nausea and weaved across the camp's macadam of earth. Found the shack, found a cot. Climbed onto it, collapsed under the heaves and her fading consciousness. Waited for Natsuki to come and stay with her like she had before. Twenty minutes, an hour, but Natsuki didn't come. The afternoon bled into evening and there was still no sign of her *unni*. Just these other girls on other cots, lost in the haze of their own injections of 606.

Meiko was out of commission for nearly a month this time. Except for the occasional soldier sneaking into the shack at night and climbing aboard her cot, she was left alone to recover. For those four weeks, she saw no sign of Natsuki. When the doctor came by to check on her, she asked about her friend. "Which one was she?" he asked. *How can I describe her?* Meiko thought. *Aren't we all the same to you, the same mounds of flesh?* "I think I know who you mean," he said. "I'm sorry, my child. She was not ill, but your friend was … she was carrying something else." He lowered his eyes. "The arsephenamine … it can kill more than just disease. If you give a strong enough dose, it can kill something else. Your friend … your friend is alone where she is, to recover. I'm sorry, but you won't be seeing her for a long while …"

It took another month before Natsuki resurfaced, floating into the girls' mess one day to collapse next to Meiko. She was as pale as snow and large chunks of her hair had fallen out. Meiko embraced her *unni* and wept into what was left of her shoulder.

"The doctor was kind to me," Natsuki said, almost in a trance. "Did you not find him kind?"

Meiko sobbed and nodded.

"He offered me a choice. The injection — or the hook."

"Don't speak. Don't speak, my *unni*."

"Stupid me — the hook would have made more sense." She ran her tongue over her bloated lips. "It's unpleasant, but only for a few minutes. They stick that wire inside you as far as it will go and then just pull the whole mess out. Instead, I asked for the injection. Why did I do that?" She sucked air through the space left by her missing teeth. "Maybe I wanted two months off."

"Did you know? Natsuki, did you even know?"

"How could I? I haven't had my period in two years. Too many diseases. But the doctor said it will never happen again. Not for as long as I live." The leathery flakes of Natsuki's face quavered. "The 606 made sure of that."

Fewer men lined up outside Natsuki's stall when she was eventually allowed to go back to work. The extra doses of 606 had left her hideous. There were days when she had no tickets to return to the manager at all. Meiko watched as her *unni* shook her empty ticket box over the manager's podium in a fit of melodrama. "What, don't the boys want me anymore?" she said. She threw her box down, then raised her skirt and waggled herself at the manager. "I still have one of *these*, you know." The manager came around the podium and kicked her to the floor, kicking her again when she began to laugh. "Back to your stall," he said. "You sad old hag. Maybe one of our brave men will take pity and fuck you like the dog you are."

Meiko was not with her *unni* on the evening she brought her empty box to the podium and found it unattended because the manager had gone on a break. Meiko was in her stall, crushed under a noncommissioned officer, her legs wrapped limply over his pounding hips, when she heard strange words reverberating down the wooden hallway. At first she didn't realize what they were, but then it dawned on her: those were *Korean* words; those were *Korean sentences*. She needed another second to realize that it was Natsuki who was screaming them.

"The ledgers! These aren't the same ledgers we had in the other house! Hey! Hey everybody! Listen to me! They aren't keeping records! *These aren't the same ledgers!*"

Meiko heard the clomping of boots in the hall even as her officer's thrusts grew toward their crescendo. *Natsuki, shut up!* she wanted to scream, but the man's lips muzzled her mouth. *Oh, Natsuki, please shut up. They'll kill you, don't you know. Shut up! Stop speaking Korean!*

More yells in the hall, more boots on the floor. "You didn't take the ledgers out of the last house, did you? You let them burn. You let our records *burn!*" The sound of the podium banging down onto the floor. It matched the sudden yelp of pleasure that the officer hovering over Meiko gave as he finished his business. When enough of his strength melted away, Meiko scrambled out from under him. Pulled her skirt down over herself and dived through her curtain.

In the main chamber she found a naked Natsuki throwing ledgers at the soldiers who had surrounded her. Other girls had come out of their stalls to see what the commotion was. Natsuki was weeping and holding open a ledger with just a couple months' records in them, wagging it at the Japanese faces closing in on her. "You lying bastards!" she sobbed in Korean. "You haven't been keeping good records. Everything I've worked for." She backed toward the corner. "Look at me. I was a *woman*. I wanted to be someone's wife. Someone's *mother*. You have taken it ... *taken it from me.* No man will want me. No child will spring from my womb. Look at what you've taken. *You haven't been keeping good records of what you owe m —*" An officer finally tackled her to the floor. Pinned her down and then raised her up.

"Everyone, out in the courtyard, now!" the manager screamed at the girls. "Every last one of you!" He pointed at Natsuki's squirming limbs as the soldier lugged her outside. "Look at that girl. Do you think this will stand? We'll show you want happens when you speak your doggerel language among these men."

This is pointless, Meiko wanted to yell at him. *You don't speak Korean and most of these girls don't speak Japanese. Nothing was exchanged here. Just let Natsuki go. Beat her and put her to bed. Tomorrow is another day.*

But the girls, in various states of dress and dishevelment, were herded out the doors, down past the muddy square, and to the edge of the easterly forest with its burnt, bare trees. The men made the girls line up in an oval in front of a large trunk, its branches a gleaming black from some long ago blaze. Meiko looked over and saw the camp doctor, the doctor who had shown her such kindness, who had given Natsuki the choice — the hook or the injection — standing on the edge of their gathering and arguing with the soldiers about what they were about to do. And the soldiers, just boys really, were *laughing* at him, laughing at his foolish pleas. Soon the manager came pushing through the oval with Natsuki over his shoulder and some hemp rope dragging behind him. Meiko watched the men tie the ropes to her *unni*'s wrists and ankles. Natsuki was screaming at them, but not with words that sounded like Korean *or* Japanese. Meiko crushed her palms into her face as the men pulled the ropes tight and strung Natsuki upside down among the lowest branches. Meiko couldn't help it — she let her fingers run down her face to stare at her naked friend, and for a moment their eyes met. *Die quickly*, she wanted to say. *Please don't fight them.* And Natsuki looked back as if to say — *Live slowly, Meiko. Live a long time, despite what you've suffered. And remember this always. Remember the records they didn't keep.*

A soldier pulled his ceremonial sword from its scabbard and climbed onto a crate that someone had set up at the tree's base. He grabbed Natsuki's left breast and hacked it off. The whole tree shook, the branches knocking together like bones. He let the breast fall to the ground like a clump of sand before grabbing her right one and doing the same. Natsuki continued to her yell her non-language as the soldier climbed back down to watch her bleed. Seconds passed but she didn't even lose consciousness. Another soldier appeared with the poker from the main building's charcoal stove, its iron point a blazing orange. He scaled the crate and then smiled down at all the terrorized girls watching, as if this were his moment of fame. He reached around to drive the hot poker between Natsuki's spread legs, shoving it into her like a penis. She sucked a glorious mouthful of air and then wailed a sonorous melody that echoed off the mud. The soldier held the poker there, tight, shaking it with little quivers of his forearm before pulling it out. Another gasp, almost silent, and then Natsuki resumed her monologue of gibberish. The soldier shook his head in disbelief, threw the poker to the ground, and then withdrew his pistol. Meiko's eyes were streaming. *Just die, Natsuki. Why have you chosen this moment to fight them? Just die.* The soldier slid the pistol's barrel into her smoldering vagina and yanked the hammer back. When he pulled the trigger, Natsuki's narrow hips blew apart like a cake dropped on the floor. The tree shook as if pounded by rain. The man climbed down and joined the others to watch. There was another beat of silence and then Natsuki picked up her soliloquy, speaking in a tongue that did not exist. The man with the sword spit out a Japanese expletive and then approached the tree with his weapon raised over his shoulders. For as long as Meiko lived, she would remember this — that it didn't look as if he *cut* her head off; it looked as if he had *knocked* it off, as if his sword were a club and her head a piece of hanging fruit. It fell and bounced like a child's ball onto the mud. And then everything was still. Everything was silent.

Where to let her eyes fall now? Not on the tree. Not on the butchered body that lived in its branches. Meiko instead let her eyes take flight like a crane to the edge of the oval. To the kind, powerless doctor standing there with his shoulders slumped in defeat. And why? *Why?* Because he was not looking at the tree, either. He had been staring at Meiko the entire time.

CHAPTER 6

Rob Cruise laughs at me, and then laughs again.

"Rob, shut up."

"You got the whole 'pull back,' didn't you?" He mimics Jin's facial expression perfectly. Justin and Jon can't help but chuckle.

"I said shut the hell up."

Rob blows cigarette smoke out my open bedroom window and into the evening's smoggy showers.

"I hadn't been on a date in a long time," I tell them.

"You *never* try to kiss a Korean on a first date."

"Rob, what are you talking about? You *slept* with her the first night you met."

"That's different."

Justin and Jon laugh again. Everybody knows things that I don't.

"Ahh, Michael, don't look at me like that. Jin and I never dated. We fucked, once. Ages ago. You're trying to date this girl. The rules are different."

"He's right, you know," Jon says. "For Koreans, dating's all about going for coffee for six months and then you're magically engaged."

"But don't get us wrong," Rob goes on. "Jin's not like that. She's a cool chick — very modern, very Western. I *love* the fact that she's fluent in English. Did you know it only falters when she's pissed off or horny?"

"Rob, don't tell me these things."

"Do you want my advice?"

"No, I don't."

"Well I'm gonna give it to you anyway. Because you're smart about so many things, Michael, but you are fucking stupid about this. Don't invest too much in Jin. I know you're sweet on her, but that chick's nuts. I mean, serious fucking issues."

"Hey, *I've* got issues."

"Just stick with me, man," Rob says. "Play the field. Let me help you. You got so much going on, Michael. You deserve *more.* More than chasing after some girl who doesn't know if she's coming or going. And more than being stuck in this dry spell," he motions vaguely at my groin, "that's gone on for *how long* now?"

"Rob, I'm not a fucking frat boy. This isn't just about sex for me."

"Bullshit," he says. "Bullshit. Bullshit. *Everything* here is about sex."

Later, we gear up for the bars. While Jon and Justin are putting on their shoes, I pull Rob aside.

"Say, Rob," I ask him, "how's your little … problem?"

Makes a sweeping gesture at his own groin. "All cleared up."

"Listen. When you and Jin, you know … is it possible that —"

"No. Not a chance. Believe me. Don't worry about it. Seriously. Don't even let it cross your mind."

I nod, and when I look back up his grin is wide. "You *are* the same," he sings at me, proud and, perhaps, relieved. "You are the fucking same."

I am a little bit the same, I think. *But I am also a little bit different.*

. . . .

Jin plays the cello. I learn this about her on our second date — dinner and a movie. I learn that she resents it a little despite her proficiency. Lessons were a childhood chore, her mother's insistence. "I hated it," she says. "She pushed me to practise every day. 'Jin-su, it's time for the cello … Jin-su, why aren't you rehearsing?' She was always bringing me out to play at parties to impress the neighbours." I laugh. "You were what we call in English a parlour trick." She lights up. "Yes exactly! I was a trick. Like a ten-year-old Mozart."

On our fourth date, we visit the Korean War Memorial in Noksapyeong. It's a huge stone museum laying out the entire history of conflict on the Korean peninsula, going back five thousand years. Jin is great at explaining her country's violent past as we move through the sequential exhibits and dioramas. How does she know so much? Afterwards, we go outside and stroll around giant black statues of South Korean soldiers in various warlike poses. I ask to take a photo of Jin with them and she agrees. I pull out my cheap analog camera — "Ohh, Michael, you should go digital!" — from my satchel while she gets into position at the base of a statue. As I point and focus, I expect Jin to flash the traditional V-sign with her fingers and let out a gleeful *"Kim'cheee!"* — the Korean equivalent of saying "cheese." She doesn't. She remains still and serious. Then, right before I press the button, her limbs burst into action as she mimics the pose of the statue above her, mimics its stony, stoic face. I think I fall in love with her a little when she does this. I ask about it after I've snapped the picture. She says she finds the cheery V-sign annoying, goofy — like the honeymooners in identical clothes. "I'd rather have the photo capture my *personality,*" she tells me.

Several dates through February and March and I behave myself entirely. I don't try to kiss her again, or anything. Jin seems fine with this arrangement — she is a paragon of personal control. I'm once again curious how Rob could penetrate that citadel of restraint. The boys offer no help: after each outing, I return to Daechi to endure their chants of "Did you fuck her yet? Did you fuck her yet?" I can't bother explaining to them that something else is happening. Jin and I are growing into each other a bit, leaving our mark on one another in gentle, benign ways, like you do with someone after a few dates. I've mastered chopsticks, thanks to her, and expanded my Korean vocabulary five fold. In turn, I've converted her into a coffee drinker following an afternoon visit to my apartment. "I was strictly, how you say, a green-tea person before this," she says, taking generous sips from one of the pink mugs that came with the apartment, "but you make excellent coffee, Michael."

Rob Cruise watches these developments from his island of sexual bravado. If he's jealous of the bond that Jin and I are forming, he hides it well. He seems stumped that I would persist with a situation that hasn't led immediately to sex. But of *course* he's stumped. He doesn't understand that my five-year dry spell has been so much more than a lack of physical contact. It has been *everything* in my life, a weight that sits atop me and will not go away. I often refer to it as my permafrost.

March 21, 2003. A date of demarcation — for me, for Rob Cruise, for the world at large. For Rob, this Friday marks his final day at ABC English Planet; he's managed to finish his twelve-month contract without getting fired, and intends to fling forth into a brand new life, into days that will finally be under his control. For me, it's my thirtieth birthday. A segregation between a decade of potential and a decade of rapidly closing doors. Still, there is a festive air in the halls of the *hagwon*, and a crew of us will be heading into Itaewon after work.

Rob has been ecstatic these last few days about his accomplishment. He has been in Ms. Kim's bad books practically since his arrival. The two of them have jousted about the school's pedagogy during countless staff meetings, arguments that leave the rest of us cringing as if doused in cold mud. For properly trained teachers like Rob and Justin, much of what we're asked to do in the classroom makes no sense. Rob has practically made a game of how far he can defy Ms. Kim — but has known, rightly, that she holds all the cards. In the *hagwon* system, the school controls your work visa, rents your apartment for you, and can fire you without cause at any time. The flipside is if you can survive your twelve-month contract, you're legally entitled to a thirteenth month's pay as severance and a free plane ticket home. This is what Rob has been holding out for, and it's vital to his "master plan." He intends to return to Canada for a couple of months, then fly back to Seoul on his own dime, teach under-the-table privates until the fall, then start the new job he's lined up for himself: a permanent position teaching ESL at Seoul National University.

At the end of the night, we all gather around for a small ceremony for Rob and a couple other teachers who have also finished their contracts. This is Ms. Kim's ritual, perhaps to show she has a *humane* side: she hands out little presents in glittery gift bags to each of the departing teachers as thanks for their year of service. Rob accepts her gift with mock gratitude, bowing deeply to his nemesis and smiling his oily smile. She won't even look at him. Then, before she's even finished handing out the other two gifts, he does the unthinkable: he pulls open the gift bag and yanks out its contents, a felt blue box. He cracks it open to find a silvery pocket watch with the school's logo engraved on the front. He takes the tinkling thing out and holds it up to show everyone while Ms. Kim tenses with horror. This is his final violation of her: in Korea, you *never* open a gift in front of the giver.

We file out of the school's office building and head straight to the curb to hail a taxi. Because it's my birthday, I've been allowed to pick where in Itaewon we're going. I've chosen a proper pub called Gecko's — no dance music or strobe lights anywhere to be found, just dart boards and wooden tables, and a good variety of beer on tap. I'm also keen that it's got a big screen TV with access to CNN. After all, March 21, 2003, is not just my thirtieth birthday and Rob Cruise's last day at the *hagwon*. On the other side of the world, Shock and Awe has begun in earnest.

Forty minutes later, we arrive at Gecko's to find the place packed; as I suspected, a crowd of GIs and foreign teachers has assembled in front of the large projection TV to watch CNN's coverage of Baghdad giving birth to balloon-like explosions. While the boys fetch me birthday beer, I find us an empty table and look around to see if Jin has arrived. I haven't seen her in a week and a half; she's been in Shanghai on business. I'm still looking when the boys return with sloshing pitchers and glass steins. Justin pours for me. "Is she coming out tonight?" he asks.

"She said she was."

"It's your birthday," Rob Cruise says. "Maybe she'll actually give you a *hug* or something."

"Hey, shut up …"

Trumpets blare and there's Wolf Blitzer in the CNN Situation Room. Iraq's government is in disarray; nobody's sure if Saddam is alive; American tanks are plowing northward from Kuwait; there are rumours of Iraq's National Guard already laying down its weapons, of ordinary Iraqis unfurling American flags in welcome. It's all framed like one big seduction, with Iraq in the role of not-so-coy mistress. I notice that the GIs here are gripped with obvious envy. They long to touch that flush of war — so much more appropriate to their training than the banal peace that has gripped Korea these last fifty years.

There's a tap at my shoulder. "Happy birthday, Michael Barrett!" I turn and see Jin hovering over me. I rise from my bar chair and, much to my shock, she *does* hug me – a big birthday squeeze. Before I can even absorb the feel of her lissome energy in my arms, it's over and she takes the empty seat next to mine.

"How was Shanghai?" I ask, sitting back down.

"Fucking awful," she replies. "Fourteen-hour days and I didn't make a single sale." She looks at the TV. "What's going on?"

"Oh, just a war," Jon Hung replies.

"Just a war," she repeats, eyeing the screen with a shadow of anxiety. She turns back to me. "Michael, I brought you a present." She digs into her purse and takes out a gift: it's an exact square (clearly a CD) and wrapped in baby-blue rice paper.

"Thanks," I say, giving it the mandatory examination before moving it toward my coat pocket.

"No, no, open it now. I don't mind."

I shrug and begin to pull the wrapping apart to reveal Romantic Classics. I flip it over: Tchaikovsky, Strauss, Liszt, Chopin. "Jin, this is grand." I reach over to hug her again and strangely, inexplicably, she tenses under the bend of my arm. When I let her go, she nods at the boys. "Did these layabouts buy you anything?"

"Hey, we're buying him drinks."

"So buy him a drink, Rob Cruise. And get me one, too."

And buy me drinks he does.

I can't remember the last time I was irretrievably drunk. You know the feeling — when your friends keep yanking you toward reality but all you want is to sink into the swamp of semi-consciousness. You drift down into a kind of wakeful sleep, but then a friend will say your name, maybe shout it out, and it snaps you up, snaps you back to notice that everyone's staring at you — *Your presence is required here.* I'm fine while the beer is flowing, but once the gin/Scotch/double shots of tequila/soju trays start arriving, I begin to phase out of my commitment to lucid conversation. Rob Cruise is a demanding raconteur, especially with the Iraq invasion unraveling on the TV in front of us. He delights everyone with his exploits in the first Gulf War, wants my journalistic insights on what's happening now, on what *will* happen. Someone puts a vodka on ice in front of me and I gulp it down, think of my mother and her obsession with the stuff, drift into the hazy fog that was her shelter from grief. Actually it's not too bad here; I find myself drumming up childhood memories; I had a plastic motorcycle as a toddler and I used to —

"Michael!"

Your presence is required here.

"He's a fucking asshole!" I say, and instantly can't remember who we're talking about. Oh right. Bush. "I wouldn't trust him with a pair of scissors, let alone the presidency."

My words attract angry stares from some GIs at the next table, and I chuff up to say something to them, something like *Don't flex your triceps at me!* I actually get up to confront them, then black out for a moment. Come back later to discover myself playing darts with Jin on the far side of the pub: I've been taken aside to "cool down." Jin is *so cute* the way she throws darts like girly-girls do, using her whole body as if trying to knock down the wall. She touches my arm, and questions bubble up from my core. So obvious what I want from her tonight, my birthday wish. I lean in and she leans away, as if I stink. I chase my disappointment down the drain, tell her how disappointed I am. She says something in return, perfect and perfectly neutralizing.

I'm hopeless, bloody hopeless. Follow her heart-shaped derriere back to our seats around the TV. A glass of beer will surely stabilize the situation.

I zone out and then zone in to find Rob Cruise in a state of agitation. A girl they all know has arrived uninvited to our menagerie. Her name is Kyla, from New Zealand. She used to work at ABC English Planet; in fact, I was her replacement when I joined the school three months ago. She's brought over a husky GI, her new boyfriend, and this seems to be what's gotten under Rob's collar. Obvious history there, none of which I'm aware of. Are we still talking about Iraq? I can't seem to follow things. Harsh jokes and crushing words. This Kyla chick is thirty different flavours of *nasty* — glass of whisky in hand, she's junkie-thin, all spaghetti-strap tank top and garish tattoos, the kind of girl you should probably wear *two* condoms with. I say something clever to her soldier boyfriend, have no idea what it is. He rebuts and Jin races to my defence. This sets off some kind of debate about the neighbourhoods we all live in. The GI won't stop talking about his fully Westernized army base — Yongsan Garrison, Yongsan Garrison. Shut the fuck up. Jin does my work for me.

"Do you know what 'yongsan' means in Korean?"

"No." Chuckle of proud ignorance.

"It means to die in a place far from your home."

BOOM. Baghdad belches another bomb on the TV.

Our arguments swirl and grow; we're all over the map. Black out, black out, come back — "He didn't even win the fucking election!" — and then black out again.

I come back again, just barely, and the mood is not good. Kyla has left and Rob Cruise is steaming in her wake. Everyone's upset — Jin included. There's talk of moving on: Where are we going? Where are we going? Limelight, Jokers Red, or hop in a cab to Hongdae? No wait, Rob says the word — hill. The Hill.

Hooker Hill. Black out, stay with us. Jin is really upset now, arguing with Rob. He's pointing at me and telling her what she should do *if she doesn't like it.* She's talking so fast, objection tripping over objection, can't follow what she's saying but so upset now, entirely encased in those black mysteries, she's turning to me and I'm turning away, don't turn away. Come back and *fuck*! Jin's gone and I don't know why. Don't know why I didn't leave with her. Why am I even here? It's my birthday. Hooker Hill. Black out.

Come back to the wind in my face and neon in my eyes. I'm wholly aware of Jin's missing presence; it's like a phantom limb. The street's a thousand noisy expats shuffling from club to club. The four of us ignore the throngs and scale the hill south from Itaewon's main drag. The saddest place in the city, an alley of impeccable grunge. Here women stand on stoops outside of clapboard bars. These are no Hollis Street hookers: they are gorgeous, leggy, teeming with feigned *joie de vivre* and a sly intelligence. They see us coming and speak in flawless English.

"Hey boys, you wanna come in for some boom-boom?"

Boom-boom. I'd laugh at the absurdity of it, except Rob is already opening a door for me. We step inside the airless hovel to see benches and old tables with candles on them, flickering in glass orbs. There's a warm hand steering me from the small of my back. Black out and return to find myself at a table with the boys, bottles of soju in front of me and a stranger's arm around my neck, her face full of immediate hospitality, a smile as soft as a plum. I take the soju and gulp it down, feel my inner world slosh and list. I want to slump forward to rest my forehead against this table and feel the stranger's arm, her false intimacy, slip from my shoulders. Just a second to close my eyes, to wait for the universe to —

"Michael!"

Fucking Rob Cruise! The girls laugh at me without a hint of pity.

There's talk, negotiations. I hear thumps and grunting from the hotel above us. I push away my soju glass, demand they give me no more.

"C'mon, it's your birthday. Why don't you —"

"Birthday? Oh then I give you *special* time, big man."

A hand moves high up my thigh, offering to venture into my permafrost. But instead it sets off an image of me like a small flame, an image of a man who's better than all of this, who will not have his wretched dry spell end here. I burst up from the table as if sucked toward the ceiling. A green soju bottle goes airbourne, its contents dousing the hookers like spindrift.

"Ah, shit, Michael, sit the fuck down!"

But I'm already hustling around the tables on my chicken legs and out the door. Out the door and down the hill. Run like I'm trying not to run. The world's spinning. My arms cartwheel in their shoulder sockets as I grab for the air and find nothing to hold on to. My knees sting with the sharpness of the street and suddenly my forehead is grinding against the curb. I am an utter mass of defeat. Wish to go sleep right here, in this strange, filthy alley. But then I feel an arm pulling me up from around my waist and a familiar voice, a familiar accent in my ear. Nova Scotia.

"C'mon, man. I'll take you home. I'm not into whores, either."

Justin.

Good man.

And then I do sleep. Sleep in the leather seat of a cab with Justin riding shotgun, staring out the window as he always does — with that acute intensity, his impenetrable sadness. I sleep and dream of the peninsula he and I no longer live on.

. . . .

Fuck. I can't find Jin's CD. Must have left it at the whorehouse.

I wake up the next afternoon and wobble into the bathroom, look in the mirror to discover a spectacular gash on my forehead and our spare pillow laid with care on the floor in front of the toilet bowl. Ah, Justin. Good man. I don't remember vomiting, but I do remember getting up from the bathroom tiles at some point in the night and toddling off to bed. I take another look at the crusted scrape streaking across my brow. How am I to explain this to my students come Monday?

I navigate the oceanic waves of my hangover to park myself on the couch. Look over to see Justin's door closed: either he's still asleep or he's left already for his tutoring session with Jenny and her mother. Best for me to be alone anyway, marinating in my own flatulence and ruminating on how I managed to lose both Jin and myself on my thirtieth birthday. I wonder if it was Rob's intention to take me to Hooker Hill all along — to drive a wedge between Jin and the Drunk Me. Could he sense that she still wasn't ready to do what I wanted us to do, but that I, under the circumstances, wanted to do it anyway and was open to other, seamier possibilities? I could ask him, call him on his handphone. I look at my watch: he'd still be at Incheon Airport waiting to board his flight to Toronto.

I don't call him. Instead I sit in the stew of my thoughts and wait for a sense of normality to return. It's in guilt-ridden moments like these that I identify with my mother's desire to be drunk all the time. It's such a passive, careening existence, a life of dulled expectations for yourself and for the world. It keeps all of the sharp corners of your mistakes under gauze, under bubble wrap.

A couple trips to the toilet and I feel much better, more like myself. An hour or two pass and I'm ready to go outside. I'm thinking about the 7-Eleven down the street where I can buy a big bottle of Gatorade and a Styrofoam plate of *kimbop*, sushi's sad cousin. I brush my teeth and put on my shoes, tasks that seem to take another half hour. Then I lurch out the door, down the stairs, and into the falling glare of this late afternoon.

I find Jin standing on the sidewalk outside my building.

She jolts in surprise and we both freeze. There's a brief radiance of body language from her: maybe she's been standing here for several minutes, arguing with herself about whether to come up and knock on my door. Maybe she had, in the very moment before I appeared, decided that she wouldn't, wouldn't bother, and was just turning to leave.

We stare silently at each other. I notice she's dressed in her business suit — has already put in a full day at work. Must have wandered down here from the COEX after she finished. In turn, she spots the loud cut on my head. Her eyes flicker to it in a momentary flight of sympathy before resuming their icy rancour.

We glare at each other for a long time. She's angry, and I'm angry because she assumes she has something to be angry about. Are we going to talk? Are we even going to bother?

"Did you enjoy your *whore*?" she asks finally.

"Jin, I didn't sleep with a whore."

"*No*? I suppose the boys took you to Hongdae instead — found you a pretty little thing in high heels and lots of make-up who'd *give it to you for free*."

So ridiculous. So unlike anything someone like me would like. And yet this is the impression I've left her with. "I'm not into those kinds of girls, Jin. They're not my type." I say this with a conviction that surprises us both.

She will not waver. "You have no idea, Michael, how offended I was when I left the bar. You have no idea how much what happened last night, how you say, how you say, *enraged* me."

"I think I do."

"No, you don't." She shakes her head. "What, are you just another slimeball, like those guys? Just another foreigner looking to take whatever he wants from my country?"

What? Where is this all coming from?

"I don't know what kind of man you are," she continues. "What kind of man *are* you, Michael? What kind of girls do you like?"

"I like girls who *don't* wear make-up." My voice floods with determination. "I like girls with long blond hair full of knots and split ends. I like girls who wear frayed jeans. I like girls who paint. I like girls who take Dostoyevsky to the beach. I like girls who can stand in the arctic in winter and still sense the beautiful poppies that grow ... that *can* grow out of all that *fucking permafrost*."

This last bit confuses her. Confuses me, too.

"I, I like to paint," she stammers.

I laugh. Thankfully, she laughs with me. "Jin, do I look like somebody who'd enjoy a hooker?"

She sighs. "Those boys got you so drunk last night. I mean I know it was your birthday, but really, they can be such a bad influence on —"

"Why did you sleep with Rob Cruise?"

She halts. Turns up those double eyelids at me. "Don't ask me that! Michael, *don't ask*. The minute I answer that for you is the *minute we are finished*. Do you understand?"

"Jin, I'm sorry ..."

"It takes a long time to build something real. Let me build something *real* with you."

"I'm sorry."

"You are not Rob Cruise. You will never be. And *that's* why I like spending time with you." She quakes. "Is that *okay*?"

"It is."

"*Is it?*"

"Yes."

"*Good.*" She sighs again. "God, you *waegookins* are so *obsessed* with sex." She shakes her head, disgusted. And yet steps up to me then and slips her arms around my torso. Her fingers make a home at the small of my back. We lean in and it's the lightest, most innocent kiss you can imagine. A mere peck. When it's over, she pulls back from me, squints one eye, tilts her chin.

"So what the hell did they do to your forehead? And what's all this … about *permafrost*?"

CHAPTER 7

It was the great irony of the rape camps: how there had been Japanese women here, too, keeping their own stalls. "The aunties," they called them. Professional prostitutes brought over from Tokyo and Osaka. The aunties had worked in the shameful calling back in Japan, were skilled and experienced in the art of pleasuring men. Yet theirs were the least popular stalls in the camps. The soldiers didn't want to take comfort from professionals and only went to them when the other line-ups got too long. It disgusted Meiko to think of it, how the men, if they had their choice, preferred to rape young, virginal girls from the lands they had conquered. Insisted upon it. But by September of '44, all of the Japanese aunties had been shipped home. The supply trucks brought only Korean and Chinese girls now, ones that had been moved from other camps. Another sign that the war was going badly.

One night that autumn, a young soldier stormed into Meiko's stall at random, clearly drunk and in a state of agitation. When she denied him service, he accused Meiko, accused all of the Korean girls, of bringing diseases into the camp and infecting the men with painful ailments that shattered their morale. Certain of this, he was, now that the Japanese aunties were gone. Convinced in his drunken hysteria that *all* venereal infections originated on the Korean peninsula. "You are the *source* of disease," he spat at her. "*You* are the source of disease," she yelled back. He kicked her in the stomach and she fell to the floor. As Meiko scrambled around on her hands and knees, the boy climbed on top of her, grabbed a handful of her hair and yanked her head back. She heard the scrape of his sword as he lifted it from his scabbard. *This is it*, she thought. But the boy did not slit her throat. Instead, he put the blade under Meiko's nose and dragged it across her top lip, so deeply that she could feel the metal grind on her teeth. Blood shot all over her face, and the boy threw her head to the floor. "I *mark* you," he said, pointing at her with the stained blade. "I mark you as a source of disease." But then, as if forgetting what he had just said, the soldier leered at Meiko's rear end pointing up at him as she flailed around in agony. The boy fumbled out of his trousers, dropped to his knees and grabbed Meiko around the hips.

Ten minutes later, in the hospital tent, Meiko sat caked in her own blood and hyperventilating on the doctor's bench. The doctor, the kind physician who had watched over Meiko while the soldiers had butchered Natsuki. He was gentle even now as he inserted a needle into her face to freeze the flesh under her nose. Once he did, he began sewing her new wound shut, pulling the long invasive thread through her numb lip until everything was as tight as a wicker basket. He clipped the end off with little scissors before running a thick, malodorous ointment over the wound to fight infection. When he finished, he gently cupped Meiko's jaw and moved it side to side to inspect his work.

"The men are told all sorts of lies about your country," he said. "Venereal diseases anger them; they know they can't get shipped home if they're infected with one."

"We were virgins, all of us," Meiko said in choppy Japanese, trying to speak around the row of hard stitches under her nose. "How could we bring these illnesses here? The men gave them to *us*, not the other way around."

"I know," the doctor nodded. "I've seen every kind of venereal disease in this place. They just revolve around the camp like little trains." He set the ointment aside. "Speaking of which, did you want me to check you — down there? Since you're here anyway?"

She stiffened at the idea, but then allowed him to lay her down on the bench and raise up her tattered skirt. He maneuvered around to look between her spread legs. She waited as he ran his thumb through her *poji* and over her bruised perineum.

"You have another infection," he said after several minutes. Meiko seized up in a panic, squashing her knees together and drawing a breath through her aching face. "Don't worry," the doctor assured her, "it's just mild. You don't need another 606 injection. Here." He moved to the glass shelf near his bench and took down a small grey canister as she sat up. "It's a disinfecting lubricant," he told her. "Rub it into yourself a few times a day. It should clear you up in a week or so." Meiko took the canister from him and read the Japanese words on the label: Secret Star Cream. *Stupid, nonsensical name*, she thought.

The doctor watched as she sat up. "My name is Yoshimi," he told her. "And yours is Meiko. Though that's not your real name, is it. It's the name a Japanese person gave you. Would you like to say your real name, Meiko? It's okay. I won't tell the manager you spoke Korean."

Meiko said nothing. Wouldn't even look at him.

He swallowed. "I understand. The girl they killed — for speaking Korean — her name was Natsuki. Not her real name, either. Did you ever learn her real name?"

She began to tremble.

"I thought you might have," he went on, "seeing how she was your *unni*."

Meiko's eyes flashed at him with surprise.

"It's okay," Yoshimi said. "I speak a little Korean. I lived in your country briefly, ten years ago, working as a school doctor at an academy for girls. So I know what *unni* means. I'd say it's important to have one in a place like this. Wouldn't you?"

She jolted into tears, as if the doctor had struck her. She turned to stare at the tent's canvas wall. "I'm sorry," Yoshimi floundered after seeing what his words had done. "I'm sorry they killed your friend. I'm sorry they forced you all to watch. I'd like to say that it's the worst thing you'll ever witness here, but I doubt that's true."

Meiko just let her tears scald her temples.

"I've been meaning to come and see you," he said, and stepped toward her. "I've wanted to tell you how sorry I am. And maybe try to explain some things. Explain why our men do what they do. Not that it will help. But I still think you deserve to know." And with that, he put a hand on her bare knee.

As soon as he did, Meiko leaped off his bench and shoved him as hard as she could. Her face was a furnace. "*Fuck you,*" she said in Korean. Then pushed past him and went out the tent door. Still crusty with blood, she headed back to the main building, back to her cubicle and the rapes that awaited her there.

He had to pay if he wanted to see her. He needed a ticket from the camp manager.

When he stepped through her curtain, she looked up dimly from where she lay freshly raped on her mat, her shoulders crushed against the wooden wall, her face shining with sweat and a new bruise. She saw that it was him. Saw the ticket he held in his fingers. Yoshimi tossed it in her box as if it were an extinguished cigarette, an indifference that mocked the ceremony of this transaction. She ignored his nonchalance. Assumed her rote position, moving down on the mat, spreading her legs and looking off to her usual spot on the wall.

"Put on a *saku*," she told him.

Yoshimi didn't move. His eyes fell first to the dull scars on Meiko's legs and then the brighter, newer one jagging across her mouth.

"This wasn't supposed to be a place of violence," he began, almost to himself. "That's what I wanted to tell you when you were on my bench. These camps were set up as an *answer* to bad behaviour. The army believed that pacifying the men's urges would promote military discipline. But the opposite has proven true. We're losing this war. We *will* lose it."

Meiko said nothing. Yoshimi was about to go on but was interrupted by the sudden scream of a soldier in the stall next to Meiko's and the guttural cough-and-weep of the girl with him. Out in the hallway came hollers of *Hurry up! Finish already! It's my turn, it's my turn!* Yoshimi cringed at the sound.

"Do you know why they yell like that? It's because they know they've survived another day and they want to celebrate. They've learned that their lives could end at any time, so they take whatever hasty pleasure they can from this world because they don't know what awaits them in the next. And that's your role in all of this. You are that little treat for them. They consider it your duty, as a servant of the Emperor."

Meiko's face was a flood. She scrunched down further on her mat and spread her legs even wider. *Violate me here*, her gesture said. *Don't violate me in places you can't see.*

Yoshimi would not let his eyes fall to the mangled genitals laid out in front of him. "Did you ever hear about the massacre at Nanking?" he asked. "No, I suspect you wouldn't have. Nanking was a Chinese city we invaded early in the war. Our men *raped* their way through it. Old women, girls, little babies. It was disgraceful. We brought an entire city to its knees by raping its women. The army denied it, but we all knew. The comfort stations were set up so that it wouldn't happen again. No more raping, no more diseases." He swallowed. "This was the Emperor's thinking."

So what do you call what happens in here? Meiko thought. *Am I not raped? Am I not diseased?*

"I enlisted as a medic after that," he went on. "I knew I'd probably never see my wife or daughter again, but thought: I can do good work. Help keep our men clean, keep them healthy. Keep them — moral. But we've lost sight of why we're here and what we're fighting for."

Meiko sat up then, stared at him. *What did you ever* think *you were fighting for? To keep the Orient Oriental, like they taught us in school? Is that what you thought when they tied my friend to a tree and carved her up like a pumpkin?*

"I'm not interested in saving our men anymore," Yoshimi said. "Maybe I want to save somebody else, Meiko. Maybe you. When this war is over, and if we're both still alive, maybe I could take you home. Deliver you there myself, back to Korea. And then I could learn your real name."

Yoshimi waited for her to reply. But she didn't. She just stared at him. "I'll be back," he said. "I'll check in on you when I can." Then he stepped through her curtain and returned to the hall. There he found one last non-commissioned officer waiting before his rank's allotted time was up. The soldier's pants were already undone, his thick member extended out from his loin cloth. As soon as Yoshimi cleared the room, the man jumped at Meiko's curtain and cackled with a laugh of relief.

She would not let Yoshimi take her back to Korea. There was only one escape from the camp that she would accept, and that was death. Death would come for her. Death would rescue her like a chivalrous older brother. She refused to allow her body, this sack of meat with its scars, with its diseases and its shame, to return to her father's house. She would die first. She would let her spirit float away like chaff on the wind.

But Yoshimi was right: Japan was losing the war, and losing badly. Meiko knew something horrible was happening when the girls had to move three times over a two-month period. Each trip took them farther south, and each new rape station was more run down than the one before. Every time they moved, Meiko hoped that Yoshimi would not be moved with them. But he always was. She came to hate his kindness, the way he paid to see her under the pretense of sex only to check in on her, bring her extra bits of food he hid in his pockets, and tend to her injuries outside of her monthly examination time.

Autumn turned to winter, winter to spring, and the war went from worse to disastrous. Meiko longed for that final explosion to come, the unexpected blast that would blow apart the wooden walls of the comfort station and rip everyone inside to shreds. The warm rains of May brought discouraging news to the soldiers: the war in Europe was over. It was only a matter of time before the Emperor would concede defeat on the Asian front. Maybe by the end of the summer. Maybe sooner.

Yoshimi increased his number of visits to her stall. What he had talked about strictly in the hypothetical before — taking her back to Korea — became more possible with each passing day. "We'll need safe passage to the coast," he said one evening. "We'll find a ship to cross the Yellow Sea to a port in western Korea, and then maybe find a train to take us to Seoul." Yoshimi's words came very close to igniting a small spark of anticipation in Meiko. But she would not allow it. She couldn't let herself imagine going anywhere except to the otherworld.

Yet how would death come now, if Japan surrendered tomorrow? Or the day after that? Was time not running out for death to slip into her stall and carry her away?

She got hold of a piece of twine. It came off a box of medical supplies that she had been ordered to unload from the back of a truck one morning. A sergeant cut the bundled rope with a pair of scissors after Meiko had set the box down, but he carelessly allowed the twine to fall to the ground and didn't collect it. As soon as the sergeant was gone, Meiko bent to scoop the twine up, bunched it into a ball in her hand, waited, looked around and then slipped it up under her skirt, all the way until she could clamp it in her armpit. Back in her stall, minutes before her first soldier of the day would arrive, she took the twine out and unfurled it. It was as thin as a vein, but strong. She snapped it a few times in her fists — yes, it would do. She went over to her tip box, grabbed handfuls of *gyumpo* bills and set them on the floor, then rested the twine near the bottom of the box, curled it up like a snake. She piled the *gyumpo* back on top of the rope until it was completely hidden.

She did not say anything to Yoshimi that night when he came to see her. He brought her a handful of walnuts he managed to sneak into the hallway; he asked how the Secret Star Cream was working. After he left, Meiko was visited by a large, foul-smelling officer whom she had serviced many times before. He arrived in the late evening and raped her quickly, silently, then fell into a light sleep on her mat, crushing his hot, doughy chest into her back. Meiko waited until deep into the night, when the officer had shifted enough in his sleep so that no part of his body was touching hers. Then she got up slowly, quietly from the mat. She moved to the tip box, submerged her hand into the *Gyumpo* bills until she felt the twine touch her fingers, and eased it out. Bundled it up again, hiding it in her fist. Moved to her curtain, slipped through it and out into the hall, which was dark and mostly silent. She walked slowly at first, out past the manager's podium and into the main room. But her gait increased as she approached the station's main door. Felt her stomach list with a kind of nauseous excitement. Out onto the building's main stoop. Hurrying now that she had caught sight of the trees with their long, sturdy branches out in the copse. Down the steps now, racing, racing.

She stumbled over a metal box set near the steps, spilling a highway of shell casings noisily onto the ground. A rustling back in the building, the sound of people waking. Voices. Ignoring the mess she had made and the clatter coming from behind her, Meiko fluttered like a bird across the field, her legs scurrying through the dark until she had crossed into the copse and found herself at the base of a large gingko tree. It arched upward, spreading its knuckled branches into the sky. More voices behind her now, thickening in the house like batter. Meiko tucked the twine between her teeth before grabbing hold of the gingko's trunk with both arms. It seemed to take forever to scale up to the lowest branch, even though it was less than a dozen feet from the ground. She was finally able to hoist her thin backside onto its rough, sturdy bark. When she did, Meiko took the twine from her mouth and tied one end into a stiff knot around the branch's bulk. The other end she looped onto itself, narrowing it into a circle and securing it with a knot. Voices now outside the building, crossing the field towards the copse. *No time now. Too late now. How long would it take?* She snap-snap-snapped the twine to make sure it held to the branch before dropping the other end over her head and patting it around her throat like a necklace. Pulled it tight against the flesh under her chin. The beam of a flashlight ripped across her torso; she looked down and saw pale grey faces approaching the base of her tree. *Too late now. Too late now. But let's see if this works.*

She slid off the branch without a second thought. The ground raced towards her and for a moment she believed she'd fumble back onto it, the twine's long slack unable to give way to tightness. But then it did — a horrendous wrench at her throat that seized her in the air and swung her like a pendulum. And suddenly Meiko was flying, lingering in space with tiny desperate kicks of her feet. The ground was still two or three feet off. She could not draw a breath through her cleft mouth — could not imagine ever drawing breath again. The pain ballooned in her head as she hanged in suspended animation. Meiko fought off the reflex to grab hold of the twine with both hands and plant her feet into the trunk. She waited for an ocean of silence, the noise of death, to flood her ears. But it didn't. Another sound came, one that made her want to weep.

Laughter.

"Ahh, *Chosunjin*, what do you think you're *doing*?"

"Cut her down!" From the back of the small crowd that had gathered. Yoshimi's voice. "Dammit, men, somebody cut her down right now."

The shake of the twine as a fist took hold of it, and the touch of a blade that instantly released the tension. Meiko dropped into a heap at the gingko's base, down on all fours as if grovelling, choking on oxygen she didn't want. Someone loosened and then ripped the twine from her throat, grabbed her by the armpit, and yanked her to her feet. She was shoved through the small crowd like a naughty toddler, the soldiers' chuckles ringing in her ears. Meiko opened her eyes and saw Yoshimi at the edge of the crowd, trailing behind it. His face had sunken with a look of betrayal. Meiko turned her eyes away from him and waited for the men to throw her back toward the building. They were in the centre of the field and she wanted to collapse down into it, feel the soft grass on her thighs.

And then came the rattle of sniper fire, snapping open the night like kindling.

Meiko was shoved to the ground. Everyone was turning, diving, aiming their weapons at the far edge of the copse where starbursts danced across the darkness. Meiko hugged the grass, kept her body perfectly flat as soldiers fired and yelled all around her. She squeezed her eyes shut. It occurred to her only later that she should have stood up, tall and proud, an easy target for a sniper's bullet to chop her down, to finish this evening's botched task.

Silence fell then. The gunfire ended as quickly as it had begun.

Meiko opened her eyes and found Yoshimi's face at eye level with hers a few feet off, half his head hidden in the long grass. He lay prostrate in the field with the same sad, dismal stare he'd had at the base of the tree. He blinked once. Concentrated on Meiko so hard — so hard in fact that he was ignoring the black, syrupy hole that had taken ownership of his throat. He gulped and strong little waves of red spurted over the grass. His expression held a thousand regrets. *I ran to you, Meiko*, it said. *As soon as the firing started, I ran to you instead of diving to the ground like I should have. What is this thing I've done?*

She closed her eyes, unable to watch the rest. Held an image in her mind of the sky opening up with a bright blare of sun shining down upon them. The sky was wide and filling with cranes, hundreds of wise cranes taking flight toward a world beyond this one.

CHAPTER 8

Little Chin-ho, ten-year-old boy in the second row, has mastered the comparative tense, and the results are hilarious. It's a Thursday evening in my Junior 4 class and we've just finished a grammar module on irregular adjectives. Riveting stuff, really — *good*, *better*, and *the best*; *bad*, *worse*, and *the worst*. The other kids get it more or less, but Chin-ho — whose English name was "Harold" until two nights ago, when he decided he didn't *want* an English name — has latched on to the term *worse* and made it his own. Now, whenever something even remotely negative happens in class, he punctuates the air with a lispy, drawn-out "Worrrrrrrse!" It sends everybody — including me — into gales of laughter. When someone gives a wrong answer, or I drop a marker on the floor, or separate two girls for whispering, or even assign grammar exercises for homework, he's right there to chastise us all with his new favourite word. I know I should punish him for this ongoing disruption, but it's just too damn funny; a moment of levity in an otherwise frustrating class. These kids are supposedly at a Junior 4 level, but really they're only about a Basic 5. This, sadly, isn't an uncommon occurrence at ABC English Planet. Ms. Kim, in her pedagogical wisdom, will often race batches of students through several levels before they're ready. It astounds me that there are children here who can recite rules to fairly complex English grammar, things some native speakers wouldn't even know — how the subjunctive tense works, where to place the comma in a prepositional phrase — and yet cannot tell me what they did on the weekend. "I is goes over our grandmothers to visit Pusan …" or some other syntactical abomination. This school treats the kids like patrons at a fast-food joint, and my language is the burgers I sling at them just as fast as humanly possible. It's awful.

Except it isn't. Surprise surprise — I find this job rewarding at the oddest moments, times when I can cut through Ms. Kim's lunatic curriculum, this *hagwon*'s assembly-line treatment of children, and get the kids to really *grasp* something. Tonight, we move on from comparatives to something I hope they'll enjoy a bit more: adverbs of frequency. I write the five most prominent ones — NEVER … RARELY … SOMETIMES … USUALLY … ALWAYS — across the length of my white board, explain what they mean, and then ask the kids to name habits or actions for each. Hands fly to the ceiling; everyone's eager to participate. The first few answers are predictably banal — *I always breathe; I sometimes cry*. Then things take a turn for the scatological: "I never eat d-d-o-n-g," says Devon, cheekily.

"Worrrrrrrrse!" Chin-ho exclaims.

Now the kids are getting into it, the personalization behind each answer.

"I usually call grandmother on Sundays," Suzy says.

"I rarely play with my brother," quips Karen.

"I always do my homework," says Eddie.

"MichaelTeacher, Eddie *never* do his homework," Erin grumbles. The kids all laugh. And me, I *get* it, finally — what all of this is supposed to be about. It's not just making them understand the concept. It's about watching those little lights turn on, about getting them to bend their brains creatively.

I have forgotten what it feels like to fall in love with someone slowly. I don't remember it being so imperialistic, your emotions stalking the other person's attributes, claiming each of them in turn, the word love sneaking into your lexicon. "You know, I *love* this about you ..." you find yourself saying; or she, apropos of nothing: "You know, I really *love* that about you ..." And on it goes until there are no aspects left to claim, and you end up loving it all — the good, the ridiculous, and especially the parts you don't quite understand, the mysteries. You love it all. "I love *you*" becomes the natural next step.

For three more weeks, Jin and I make these concentric circles around each other, snatching up more and more characteristics as we go. I love the way she sticks out her bottom lip when she's thinking hard. She loves the way my brow furrows when I'm reading something good. I love the flutter of her eyes whenever I say something foolish. She loves my beard, its scruffy coarseness framing my jaw. I even love aspects of Jin that I would normally find untenable in a girl, like her total inability to accept a compliment at face value. She treats blandishments from me not so much with suspicion as with supreme exhaustion, like she's heard it all before. Is it weird that this causes a strange flush of yearning in me, a bubble of desire?

I even love the way she strings me along, keeps me guessing. One Friday night, we join a group of her girlfriends for dinner in Apujung, Seoul's ritziest, most celebrity-rich neighbourhood. The drinks flow and Jin is charming, running circles around these girls, all of whom are giggly, sweet, brittle, and not very fluent in English. I'm enamoured with the deference they pay to Jin, to all she has experienced, the envious curiosity they show over the fact that she has a *waegookin* boyfriend. By the time Jin and I head back to the subway together, I'm feeling brave. Mildly drunk and full of desire for her. "Do you want to come back to Daechi?" I venture.

"No, I have to work in the morning."

"Yes, at the COEX," I reply. Implication: a twenty-minute walk from my apartment.

She turns to me, her look inscrutable. "My mother is waiting at home," is all she says. We descend the subway stairs, buy our tickets, and prepare to be triaged to opposite sides of the platform. "I'll see you next weekend, Michael," she says lightly, then hustles off without so much as a goodnight peck on my cheek. Before I can even mount a protest, she already has her handphone out and open, her eyes narrowing over its screen as she sends out a text message, probably to her mother. I stand there, watching her go, full of a lust I've never felt before.

And there are attributes we love because we think we can change them, make them stronger. She detests the food I keep in the apartment fridge — can't understand my penchant for bland bags of white bread and sad cartons of skim milk, silvery bags of pre-made kimchi, and store-bought packages of dried seaweed for snacking. Every meal out with Jin becomes a matter of correcting my lazy tastes, with her explaining the intricacies of each dish with little jabs of her chopsticks. From my end, I begin probing the hang-ups she has about her family and stop hiding the fact that I want to meet them, to be introduced to this father who never sleeps and this dragon-like mother who still treats her like an adolescent. Jin gives no quarter on these queries, though mentioned in a moment of weakness that she has no desire to marry a Korean man. She longs to live aboard, like her younger brother "Carl," who is away studying at a chef school in Los Angeles. Jin would love to move to an English-speaking country, maybe even Canada. She says this one day while squatting down in front of my open fridge to critique the contents of my vegetable crisper. She stands back up and swings around to face me, her hair a-flutter, her eyes falling into mine. "Yeah, I think living in Canada would not be too bad," she flirts. "What do you think?"

I think: *Don't you dare fucking tease me.* I think: *I love the way you tease me.*

Three weeks and then it happens. The Saturday starts in a swath of innocence. We've been invited to dinner at the home of a young married couple with whom Jin is close friends. "Jack" and "Mindy" live near Wolgok station in the far north end of Seoul. It's a horrendous subway ride from my place in Daechi, involving several transfers. Jin meets me after she finishes work so we can make the trek together. She has explained that Mindy is a literature professor at a nearby university and Jack edits a tourism magazine. "You'll love them, Michael. Fluent in English. Very literary and modern. They're your kind of people." On the way, Jin asks me why she didn't see Justin in my apartment when she stopped by to get me.

"He's away this weekend," I tell her. "He went to Seokcho to go hiking with the family he tutors."

She nods. "He'll be going up Seorak Mountain, obviously," she says. "Seokcho is very beautiful — right on the ocean." She gives me a look I can't read. "When does he come back?"

"Not until Monday," I answer. And she nods again.

We finally arrive in Wolgok and make our way to Jack and Mindy's condo building — a gleaming, silvery edifice standing over a mélange of more run-down apartment tenements. Jack and Mindy buzz us in and we ride the smooth, silent elevator up to their unit on the eighteenth floor. The smiling couple is already waiting for us at their threshold. They welcome us in to the first spacious Korean home I've ever seen. Full wraparound living room leading to an alcove dining area, a large galley kitchen, and a hallway leading down to bed and bath. The floor beneath our feet is not plastic *ondol* covering; it's actual hardwood with a nice cozy heat radiating up from it. There's a massive flat-screen TV on the wall in the living room, surrounded by shelves of neatly stacked books.

Jack and Mindy speak to us in unwavering English, which puts me immediately at ease. A glass of wine appears in my hand and we seat ourselves around their dining room table, with Mindy making occasional trips to the kitchen to tend to whatever food is making that delectable smell. They check in with Jin about her job before turning to ask me how I like teaching children at a *hagwon*. I put a polite spin on my days of slinging English at exhausted kids, and Jack and Mindy nod knowingly; like Jin, they too went through their *hagwon* paces as children, know the Sisyphean stress of it. Jin mentions to Jack that I had worked as a journalist back in Canada, and this allusion causes my spine to kink, that old reminder of a deliberately destroyed career. If he picks up on my discomfort, he doesn't let on; merely mentions that he works with a lot of journalists, though struggles to find good writers in English. Am I a good writer?

Over two more glasses of wine, I learn that Mindy teaches courses on Hemingway and Fitzgerald at the local university, but her true passion lies in what she calls the "linguistically ambitious"; she can draw a straight line from Evelyn Waugh and Anthony Burgess up through Martin Amis and Will Self. "We grabbed each other over Milan Kundera," Jin pipes up, and I nod in agreement. I'm in a stew of engagement here. Jack seems a little left out; he hasn't read nearly as much as the rest of us. Eventually, Mindy dresses the table with our meal — a rich pork-bone soup, Korean dumplings seared to perfection, and the freshest, spiciest kimchi I have ever tasted. It all goes down nicely with the wine, with the stories we tell and the jokes I make, the generous laughs all around.

After dinner, we move to the couches in the living room. Jack is glowing pleasantly from the wine, slurring his words, and nearly spilling his drink on the white upholstery beneath him. The rest of us playfully chide him about it. He responds by growing a touch more serious: he wants to talk about the news — specifically what's been happening in Iraq since the invasion started. He's impressed, he says, that the Americans took Baghdad so quickly, and they did excellent work rescuing that poor Jessica Lynch girl. Still, he's worried about the outbreaks of looting and violence that have started plaguing the city. I propose that these are not random acts, but rather the beginnings of an insurgency. Jack disagrees; chimes in perfunctorily about freedom, about the Americans yanking the Iraqi people out from under Saddam's thumb.

"Isn't *that* what this is really about?" he sloshes. "Won't all this be a liberation in the end, no matter what America's really there for?"

"No, Jack," I say. "Every invasion is a rape." As soon as the word leaves my mouth, there's a gasp in the room. It's Jin. I look at her, there on the other side of the couch, clutching her wine. Her mouth has gone slack and she's staring right into me. I swallow. Turn back to Jack. Continue tentatively. "I mean, maybe not every invasion, but this one certainly could be. I don't think it counts as a seduction if your victim is an unwilling participant. There are *always* consequences when you force violence on a different culture. Trust me, this won't be a simple seduction." Jack opens his mouth, but then closes it again. Sips his wine.

I look back at Jin. Her gaze is locked into me, but not unpleasantly so. She says nothing while the rest of us natter on for a while longer. She turns to Mindy. "Can I use your washroom?" she asks.

"Of course," her friend replies. Jin sets down her wine, gets up from the couch. But as she does, she digs out her handphone. Flips it open and dials a number, tucks the phone under her hair

132

as she disappears into the hall. Who on earth is she calling from the bathroom?

It's very late, past midnight, before we finally call it a night. Jack and Mindy shake my hand at the door and tell me I'm welcome back any time. "He's *fascinating*," Mindy tells Jin, but Jin just nods and looks at her toes. We say our goodbyes and then ride the elevator down to the lobby. When we hit the street heading to the subway, Jin takes my arm and pulls me close.

"Hey, you were pretty quiet there by the end," I say. "Is everything okay? I didn't overstep my bounds with your friends, did I?"

"Of course not," she replies. "I just love it when you're in *that* mode, Michael. I didn't want to interrupt you. I just wanted to *listen*. I love … I love *it*."

As we approach the subway stop I'm about to ask when I'll see her again — perhaps next weekend? But before I can, Jin says, "So what are we doing now?"

I startle with surprise. "I, I don't know. What *are* we doing now?"

"Can we go back to Daechi?"

"Sure," I sputter. "Sure we can."

So south we go on the subway, the long parade of stops and transfers. Jin is silent through most of the trip, pulled deeply into herself. If I didn't know better, I'd say there is a tinge of fear in her body language, or at least an inner debate going on. Each transfer point we pass is another closed door, another lost opportunity for her to bail on what's about to happen. She doesn't bail.

Back in Daechi after nearly an hour, and we walk up the deserted main drag. She asks if we can stop at the 7-Eleven to get beer. We purchase two massive bottles of Hite lager, and I carry them for us in a plastic bag. In the apartment, I ensure the door is locked behind us as she moves into my cramped little bedroom. At the kitchen counter, I open one of the beers and fill two glasses, then bring them into the bedroom. I find she's already put on some of my music — John Coltrane — and made herself comfortable on my floor.

We drink in silence for a while, our legs touching, our backs resting against the edge of the bed. She won't look at me — just lets her dark hair fall over her face as she burrows a gaze into her navel and takes pulls from her glass of beer. I'm tracing a finger along her denim leg, from the high point of her thigh down to the bump of her knee, and then back up again. Her breathing is methodical, as if she's making a point of controlling its cadence.

"You're very different now that Rob Cruise is away," she says. "Have I told you that?"

"Different how?"

"You talk more. You reveal more of yourself, now that he's not around." A blush of brake lights smear across the frost of my window, the quiet surge of a late-night car moving on. My finger grows a touch heavier on Jin's thigh. "Whenever he hangs out with us," she goes on, "Rob needs to talk over everybody, to *own* the room — all the time. At first that is very attractive, but then it gets annoying. I noticed right away that you don't fight with him for your place in the room. You don't go down to that level. You — how you say … how you say …" Her English fails, and so I steady my hand a moment. "How you say, pick your spots. That's what I liked about you from the very beginning — that you don't talk just to talk. You only speak when you have something wise to say. I find that so rare."

"Jin …"

"And now that he's gone for two months, you seem more relaxed, ready to share yourself. And that's what I find attractive now. Like tonight — all I wanted was to sit and listen to you fit in so well with two of my dearest friends. I mean, if I brought

Rob Cruise into that environment he'd offend them in about five seconds, just by being himself."

I cup her behind the knee, pull her close enough for our chests to almost touch. Her chin is pinned between her collar bones. She still won't look at me.

"There are many things I want to tell you," she says. "Things about my family — things I think you'd understand. But it *scares* me a little, to think that y —"

I wait no longer. I steer my head between the curtains of her dark hair, pull her face up with mine. No weak little peck on the lips this time; my mouth sinks into hers, parts it like water. Her breath grows frantic as my tongue strokes hers, and she quivers all over. Our heads sway like buoys as we kiss fully, properly, wondering why we waited so long, wondering if we should wait longer. But then her hands slip up under my shirt with a confidence that startles me, and she's pulling it up and over my head. I do the same for her. She looks down at me in the dark. "Ohh, you're very hairy!" she whispers, running fingers through the forest of my stomach, and we laugh, touch foreheads. Then I'm kissing her again, serious, can't believe that she's letting me kiss her.

And then I have her in the air, lifting her off the *ondol* floor in a rescuer's embrace. I set her down on the bed, let her sink into my sheets and pillow. She stretches out to welcome me. I reach behind her for the clasp of her bra and she arches upward. I struggle; I'm useless, useless. She helps me out, an expert unclipping, then lets her shoulders go limp so the garment can fall away. Her small breasts look silver in this light. As I work my way down to them, she lets out a delighted noise, but also tinged with doubt. Still with the doubt. So I kiss her mouth again. The room is so hot now. Our hands move lower and grow busy. The rattle of undone belt buckles knocking together, the swish of our jeans, the sound of them falling heavy on the floor. She strokes my shoulders and neck while I kiss her throat. I work my way back down again, breasts and sternum and stomach. Discover her underwear, just a thin cotton ring around her hips. I tuck my thumbs under either side, prepare to ease them off. But she seizes up, seizes up for just a moment, a final groan of uncertainty.

I stop. And the fact that I stop swings the pendulum: she relaxes completely, sinks deeper into my bed. I gently pull the panties from her hips, down legs, over ankles, and onto the floor. There is a kinetic energy to her limbs as I return. Pulling her to me, I kiss her lower stomach. I can't stop kissing her. I move even lower. Jin immediately takes my head in her hands and pulls me back up, lets out the littlest "Uh-uhh …" I moan a small disappointment, genuine. As if to console, she bites her bottom lip and leans into me, moves her hands over and then into my tented boxers, her fingers on my flesh. I pull my boxers off. Then I raise her legs by the back of her knees. She fidgets, pleads, "Michael … Michael, you better …" I get it. I reach over her, bang open my night-side table. The rustle of cardboard, square tinfoil in my hand, a rip and pull, liberating that wet little ring, then a slow, tight roll. She's fighting her doubt, helps me push the thing all the way down. I raise her legs up again. She's hovering in a place between close and very far away. "Michael, please … Michael, please …" She's nearly weeping under the weight of her indecision, begging me to carry it away like something toxic. I am struck by a stroke of genius. I take myself in my hand and begin slowly rubbing her, *there*, with the point of me.

"Jin, how much of me do you want?" I say in the dark. Deadpan it, to create the illusion that I could go either way.

"Huuh? Hohhh …"

"Do you want just a little of me?" And with that, I move in on her, just enough to give her a taste. Refuse to go deeper.

"Hohh, hohh, hohh …"

I pull back out, resume my cruel rubbing, my slow circles. She coils like a spring. "How much of me do you want?" I ask again. "Hmm? Do you want just some of me?" I squeeze back inside her, slide myself in half way. Hold it.

"Hahhhhh … huhhhhh …"

This is more difficult than I thought. Fighting every instinct in my body, I slowly pull out again, return myself to that nub, gently lap it like a tongue. I feel like I'm going to break right through the condom. "Was that enough?" I ask. "Or do you want more?"

"Michael … Mi*chael*!"

"Do you want just some of me, Jin? Hmmm? Or do you want *all* of me?"

A slow languorous sink all the way to the ocean floor. She sucks every molecule of air from the room, releases a scream. I hold myself there, feel the little tickle of her cervix on my tip. Then, fighting the weight of the world and Jin's desperate grip on me, I pull back up, back out, and return to my teasing. She gives me the sound I've been waiting for — a holler of shattering disappointment.

"How much of me do you want?" I beg, rubbing, rubbing.

"Ughhhuuu … arrrghhhuuu …"

"Jin, how much of me?"

"All of you … all of you …"

"Are you sure?"

"*Yes.*"

And with that final beseech, I plunge back in. Back in to stay. And I think: finally, after all these years, somebody finally wants me. Wants all of me.

We're on the cheap leather couch in the living room for Round Two, an abandoned trip to the kitchen to freshen our beers. As

Jin dances above me, I briefly worry about Justin coming in the door then, home early from his trip to Seokcho, to see Jin's breasts flying and my mouth at her throat. Of course he doesn't, wouldn't. It's something like three in the morning.

After we're done, we're locked on those narrow cushions in a semi-comfortable embrace, legs twined and faces turned up at each other. I take a casual glance at my watch. "Won't your mother be angry you're out this late?" I ask.

"No. I called and told her I was staying at Jack and Mindy's."

Ah yes, the call from the bathroom. I beam down at her. "Did you now?" She gives a mischievous shrug, like a teenager. "And if she knew the truth," I ask, "would you be grounded?"

"Grounded?" Her mind flips through vocabulary until she finds it. "Oh shut up!" she barks. And I laugh.

With our passion sapped and the memory of it fading behind us, I already feel Jin pulling away from me. Shoals of doubt, shoals of distance, shoals of *What the hell just happened?* swimming between us on the couch. She sits up, pulls her legs under her. Finds the remote control, pops on the TV.

"Jin, c'mon, turn it off."

"No. Let's watch something." She surfs through the channels — talking heads, noisy action movies with Korean subtitles, over-wrought singing contests. I can't bring myself to watch. Instead, I stroke her hair, trace a knuckle over her shoulder and down her long, lean side. She doesn't respond, doesn't even look at me. She's so beautiful. I'm scared to tell her how beautiful she is.

Her face tightens just then. "What the hell is all this?" she asks.

I turn to find myself once again staring into CNN. The news ticker rushes along the bottom of the screen, and above it a stony image of Saddam Hussein. Not an image. A statue. We watch as the camera switches to a long shot, showing his body in full: A single arm raised in avuncular salute over a square packed with people. There is a thick rope and pulley hanging loosely over the statue's neck and shoulder.

"What's going on?" Jin asks.

"I don't know."

We watch a long preparation, U.S. soldiers in beige desert wear working and then clearing out. At first nothing happens, but then the rope grows taut, tightened by the pull of an armoured vehicle. Another moment and Saddam begins to bow to the crowd. His fall is slow, incredibly slow at first, but then picks up speed as his legs break and he slumps drunkenly over his own pedestal. The statue hangs there for an eternity, detritus and shoes flying through the air at its head. Jin and I watch in a kind of silent sobriety.

"Michael, do you think …" she says. "Do you think it will …"

And then it does. Breaks loose of the pedestal and comes crashing to the ground with a heavy lurch. The crowd rushes it, leaps onto it even before the torso comes to a full stop. The tall arm waves at the sky. The people are plowing onto the statue, dancing on it, stomping it, smacking it with the soles of their shoes. Jubilation and tears and arms pumping in the air. The CNN commentators have caved to their jingoism: this is why they believe America has come.

"Do you think it's staged?" I ask.

"Staged? What does this mean?"

"Do you think they're —" I clear my throat. "Do you think they're *faking* it?"

Jin looks at the TV, then back at me, a kind of once over, then to the TV again. I'm suddenly very aware of my naked-ness. She blows a hair out of her eyes as the dancing and cheers go on. "No, it looks genuine. But I'm thinking of what you and Jack were talking about tonight. I still say he's wrong and you're right. This," — and she nods at the happy images glowing at my living room — "this isn't a simple ... a simple — what was the word you used?"

I hesitate. "Seduction."

"Right. This isn't a simple seduction. This won't be simple at all."

The TV eventually comes off but we're too lazy to move back to my bedroom. Jin curls on the couch to sleep, but in an unwelcoming way; there really isn't room for both of us. So instead I move to the cold floor, sit with my back against the chilly wall. I'm not going to sleep. I'm going to sit exactly like this for the whole night and watch Jin as she dozes. A few hours pass and then she stirs, opens her eyes to find me staring at her. She sits up and stretches. Then, without a word, slips off the couch and heads to my room. From the darkness, I hear her pulling her clothes back on. She takes forever. When she finally comes back out, she's got her handphone open, looking at the screen and pressing buttons. Sending a text message, to her mother I suppose. She sits back on the couch, her knees together. Texting, texting. Not looking at me.

"Jin ..."

She claps the phone shut. "Hey, did you sleep at *all*?" she asks.

"I didn't want to sleep," I reply. "I wanted to kiss you until the sun came up."

Corny. So corny. A wave of unease passes through her. She's resumed that bashful, closed-off stance from last night, chin down and buried, hair falling in her face.

"Michael, I have to go. I have places I need to be."

"Jin ..."

She shakes her head, but then grows still. Sighs. "Ask me," she says. "Go on and ask me."

"Jin, are we going to try to love each other?"

She looks up but not at me.

"You're afraid to love a *waegookin*," I say.

"I *am* afraid," she clips, turning to me. "Is that so wrong?"

"I'm afraid, too. But so what? Jin, there are right decisions and there are wrong decisions. But you can never make a right decision from a place of fear. You know that." I lick my lips. "So fuck fear. Fuck it. Throw your fear out the bloody window, for Christsake. And then give your *heart* to me." It sounds almost like an order.

Her bottom lip comes out. She's thinking hard. Eyes me up and down in my nakedness. But then nods. She nods.

Yes.

Yes?

Yes.

And I collapse into relief without showing it. Without knowing what this victory will mean, what these words, this conquest, will really lead to.

CHAPTER 9

The sound of tears mixed with the sound of laughter. That's how it rang out in Meiko's head, a percussive echo swelling in the silence that had descended on the camp. Her laughter at the men's misery; their tears over the bomb, their *pock'tan*. This was the abandoned month of August, the reversal of fortune. The silence she had prayed for.

Evidence of the soldiers' desertion lay strewn through every crevice of the comfort station. Wooden crates were left to rot in the long grass of the field. Shells and other ammunition were stacked like cordwood along one wall, never to be fired. Crumbling army boots, soles gaping with holes and laces limp, lined up like urchins along the north stoop. The camp's charcoal stove, littered now with the ledgers' ashy remnants, had fallen cold.

It took a while for the girls to organize themselves after the men had left. They came peeping out from behind their curtains, faces ripe with disbelief. *We are alone*, they communicated to each other, to themselves. *Who will take care of us now? We'll have to take care of each other.* The girls latched on to Meiko almost immediately; to them, her scarred legs read like a map of sedition, her laughter at the soldiers a proclamation of bravery. Of course *she* would know what to do. Of course she would take charge.

There was the issue of food. The men had left them virtually nothing. Just a smattering of stale rice balls and soggy radishes. They gathered up what they could find; it filled half of a table in the mess. How many are we? they asked, and counted themselves in Japanese. A dozen. A dozen girls. This food would not feed twelve girls for long.

They bickered briefly over what to do. One girl, named Hiri, still too terrified to speak, pantomimed her opinion, patting the air with her open palms: We need to stay here. She mimicked the actions of a sniper, but Meiko was uncertain what she meant: We leave and run the risk of getting shot? Or the enemy knows of this camp and we should stay in the hopes of being found? *Just say it in Korean*, Meiko wanted to bark at her, but could tell Hiri was too frightened, even though the camp manager was long gone. Another girl, named Akiko, came to their gathering with her box of Gyumpo bills. Flapped a handful of them in the air. *We are flush with cash*, she seemed to be saying. She pointed sternly out the window, to the Chinese landscape beyond it. Obvious what she wanted: to take the money and find a village to buy food and passages home. The girls turned to Meiko, as if only she could cast the deciding vote. She nodded. "We'll die if we stay here," she said. The girls flinched for a moment at her use of Korean. But then nodded in agreement: it was okay, now, to speak their native tongue. "If we stay and this food runs out, what then?" Meiko went on. "We can't eat Gyumpo bills. Better to use this food to get us to the nearest village, and then this money to get us — to get us to whatever awaits after that." Her words caused many of the girls to redden in shame. *To whatever awaits? We're washed-up whores, all of us. What could possibly await us after this?*

But it was agreed they would leave. The question was, in which direction? They had to piece together the best plan, like a mystery, from what the soldiers had rambled about in moments of indiscretion to the few girls who understood Japanese. A consensus bubbled to the surface: the village of Xingshuan, to the south of them. The men had talked about it, this nearby oasis of good sake and good music, a town that excited them upon their return from battle because it meant their convoys weren't far from the comfort station and the girls who awaited them there.

So it would be Xingshuan. How many days by foot? Three? Five? Five would be too many — their food would run out. It would need to be three. And they would need to leave right away.

The girls prepared themselves. Drew jugs of water from the well in the courtyard. Gathered up whatever clothes they could find — discarded tunics and old blankets left in wooden corners. They loaded their supply of rice and vegetables in canvas sacks. And most importantly, they gathered up their boxes of Gyumpo — these bills, given to them in the lightest gestures of remorse, accumulated over countless months of rape. The girls would carry them through the wilderness clutched to their chests.

They left the camp behind to trek through scorched hills and bare ginkgo trees. Along the way, they encountered burned-out army trucks and bullet-riddled bodies half-buried in muck, and deep pockmarks in the ground where shells had fallen. The late summer heat soaked the girls as they worked their way around these horrors. "Keep the morning sun to the left," Meiko chanted as she led them, more a distraction than an order, "and keep the evening sun to the right." Each night they settled into a ditch with their blankets and slight rations of food, fearing the appearance of bandits or worse, broken-up Japanese platoons looking for one last plunge into conquered flesh.

The village of Xingshuan appeared to the girls after three hard days of hiking. It stretched over a plateau on the south side of a broad, babbling creek. They walked the iron bridge into town to discover a hybrid atmosphere of jubilation and chaos.

Thick pillars of smoke rose into the air from burning homes. Streets were strewn with abandoned corpses and shattered glass. And yet people were out in the streets dancing, singing folk songs, burning Japanese flags and pictures of Hirohito. The girls wandered into the village like their own small army and drew less-than-welcome stares from the locals.

They found a street market near the centre of town. Wandered into a mad avenue of haggling to discover a modest ransom of food for sale, more than they had seen in months. A couple of the girls rushed to the first table they saw, lined with root vegetables and shellfish. Taking out their boxes of Gyumpo, they grabbed handfuls of bills and began trying to communicate to the tired-looking man behind the table. He did not move when he saw the money; his face connoted nothing. They waggled the bills at him. He shook his head, said something back to them in Chinese, which they didn't understand. They flapped the bills at him again. The man raised his arms angrily. The girls pleaded with him, their Korean falling out of their mouths in long rambles. The man practically spat at them, then folded his arms tersely over his chest, not willing to spend another second dealing with these girls who had wandered in from God knows where.

They moved back to their group, tremulous. How to express what had just transpired? They didn't need to: Meiko could tell what had happened. She turned to the other girls. "Worthless," she said. "He's not taking any Gyumpo. These bills are absolutely worthless."

Tears began to well over their starved faces. They moved from table to table, their Gyumpo bills out and presented like hats begging for alms, but each proprietor met them with the same reaction. One woman selling bags of rice was able to speak to them in broken Japanese. "You giving me Gyumpo? No!

Nobody take army money anymore. War is *over*. You have yen? You have yen? I can take yen. No yen? Really? Not twenty yen among you? Then no rice! No yen, no rice! Japanese bastards gone! Army money is no value. No value at all …"

The girls drifted from stall to stall, their Gyumpo bills falling like leaves at their feet. Each rejection caused their hunger pangs to swell up inside them like little fires. They turned to Meiko, expecting her to provide some wisdom that would make this situation dissolve like mist. But she had nothing for them. Her words were as worthless as the Gyumpo bills they had lugged all this way.

The girls moved to Xingshuan's outskirts; there, they could see where the war had drawn its final lines — deep trenches through the woods, the shells of burned-out houses. The girls, filthy and starved, wandered among these homes trying to find anything edible, anything of value that they could sell or trade for food. But it looked as though others had come before them and picked these homes clean.

Meiko led her little army beyond the town's edge. There, they roamed like exhausted ghosts through the remains of a large house by the creek that had been reduced to rubble. Meiko kicked aside a blackened chamber pot, watched it sail across the debris. It landed with a strange sound — the hollow thump of wood. She ran over and began clearing away chunks of brick and concrete to find wooden doors sunken in the ground a few feet outside where the foundation had been. She pulled the doors open and the stale air of a cellar struck her face. She called the girls over and they descended down together out of the rain.

Through the pale afternoon light falling in, they could see sagging wooden shelves along the cellar's earthen walls. And on them, lined up like pig's heads, stood large glass jars coated in dust. Chinese preserves. The girls gasped in glee. A veritable banquet. Pickled plums and cabbages, floating shark fins, bean curd and pickles. They yanked down some jars, unscrewed the tops and sat eating feverishly on the floor, a moment of weakness before realizing that they should pace themselves. Sated, they sat in joyous silence, almost wanted to laugh at their luck. Here was shelter, here was food, and here was darkness to mask them from marauders.

In that hole in the ground, they were free to live as themselves. They relished in their safety, the lack of fear. In the cellar's darkness, they entertained each other with stories, sang folk songs, created games to play with pebbles and sticks. Above ground, on the hunt for supplies, the girls became ghosts again, lost shadows trapped between the living world and the dead one.

Groups of them took turns each day making excursions beyond the cellar to gather water and anything else to help them survive. On one trek, a girl found an old iron pot half-buried in mud, and after giving it a wash in the creek, they had something to cook with. They built a small fire just outside the cellar doors and made a thin stew with some of the preserves. There was a raucous celebration one day when a group of them came back from another trek with a large crow they had caught and strangled. They plucked and gutted the animal and had fresh meat in their evening stew.

It was on an early morning touched by autumn's chill that Meiko bent the rules and ventured out of their hiding place on her own. She woke with a distended ache in her bladder. Instead of waking one of the others to go with her, Meiko climbed the stairs on her own and stepped out into the cool morning air. She headed to a thatch of long grass and squatted down, hiking up her ratty dress. As usual, the urine burned all the way out of her swollen genitals. When she finished and straightened herself, Meiko decided to take one of their jugs, stacked in rows by the cellar doors, and fetch their morning water. She walked to the creek's edge, dipped down and submerged the jug in the water. Pulled it up when it was full and capped it.

Then she turned, and saw a group of men watching her.

Meiko froze, dropped the jug. She saw the men's uniforms before she saw their faces. Japanese army fatigues. She tried to scream, but her voice merely crackled out of her like static. She felt abruptly naked as their eyes fell on her, her rags melting away to expose a broken body primed to be broken again. Five men. She could not raise her head.

One of the soldiers stepped forward, took off his dirty, frayed cap and gave her a little bow, nearly bashful.

"Hello," he said in Korean.

Meiko looked up at him. His was not a Japanese face. The man wore the clothes of the Emperor's army but he was Korean. A *Korean man.* It had to be an illusion, a trick of the eye, a symptom of her illnesses, her hunger and lack of sleep. Meiko looked again. No. All five of them were Korean. And she let her mind slip back to thoughts of her two brothers conscripted into the Japanese military so long ago. She hadn't seen a Korean man since her abduction to China. If there had been some in the platoons that visited the camps, they weren't allowed anywhere near the girls.

Meiko trembled all over. She was certain of what was about to happen. A Korean face ... but a Japanese uniform. *What will they want? Will they hold me down and rape me right here at the creek, taking what the Japanese had denied them? Will my noises bring the girls out to see what's happening, and will the men chase some of them down while the others flee into the forest? We'll scatter like dust. It's over. Our little lives here in the cellar are over.*

The soldier cleared his throat. "You have no reason to be afraid, my child," he told her, again speaking in Korean. He gestured toward the cellar doors in the distance and the jugs lined up there, the cooling fire, and the blankets drying on chunks of concrete. "You have friends?" he asked. She didn't answer, but he nodded anyway. "How many are you?"

Meiko did not speak, would not betray the girls. She looked hard at the men, her eyes turning sharp. They didn't react to her hostility, and this made Meiko even angrier. *Why are looking at me so innocently? Why are you ignoring what I so obviously am? What do you want? Shall I jiggle my cunt at you? Shall I lay in the mud and let each of you have me? What do you want? What do you want?*

The man turned back to his comrades, gave them a nod of understanding. They nodded back. *We can help her.* The man returned to Meiko, looking as if he wanted to take a step closer to her, but wouldn't.

"We've been discharged," he said gently. "We have a transport coming to Xingshuan the day after tomorrow, to move us to a port city. I can't remember its name, but we will have passage home. Back to Korea. Back to *Chosun*." The cellar doors suddenly squeaked open and a few of the girls peeked out. Meiko turned to them, then back at the soldier. He held his cap at his waist. "Let us help you," he said to her, then repeated it to the girls, calling over to them. "Let us help you. We can take you home."

And Meiko thought: *What is this I'm sensing? Is this death creeping in? Are these the chivalrous brothers I've been waiting for?*

Meiko was surrounded on all sides by her people. Korean girls staring up from the hole in the ground in the distance. Korean men hovering over them.

"What is your name?" one of the other soldiers asked Meiko. "Child, what is your name?"

And so Meiko raised it high, like a treasure she had kept hidden from everyone.

"Eun-young," she muttered, drawing out the name that her mother had given her, a name to be spoken only behind the closed doors of her family house. She said it again with more conviction, finding her voice.

"My name is Eun-young."

PART 2

. . . .

THAT SHE WOULD ABANDON A GOOD MAN

CHAPTER 10

The Japanese couple watched the young girl as she watched the sea. The girl stood at the metal rail on the starboard side of the ship and stared out at the black water as it parted with eerie quiet beneath the ship's bow. The Japanese couple had been watching her for a long time and knew what she was thinking. The girl trained her eyes onto the northeast point of the horizon, the direction in which the ship was headed. The couple was sitting behind her a few feet off on a wooden bench bolted to the wall near the galley door. The girl had her back to them as she watched that horizon, waiting for the first faint sign of land to rise out of the fog.

I'm going home, the girl thought. *My name is Eun-young. I'm going home. And I'm going home a whore thirty thousand times over.*

She placed her feet on the bottom rung of the rail, raised herself up, the sea wind blowing her hair to one side as she took in a breath of spindrift. At the sight of this, the couple behind her rose suddenly, the man stepping ahead of his wife ready to rush across the deck. Eun-young let her eyes fall all the way down the ship's iron hull and into the whispering foam below, the deep, lulling darkness. She trembled a little, tightened her toes around the rail, lifted herself higher. But then, as quickly as she made her ascent, she backed off. Stepped down from the bottom rung and returned her feet to the deck's wet surface. She turned and was startled to find the Japanese man almost upon her, his face full of concern, his wife stricken with feminine panic behind him.

Eun-young just shoved past the couple, back toward the galley door. *Not tonight*, she sniffed at them with a glance. *Not tonight. But maybe tomorrow.*

There were just eight of them left now. Three girls — Takako, Eri, and Nako — had hanged themselves before they had even left China. A fourth, named Akemi, had flung herself over the rail of the ship just a few hours after it had pulled away from the pier. That's why the other passengers were watching the girls so closely now. Which made no sense to Eun-young. *What difference does it make to these people if we end our lives?* she thought. *Why are they so determined that we see Korea again? They think the battle is over. But it's not over for us. The possibility of a future is waging war against the shame of our past.*

The girls did not speak much to each other on the ship, even when they sat together in the galley for meals. It was like a silent agreement: They would not air what each of them was thinking of doing as the ship moved across the water. So Eun-young watched the other passengers instead — the smattering of discharged soldiers and the Japanese civilians travelling to Korea before moving on to Japan. Funny, how these passengers could keep an eye on the girls without actually looking at them. Was there any doubt as to what they were? The filth, the obvious trace of disease, the hair choked with lice, the way they lowered their eyes whenever a man walked by. *Fuck you all*, Eun-young wanted to say. *The shame should radiate from you, not from us.* Mostly, though, she just watched the Japanese couple who had confronted her at the rail. During one meal, the two of them were eating together on the other side of the galley when the ship listed hard to the left.

Eun-young watched as the wife's glass of juice pitched over, the liquid racing to the table's edge and into her husband's lap. The woman was so apologetic, getting up with her napkin at once — and Eun-young expected a brief flare of anger from the husband. Was anything else, after all, possible from a man? Instead, he laughed. Cupped his wife's head in his hand, pressed his forehead into hers, wouldn't even let her sop up the mess before he kissed her. And then they laughed together. This benign moment between a husband and his wife left Eun-young feeling hollowed out, a husk sitting there in her chair.

She saw them later, walking arm and arm on the deck. The man hadn't even bothered to change his pants.

On the last day of the journey, Eun-young woke early and found herself wandering the upper deck in a state of near hypnosis. She started to imagine what would transpire once she saw her family again. If her brothers were still alive, they would not be able to look at her. If her mother was still alive, she would fall to her knees at Eun-young's feet and pour out a symphony of thanks. If her father was still alive, his face would crush up in disgust at the sight of her. And if her baby sister was still alive — well, she didn't know. Ji-young had only been ten years old when Eun-young, five years her senior, was taken away. Would she have gone through these things, too? It was a question Eun-young had sometimes thought about at night during the quiet times in the camps. *Is Ji-young being raped, too?* Surely she had been too young. Surely the monsters who had done this would have left her alone.

Eun-young was snapped out of her daze by the sudden blare of the ship's horn. It rang out in a seemingly ceaseless bellow. Eun-young found herself hurrying to the front of the ship before the horn even stopped, nearly crashing into the rail when she got there. She looked out over the blue-green water. In the distance was the thin line of land that she'd been watching for before. Jags of mountains. Fog. The slightest wisp of rambling green hills. For an instant, she doubted where this place was, where the ship had taken her. Her heart heaved a little. It wasn't until she could see Pusan Harbour, its long lean piers, its buildings snuggled into the mountains, that she guessed where she was.

It took another moment for her to realize she had once again placed her feet on the bottom rung of the rail. She clung there for a bit before stretching her torso out, dangling it over the distant water. Her feet scrambled onto the second rung, and then the third. All she had to do was pitch her weight forward and gravity would do the rest. Send her down the side of the hull like a coin dropped for good luck into the rushing foam below.

A hand seized her just above the elbow. Yanked her back to the deck. Of course it did. She turned to see the Japanese man. He pulled her as far from the rail as possible. Practically threw her against the wall of the ship, though there was no malice in his strength. She glanced around, but the man's wife was nowhere to be seen. Probably she was still below deck, still in bed. Eun-young could not look at the man. As daft as his gaze was, she still cowered below it. He took her by the arm again, led her back to the rail. She let him. He held her in place. Pointed at the land as it crept closer to the front of the ship. Spoke to her in serviceable Korean.

"It's yours now," he said meekly. "All of it — it belongs to you. Don't throw it away, like your friends did."

Mouth quivering, Eun-young pulled herself out of his grasp. Spoke to him in flawless Japanese. "You have no idea what they took from me," she choked. "Why live? Why, when I will never experience a fraction of the joy *you give your wife*?"

. . . .

If it all belonged to her, it was hard to tell. The girls did not encounter a single Korean face after disembarking and moving through the long lines at the pier, where they were herded like bovines into a narrow garage overlooking the sea. Instead, they were greeted by a small band of American soldiers. Tall in their green fatigues, they were talking in the clumpy staccato of what Eun-young assumed was English. They acted as if they owned the whole country, lining the girls up in a row on the concrete floor of the garage with gruff, incomprehensible instructions. There, an army doctor moved from girl to girl, checking her head for lice. When he finished, he nodded at the men and left the room. A few minutes later, he came back lugging a large plastic tank with a long rubber hose and a spout as thin as a pencil. The soldiers straightened the girls up and then pantomimed them covering their noses and mouths and squeezing their eyes shut. They did what they were told. The doctor moved from girl to girl, spraying each of them with a colourless powder reeking of chemicals that shot out of the spout in a throat-choking cumulus. It filled their hair, their ears, the pores of their skin, ran down the front of their throats and into the tattered clothes on their bodies. Decades later, Eun-young would learn that this horrible mist was most likely DDT. The doctor was generous with it, ignorant of what it could do to the human body. The girls didn't complain. The stuff did an excellent job of killing the lice.

Moved to a different part of the garage, they were showered, given fresh clothes to wear, then taken to a small cafeteria in an adjacent building. There, they ate grey, flavourless food among American soldiers, who eyed them up and down with interest.

When they finished, the girls were taken back to the garage and lined up again. There, they found a Korean man waiting for them. An administrator of some kind, wearing an American business suit. Once the girls were lined up in front of him, he gave them each one thousand won and told them to take it to the nearby train station, where they could buy tickets home to their towns and villages.

The girls did as they were told. It was the late part of the evening before they arrived at the Pusan train station. There was a large chalk departure board at the front displaying different destinations written in Hangul. Eun-young could not remember the last time she had seen the Korean alphabet. She pointed out various locales for the girls who could not read. Then they moved to the tellers' booths to purchase their tickets. Kwangju, Kyungju, Seokcho, Suwon, Seoul. The girls would be parting company now, finally. They did not make a huge performance out of saying goodbye. There were Koreans here at the station, hundreds of them, and the girls didn't want to attract undo attention with a weepy, dramatic end to this, their unfathomable ordeal together.

Eun-young's train to Seoul boarded just before midnight. She sat a window seat in the front row of the first car. There were both Americans and Koreans filing into the seats all around her. She could not look at them. She just stared out the window and waited for the train to begin moving.

Dawn in Seoul. The streets were just coming to life when Eun-young stepped onto them for the first time in two and half years. It was hard finding her precise way back because the street signs, written in Japanese for her entire life, were in the process of being torn down and replaced with signs written in Hangul. There were also, she noticed, many signs in English now.

A steep hill led from her neighbourhood's main street all the way down to her parents' small house. It was paved with broken cobble, littered with trash, and laced with laundry lines strung from one iron-tiled roof to another. As Eun-young made her descent, she remembered how her mother would look up this hill for hours at a time in those months before Eun-young was taken, waiting for her sons to return from the war. This ritual would no doubt have extended to Eun-young after she was taken. How many mornings would her mother, in great grips of despair, have waited outside their door, hoping that Eun-young would complete this very act — to walk down the hill alive, returning as suddenly as she had vanished.

When she arrived at the bottom, she found the small windows of her family house darkened, greasy, and the garden on the side lawn bare. She looked around but her mother was nowhere to be seen. Eun-young waited, trembling near the stoop. *I should run*, she thought. *My life ended here two and a half years ago. I am dead as far as this place is concerned. I do not exist. I do not even —*

A young girl came around from the back of the house carrying a basket of laundry. She stopped when she saw Eun-young standing in the narrow street. It took a moment for Eun-young to realize that this was her baby sister, Ji-young. It took just as long for Ji-young to realize that the disheveled urchin standing at their door was her older sister. The basket of laundry fell. The girls' bodies crashed into each other, nearly becoming one. A wail boomed over the neighbourhood like an old iron bell. The girls collapsed onto the cobbles, nearly wrestled on the ground. Tears flowed down Eun-young's throat and she struggled to find her voice. She pried a convulsing Ji-young away, held her by the shoulders.

"Mother," she said. "Where's Mother? Has she not been waiting for me?"

"*Aigo, aigo*," Ji-young spewed. "She waited for you every day. She did. *Aigo*. Eun-young, you are ten months too late. Why didn't you come home sooner? *Aigo*. Mother couldn't wait any longer. Her heart — her *heart* could not wait any longer."

And everything crushed inward then. A shock like a river, and a grief like rain. The loss of a mother to a heart attack. The loss of brothers to the anonymous death of war. The two girls wailed and wailed together. A red and blue flag, hanging out of a neighbour's window, snapped in the wind.

Their noisy anguish soon turned into the silence of mourning, a kind of shame. They took their grief inside the house, away from the eyes of neighbours, and Ji-young made them breakfast. She went to the iron stove to boil a pot of rice, standing in that slight groove in the floor where their mother always stood. Eun-young watched as Ji-young lit the stove, set the pot of water, measured the rice in an old tin cup, poured it in, and began stirring. Her sister was still just a girl, Eun-young noticed, her body flat and shapeless, yet holding a nascent litheness and certainty that would attract men's stares before long. She was showing off a twelve-year-old's expertise at the stove.

"You've become domesticated," Eun-young said.

"I've had to be," Ji-young replied. She smoothed her hands over her dress before joining her sister on the floor at the table. "It's been just Father and me," she said, her words quaking, "since Mother's heart gave out back in December. I've had to take care of him."

"Where is he?"

"He worked the night shift at the factory. I expect him home any minute."

A silence fell between them. Eun-young felt a tightness grip her shoulders.

"He said *you* were taken to a munitions factory, in China," Ji-young went on. "Is that true? Very dangerous work, I assume. Is that how you got that scar over your lip?"

Eun-young turned her face away.

"Hey, don't be ashamed of it," Ji-young said. There was an innocence to her tone, to the way she touched Eun-young's hand. "I'm sure however it happened, it wasn't your fault."

"Did the Japanese not come for you?" Eun-young asked.

"They *did* come for me," Ji-young replied. Her face grew stern. "The *Jungshindae* came by every week. But mother and father hid me in the cellar each time they did. I haven't seen anything beyond our front door since you left. They weren't going to lose *another* child to those bastards. But they're gone now. And I'll be starting *school* soon. Father said it was okay, now that the Japanese are gone."

Lose another child. I am a lost child. Eun-young let her gaze fall to the table.

Ji-young squeezed her hand. "Don't think about it. You're home now. It's over. The Japanese are gone. Our country is going to belong to *us* again. We can start everything anew." She tried to smile at her older sister. "You're seventeen now. We'll have to talk to the matchmaker and find you a *chungmae*. It's time."

Eun-young found her head shaking involuntarily, her face cresting into a frown.

"Oh, Eun-young, please don't tell me you're still holding out for a *yonae*. You know that you —" Fresh tears spilled out of Eun-young's eyes. Ji-young startled. "Eun-young, I didn't mean … I'm sorry. I didn't mean …" The rest was written on her face: *I didn't mean you're too ugly now, with that scar, to find a yonae.*

"I'll get the rice," Ji-young said meekly, getting up from the table.

They ate in silence, rice and kimchi. The kimchi hadn't been left long enough to ferment; Ji-young was still learning. They had just cleaned their plates when they heard a rustle outside the door. The girls stood. The latch lifted and their father stepped in, his head down.

"Ji-young? Ji-young?" he called out, his voice heavy with exhaustion. "Why did you leave the basket of laundry in the street? Are you mad? Did you —"

He stopped when he saw two girls, not one, standing in his home. His whole body went slack when his eyes met Eun-young's. It was like he was staring at a ghost. Eun-young moved her arms over her chest, as if pulling closed an invisible coat. Certain he could read every shame written upon her. She looked into his face and for a moment thought she saw the slightest hint of kindness there.

But then his mouth turned down. He marched up to Eun-young and paused. Then he struck her as hard as he could.

Eun-young crashed to the floor, nearly hitting her head on the table. As she fumbled around, her dress hiked up around her hips, revealing the graffiti of scars on her legs.

Ji-young screamed. Went to their father. But he shoved her away, ignoring her wordless pleas. "Stand over there, Ji-young. And don't say a word. Not one word — or your fate will be hers." He hovered over the prostrate Eun-young, looking down at the legs spread into a crawl in front of him before she could pull her dress back down. The sight seemed to confirm everything. He grabbed her from behind and tossed her to her feet. She stood before him, not daring to touch the syrupy blood that tickled under her nose.

"You are a *whore!*" he bellowed. Wiped his mouth, moist with anger. "Do you even understand the *disgrace* you have brought to this family? Do you even *know*?"

"Father please …" Ji-young wept from the corner.

His eyes would not leave Eun-young. "Slut! Fox! Diseased vixen!" He shook all over. "You had to be out there in the *world*, didn't you? You had to ignore me. And now look at what has come to pass. Look at *you*!"

He took a step closer to her and she recoiled into herself. "You killed her, do you know that? You killed your mother, Eun-young."

"Father, no!"

"She waited outside that door for you, staring up that hill for you. Every day. Thinking that you would one day come back down it. But you never did, Eun-young. You never came back, and it *shattered* her heart."

He was trembling now. Looked like he had finally finished. But then he struck her again, harder than before.

Eun-young crumbled to her father's feet. He floated over her before grabbing a handful of her hair. Pulled her back up. Placed his face near hers, as if he were about to kiss her.

"I cast you out," he moaned. "I cast you out of my house like the *ghost* you are."

He dragged her to the door by the hair, with Ji-young screaming and following behind them. He raised the latch, threw open the door and tossed Eun-young to the street.

"You wanted to be part of the world?" he barked as she got to her feet and began walking away. "Well there you go, slut. You belong to the *world* now." He kept yelling even as she hiked back up the hill and out of earshot, even as he held a screaming Ji-young back with one arm. "You belong to the world now!"

I may belong to the world, she thought in those first hours, those first days on the streets of Seoul, *but who does this* country *belong to*? As she searched for a way to survive, Eun-young could not ignore that foreigners were once again deciding the fate of her homeland. A line had been drawn, she found out, just north of Seoul — *temporary*, people were saying — until the Americans and the Soviets could decide what to do with this strange, crucial peninsula.

The Americans were everywhere in Seoul, she noticed. They were running things, along with Koreans who had obviously been Japanese collaborators during the occupation. Still, Eun-young was grateful to this new administration: it offered her a job right off the street, cleaning government buildings and the homes of rich diplomats. She couldn't believe it. The work paid poorly and forced her to live in a squalid rooming house full of prostitutes and paupers, but still. She had her own room. She had food to eat. She *would* survive.

Her new neighbourhood was soon littered with all manner of competing pamphlets. Rife with garish slogans and propaganda, they choked the gutters and hung like leafy scales on trees and power-line poles. Both sides had an explanation for recent terrorist attacks — blamed on Marxists — that rocked various sections of Seoul; both sides had their definitions of what *Korea for Koreans* meant. Eun-young began collecting these pamphlets, taking them back to her room to read at night. She used the blank spaces on the back to write letters to Ji-young, explaining where she was now, describing her long, anonymous days in the government buildings cleaning toilets and scrubbing floors. She also saved a paragraph to comment on whatever absurd propaganda blared across the reverse side of the page. *Are these idiots really advocating civil war?* she asked.

At first Eun-young mailed these to Ji-young through the regular post, but months passed and she never received a response. She imagined her father intercepting the letters, ripping them up before Ji-young could see them. Eun-young eventually got the idea to walk to the family house in the middle of the night and slip her letters under the door. Their father would either be asleep or working at the factory. The plan succeeded: within days, Ji-young's first letter arrived at the rooming house. It was not written on the back of pamphlets and made no reference to Eun-young's commentary on the propaganda. It was written on plain rice paper and, much to Eun-young's surprise, talked about *boys* that Ji-young was discovering at school. About how she was beginning to think that a *yonae* would "actually be not such a bad thing."

One day, Eun-young was emptying garbage cans in a civil servant's office when waves of pain suddenly overtook her. They clenched her guts, nearly doubling her over. By the time she finished her shift, she could barely walk back to her room. She had been sick like this before, mostly at night. The fevers, the heavy, crawling itch between her legs, the painful swelling of her private places. The next morning she forced herself out of bed, desperate not to be late for work, and left a stain of discharge on the sheet below her. She arrived late anyway and was threatened with dismissal. Worked her way through the pain, all day long, practically weeping as she scrubbed and cleaned.

For months she tried to ignore these days. Her body was fighting with itself, waging a war between health and sickness. Eun-young kept believing that time alone would heal her and that the periods of health would soon outlast the periods of illness. *How long since my last rape?* she often thought. *Surely one day there will be no trace of the Japanese and their diseases in my blood.* But that day never came. And soon she was late for other shifts. The threat of termination hung over her constantly. Eun-young could not bring herself to visit the clinic set up by the U.S. army near the government building. She didn't want American doctors probing her down there and discovering her shame. So she instead turned to a Korean folk healer, an old woman who kept a ginseng shop in a back alley near the rooming house. After Eun-young gave her a vague description of her symptoms, the *a'jumah* prescribed foul-smelling ointments, bitter-tasting teas, and a nightly ritual of standing on her head with her legs spread out like airplane wings. For a few weeks the treatment seemed to work. But then the symptoms returned, and worse than before. Eun-young ignored them for as long as she could, the randomness of them. On a particularly bad day, one of the prostitutes in the rooming house gave her a small sample of penicillin. *The Americans are giving them out like treats!* she exclaimed. *You should go see them about your problem.* And could not understand why Eun-young wouldn't. *I am not like you*, she wanted to say. *I don't want an American doctor thinking that I am, or ever was, one of your ilk. Because I wasn't.* But she had to admit, the penicillin helped for a while. But then the flush and aches and night sweats returned.

By the late summer of '48, it was official: There were two Koreas now. The demarcation at the 38th parallel had become a heavily armed border. Strangely, the American presence in Seoul was receding in the face of this mounting tension, the rumours of war, impromptu terrorist attacks, and news of guerillas hiding in the mountains beyond the city, ready to strike. Eun-young wrote letters to her sister about what she was seeing. *What can come of this? The Americans have put thugs and Japanese collaborators in control and expect us to support them. Meanwhile, the Soviets have Kim to impose their version of communism on the North. This cannot end well.* Ji-young, fifteen now, had no interest in politics. She wrote back with long, flowery descriptions of her days at school and the boys she was discovering. Working hard, she was, to secure a love match for herself before all the good boys disappeared into a life in the army. Eun-young wept over the stupid innocence of these letters. She was so jealous. She walked to work one day trying to shake off these resentful thoughts, images of her little sister maturing into a life — marriage and children, family and a home — that Eun-young herself never would. It was unbearable to think about for too long.

But when Eun-young arrived at the office, she discovered that the windows of the first floor had been blown out by a terrorist's bomb, and there were dead bodies on the ground.

The prostitute kept leaving fresh samples of penicillin in her mailbox. *Stop being so stubborn and go ask for help,* her notes invariably read. There was no doubt: this penicillin was a miracle drug. Eun-young couldn't help but remember its predecessor, the dreaded 606 injections in the camps, and how sick it always made her, poisoning the diseases out of her blood. This penicillin was infinitely better. But Eun-young couldn't help it; still couldn't bear to drag herself to the clinic. Couldn't bear to let the diseases inflicted by one group of foreigners be cured with the solutions of another. Even if those solutions were ultimately for the best.

Skirmishes, the newspapers called them. The word sounded like a game, a kind of child-like horseplay. It was not. These fights were legitimized now — a genuine clash between rival nations. The streets were choking on ideology. Kim and Rhee. Communism and whatever you called the system that the Americans were leaving behind. Talk of war and reunification. The history of

Japanese aggression hung in the air, leaving the entire peninsula sick and splintered.

The eyes of the world are watching us now, Eun-young wrote to her sister. *Our little peninsula is in the crosshairs of history.*

She was not surprised when Ji-young wrote back and compared the conflict to some rivalry that she had drummed up with one of the girls at her school.

The worst day came, and Eun-young could no longer bear it. A fever that left her limp and sweating on her bed. Her genitals and anus had swollen almost completely shut, making trips to the bathroom an exercise in agony. Welts appeared around her groin and her joints ached as if she were a decrepit old hag instead of a young woman of twenty-one. Eun-young gave up on her fears, and dragged herself to the army clinic near the government building. There, she was surprised to see that it was a Korean doctor, not an American one, who treated her. He gave her a thorough, silent examination. There was a coldness to his touch, and she wondered if he was secretly judging her. When he finished, he prescribed a regimen of penicillin and other pills that she had never heard of before. "Compliments of the Americans," he said when he saw the wad of bills that she had saved up to pay for the drugs. "Put your money away."

Eun-young went home, and followed the regimen that the doctor had prescribed. It took seven months, but eventually the worst of her symptoms subsided.

But then the war broke out.

There was no time to prepare. Her identification papers clearly marked her as an employee of the fleeing regime. As the tanks rolled in and the Communists took control, she would need to escape as well. Imprisonment or even death awaited her if she didn't.

No last letter to Ji-young; no final sojourn through the late-night streets to slip a note under the family door. *Father will not let you run. If I know him at all, he'll hold his ground even as the bombs fall and the killing begins. Stay safe, Ji-young. Stay out of school, stay in the cellar, stay underground with your diaries and your daydreams of boys for as long as you can.*

Eun-young needed to pack whatever belongings she could and escape to the roads that led southward. She was not alone. Streams of refugees clogged the streets leading out of Seoul. People travelled any way they could — on foot, by bicycle, in cars or trucks — to stay ahead of the advancing North Korean army. In Suwon, Eun-young found an abandoned motorbike in a back alley next to a bakery. When its fuel tank ran dry just north of Kwangju, she hitched a ride with a family in a pick-up truck; they had just enough space for her to squat down in the back.

The long, sad streams of refugees were pushed south, and then farther south. *Will they shove us into the sea?* Eun-young thought. *What happens if we run out of land to flee to?* Within a few days she found herself back in Pusan, the last holdout of the Republic of Korea. Word spread that the Americans had made an audacious landing at Incheon, cutting off the North's supply chains southward.

CHAPTER 11

In retrospect, it was probably in poor taste to show up drunk at my mother's funeral after she had died of cirrhosis of the liver. There are regrets in a man's life that he feels less keenly than others — a mere sprain rather than something broken, something poorly set that never heals right. I remember thinking this as Cora and I staggered up the steps of St. George's church in Halifax on that slushy afternoon in January 1994. *I'm going to regret this later*, my mind had warbled, *but not much*. Thank God for Cora. She had not dissuaded me when I suggested we go down to the Nautical Pub when it opened at 11:00, giving us three and half hours of solid drinking before I was due at the church. She and I had been dating for about four months at this point and were still tentative with each other — not *sexually* mind you, but tentative in the sense that we wouldn't yet criticize the things that annoyed or alarmed us about the other. If she was worried by the sight of me pounding back a succession of pitchers in my jacket and tie there at the Nautical, she didn't let on. Just watched me with her silvery blue eyes and steeled herself against anything that might erupt from my sadness. I appreciated that, the way she allowed me to talk in bursts and then fall into long silences, did not grow impatient when I took lengthy stares out the window at the lazy grey harbour, at the container ships heading out to sea. Now, on the steps of St. George's, she felt compelled to parent me a little. Actually straightened my tie and patted down the cowlick I would lose to baldness years later.

"Are you ready?" she asked.

"Of course," I replied. "You only get to bury your mother once."

We moved through the narthex to stand before the rows of pews beneath the tall white dome. There, sitting in the front bench, was my older sister Heidi. She was surrounded by the minister, and the funeral director, and several altar boys. In the grips, she was, of one of her many fanatical outbursts of grief since we had pulled the sheet over Mom four days earlier. Her body was hunched, her shoulders bouncing, the minister kneeling in the aisle by her side with her hands in his, and Heidi's seven-year-old daughter, Soleil, sitting next to them and looking a bit stunned at the sight of her mother's grief. I stood there and watched Heidi in her performance. It had been ten years since she had run away from home, and I had seen her back in Halifax only a few times since and always at her worst, always at the apex of some personal catastrophe that she took out on Mom. I thought about all those arguments that had practically taken on a callisthenic property. And now here Heidi was, jiggling in regret like Jell-O. Not so much, I suspected, over the tragic end to our mother, but at the solipsistic remorse that her death kicked up like mud. And I blame the beer for what I thought then, for what I nearly hollered aloud down the empty pews: *You fucking fraud.*

We walked up to face them. Heidi, at this point in her life, was at the peak of her tattoo phase: beneath her frilly black dress, I could see the shadow of eagle wings around her collarbones, the silhouette of a spider's web on her shoulder. Soleil gave a shy little wave when she saw us, her tired blond hair the colour of mashed bananas and falling all over her own black dress. When Heidi looked up, her face was a rosy red carnival of tears.

"Where have you *been*?" she barked at me. Looked at her watch. "Michael, it's nearly three. Could you not have gotten here sooner?"

"Sorry, I spent the morning …" and here had to choose my word carefully, "… thinking."

The minister stood and looked to ease our tension with his hardened Anglican calm. He shook my hand and offered his condolences. "We have some business to take care of before your guests arrive," he said. "Shall we go into the other room and say goodbye?" So off we went to see Mom one last time in her open casket, all tucked in and tarted up.

An hour later, the pews were barely peppered by the family and friends who bothered to show up; their scant numbers seemed even smaller in that massive house of worship. Throughout the service, I kept twisting with great drama around in my seat to cast a glare from one near-stranger to another, these benighted uncles and dim-eyed cousins who had stayed eternally on the sidelines while my mother destroyed herself. *Haven't seen you in five years … haven't seen you in two … I don't even know who that person is …* A dishevelled half-uncle of mine had shown up wearing a checkered lumberjack coat — a Cape Breton dinner jacket, we called it — and a crust of dried toothpaste around his mouth. The sight of him filled my eyes with tears. "Fucking asshole," I slurred. "Could he not have shown her some respect?"

"Shh-shh," Cora just said, patting my arm.

With rituals done, we made a slow procession over to Camp Hill Cemetery. One more quick prayer over the green brands and then we lowered Mom down into that rectangle carved in the slushy earth. An aunt offered to have everyone back to her place for coffee. Heidi trembled her acquiescence — she and Soleil still had a couple of hours before they were due at the airport for their flight back to the west coast. Gazes turned to me. Cora straightened me up from where I was leaning blasphemously against a gravestone, and I looked from face to face. Saw genuine welcome there: this paltry ensemble of my family were finally, after ten years, reaching out to help me. And maybe I do regret it, not accepting their rare offer of fellowship. But can you blame me? I was twenty going on twenty-one — hotheaded and stupid. Maybe if I *had* taken that olive branch, then other things, *the whole thing*, would have worked out differently — to have family around years later when my life really fell apart.

I shook my head. *No.*

"*Michael* …"

No, Heidi. Who you turn to when your mother dies speaks volumes about where your heart is. And my heart wasn't with these people. I squeezed Cora's arm. *This* is where I am. Only here. And so we walked away, dispersing as if I were just another family acquaintance.

"What do you want to do?" Cora asked as we milled on the icy sidewalk outside Camp Hill.

"Let's go get a *drink*," I said cheerily.

"I think you've had enough."

I sighed. "Can we go back to your place?"

"That's more like it."

So we crossed the road to her bachelor apartment on Summer St. I always loved walking into that delightfully feminine nest, so bursting with Cora's lovely smells and competent decor. After we settled in, she cooked me dinner and we watched the news, like the good journalism students we were. Afterwards, I allowed her lead me by the arms over to her bed. How quickly my disposition changed — limpid grief transformed into ferocious lust. And what of those milestones we achieved in bed that night? For the first time, we had sex without a condom. For the first time, I told her that I loved her – weeping out those words, in cliché fashion, at the explosive peak of my excitement. But she grew distant as we ramped down together. I think I may have apologized. "Hey, it's okay," she said, kissing my wet face. "I'm on the Pill. Hey, hey. It's alright." She disentangled herself from me and toddled off the bathroom as if trying to walk while holding a bar of soap between her legs. She returned a few minutes later to find me on my stomach. Eased herself onto my back and stretched her arms out over mine. "Of course I love you, too, Michael," she whispered into my neck. "Of course I do." Convincing herself, I suppose.

Even after five years together, I felt like I had bore witness to only a small portion of Cora's mysteries. Sometimes you learn things too late about a woman, about how her emotional response can be so tied to seemingly innocuous sensations. The colour of the seats on a bus, the smell of stale coffee, the feel of rough stone. They can set things off. Cause a churning.

I would love to know what sensation set off Cora's final conclusion: *I don't love Michael.* I imagine it a simple thing, happening as it does in some purple-prose short story: the texture of an undercooked pepper from some evening's pasta sauce, or maybe the sound of the newspaper hitting the landing in *just a certain way.* Whatever it was, it triggered a remorseless instant of emotional truth for her: *I don't love Michael. And I'll be ruined in a thousand little ways if I stay with him.* And I would love to know what sensory experience caused her to fall so completely in love with her Quebecois coworker, Denis-never-Dennis. Again, something very basic. The way he raised his wrists while typing up his radio stories, maybe, or the gleam of the gel in his hair under the newsroom's fluorescent lights. All I know is that she took him deeply inside her, made him the centrepiece castle in her busy emotional aquarium. *He is IT*, she realized one day with irrevocable certainty. *And I've got to have him.*

At least, that's how I imagined it going down.

I mark the ten-year anniversary of my mother's death in a *Jokki-Jokki* bar in Daechi with Rob Cruise and Jon Hung. We sit at a wooden table with glasses of beer and little rings of puffed rice set out in bowls in front of us. Asian lanterns hang everywhere and frantic K-pop jangles from the speaker above our heads. Rob has summoned us here for a "business proposition," though he's being coy about what it is. He's holding off on details until Justin arrives, as well as a new friend that he's made at the university — a guy named Greg Carey. While we wait, I break the news to Rob that I've signed up for another twelve months at ABC English Planet. His reaction is predictably hysterical.

"Are you kidding me? Are you *fucking kidding me*?"

"No, I'm serious. I signed the contract yesterday. I've begun to like it, Rob. I mean Ms. Kim is still insane, but I like teaching the kids. I ... I *really* like it."

"Ah, *fuck me*, man!" He leans back against the wall, his shoulders taut with genuine disappointment. It gets to me. Even after a year of knowing Rob, of knowing *what he is*, I still feel that need to seek his approval. "You're a brilliant man, Michael," he says almost to himself. "I can't believe you're going to rot away in that shithole for another year."

"I can't believe you're quitting your university gig," I counter. "It's twelve hours a week, Rob. What, you can't handle twelve hours a week?"

He leans back in, grabs his beer glass, eyes Jon and me both. "You guys think university gigs are the bomb, but it's a fucking lie. First of all, the pay is *crap*. When I'm not on campus, I'm hustling all over this city for privates. I work harder now than I ever did. Second of all, the students are *shite*. This country is so ass backwards: they work little kids to the bone all the way up through high school; they get to university and know they've made it, and don't want to do *fuck all*. I'm sick of it, man."

"You seem to get sick of a lot of things, and rather quickly," Jon Hung points out. He himself left the *hagwon* a few months ago and now works for the KOSPI, doing some sort of English-based stock analysis. "Rob, you're like a seagull looking for a rock to land on, and crapping over everything as you go."

"Hey, shut up, I definitely need you for this. You've got half an MBA. You're gonna run the business end of things."

"Rob …" Jon sighs at him.

"Look, just hear me out. Trust me, this is an excellent idea. We're all going to make butt-loads of money. Where's your entrepreneurial spirit?"

Just then, the notorious Greg Carey comes through the door and joins our table when Rob waves him down. I say notorious because, though this is my first meeting with Greg, Rob has regaled us with tales about him since they met five months ago. They've already taken two holidays together to Puket, Thailand, and the priapic adventures that resulted are beyond anything I could imagine. This man has achieved a level of legend in my mind. He's in his late thirties, even older than Rob, and has been Korea for seven years. He worked in a succession of shitty *hagwons*, survived the IMF crisis, and has now become the epitome of everything Rob wishes *he* could be: an expat Canadian who works very little, makes obscene amounts of money under the table, and flees to the whorehouses of Southeast Asia at every opportunity.

"Have you told them our idea?" he says as he sidles up to our table.

"*My* idea," Rob corrects him. "No, we're still waiting for one guy to show up."

I eye Greg up and down as he slips out of his winter coat and drops it on a hook on the wall. He has fiery red hair, a face covered by a galaxy of freckles and an unfortunate mustache.

Before we can go on, Greg begins snapping his fingers in the air to summon our Korean waiter. "Hey! *Hey!*" he yells.

The guy comes over in his apron and smiles politely.

"Bring-ah me-ah some a beer-uhh," Greg chimes at him. The waiter looks confused but continues to smile. "Some beeeer-uhhh," Greg repeats. "Bring-ah me some a beer-uhh. Some beeer-uuhhhh." The waiter, still smiling, blinks and looks to the rest of us for help. Rob has burst into braying laughter over this — I would expect nothing less of him — but shockingly, so has Jon Hung. Perhaps he's forgotten that he himself is half Korean.

"*Jeo'ghee'yoh.*" I nod gently at the waiter. "*Maek'ju jusaeyoh. Cass. Oh'bec cee-cee, yo.*"

He bows at me, still smiling. "*Neh, meak'ju, neh.*" And goes back to the bar to fetch it. Rob Cruise leers at me, oleaginous. *Ahh, I see Jin has trained you well.*

Greg puckers his freckled face and spits as he talks: "Bah, he knew what I *meant.*"

I turn to a grinning Rob. "Can we get this thing started?"

"No. Where the hell's Justin?" He looks at his watch.

"Rob, he's with his private tonight. He said he'd be late."

"Fine, we'll start without him." He reaches down to pull his satchel off the floor, opens it and takes out glossy brochures and business cards that he and Greg have had printed up. He lays them out on the table and Jon Hung takes one up. "The Queen's English," he reads. "Holiday Camps for Kids." He shrugs. "This is the dumbest idea I've ever heard."

"Look, would you give us a chance?" Rob straightens up in his chair. "We all know Korean parents force their kids to study even harder when they're on vacation. They send them to English camps anyway. Why not one owned, organized, and run by native speakers? It only makes sense."

"So you guys are quitting twelve hours a week at the university for *this*?" I ask. "Rob, I don't think you grasp how much work this would be."

"It's a *summer camp*. Even with all the prep, it'd only amount to about four months of work a year. We can charge millions of won per kid, and with hundreds of kids signed up we'd make a killing."

"I think you've confused gross with net," Jon says.

"Exactly." I nod. "I mean, where are you going to hold this camp? What are the kids going to eat? Where are the books coming from?"

"Look, irregardless of the expenses, I still think —"

"*Irregardless*?" I laugh at him. "Rob, dude, if you're going to name your company The Queen's English, you should at least learn to speak it."

"See, this is why I need you on staff, Michael. You have a journalism degree — you're like fucking grammar god!"

"Where's the start-up money coming from?" Jon asks.

"Well, that's what we need from you," Greg pipes up, stroking his unfortunate mustache. "We're each going to invest 2.5 million won up front."

"Oh, you *are* out of your fucking mind," I say to Rob.

"Look, we got tons of teachers around Itaewon interested in this," Rob says. "But you are my *boys*. I want to get you in on the ground floor."

I'm about to respond, but just then Justin lumbers through the door, his shoulders slouched, his head down. He pulls a chair up to our table. Looking into his face, I can immediately tell that something is wrong. He doesn't make eye contact at us. *"Yogi yo,"* he calls to the waiter and orders a beer.

"You're late," Rob says.

He still won't look at us.

"You had a private with Jenny?" I ask. "On a Saturday night? That seems strange."

"I *thought* I had a private," he replies.

"It wasn't a private?"

"No. Turns out Jenny and her dad are down in Kjungju for some festival. It was her mom, Sunkyoung, who invited me over. For dinner." He swallows very slowly. "Dinner — and a proposition."

Rob and Jon's eyes light up like Menorahs. "I *knew* it." Rob beams. "I fucking well knew it!"

"Rob, shut up," Justin says with a point of his finger. "I swear to God, if you say one fucking word I'm going to rip your asshole out and feed it to you."

Rob just cackles. Cackles at the wit of it.

"What happened?" I ask.

Justin's beer comes and he takes a pull. "I got there to find that Jenny and her dad were nowhere around. Sunkyoung had the table all set, just for the two of us. Kept plying me with red wine all night long. And then asked, in this weird matter-of-fact way, if I would consider being her *boyfriend*."

"You must have an inkling that this could happen."

"I suppose. She's only a few years older than me, and her —"

"Is she hot?" Greg Carey asks.

Justin sighs. "Yeah she's hot, as Korean moms go." We all can't help but laugh. "Look, this is serious. I've been tutoring Jenny for over a year. This family has practically adopted me."

"Look, this is no big deal," Jon Hung tries to assure him.

"Tons of Korean housewives keep boyfriends on the side. You were telling us that Sunkyoung's husband works, like, ninety hours a week. She's probably not getting *any* at all. I say shag her. She'll probably feel guilty after a few times and break things off. Sure you'll lose the private, but there's tons of other work out there."

"But I *like* tutoring Jenny. She's a good kid. And I like her family. It, it reminds me of ..." But he trails off.

"Did anything actually happen tonight?" I ask.

"Well, we polished off two bottles of Merlot, and the next I know she was sitting in my lap."

"What can I tell ya?" Greg chuckles. "Never underestimate what loneliness and red wine will do to a woman in her thirties."

"I'm sorry, who the fuck are you?" Justin snaps. But Greg merely grins at him. "Anyway, I just pushed her off me and fled. I felt bad, but didn't know what else to do."

"Man, you're a fucking chickenshit," Rob finally says.

"Yeah, Rob, I'm a chickenshit." Justin drains his beer, sets the glass down, puts five thousand won on the table and stands up.

"Hey where are you going? I didn't tell you about my —"

Justin glances at the brochures and business cards. "Yeah, whatever it is, Rob, I'm not interested. Have fun in Itaewon, boys." And then shambles back out the door.

I'm not sure why, but I sit there for a bit longer, chewing on what happened. I'm not even listening as Rob goes up and down his plans again. Finally, I stand up, too.

"Hey, where do you think *you're* going?"

"I'm going to check on him."

"Please. He's *fine*. What the hell?"

"Rob, do you even know why Justin's in Korea in the first place?"

"Oh, fuck off, Michael." He folds his arms. "Whatever."

Back at the apartment, I find Justin in his room cast in the faint light of a single lamp. He's on his bed with his shoulders against the headboard and his big feet dangling over the edge. He looks almost angry, resentful in his solitude, but when he sees me at his door he softens.

"Hey," I say.

"Hey. No Itaewon tonight?"

"No. I changed my mind."

"Is Jin not around?" he asks, looking at the wall.

"No, she's in Shanghai for the week. She's back on Tuesday." I swallow. "I kind of wish she was here tonight."

"Oh yeah? Why's that?"

"Because today is the ten-year anniversary of my mother's death."

He turns to stare absently at the photos of his son Cody, forever frozen at age six, taped to his headboard. That look of resentment comes back to his face.

"You know it's okay to admit," I say, "that this thing with Sunkyoung has a lot to do with Cody."

He looks at me. "I can't remember how much I told you, Michael."

"A little," I reply.

This is what I know: By age twenty-three, Justin had earned his education degree, had married his university sweetheart Kathy, and was teaching at a high school in Halifax. A year later, their son Cody was born. In the year 2000, the three of them took their first big family vacation together — a hiking trip to Gros Morne National Park in Newfoundland. Negligent, perhaps, to take a six-year-old on such a difficult trek. Distracted by the majesty of those gorges and mountains, they allowed the little guy to get away from them for a few seconds. The seventeen-metre drop beyond a safety rail killed him instantly. Within a year, Justin and Kathy had split up, and within a year of that Justin was in Korea, teaching at the *hagwon*.

"Did I ever tell why Kathy and I got divorced?"

"I've had my hunches."

"It's because I had an affair." He sits up. "It happened about four months after Cody died. It was so fucked up, what I did."

"Tell me about it."

"It was so stupid," he says, running his fingers through his hair. "It happened with another teacher at the school. This brief but really intense … *fling*. That's all it was. But that's all it needed to be. I look back now and can't believe the lack of control I showed. I just dove into that opportunity, you know? I needed to do something really destructive, so I could feel like I had power over myself again. That I wasn't just a man who let his son die. You know? I mean, I never realized how destructive sex could be. And the ironic thing is — *the sex was so good*. Like, ridiculously good. The kind of fucking that will cost you a damage deposit." He laughs but his eyes have gone shiny. "I mean, that woman, the other teacher, made noises with me that Kathy never made in our eleven years together. And the whole time I'm thinking, *You're wrecking everything. This is going to destroy Kathy*. And now look at me, Michael: I'm teaching in fucking Korea, and *everything* here is sex. Itaewon, Hooker Hill, Hongdae. It's all sex, sex, sex. But I don't want to leave, because I don't want to go back to Halifax and face my people. I don't want to face the fact that I willfully destroyed my life."

"So Kathy found out?"

"Of course she found out. We all taught at the same school. Shit gets around. I tried to protect her — she'd already been through so much over Cody — but she *wanted* me to tell her everything, every fucking fleshy detail. It was as if hearing about me fuck another woman made her grief complete, girded her for what she needed to do. And what she needed to do, she went about so clinically. The lawyer, the dividing up of our stuff, the taking back of her maiden name, all the rest. It was so *amicable*, only because she had closed the door to the idea of not doing it. I thought divorces took forever, but it didn't feel like forever: it felt like one day she was my wife and the next day she wasn't. She was just so *clinical* about it." He takes a deep breath. "And that's what I saw tonight with Sunkyoung, too. She had that same detached approach when she solicited me, as if asking if I'd help put down new tile in their bathroom or something. Her English isn't great; I thought I'd misheard her. But, no. She was proposing that I become her, her …"

"Her gigolo."

He laughs. Thankfully, he laughs. "Yeah, her gigolo. And I'm not gonna lie: I am attracted to Sunkyoung. She's sexy, you know, in that Asian way. In that way that Jin is sexy. But I …"

He looks back at his headboard. In the photos, Cody looks so alive, so bursting with little-boy energy. I think he and Sunkyoung's daughter, Jenny, would be roughly the same age.

He turns back to me. "I'm not going to break up another family. I'm not going to allow *sex* to break up another family."

"Then don't," I say.

He nods. Looks up at me. "Michael, I'm sorry to hear you're marking such a grim anniversary tonight."

"It's all right," I reply. Lost for a moment in my thoughts, I find myself frowning. "Did I ever tell you," I ask him, "that I showed up drunk at my mother's funeral?"

"Really?"

"Yeah. I've been feeling bad about that all day."

He chuckles. "In the grand scheme of things, that doesn't seem so awful."

"Yeah, I know. Still. I wish Jin were around tonight. I could really use her company."

He nods again. "So you've signed up for another year at the *hagwan*?"

"I have," I shrug. "Ms. Kim offered and I accepted. I was telling Rob, I like it. I sorta think I'm becoming a proper teacher."

"So one more year of slinging English like hamburgers, eh? And then after that?"

"I dunno. I have to give it some thought." I scratch my nose. "I suppose *Jin and I* have to give that some thought."

CHAPTER 12

She fell from the anonymous role of a cleaning girl and into the anonymous role of a cook in a greasy Pusan diner. The proprietor took one look at the scar on Eun-young's face and refused to let her serve customers — the ROKA and UN soldiers and the few Pusan civilians allowed to mingle with them. "You'll scare them off with that wound," the madam said. She sensed something unwholesome in this girl who came begging for a job, something that would need to been hidden away from Korean eyes. So she put Eun-young in the kitchen to work in perfect anonymity over the long row of cast-iron stoves, chopping vegetables, cooking rice, setting stews to boil. The only contact Eun-young had with the dining public was when she set completed dishes on the window counter for the madam to carry off to customers. Each time she did, Eun-young would steal a glance over the tables of soldiers, trying to spot a single face that had been in the diner before. There never seemed to be any. These soldiers ate and then moved northward to join the fray. It made her think of the men in the rape camps, enjoying a moment of peaceful pleasure before disappearing, and most likely dying, in the throes of battle.

When the South took back Seoul for the final time, Eun-young resumed her letter-writing to Ji-young. Even if the mail service between their two cities was working, she had no faith that her notes would get through. For the longest time no response came, and Eun-young feared the worst. But eventually a letter did arrive at the rooming house where she was living, the address written in Ji-young's florid scrawl. The war had changed very little about her sister's obsessions. She was eighteen now — and finally engaged. "His name is Chung Hee and he's an army mechanic," she wrote. "He's got flat feet so he can't be a soldier proper. But he's a genius when it comes to the modern engine and *he's very good with his hands*." She underlined this part with a teenager's glee. "He promises to marry me as soon as this war is over. I hope he survives!" Eun-young frowned at the note. *All out civil war, death, and destruction, Seoul being blown to bits, and she's still fixated on finding a husband.*

In her next letter, Ji-young raised the inevitable question: "And what about you, dear sister? You are still a marriageable age. Please write and tell me you've found your own man to love and take care of you." Eun-young tore this letter into little pieces. *You know nothing*, she wanted to write back. *Haven't you figured out yet what I was, Ji-young? You have no clue how lucky you are, to have been born five years after me and not have this disgrace written all over you.*

Her anger carried itself over to her work in the diner. She often looked out from the kitchen to the bowed heads of soldiers eating, who never once looked up at her or smiled or asked her name. To them, she was but a mere shadow moving pots and pans around the kitchen. She looked out over them and thought: *Eat your dinners, and then go meet your deaths already.*

Evidence of the armistice came almost immediately. Within a couple weeks of the conflict's end, Eun-young noticed that customers *had* started to become familiar faces, had begun returning to the diner on a regular basis. At first these men continued to wear their army fatigues, but before long they began showing up in civilian clothes — just regular customers happy about their return to Pusan and the passage into shaky peace with the North.

To celebrate the armistice, the madam bought the building next door and knocked out the wall between it and the diner in order to turn the new space into a singing room. Eun-young continued working for her, putting in even longer hours. (She didn't even ask for time off when the letter came announcing Ji-young's wedding date; Chung Hee was free of the army and kept his promise to marry her right away.) The restaurant got so busy that the madam even began allowing Eun-young to inter-act with customers, letting her clear dirty dishes from the tables. Eun-young was happy for these moments of freedom from the sweltering stoves in the back. She kept her head low as she cleaned up after patrons, her hair over her face. She even refused to look up when one of the regulars, a young man, a boy really, tossed a curious smile her way. What does *he* want? What's *he* smiling at? She ignored him. Ignored how the boy's eyes would follow her whenever she limped back to the kitchen with her heavy tray of dishes propped on her shoulder.

The construction of the singing room disrupted things for several weeks. The drilling, the hammering, the thin mist of dust hanging in the air annoyed the regulars constantly. The sudden blast of banging would break conversations in mid sentence, send the patrons into a sea of silence until it stopped. Every day the regulars threatened not to come back until the work was done and every day Eun-young mumbled that they should take their complaints up with the madam who owned the place.

One night, just before close, the madam was in the other room arguing about something with the builders, and Eun-young was left alone in the kitchen to wash up for the night. She stood at the metal sink scrubbing down the wide cast-iron woks before drying and hanging them on hooks on the wall. She moved to the cupboard to fetch a fresh drying towel, and discovered with a start that one of the regulars had wandered back into the kitchen. It was the boy she had noticed staring at her, the one who had attempted smiling. He stood in front of the curtain over the doorway, his cap in his hands. He had a podgy face, as if full of baby fat, but his hair was still carved into the crew cut of a brutal soldier.

"Excuse me," she barked from behind her hair, "but you're not allowed back here."

"I have a question."

"If you have a grievance, take it up with the madam."

"I don't have a grievance," he said. "I have a question."

Eun-young just kept her head bowed.

"Do you sing?" he asked.

Her surprise caught in her throat. She nearly looked up, but didn't.

"When the room next door is finished," he went on, "will you be singing in it?"

Her hand moved to rub absently at her neck. "No. I don't *sing*." A mumble so low she wondered if he heard it.

He lowered his head a little, trying to catch her eyes. "What's your name?"

She said nothing. Felt her *han* swell and squeeze her. Felt that familiar flush of shame on her skin. He waited, but she wouldn't answer.

"Mine is Po," he said. "Don't let the haircut fool you — I'm not a soldier anymore. I'm moving into construction work. I'm very fascinated by what they're doing next door." He shifted his cap in his hands. "What's your name?" he asked again, and took a step closer.

The rush of *han* overtook her. Eun-young did raise her face then, threw back her hair so this Po fellow could get a good look at the scar that cleft her lip. "You're not allowed — in *here*," she spat, giving him a full view of her ugliness.

She waited, but his eyes wouldn't fall to the scar, not for a second. And his smile wouldn't slip away. "Okay," he said pleasantly enough, and nodded at the curtain over the door. "Maybe I'll talk to you out there, then."

And talk to her he did. Po was in three or four evenings a week, usually with friends, and he would always break free of their banter to speak to Eun-young whenever she was out clearing tables. She in turn refused to acknowledge him. He learned her name only when the madam yelled at her after she accidentally dropped a stone pot on the tiled floor, drawing noisy attention to herself. One day, as Eun-young was wiping down a table near where Po was sitting, she thought she heard one of his young friends chuckle at him: "Why do you keep staring at her? What do you see in that *old hag* anyway?" She returned to the kitchen in a fume of humiliation, tossing her dish cloth into the corner. *Old hag? I'm twenty-five. I'm not a* hag. *I'm … I'm …* What was the phrase that Ji-young kept using in her letters? *A marriageable age. I am still a marriageable age.* She wanted to go back out and scream that at Po's friends, yell it right in their faces.

That night, a letter from Ji-young arrived at the rooming house. Eun-young opened it to find a wedding photograph included inside. The black-and-white image showed Ji-young and Chung Hee dressed in traditional wedding garb — thick robes of silk and elaborate headgear — and sitting on a small, plush couch. They were barely touching and their faces held a stony Korean austerity. Yet Eun-young sensed a sweet mystery sweeping under her sister's chastity. A riptide of triumph.

. . . .

The alcohol was flowing on opening night of the singing room. There were to be four performers — Po included — and a master of ceremonies, a hulking former army sergeant, to introduce each of them. But the MC had been drinking *baekseju* since the early afternoon, one golden bottle after another, and by the time the crowd had filled the singing room in the evening, he was barely able to get up from the table in the diner. The audience, seated in wooden chairs in front of the stage in the next room, was growing impatient. Finally the MC rose from the table and wobbled his bulk through the adjoining door. He took the stage and began slurring into the microphone, welcoming everyone and blathering about how grateful he was that this city, this country, had achieved enough peace to allow a night like this to happen. Eun-young moved among the audience with her tray on her hip, passing out bottles of beer and *soju* and *baekseju* as the first singer took to the stage. He strapped on the guitar that was waiting for him and stood under the stage's bright, colourful lights.

He was horrible. He introduced his three Korean folk songs with lengthy, disjointed preambles that lasted longer than the songs themselves. His voice was shrill and out of tune as he sang ancient tales of their ancestors fighting off foreign invaders. The second singer was just as bad. He clearly didn't know his selection of tunes well enough and kept restarting them each time he flubbed on the guitar. The third performer opted to belt out an off-key medley of American jazz tunes, stuttering through the English.

By the time Po took the stage, the audience was agitated. Eun-young stopped serving and found a darkened corner of the room to stand and watch him, away from the madam's vigilant gaze. Eun-young's eyes followed Po as he jogged up to micro-phone. He strapped on the guitar, tuned it gently, nodded once, and then launched into a fitful but competent instrumental piece. It started with a slow, methodical tempo but then climbed in its pace. When he finished the tune, the audience members set down their various bottles and applauded loudly. Po played three more short tunes, singing out lyrics that echoed over the room. But then he set the guitar aside and began climbing back down from the stage without so much as a bow. The drunken MC dashed to his feet from his place in the front row, applauding until he could get a hold of Po's arm and pull him back up. "Play another!" he sloshed. "Play another!" And so Po did, bashfully. And then tried to leave the stage again. The audience joined in the MC's chorus. "Play another!" So Po played another, and then another, and then was finally allowed to sit.

It wasn't that he had stolen the show. His playing had been merely competent, not extraordinary. But it was what Eun-young saw Po do afterwards as she resumed her serving, manoeuvering around chairs and tables, that caused her to pause. She watched as he mingled with the other singers and bowed to audience members who came up to greet them. When one of them became profuse in his praise, Po would not relish it or puff up his chest, even a little. Instead, he paid a magnanimous but unnecessary deference to the *lesser* singers. He was doing this, she saw, out of a sense of genuine civility, a deep well of kindness that nour-ished his every action. *He is the rarest of men*, she realized as she watched him. *He is decent — more decent than even he realizes.*

Whenever Eun-young passed by with her tray, Po would look up from where he was chatting and throw a tight, knowing smile her way. And when he did, Eun-young would look at the floor and grit her teeth, suffocating under the weight of a new sensation that she could not name. *Oh my dear sister*, she heard

Ji-young's voice ring in her head. *What you're feeling* does *have a name. It's called desire.*

And so just once, she did look up into Po's plump face and return his smile, wondering: *Is it possible for a soldier to be this gentle?*

He asked her to go for a walk with him on her day off, and she agreed.

It was a Sunday morning and they strolled together through the busy fish markets of Pusan harbour. As they walked along the wooden wharfs and past the long metal fences that opened out to the sea, the two of them watched the morning's chaos unfold around them. Fishermen just coming off their late-night boats lugged ship-to-shore boxes teeming with their catches; and the women working the markets stood ready to haggle with them in great animation. It was like a symphony of wheeling and dealing, a vibrancy that put Po at ease. They would have stayed and soaked it in all morning, except they were shooed away by a grouchy fishmonger when it became apparent they weren't going to buy anything.

Po and Eun-young stopped at a small restaurant just beyond the market's edge for a late breakfast of king crab and rice. They sat on the floor at a low table and manoeuvered their chopsticks around the food, Po stopping to break up the crab shells for Eun-young without asking. As he did, he said: "I never noticed before, Eun-young, but you have a Seoul accent."

She nodded. "Yes. I am from Seoul." She explained about her job with the provisional regime and how it had meant fleeing south to Pusan like so many other Seoulites once the North rolled in.

Po seemed to think hard about this. "It's so strange."

"What is?"

"I always thought you were delivered to me from the sea, not over land. Like you should be from somewhere on the water — Jeju Island or somewhere even farther. I perceive a great ... a great sense of the sea in you."

Delivered to you? I have been delivered to you? She turned her face away a little, moved a piece of crab into her mouth with her chopsticks. On the opposite side of the restaurant, a noisy group of fishermen sat at a table in the corner over a huge feast. They were already drinking despite the early hour, the green bottles of *soju* lining up around their dishes. The alcohol was making them bombastic. A few of the fishermen looked over at the young couple. They eyed Eun-young with what she thought was disapproving curiosity — at the scar on her face, at her cracked teeth, at the awkward way she sat to keep her weight off her pelvis, which still ached on cold mornings such as this. She flashed an angry stare at the men: *What are you looking at?* And she read their gazes back: *We're looking at you — and wondering why your boyfriend can't see what we see.*

She turned back to Po but looked at the table. "No, I am from Seoul. I always lived in Seoul."

He smiled at the way she wouldn't look at him. "You're very shy," he said.

She just let her hair fall in her face and thought: *Don't stare through me, Po. See what's there, not what you wish to see. Or else you'll know nothing.*

After their meal, they walked north from the waterfront and up the steep climb rising over Pusan's lower districts to find a park in which to sit. Behind them, the jagged jaws of Pusan's mountain range gaped out of the mist above them. Down the hill from the park, they could see the inchoate structures of newer neighbourhoods bursting into existence. All around them, seniors were out in the park, shuffling along the stone paths or performing *tai chi* on the grass in the late morning sun. Not far from where Po and Eun-young sat, a tall metal pole carried South Korea's new flag, proud and defiant against the sea's winds.

"I never thought I'd live to see all this," Po said. "During the worst days of the war, I came to believe that I'd die before I could ever do anything as simple as this."

He stopped like he was waiting for her to say something, to contribute the same thought. He turned and for the first time acknowledged the scar on her face. "*You* know what I'm saying," he said. "You understand, don't you, the marks that war can leave on a person."

She refused to follow along. "Po, tell me — what makes you think that I've been, as you said, *delivered* to you? I haven't been delivered. You must know this. I'm not some gift that fell out of the sky just for you."

"Not out of the sky," he said, almost child-like, "and not over the sea, like I imagined. But over land. You were brought to me over land."

"Po, please be serious."

He fell silent for a moment, training his eyes over the city. "I don't want to be part of the past anymore, Eun-young. Can you understand this?" He took a breath. "My father was a sea captain. He was killed on a run to Shimonoseki, ten years ago. I was twelve. For years I thought I could go on without his guidance and live a life of honour, no matter what happened to our country. But then the war broke out with the North, and I was proven wrong. I did not live with honour, Eun-young. *You* must know *this.* I was told to murder our own people. People who wanted nothing more than to enjoy the kind of simplicity we're enjoying *right now.* And I did it — I murdered, over and over. You would never believe that someone like me could do such terrible things.

But I did them because I was ordered to. I did them because I was a soldier and that's what I thought honour *meant*."

Eun-young wanted to weep, but couldn't.

"So now, I want nothing more to do with the past. I am done with it. And you ask me why my eyes have fallen onto you? Because I knew, Eun-young, right from the moment I saw you, that you carry the same kind of wounds from the war. I don't know what the North did to you before you managed to flee, but whatever it was you carry your wounds as deep in your heart as I carry mine." His eyes rose to the neighbourhood that unfolded below the park. "Look at what's happening here, Eun-young. Not six months after the armistice and we're already rebuilding ourselves. *Renewing* ourselves. We will be a great country one day. And that's what I want to be a part of. I want to *renew* this country. I want to help build it."

He shocked her by taking her hand in his. She quavered, nearly pulled away.

"It's time to renew," he said. "Eun-young, listen to me. The past, it cannot touch us. If we are strong and proud, we cannot be driven down by the marks that others have left on us. Do you understand? I want to renew myself — with you. Do you understand? The time has come to *renew*."

She did weep then. Not because she had to say no, but because she knew she could not say no. Every pore in her skin thirsted for something as simple as this. The love of a decent man.

Eun-young leaned her head low, and Po took it as a sign of her chastity.

CHAPTER 13

So here is me in my classroom. After a year and a half of this teach-by-colours curriculum, I've pretty much gotten a handle on it. I've become a conscientious teacher, tacking student essays and drawings to the wall by the door, using the white board and coloured markers to great effect, standing more often than sitting, making grammar come to life with silly stories from my past, performing magic tricks and telling jokes that leave the kids giggling or groaning. All of this has helped put me in Ms Kim's good books, which is why she offered me a second contract. She sees me as a "senior teacher" now, and as a result assigns me more than my fair share of upper-level courses. I love it. The big purple textbook I teach from has Hemingway short stories and excerpts from *The Joy Luck Club* and *Roots*. The kids in these classes are not necessarily older, but their English and critical-thinking skills are as strong as they come at a *hagwon*. I'm required to be tough on them, cruel even, but in my heart I admire each of these children so much. There's one boy in particular, his English name is "Joe," who brings to my Senior 5 class an unwavering meticulousness and a genuine joy for learning. Twelve years old and cursed with fish-bowl glasses, he is nonetheless imbued with confidence, an assuredness about what he wants to be when he grows up — an international diplomat. He happily puts himself through English grammar drills each night, and his essays teem with his unique interpretation of the world.

He's also insatiably curious about *everything*.

"So as we can see in this paragraph," I say, pacing in front of the kids with the textbook open on my arm, "Roland and Barbara are married, but do they love each other?"

"No!" the class chimes in unison.

"Exactly. They don't love each other. So then why are they married?"

The kids ruminate on this for a bit. Joe raises his hand. "MichaelTeacher, I have a question."

"Go ahead, Joe."

"Are *you* marry?"

Am I merry? Oh wait, he's confused by the adjective, that revealing mix of present and past tense in a single clause: *Are you married*.

"No, I'm not married," I sigh.

"Do you have girlfriend?"

A few snickers chase their way around the class. I hesitate, chew on my smile. Big mistake.

"MichaelTeacher," pipes up ten-year-old Tony, "are you a *player*?"

"RobTeacher was a player," points out thirteen-year-old Jinny, as if she'd know.

"Alright, back to the story!" I say.

Nine-year-old Susan looks confused. "'Player'? What's mean? What's mean 'player'?"

One of the older, dimmer boys in the back, Dylan, begins answering her question in a litany of forbidden syllables.

"No Korean, please!" I bark, and the class snaps silent. I give Dylan the evil eye, then march over to the tray at my whiteboard, seize a marker, uncap it, and write Dylan's name in the far right-hand corner of the board. There it sits for the whole class, and the closed circuit camera hanging in the corner (and thus

possibly, eventually, his mother, whom he would fear worse than God) to see.

I turn to Susan. "A player is a guy with many, many girl-friends."

Jinny hikes up a dainty elbow. "MichaelTeacher, can a girl be a player?"

"No. There's a different word in English for a girl with many, many boyfriends."

"What is it?"

"I can't say in front of children. It's a bad word."

"Ugh! Bad word for girls, but not for guys? Ohhh, *sa'ghee!*" she says, using the Korean word for *unfair*.

"Jinny, no Korean!" I march over and write her name under Dylan's, just to prove that I believe in equal wrongs as much as equal rights.

We finish examining the story and then I assign an essay topic and grammar exercises for homework. The kids fall over their notebooks to get it down, scribbling and scribbling. When they finish, there are still a few seconds left to the class.

"MichaelTeacher, do magic! Do magic!" the kids demand as they pack up.

This is a thing I've started: Based on my digital watch, I know the precise second when the bell is going to ring. Smiling, I float my right arm upward while keeping an eye on my watch, splay out my hand, twiddle my fingers, make a low, mysterious groan in my throat, and then, at exactly the right moment, I thrust my arm at the speaker in the ceiling and yell out "Pow!" *Mary Had a Little Lamb* chimes just then, and the kids cheer as they bolt for the door.

I pack up their workbooks and essays from the previous night and slip them into the plastic tray on my windowsill, glancing at Seoul's nightly traffic as it moves through the street four storeys below. I wipe down my board and then go around the empty room, straightening chairs and looking for rogue pencil cases. Then, throwing my satchel over my shoulder, I saunter out to the school's lobby where I find Jin already waiting for me.

"Hello there, Mr. Teacher Man," she beams. We share the slightest of hugs, just a brief placing of a hand on a hip. But unfortunately there are a number of my students, including Joe, loitering together in the lobby. "Ohhhhh MichealTeee-chorrre!" they sing, and scrape one index finger over the other: *tsk tsk …*

Joe walks up to us. "MichaelTeacher, I have a question."

I brace myself. "Go ahead, Joe."

"Can I write you *two* essays this weekend?"

"Of course you can. But that's a lot of extra work."

"I know. But I want to write about my trip one month ago to Pusan to visit my grandmother. Can I? I will write your assignment, too, of course." He looks up then at Jin. "Who is this?"

"This is Park Jin-su."

"Anyeong," she addresses him, but then cuts him off before he can pose his next obvious question. "So tell me, do you like attending this *hagwon*?"

Joe nods vigorously, his eyes undulating in their lenses like poached eggs.

"And what do you think of *him*?" she asks, tilting a chin at me.

Joe begins answering her in Korean, but she cuts him off. "No, say it in English."

He squishes up his face in mock-annoyance. "Ohh, MichaelTeacher is very crazy — but also … *super genius!*"

She bursts out laughing. "Really?"

"Yes. He knows all about America, and Canada, and Michael Jackson! And he tells very good jokes about President Bush."

She gives me an approving look.

"All right Joe," I say, "I'll see you on Monday. Have a good weekend."

"You, too!" he croons at us. He starts to leave, but then hurries back and addresses Jin, measuring each word methodically. "By the way — What. Are. You. Eating. Under. *There*?"

"Under where?"

"You're eating *underwear*?" Joe explodes into laughter, and jabs a finger at me. "He taught me that!" Jin and I watch him hustle out the glass doors with his backpack pulled tight on his shoulders, a little Sherpa ready to scale another mountain of weekend homework.

We just sort of grin at each other for a moment after he's gone. "So what should we do now?" I ask.

Her eyes fall briefly to my mouth. "Let's go back to your place ... *super genius*."

We need to have a discussion about what's going to happen tomorrow night. I am to show up at the Park apartment at seven o'clock. I am to bring a gift — something small and inexpensive, but it must be wrapped. I am not to take offence when her parents set the gift aside rather than open it in front of me — it's not the Korean way. I am to keep in mind that her parents speak very limited English, and that Jin will translate when necessary. And I must also remember that they're still coming to terms with their daughter dating a *waegookin*. It was difficult for them to hear the news, and more difficult to agree to have me over. Her father will be okay with it. He will be fine. Her mother's a different story. The Korean term for what we're doing is *mool heurinda*: "muddying the waters."

Saturday night, and I sit with a book on the subway en route to Jin's neighbourhood of Mangwon, listening to stop after stop go by, and hold the gift I'm bringing in my lap. It's a small crystal bowl, good for candy or spare change, wrapped in rice paper and tucked inside a glittery gift bag with strings. When I arrive at Mangwon Station, I find Jin waiting for me outside the turnstiles. Her hug is cool, disinterested. I get the message loud and clear: we must suppress any and all signs of physical affection in front of her parents.

"My father is still at work," she grumbles as we head outside.

"It's seven o'clock on a Saturday night."

"I know. Mother is not pleased with him. And neither am I."

I'm not sure what I'm expecting from the Park apartment before we arrive. I imagine it huge, sprawling, glimmering hardwood floors and giant windows overlooking the busy Seoul skyline. When Jin welcomes me in after a twenty-two-storey ride in the elevator, I find something different. Her family home is not that dissimilar to the cramped apartment that Justin and I share: it's a bit bigger, a bit nicer, and more lived-in, but still very Korean with its faux-wood flooring, wallpapered cement, and LG air conditioner hanging like a barge over the living room. There is a venerable forest of potted plants on the marble ledge overlooking their balcony. Off to the side, in an alcove, I see the glowing green digits of the washing machine that Jin has spoken so derisively about. The beast is enormous, and far more elaborate than the oversized bread maker that Justin and I do *our* laundry in. Jin and I take our shoes off in the entry and she calls to her mother: "*Umma! Umma!* Come meet Michael."

Jin's mom comes out of the kitchen in a cloud of delicious smells. She wipes her hands on her apron and bows once to me.

"*An'yon hashimnigga,*" I say carefully, addressing her in the more formal tongue, and hand her the gift. She barely looks at it before setting it down on a small table by the door. "Well come, well come," she says, measuring her own words. She says something to Jin in Korean. Jin turns to me. "Dinner won't be ready for nearly an hour. Father's running very behind. Come. Let me give you the tour."

Jin shows me the bathroom (they have a *tub*, I notice jealously), the kitchen (countertops lined with an armada of expensive appliances), her brother's empty bedroom, and finally her own bedroom. She pops on the light as we step inside. "We won't be able to stay in here long," she says. "Mother will get nervous."

"Of course."

This space is still very much a teenager's bedroom. The single bed against the wall has a bright purple duvet with a golden sun star embroidered on top. Her bureau and nightstand are littered with books and jewellery boxes. There is splay of girlish magazines on the floor — *Cindy the Perky* and *Korean Vogue*. On the walls, she's hung an assortment of paintings. I walk over and take a look at the garishly colourful pictures. There's one of the Eiffel Tower in Paris and another of a Korean rural scene — jagged mountains in fog, a Buddhist temple with its dragon-backed roof off in the distance. The compositions are a bit jumbled — the warped perspectives of Van Gogh mixed with the vagueness of Impressionism. The colours are so bright they practically hurt my eyes.

"You did these?" I ask.

"Yes. I told you I like to paint."

Jin sits on the edge of the bed and I'm about to join her when I spot another picture. It's hanging in the corner over her nightstand and is smaller than the others — no bigger than the size of a magazine cover. Unlike the others, it's in black and white, a charcoal sketch. I walk over to it.

It's of an old Korean woman.

"Michael —"

Jin comes up behind me as I take the drawing in. The old woman is dressed in traditional *hanbok* and hunched a little at the waist, a Quasimodo stance. Her hands are collected on the butt of a cane and her eyes are downcast in an incomparable sadness. I take a closer look and sense anger there, too — a tightness to her shoulders and the stare in her eyes that hides something so deep it frightens me a little. Jin has caught that hybrid essence of sorrow and fury with just a few hand strokes.

There is also what looks to be a scar running under the old woman's nose.

"Your grandmother," I say.

"No. That's my *eemo halmoney*. My great-aunt. She's my grandmother's sister."

I point at the line running above her lip. "How did she get that scar?"

"She got it in the war."

I turn to her. "What, she was a soldier?"

"No, Michael, she wasn't a *soldier*." Jin's looking at the floor. "She was a *wianbu*, a comfort woman." She turns back up at me. "Michael, do you know what this means?"

I can do nothing but blink. It's like a flower has opened up inside my mind.

"It means she was a sex slave for the Japanese during the w —"

"I know exactly what it means," I say. I point at the sketch. "A member of your family?"

"Yes."

"You *wanted* me to see this. It's the real reason you brought me here, isn't it."

She hesitates, but then nods. "Yes."

And suddenly I understand so many things that I didn't before — things that happened, or didn't, at the beginning of whatever it is that we have now, between us.

"What was her name?"

"*Is* her name — she's still alive. Her name is Eun-young. Though that's not what they called her during the war. She had a Japanese name back then: Meiko. Everybody had a Japanese name back then."

"Jin, why didn't you say something? Why didn't you tell me?"

"I don't know. It's hard, figuring out when to mention something like that. I mean, at what point in a relationship do you say 'I have this relative who was raped thirty-five times a day for two yea —" She cups her mouth in surprise. "You're the first guy I've ever said that to. That was the first time I've ever expressed that in English."

Tae is suddenly yelling from the kitchen: "Jin-su! Jin-su!" She rhymes off a big, complicated sentence.

"I have to go help her," Jin sighs. "You should probably come and wait in the living room."

"Of course."

"And Michael, don't say anything to my parents about —" and she nods at the sketch on the wall. "My mother would be very angry if she knew I told you about Eun-young. We don't, we don't … talk about her in this family."

And the rose in my mind blooms even further. "I understand," I say.

We go back out and Jin flutters off to the kitchen to take orders from Tae. I sit on the couch alone, trying to relax, trying not to relax, trying not to touch anything, upset anything. And trying very hard not to think about what Jin has just shared with me. After a bit, the front door opens and her father, Minsu, comes in. He's wearing a full business suit, the tie not even loosened around his neck. He sees me on his couch as he slips off his shoes, and breaks into a smile. He comes over to pump my hand up and down and bow. "Hello, chief! Hello!

Welcome to my home." He points at my face and motions to his own. "Oh, Jin *said* you has a handsome beard."

Minsu heads off to the master bedroom to change while the women set the table and begin adorning it with the savoury meal that Tae has prepared. I offer to help but Jin tells me to just sit. This table is in the traditional style — low to the floor and no chairs. Because I'm about as flexible as a two-by-four, I've never been able to sit on the floor comfortably at a table like this. Koreans, on the other hand, do it as naturally as breathing. We all settle in and our chopsticks begin making the rounds, dipping into dishes and pulling towards our mouths the marinated beef strips, fried dumplings, spicy leaves of kimchi, pickled zucchini. Tae pours me some ice water, but I seem to be handling the spices well.

Jin's parents begin asking me questions that reveal just how little they've been told about me, and Jin does the translating. "Where are you from in Canada?" The east coast — Halifax. "What did you do there?" I was a journalist. "Why did you come to Korea?" To pay off some loans and see a different part of the world. "Do you *like* Korea?" Yes, very much: I love the food, the language, and the people here are very nice. "Will you go back to Canada?" Yes, I think so — eventually. "*When* will you back to Canada?" Jin hesitates before translating this one. After she does, we sort of look at each other. "Tell them I haven't decided yet." Her parents spot the awkward body language between us. Tae's face is a forbidding calm.

Minsu gives her a stern look, then smiles at Jin and nods at me. "Hey, chief, Jin's brother is went to America." He gives a jiggling thumbs-up. "Very good! We proud. If Jin go somewhere, too, we … we …" He turns to Jin and finishes in a flurry of Korean.

"What did he say?" I ask.

"He says if I decide to move to Canada, they will support it." I flash my eyes up at Tae — I can't help it. Her face is bare of emotion. Her icy stillness speaks to her *real* position here, the true head of this household. I keep waiting for those words to appear in her eyes: I. Will. *Not*. Allow. This.

We eat and eat. I try to ask Tae thoughtful questions about the food with Jin as my proxy. Her answers come back polite, but abbreviated: she clearly doesn't think I'd grasp the nuances of these culinary acts. I switch gears and ask Minsu about his job. He huffs and makes another earnest effort at English. "Oh, very hard. Every day long day. I will be old man soon." He winks at Jin. "But important!" When the meal is done, we stand and begin collecting bowls and plates from the table. I limp around, my hips and thighs aching from sitting on the floor. Tae comes over and takes the dishes out of my hands, insisting that I not help. She turns up to me and speaks more English than I thought possible of her. "Michael — maybe you want go on balcony for cigarette with Jin."

"*Umma!*" Jin snaps at her, rattling the dishes in her own hands. "I told you: I don't smoke!"

"She *do* smoke," Tae says. Then she lobs a full Korean sentence at me as if I'd understand.

I turn to Jin. "What did she say?"

Jin sucks her teeth. "Ugh. She says I'm not very *Korean*."

Minsu and Tae are adamant that we don't help with the cleanup. So Jin and I do find ourselves out on the balcony. This high up, we have a fantastic view of the lolling Han River and the manic city lights that embrace it.

"Things seem to be going well," I say.

"You must forgive my mother," she replies. "She does like you. But she's uncomfortable. And she gets extra strict when she's uncomfortable."

"I'm sorry I make her that way."

"It's not you that makes her uncomfortable. It's, how you say, the *idea* of you. What you represent — to me."

"And what's that?"

She just shakes off my question. "Mother has very fixed ideas about what she wants for me. She tries to be open-minded, but deep down she just wishes I would marry a Korean and end up with the same life as her. Because it's safe. Mother is all about what's safe." Jin leans over the rail, lets the summer wind blow back her hair. "But the *world* is not a safe place. And I don't want to be *safe* in it. I want to be myself in it, and let — what's the phrase in English? — let the chips fall where they may. That's the only real way to be safe." I notice only then how angry and hurt she is. "Who is she to say I'm not very Korean? Does it matter that I'm 'Korean' enough? What about that I'm *happy* enough? Isn't that more important?"

I swallow. I feel awkward here. "You know, they love you very much. They're only looking out for your future. But at some point, we're going to have to talk to them about it. We owe them that."

She comes over. Glances through the window to make sure that her parents are away in the kitchen, and then she kisses me, pressing her lithe body into my frumpy one. "You are a very decent man," she says, but says it like she's quoting somebody else. "You are more decent than even you realize. Come on, let's go in."

So we do, and soon the evening winds down. As I'm gearing up to go, Minsu addresses me with curiosity on his face. "So, Michael, you come to birthday party next month?"

The women freeze, stiffen.

"Birthday party?" I ask, and look at Jin.

"Yes, it's for my grandmother."

"Your ...?"

"*Grandmother*, Michael. Ji-young. We're having a birthday party for her next month." She looks at me quizzically. "Do you *want* to come?"

"Yes, please come," Minsu says.

I turn and look at Tae. Her expression is impenetrably neutral. Then back over at Jin. Arms folded. Head tilted. And all the mysteries she continues to keep from me.

"Yeah," I say. "I want to come."

CHAPTER 14

They were set to marry in spring of 1954. It was an instant scandal, a collective air of disapproval among Po's family. Eun-young said nothing, would not defend herself when Po's mother and siblings grilled him over what he was doing. Who *was* this little woman of mysteries whom he had taken as a *yonae*? Who was this greasy-diner waitress who spoke with a Seoul accent, who had a scar over her mouth, and was plagued with vague, intermittent illnesses? Was she an orphan? She didn't seem to have any kin. And she was three years Po's *senior*. How could he marry an older woman, one so damaged and yet seemingly without a past? The bulk of the vehemence came from his older sister, Pan-im: her face seemed to curdle at the very mention of Eun-young's name.

Thankfully, Ji-young and Chung Hee came down from Seoul for the wedding. When they embraced at the train station, Eun-young could barely get her arms around her baby sister: Ji-young was heavily pregnant with her first child.

"My in-laws hate me," a teary Eun-young whispered in her sister's ear.

"Oh, they'll warm up to you, don't worry," Ji-young replied. As she was right: The arrival (and thus evidence) of some kin from Seoul did thaw out Po's family a little. Despite their objections, they sent Eun-young the traditional box of *yemul*, the bride's pre-ceremony gifts that come a few days before the wedding. Inside, the sisters found everything Eun-young would need to dress for the ceremony: ribbons of blue and red to tie in her hair; an array of beads that she would assemble into jewellery; and a blue satin dress, as long as a river. But the items were tarnished and frayed, obvious hand-me-downs from someone else's wedding. They sisters chalked it up to poverty. The war had made everything in short supply.

Another scandal: They could not hold the ceremony in the bride's home as per tradition, because Eun-young lived in a grimy rooming house. They had to rent a hall not far from the groom's family home. Po and Eun-young sat at the front in modest splendour, their colourful garb gleaming under the hall lights. Po failed to catch the mounting unease that gripped Eun-young after the wedding rites had passed — the deep, loving bows, the sipping of tea from stone cups, the stoic stares as the minister performed the rituals that forged them together as husband and wife, the eating from the paltry feast in front of them, dried persimmon and nuts and rice cakes. Eun-young's eyes kept falling with dread to the table's centrepiece display, the most important gift of all: two wooden ducks, elaborately carved and facing each other in a gaze both innocent and cheeky. Ducks — the Korean symbol of conjugal affection between a man and his wife.

The wedding party made its short procession back to Po's family home. There, everyone gathered to drink and eat in celebration. Eun-young, propped on display in the front room, watched as people plied her new husband with beer and *dong dong ju*, more alcohol than he could handle. She knew the party would continue into the evening, until that moment when the newlyweds slipped upstairs. And then the guests would gather in the stairwell and grow naughtily quiet — to *listen* for the sound of a consummated marriage. Eun-young tried not to think of what this old tradition reminded her of now: the thin wooden walls of the camps, the men lined up outside the curtains and listening to the noises coming from the other side. The vicious bangs and groans, the screams and pleas of the girls with the soldiers.

When that hour arrived, Po came to where Eun-young sat, his eyes varnished with drink. He looked like a little boy as he beamed down at her. He extended his hand, and when she trembled at the sight of it, he smiled. He took Eun-young's arm lightly and raised her to her feet. They walked through the party to the wooden stairs that led up to his bedroom. As Eun-young passed Ji-young on her way, she could feel her sister's eyes fall on her, but she would not return the gaze. She would not look up at all.

Po and Eun-young climbed the stairs and went into his room. A small, low bed awaited them. On the window ledge, a single candle was already lit, its stiff flame searing at the darkness. By the time Po sat her down on the bed's edge, Eun-young had begun to weep. He kissed her deeply on the mouth, her tears dabbing his cheeks, and trembled under his own nervousness. "Don't be afraid, my wife," he said when their mouths parted. "I'm just as new to this as you are." She would not look at him. He began to undo the straps of her bridal headgear, raised it up and off her head. He took a long, slow look at the ribbons tied just so in her hair, and then began to undo them one by one, savouring that steady removal of these symbols of her virginity. When he finished, he stood and undid his wedding jacket, slipped off the shiny silken garb and removed the shirt underneath. His chest did not look like it belonged to the chubby, boyish face above it: it was still hard and lean from his years in the army.

He reached out to undo her bodice but she recoiled from him. "Po, please …" She shook all over. "I have … I have scars…"

"I know," he said and caressed the cleft that ran under her nose.

"No, I have *other* scars."

His face softened with curiosity. "Let me see."

"*No*." She shuddered.

He moved closer to her. Cupped her side. Held her. Waited. "May I?" he asked once her muscles had relaxed. He slid his hands into her satin dress and began to ease her body free. She was too terrified to fight his respectful touch. When her bare legs slipped out from under the satin, his eyes fell on the faded pink gashes embedded into her skin. She could see that flash of curiosity return to his face, but she could also see him fight against it, instantly. Struggling not to ask the questions he wanted to ask. But he didn't question her, and she was stunned.

Look at me, Po, she thought. *Here, cast your eyes down on my ...* poji. *What's wrong with you? Can you not tell that hundreds of men have been here before?*

"I have never seen a woman naked," he whispered, as if to answer her question.

"Po, I am disgusting."

"You are *not*." He gave the lightest laugh. "Eun-young, you are my wife," he said. "These scars don't frighten me. I'm going to teach you how to ignore them, as I will. I will teach you how to be completely unselfconscious." He eased her onto the bed. His mouth moved over her then — her shoulders, the inside of her arm, her breasts. She was suddenly very hot, as if a stove had burst to life in the room. She heard the swish of the rest of his wedding costume as he liberated himself from it. Then he climbed between her legs. Eun-young waited for his blunt hardness, that violating club, to slip through her flesh. Po did touch her there, moved in on her. But he was not hard. Not enough. He repositioned and tried again. And again failed. He pulled back and attempted to laugh. "Give me a moment," he said.

"Po, it's okay ..."

"No, it's all right, just give me a moment. I'll be fine ..." He tried a third time, fell onto her, his flesh meeting hers, and for a second it did go in a little, but then slipped out. She remembered this sort of thing happening on occasion in the camps, and she was expected to console the soldiers when it did. She reached out for Po but he pulled away. "No, it's okay, please just give me a second ..." He let out the smallest mutter of frustration — and then began stroking himself with jerks of his hand. This went on for more than a minute, until she couldn't bear it. She sat up and moved his hands away, grabbed him by the shoulders and laid him back down. He sucked a noisy breath through his nose. "Eun-young, I'm sorry. It's ... I think it's the alcohol."

She kissed him on the mouth and looked into his eyes, gone dull with embarrassment. "You are my husband," she said. "I will teach you to pay no heed to this, as I will."

She sat up then and faced the bedroom door. "He is my husband!" she yelled out into the stairwell, to all those who were listening for the noises of their love.

But their marriage soon became a small scandal, and not just with Po's family. Gossip began circulating like currency through the streets of their new neighbourhood as people began asking questions: why had this bashful young man taken an *older* woman for a wife? Who was she? Who was she really, and where did she come from? Po's friends, the men he worked with on construction sites, mocked him for his attraction to Eun-young, couldn't understand why he'd hurry home at the end of the day to be with her instead of going drinking with them. For Eun-young's part, she had raised the suspicion of other wives in the neighbourhood by not joining in their kimchi-making circles or afternoon card games. She preferred to be alone during the day while Po was working. When she did go out, to fetch food from the markets or books from the library, she spoke to no one. Kept her head down. Floated around people like a ghost.

The gossip shifted when a few years passed and they still hadn't produced any children. Other young couples were breeding, and Pusan's streets soon teemed with new mothers toting babies on their backs or gaggles of children rushing off to school. Po's coworkers had a new thing to chide him about. "Rebuilding this country takes more than putting up highrises," they joked. "Where are your wee ones? What, does your wife keep them hidden in her kimchi barrels?"

The truth was something that Eun-young carried around like stones in her pockets. She suspected that the camps had left her as barren as a rock, but this was just another secret that she kept from Po. Of course, he harboured his own secret, the most obvious reason for their childlessness, away from the wagging tongues of the neighbourhood. He continued trying to consummate his marriage, several times a week. For months. For years. Each time, Po would come to their bed in a cloud of desire, kissing Eun-young passionately, touching her in ways that warped her flesh with longing. But when the moment came to do what he had to, what every husband in every house all around them was doing, he could not. His mind would flood, he often confessed to her later, with the most unsettling thoughts, from the war — the callous slaughter of his own people, and his role in it. Such visions bred a looseness to the strips of flesh that he imagined existing deep in his pelvic bone. *A loosening of the strings*, he called it. He tried to joke about this with Eun-young in bed — *I'm trying to tighten the strings, to raise myself up*. She never said a word, but merely touched him with wifely duty. *Please don't my dear just wait here give me a minute touch me there no not like that like this there there there okay — dammit! sorry ha-ha I'm sorry I'm sorry I'm sorry …* It pleased Eun-young that they had this little problem. It went a long way in concealing from Po that the Japanese had ransacked her womb.

Their lives outside the bedroom were much more enviable. As far as Po's friends and relations were concerned, theirs was an incomprehensible love — incomprehensible because it didn't result in children. This bred a condescending curiosity. *How do you two spend so much time alone? How do you possibly celebrate Chuseok each autumn without little ones?* Po and Eun-young revelled in their freakish solitude. They had more free time than other couples, and spent it at the cinema watching Korean films or going to the park to read books or newspapers in the summer sun. Po doted on Eun-young, and this drew jealous stares from other wives, even as they denounced it among themselves as unnatural.

There were other secrets, though, ones Po could not ignore or hide. They weren't just the occasional sicknesses that afflicted his wife, incapacitating her for hours or even days at a time. There were also emotional outbursts, erupting either in private or when they were with his family. The smallest, most innocuous thing could trigger one. A simple bowl of miso soup on a messy table could send Eun-young into a fit of despair, and she'd lock herself in the bathroom for hours, weeping madly, and with Po knocking and pleading for her to come out. Or she'd learn something from the radio or newspaper, something about Korea's development as a nation, and she would grow unfathomably enraged, banging pots and pans around their kitchen. Po might sidle up to comfort her but she'd shove him away, hard, slamming her palms into his chest and crying. When he refused to return her rage, when he merely looked back stunned and confused, she would turn instantly remorseful and take his face into her hands. "I'm sorry, Po."

"What *is it*, my wife?" he'd beg. "What brings about these sparks of anger in you? Please tell me."

But she would just lower her head in shame and say nothing.

Po became convinced that lovemaking would solve all their problems, if only they could achieve it. How impossibly complicated the sex act seems, he'd think, when you can't get your body to do what you want. He blamed certain thoughts he couldn't keep from seeping into his mind: *I am a murderer. I killed my fellow Koreans. I did. I tied their hands behind their backs with communication wire, made them sit on the ground, and then shot them in the back of the head, like they were animals. I have done this. I have I have I have …* His impotence manifested itself in other ways. One night, Pan-im and her husband came for dinner. Eun-young had cooked all day in anticipation, but when they sat to eat Pan-im barely picked at the food. She pointed out how ironic it was that her brother had found his wife working in a diner and she still couldn't prepare a decent meal. Eun-young's eyes moistened and she looked to Po to defend her honour. But he merely muttered something noncommittal, looking to make peace. After their guests had left, Eun-young yelled at him. "You were a *coward* not to defend me in front of Pan-im." The word snapped like a sheet in the wind, and she watched as Po tried to take offence at her use of it. His struggle to summon some rage was almost comical. He nearly got it, but then the muscles of his face collapsed.

"I am weak," he said.

"Po — I'm sorry. I didn't mean it."

"No. You're right. I am a coward. It's okay, Eun-young. It's okay. I know you don't see me as a real man."

"Ah, Po, why do you say such things?"

"Because it's true. I'm not a real man. I don't please you, do I, Eun-young?"

"Po, don't be silly. You please me in so many ways."

"But I don't *please* you." He did turn angry then, for just an instant. And she recoiled a little. He cupped his mouth and calmed back down. "Eun-young, what are we going to do? I feel so ... so sundered from my own body."

But this only struck her as ludicrous.

In the fall of 1960, Ji-young and Chung Hee travelled to Pusan to pay a visit. They had three small children now: a six-year-old, a four-year-old, and a fifteen-month-old. Poverty had kept them away, but now there was a reason to come to Pusan: Ji-young had lingering worries about her sister, a concern that revealed itself in the same question that Po's relatives and coworkers kept asking: *Why hasn't she produced any children?*

They arrived on a late-afternoon train and soon filled Po and Eun-young's tiny house with sounds it had never heard before — the raucous noise of a young family. The children took an instant liking to their uncle, especially Ji-young's eldest, Tae. The six-year-old girl was all over Po, climbing him as if he were monkey bars and wanting to show him things she had been taught at school, how to write her name in both Korean and Chinese characters and how to sing the new national anthem. She drew him pictures of rabbits and giraffes she had seen at a zoo in Seoul, and Po put on great airs about her crude, bulbous drawings. The sight of him with the children at bedtime on that first night, reading one of the storybooks they had brought from Seoul, put an enormous smile on Ji-young's face. "He is a natural father," she whispered to Eun-young as they watched him from the door jam of the adjacent room, and then tossed her a look of curiosity, tinged with censure.

"We are *trying*," was all Eun-young could say.

The plan on the second day was to go on a hiking trip up the nearby mountain, but Eun-young awoke to discover her body in sudden rebellion, a sickly stabbing to her kidneys. "I'm not well today — you'll need to go without me," she informed the six of them over breakfast. "Oh, but we couldn't!" Ji-young exclaimed.

Eun-young just shook her head. "Don't worry, you'll have fun. I'll make sure to have dinner ready when you get back."

Ji-young protested again, but Po came to Eun-young's rescue. "You must forgive my wife," he said. "She is not always the healthiest of people. It's one of the trials of getting old." He meant for this to sound ironic, but Ji-young and Chung Hee just furrowed their brows. *What are you talking about, Po? She's only thirty-two …*

While they were gone, Eun-young spent most of the day in the bathroom, huddled over the ancient throbs that ricocheted through her nether regions. These bouts of random illness had become more frequent in the last few years, a constant reminder of what she hid from everyone. When she was finally well enough, she moved back out to the kitchen to begin preparing the evening meal. Her family returned from their hike with happy faces crimson from the sun and boots caked with mud. When they came through the door, Eun-young saw that Po was carrying a giggly, squirming Tae on his shoulders.

On the third night, after the children had gone to sleep, the men sat in the main room with glasses of *soju* and talked politics while the women cleaned up in the kitchen. Chung Hee had no stomach for the fledging but incompetent new democracy that was making a mess of everything, and was convinced that the nation would collapse into communism without decisive leadership. He was in favour of the army general who shared his name — Park Chung Hee — taking control of things.

"So you believe the army should be running the country?" Po asked in disbelief.

"I *don't* believe that," Chung Hee replied. "And neither does General Park. He's been very vocal about getting the military out of politics. But we must do *something* to keep our economy, our society, from spiralling out of control. The Marxist-Leninists are still here, hiding in their basement apartments and holding their secret rallies — and they thrive on chaos, like worms on a corpse. I ask you this, Po: What did you and I fight for, kill for, if our country turns communist and simply merges with the North? *Nothing*, that's what. General Park offers our best chance at stability."

You didn't kill anyone — you were just a mechanic, Po thought. "The Americans will not allow Korea to fail."

"The Americans have their own problems. Besides, it's time for Korea to stand on its own. We cannot be cloistered and isolationist. That's the North's path — and it will lead only to dictatorship and poverty. I'm *tired* of being poor. We need to be a strong and wealthy country. We do." He took the last sip of his *soju*. "We could start by normalizing our relationship with Japan."

"Oh, Chung Hee …"

"No, I'm serious. There are great trade opportunities between our country and theirs."

"I can't see it happening."

"But it *must* happen. General Park believes this. The occupation ended fifteen years ago. Why are we so stuck in the past? We need to make our peace with the Japanese before we can move forward."

Chung Hee said this just as Eun-young was limping over from the kitchen with the bottle of *soju* to freshen up their glasses. She stopped, frozen at the sound of her brother-in-law's words. She held the bottle limply in her hand. Chung Hee extended his glass without looking at her.

"They raped us," she said.

The two men flashed their faces up at her from their place on the floor.

"Eun-young …?" Po was staring at her like he didn't know who she was.

Are you about to do this? Will you tell them, now, everything? Every last bit of it? Ji-young had moved out of the kitchen, as well, and was looking at her sister.

"They raped our country, I mean," Eun-young went on instead. "Have you forgotten, Chung Hee? They burned down our temples and monuments. They refused to teach us our language, our history. Their army conscripted my brothers and sent them off to die in China. In *China*." Her tongue took a trip across the scar over her lip. "And you wish to make peace with these people?"

Chung Hee looked at Po as if to say, *Does your wife speak to you this way?* He turned back to her. "Eun-young, please — politics are no place for a woman."

She tried to keep from shaking. Chung Hee offered his glass again, jiggled it. So she poured the *soju* — but didn't fold her left arm over the right in the respectful, traditional manner. When she finished doing the same for Po, she waddled back to the kitchen, bumping shoulders with Ji-young as she did.

Their last day in Pusan was one of sadness and long goodbyes. The children didn't want to leave. Tae climbed into Po's lap and clung to him as if he were a life preserver, beginning to cry in that way that small children do when fun times are about to end. Eun-young watched her husband display an avuncular grace with the child. He patted her head sweetly, told her that she needed to be a big girl and not cry, that he and Eun-young would come to Seoul and visit just as soon as times got better. Tae eventually slipped out of his lap and resumed her place at her mother's hip. Ji-young tousled her daughter's hair and asked if she wanted to give Po and Eun-young the new picture she had drawn. The child bolted away to her bag, then hurried back to present the long piece of paper to her aunt and uncle. Po laid it flat on his legs as Eun-young looked over his shoulder. There were seven rough stick figures drawn across the page, with Pusan's jagged mountains in the back. Tae took great care explaining who each figure was. Only the sketch of Eun-young carried extra detail: she floated above everyone, like a phantom, smaller than the other adults, as if in the background, and there was what looked to be a lightning bolt streaking across her face.

That night, with the house silent after a week of guests, Po came to their bed naked and eager. This was one of his favourite expressions, and he often wished Eun-young would do the same for him, sometimes. "I long for *you* to come to *me* naked and eager, every now and then." Tonight, she lay on their mattress as limp as a wet leaf.

"Don't be sad," he cooed as he caressed her. "We'll see them again soon. In the meantime, let's try to fill this house with our own noises."

Eun-young said nothing as his hands and mouth moved over her body. His breath quickened as his back arched downward and his arms folded around her head. He moved between her scarred legs and took himself in his hand. She waited. And waited. And waited.

"Dammit," he muttered. "C'mon … c'mon … c'mon …"

"Po, it's okay."

He collapsed on his side of the bed and let out that long, pitiful moan of his. He fell silent for the longest time. Then finally spoke again. "He never killed anyone."

"I'm sorry?"

"Chung Hee. He never killed anyone. He was just a mechanic."

"Po …"

He turned and looked across the bed at her, his face full of humiliation. "Eun-young, I want to tell you something."

"Po, just go to sleep."

"No. I want to tell you. I am willing … I am willing to turn my back. I'm willing to turn my back for you."

"*What*?"

He cleared his throat. "If you wish to take a boyfriend behind my back, I — I will understand."

"Ah, Po, just go to sleep!"

And she rolled all the way over on the mattress, as far away from him as she could.

CHAPTER 15

I am remembering something that Rob Cruise once told me: that contrary to the popular axiom, every man *is* an island, floating out there alone in the sea. This has been his guiding principle while navigating the sleazier side of Seoul's nightlife — cutting himself off from the mainland of bigger meanings, a larger purpose. Thirty-four years old and he's getting worse, not better, as time goes on, regressing into his late adolescence, a period of big mistakes and zero expectations about his future. When you hang out with Rob, it's easy to be lured in by his philosophy, to see Korea as an island of ideal hedonism. The work here is plentiful, the drinks are cheap, the women are beautiful, and there is nothing waiting for any of us beyond these shores. I'm convinced Rob will be here forever; he makes being here forever sound like the only option any of us has.

I am remembering this as I find websites about Korea's comfort women. I sit in the smoky dimness of a PC Room not far from my apartment, surrounded by pimply teenagers — and grown men — playing video games here in the darkness. I ignore the racket of their laser blasts and watch as a grainy, hidden history downloads in front of me. Pictures of young girls and the old women they would become. Photos of grinning Japanese soldiers lined up outside stalls, outside cubicles. And endless, endless testimonials in rickety translation about what happened in those curtained-off rooms. A new wisdom takes hold of me. A voice. A story I want to tell. The truth of this place is not in its dance clubs and brothels. The truth is something cryptic and lost. There is a sorrow here that I can barely comprehend. Korea is not an island. It is a peninsula. It *is* attached to something larger than itself. This is a story I want to tell when I finally decide to leave this place. Jin once said: "Michael, you're in Korea. You don't know what real shame is." So show me real shame, Korea. Show me the disgrace that splits you in two.

And man, does it ever. Those pages download from the Web and I can hardly believe what I'm reading.

I buy a digital camera on the night of the birthday party and take it with me. On the subway back from Yongsan Electronics Market, I play with my new toy as if discovering the technology for the first time. I mess with the settings, draw Tetris shapes in the air, watch pixilated commuters and overhead ads undulate through the viewfinder. This is far more fun than reading the English-language newspaper I brought along for the ride. Everything is Iraq, Iraq. It's the summer of 2004 and Baghdad is burning.

The restaurant is at Yeoksam Station. I exit the subway and follow Jin's directions until I locate it. It's a massive, traditional Korean structure, like an ancient temple: piled-stone foundation, looming pagoda roof, a cedar-wood portico out front. I find Jin waiting for me underneath it.

"You bought a camera!" she exclaims. "About bloody time, Michael. You've been here a year and a half!"

I point the camera at her and she strikes an immediate pose between the pillars, arms stretched to embrace them, head tilted and lips crushed into a come-hither pout.

"Have things started in there?" I ask after I've taken the picture. She nods. "It's time for you to meet some people."

I soon realize that this is more than just a restaurant. It's like a compound, actually, a fort, a place with private rooms in the back for private parties. The hostess at the door, standing at her podium, exchanges a few sentences with Jin and then motions to the hallway at the back. On our way, we wander past casual diners sitting at Western-style booths. The lights are dim here, flickering faux torches in the corners. Jin and I enter the long wooden hallway leading to the back.

This is what I notice: On either side of us are sliding paper doors with wooden frames. Behind each door is a private room. Like cubicles. Like stalls. I halt for a moment there on the hardwood. Behind the doors I hear the sound of revellers – the clinking of *soju* bottles, the clacking of chopsticks, and hearty laughter that sounds almost like weeping. Jin is walking but then turns, comes over.

"Michael, what is it?"

I don't know what it is. There is something about this hallway, a reminder so recent. A reminder of what I've been reading on the Internet in the last month. My little bit of research. I'm suddenly very creeped out.

"C'mon, let's go," Jin says. "There's no reason to be nervous. Everyone will like you. I promise."

She leads me by the arm to the back and slides open the last door on the left. I release my breath as we step inside. Her family has rented the largest room in the place. A low cherry-wood table goes from one end of it to the other. Jin's extended family is seated on mats around the table; and at the centre, an old woman, the guest of honour. Ji-young. Her grandmother.

People turn to look as we slip off our shoes in the entryway and climb up onto the elevated floor. Hellos flutter through the air like swallows — the only English word everyone knows for sure. I nod and toss my own hello back; I feel uncomfortable speaking even the most rudimentary Korean in front of these staring, curious people. It's like my presence has abruptly crashed their party, put hamstrings on their conversations because I'm not fluent in their tongue. Jin leads me to the centre of the table and introduces me to Ji-young and her husband, Chung Hee, down there on the floor. Ji-young is in her early seventies, a small and fragile-looking woman, her pewter-coloured hair cropped close to her skull. She smiles at me, her eyes vanishing into the wrinkles of her face. She speaks in Korean and Jin translates. "She wants to thank you for coming. She's never had a *waegookin* at her birthday before."

I nod, then scan the room quickly, hunting for the person I've really come here to see. I spot young faces and middle-aged faces, but no other elderly faces than the two in front of me. "Is everyone here?" I ask.

"I don't think so," Jin says, scanning the room herself. "Come on. Let's settle in."

We find a place farther down the table where Jin's parents are sitting. "Hello, chief!" Minsu exclaims. He waggles a bottle of *soju* in the air. "Please, come. You must get drunk with me." Tae gives him a stern look as I put myself down on an empty mat. Minsu passes me the bottle and waves at two small, empty glasses on the table. Since I'm younger, I am to pour for us both. I do so, folding my left arm over my right as the clear liquid glugs out of the bottle. Approving stares stream down the length of the table at my gesture; Jin has trained me well.

I turn to her. "You want some?" She raises her own glass and tosses an impish leer at her mother.

I can't engage all that much at the table as conversations resume in Korean. Jin tries to translate, but it's hard work. Family banter takes her away for several minutes at a stretch. It doesn't matter. Each time the sliding door opens, I startle a little. A few more guests drift in — cousins smartly dressed in pastel colours, a mom toting a toddler on her hip. But I'm waiting for someone else's arrival. I know I am. I'm jumpy.

In the meantime, I can't help but notice the hierarchies that stretch over the room. Ji-young and Chung Hee are the centre of attention — not just because it's Ji-young's birthday, but because they are the oldest here and draw a quiet, almost Confucian respect. Below them in this familial pyramid are Tae and Minsu, and Tae's siblings and *their* spouses. And below them, the assemblage of cousins, the younger generation of which Jin is a part. Some have babies of their own, some are students; and a few, I find out, are unmarried and still live at home, like Jin. Yet I notice through their chit-chat that Jin stands out in this familial hierarchy. It's not much; just a touch of exclusion. A bit of body language; the way her cousins don't fully engage with her. I assume it's because I am here. The fact that Jin has a *waegookin* boyfriend reinforces to the hierarchy that she is the black sheep of the family.

The paper door slides open again, and again I jump. It's the food coming now — the waitresses, dressed in traditional *hanbok*, cart in dishes and trays, plates and bowls, and begin loading the table with them. The colours of their hanbok are ferociously bright, garish, a little ridiculous. Watching the waitresses as they work, I think what every foreigner thinks when he sees these tent-like dresses: *It looks like maternity wear.* I raise my camera, turn it on, and snap a photo of them.

"Michael," Tae asks, "you like *hanbok*?"

"Sure," I stammer, then turn to Jin. "Do you ever wear it?"

"No, I *never* wear *hanbok*." She smirks. "It's not flattering. You can't tell what a fantastic ass I have."

A couple of cousins who speak enough English giggle at this, covering their mouths. Tae looks at Jin with confusion, and Minsu looks at Jin without confusion, but graciously pretends that he is confused. Jin spouts something in Korean at her mom, clearly a lie about what she has just said in English. Tae is dissatisfied. She scowls a little, at me.

I can pay no heed because the food is in front of us now. Elaborate, spicy *japchae* noodles, steamed ox leg soup and barbecued beef ribs, bowls of dumplings, and long plates of mottled fried rice. The aroma is inebriating. The little porcelain dishes of kimchi ring out on the cherry wood as the waitresses lower them from their trays. I need to stand to take the photographs I want. Everyone's looking at me as I snap and snap and snap. Jin tugs at my pant leg, smiling. "You should sit and eat." And so I do. My silver chopsticks fling forth with an expertness that I had once thought unimaginable. I impress Minsu when I order a bottle of *baekseju* from a passing waitress; he gives me one of his cheerful thumbs-up. The golden bottle comes and I pour and pour. We drink and eat, eat and drink. I understand none of the conversations that fly across the table, but I don't need to. I think: *I could do this — I could make these people my new family.* I want to lean over and kiss Jin for what she has brought into my grey little life. But of course I don't. I know the etiquette on public affection. It doesn't matter. Only this food matters. Soup splashes a little on the table around my bowls and plates; the edge of my hand is stained with red sauce. Minsu chuckles at my minor clumsiness, pours me another drink.

The sliding door opens and I forget to jump. I *should* have jumped, because now there is another old woman here to join us, standing at the room's threshold. Conversations cease. The *clink* and *click* of our dining pulls back, like a tide. Everyone, including me, looks up at her. My heart plummets at the sight of this woman, the confirmation of her existence. It's her. Eunyoung. The woman in Jin's painting. There is no mistaking the scar that streaks like a thin, pink ribbon across the wrinkles of her mouth.

"*An'yon haseyo,*" she bellows into the silencing room. There is a deep timbre to her voice, like a man's; her greeting comes out almost like an admonishment. Nobody says a word in return. The woman's hair and clothes are so grey that she is nearly translucent in them — like a ghost. She's hunched over at the waist and leaning on her wooden cane, just like in her painting. From her place at the threshold, she exchanges a few sentences with Ji-young, her sister. Perhaps a polite birthday greeting, one elder to another. Then she slips off her footwear — soft, old lady shoes, almost like slippers — and staggers in. She struggles. Her hips jerk awkwardly, one after the other, as she tries to negotiate the floor's elevated lip with her cane. She's like a scarecrow being walked across a field by mocking children. Jesus. *Jesus.* She's going to fall. She's going to fall, and yet nobody moves to help her. In Korea, being an elder is *everything*. It is the *top* of the family hierarchy. And yet for that one beat of time, not a single person moves to assist her.

Jin sucks her teeth at her family as she climbs to her feet. "*Eemo halmoney!*" she exclaims, followed by another phrase I know: "*Jo'shimhae!*" — *Be careful now.* I watch my girlfriend flutter across the *ondol* floor to assist Eun-young as she wobbles. There is something like an embrace between them, and then Jin is petting the old woman's hands and saying sweet things to her in Korean. Eun-young nods at her grandniece, but doesn't smile. Jin takes her arm and helps her over to the table, braces her withered hand as the old woman lowers her bones to a mat on the floor. Jin squats down next to her, talking and talking, and then begins organizing a plate and bowl in front of her. She points at dishes and Eun-young either nods or shakes her head. The bit of food she accepts would not be enough to fill a sparrow.

Jin is suddenly waving her hand forward at me. "Michael — come come come." I get up and walk over, sensing a pair of nervous eyes follow me as I do. Tae's. She's holding her breath as I approach Eun-young, listening for every word we're about to utter. I hover over the old woman as Jin makes introductions. Again, Eun-young nods, but doesn't smile as she looks up at me. I catch very little about what Jin tells her about me — I hear *Canada* and *hagwon* and maybe the Korean word for journalist. Eun-young's eyes narrow a little.

We eventually return to our own mats and discover that conversations and dining have resumed, though much more subdued. Why? Is it out of respect or — no, it's discomfiture. Eun-young's presence here weakens everything, makes what was hard and secure now wobbly and trivial. I can sense it in the table's banter. Eun-young eats silently except for a few occasional words passed to Ji-young. She doesn't even acknowledge the younger generation here. I wish I'd brought a notebook with me. I'd be jotting furiously, trying to capture what I'm seeing. Nothing I've read on the Internet has prepared me for this.

I look down at my digital camera. I turn it on and move it to the edge of the table, trying to hide it as best as I can. I clasp it between thumb and finger, turn it to my left, look down through the viewfinder. Turn it, turn it, and then there Eun-young is, streaming across the screen in a pixilated image. I press the button quickly before I lose her. When the flash has finished, I return the camera to my lap. The screen goes black for a moment, returns, and then there she is, frozen at a badly blurred angle, captured in all her torturous dignity.

I look up and see Tae glaring at me with unmistakable contempt. I sip my *baekseju*. Jin touches my arm, leans into me.

"Michael, put the camera away," she whispers.

. . . .

Much later, Jin and I are alone outside the restaurant saying our goodbyes. The party is breaking up and her parents are waiting inside to drive her home. A brief silence falls between us, this moment of privacy.

"I feel guilty," I say finally.

"For what?"

"I feel if I get what I want and you follow me back to Canada, I'll be taking you away from all those people."

She looks away, says nothing.

"You did the right thing tonight, by the way."

She perks up. "What did I do?"

"You helped an old woman when nobody else would."

She just glances at her feet, hair falling in her face.

"Jin, I'd like to speak to her."

She looks back up. "*What?*"

"I'd like to interview Eun-young, if I can. You could translate. I think it would —"

"Michael, *are you out of your mind?*"

"Just hear me out. I know it's —"

"I told you: we don't talk about her in this family."

"I know, but —"

"*She* doesn't talk about *herself*. Ever. The only people who know what she went through are the people who were in that room tonight."

"Jin —"

"The only people, Michael. She has told nobody else. *Nobody.*"

"Yeah? Well *maybe that should change.*"

Jin's a bit shocked by my forwardness. She steps up to me, gets right into my face. "What, all of a sudden you think you're a journalist again? You don't understand *anything.*" Then sees the hurt she's caused me, and so she squeezes my hand. "You know I love you, but you don't understand. Michael, you don't."

"But I want to," I reply. To this, she has no answer.

A few minutes later, I'm on my way back to the subway. I'm almost at the station when I freeze abruptly, there in my tracks. I pat madly at my pockets. Rifle through my satchel. Ah *shit*. I hustle back, all the way to the restaurant. Up the steps and through the door. Jin and her parents have already left. I bow to the hostess at her podium and motion to the back. She nods her understanding and lets me through. I hurry into the hallway and aim myself at our room, the place at the table where I'd been sitting.

I don't make it.

We meet each other in the hall. Face to face and alone. She, hunched on her cane and wobbling. And me, slumped shoulders and gawking. She turns her gaze up to mine. Recognizes me instantly.

"An'yon hashimnigga." I bow, but she seems unimpressed.

"Ka Meh La?" she asks, forking an eyebrow.

I shrug lightly: *I don't understand.*

So she reaches with her brittle hand into the pocket of her dress and takes out my camera. Must have picked it up after we left, must have been on her way to give it to the hostess. Now she lets it float there, like she's not quite ready to relinquish it to me. But then does.

Our fingers touch as I take it from her. I bow again. *"Kamsa'hamnida."*

But she says nothing more. Just shoves past me in the hall and on her way, alone. I watch her go with ten thousand questions sitting at the bottom of my throat.

Later on the subway, I flip through the evening's images.

Son of a gun.

She deleted the one of her.

CHAPTER 16

It often seemed to Eun-young that she was the only person of her generation who used the Pusan Municipal Library. If she came during the day, the place was nearly dead except for a few old men poring over ancient scrolls rolled out on tables. If she came during the evening, the library was swarmed by young people doing their homework. Never did Eun-young see another housewife in her thirties in here. She sometimes wondered what her mother would make of this library, these shelves straining under the weight of information. If her mother had had access to such a place, Eun-young imaged her doing what *she* was doing — reading voraciously, indiscriminately, sucking up the sustenance that fed and quelled and distracted her mind. *Facts are everywhere*, her mother would have said. *Anyone can absorb facts. But real wisdom lies in the gaps between things, in the pictures you draw from all the little pieces.*

Eun-young's favourite books were the poetry. She would often take out whole stacks of anthologies — ancient poems, contemporary poems, poems written during the occupation. For her, they distilled knowledge into pure wisdom. She loved the way a poem could drop a stone down the canyon of her soul and send that slight but irrefutable ping of Truth reverberating back up.

She often read verse to Po at night in bed while he kissed the scars on her legs.

• • • • • • • • • • • • • •

In the spring of '61, at the height of Korea's political chaos, General Park Chung Hee pulled off a dramatic *coup d'etat* and seized control of the country. To legitimize his new regime, he ran in a general election two years later and won a narrow majority. The newspapers and radio heralded this as a new dawn for the Republic, one that secured its economic and political future. But ordinary Koreans were still uncertain, still nervous that they remained, technically, under a police state.

Po and Eun-young never discussed how they had voted in the 1963 election, but Eun-young was sure that her husband had acquiesced to her brother-in-law's argument and voted for General Park. Po had come to believe that stability was better than instability, no matter what the cost. He longed to hide beneath mundane things: his work on construction sites, his weekends taking Eun-young to the cinema, their nights in bed when he would try his best to be a man, to force sounds of pleasure from her with the earnest efforts of his tongue and hands. He was willing to believe in anything, so long as it didn't disrupt the tenuous rhythm of their days.

But as the months and years passed, Eun-young spent more and more time in those places where Po could never reach her. There were nights when she would burst awake in bed, slimy with sweat and panting from some nightmare. When this happened, she would not allow Po to speak or touch her, to infiltrate her terror in any way. There were times when she spent untold hours locked in the bathroom under the twist of another vague illness, and would not tell Po what was wrong once she finally emerged. And there were evenings when he could not pry her away from the newspapers, or the books she borrowed from the library. She pored over them as if researching something, as if burrowing down into all those words on the hunt for some buried truth. She was keeping track of her country as it moved on, moved up in the world.

Of course, Po believed that these widening distances had a lot to do with his ongoing inadequacies. He would often find ways to broach the offer he had once made to her. "Did you meet anyone interesting when you were out today?" he asked one evening in their sitting room. Eun-young was engrossed in the newspaper and hadn't spoken to him since supper.

She looked up and squinted, as if he were a stranger. "I'm sorry?"

"I said did you meet anyone … *interesting* when you were out?"

A bemused frown fell onto her face. But then she got up, set the newspaper aside, and crossed the room to where he was sitting. She knelt at his legs, rested her arms on his thighs. "Po, we've been through this: I could never touch another man."

"Eun-young, I'm just saying — if you wanted to, I wouldn't —"

"*Po* — I could never touch another man."

He didn't believe her. There were too many secrets that she kept from him already. He knew this, a doubt he couldn't restrain no matter how hard he tried. When she kissed him then, he refused to acknowledge the assurance behind it. It felt perfunctory. A wife's duty to her doubtful husband.

She couldn't remember what had compelled her to wander into the foreign-language section that afternoon in 1964. For years, she had ignored that single aisle of books in the far western corner of the library's ground floor, as if it were a dark cavern full of unsafe mysteries. What was it on that day that had caused her curiosity to get the better of her? Was it boredom? Was it something she had read in the paper that put a nettlesome bug in her mind? Whatever it was, Eun-young found herself drifting into that aisle. When she did, it was like she was transported to a different country, surrounded now by multiple foreign languages. There was a row of English grammar books, a row of French novels, but the bulk of the selection was in Japanese. Entire yards of flaking cardboard covers lined up on either side of her. Seeing that alphabet etched on the spines, characters she hadn't read in nearly twenty years, made her pulse quicken. She was suddenly tremulous. She tried to calm down. *It is just a harmless alphabet*, she told herself. She pulled a book from the shelf at random, a Japanese novel for teenagers, an anodyne tale of young love and young jealousies. *See?* she thought. Stupid. *It's just a language, one that no longer holds any dominion over you. These are just characters on a page.* She put the book back.

Farther down the row of Japanese texts, she saw a huge tome jutting out from the shelf — its glossy hardcover gleaming under the library's lights. She went over and looked at how its sheer mass stood out from the other books on the shelf. She reached up and pulled it down. The book's surprising weight nearly overtook her as she moved it around to look at the cover. It was a Japanese history book for high-school students. She could tell it wasn't very old: the corners were uncurled and its spine was still strong and unwrinkled. Eun-young rested the book on the underside of her forearm so she could open it to the publication page.

Copyright 1956.

She carried it out of the aisle and over to one of the library's tables. Sat down and opened the book to a random chapter. Each page was divided by two dense columns of Japanese text, broken up with images — a few ancient illustrations, but mostly more contemporary photos of Tokyo and Osaka and other places. She snapped the book shut. *Go put it back. You don't need to do this. There's nothing in here you want to see.* But then her mother's lilted voice rang out like a bell in her mind. *Don't ever be afraid of knowledge, my little crane. Always be as wise as you can be.* Eun-young looked at the book again, then reopened it, this time to the table of contents. Found the section on the twentieth century. Took a breath, and flipped to it.

Her Japanese was rusty and she had to muscle her way through the vocabulary and grammatical structures. There was so much here to read. She found herself skimming, her eyes flowing over column after column, hunting for any reference to Korea. Surely there had to be *something*.

She wouldn't have time to read it here. She closed the book again. And was overcome by a decision that felt like it could split her soul in two. Go put it back — or check the book out.

Go put it back.

Or check the book out.

She lifted the tome off the table, cradled its weight in the crook of her arm, and carried it to the front desk.

The newspapers were left forsaken in their little alcove by the front door. Days would pass when she would not bathe or even change out of her night clothes. Po would come home from construction sites dusty and starving to find the wood stove in the kitchen unlit, their dinner for the evening not started. When this happened, Eun-young would emerge from the sitting room surprised to see him home, then look at the clock, realize what time it was, and bolt into action. "I'm sorry Po I'm sorry I lost track of time here let me get some rice and vegetables on I'm very sorry …" But if he showed any annoyance at all, or even questioned what she'd been doing all day, she'd get defensive and snap at him. "What, do you think it is *easy* being a wife? To be cooped up in here all day cooking and cleaning for *you*?"

But his face just softened with concern. "Cooking and cleaning for *us*," he ventured. And this just made her all the angrier.

One evening, he came in with the day's mail and handed Eunyoung a card out of the thin pile in his hand. "What's this?" she snarled from her place at the stove, trying to get it lit. "It's a notice from the library. It says you have a book overdue." She ripped the little card in two without looking at it and stuffed the pieces down the stove among the kindling and newspapers. "Dinner won't be ready for another hour," she said without looking at him. He just stood there coated in the day's dust, watching her. "Go take your bath, Po," she sniffed. "Your body stinks of progress."

She checked out the history book so many times it felt like it belonged to her now. She vandalized the section on the twentieth century with a pen, underlining whole passages and writing angry notes in the margins: "Liars!" and "They were protecting their colonies from *what*?" The book whitewashed everything, talked about Japan's noble intentions in Asia and how they'd been corrupted by extremists in the Emperor's government, how the West had misconstrued everything. It made no reference to life on the Korean peninsula in the thirty-five years of occupation. It certainly made no reference to the thousands of girls coerced from their homes and taken to China. Not one mention, not one inkling. And worst of all, the book's final chapter droned on and on about the dropping of the atomic bombs, how Japan had been a victim — a *victim* — of American aggression. She read the section over and over until it carved out a deep cavity inside her heart, one she vowed never to fill. *They see themselves as victims. They honestly do. This is what they're teaching their children.*

One night, during those weeks when the book held Eun-young hostage, Po came to her in bed more assertive than usual. He moved up on her from behind, ran a hand down the length of her body and squeezed his face into the crook of her neck. She curled in on herself, away from him. He sang out her name, but she would not relent. When he finally gave up, he fell back on his side of the bed and looked up at the ceiling.

"Eun-young ... Eun-young, I need to ask you."

"Po ..."

"You've met someone else, haven't you? Eun-young, I need to know. I *deserve* to know. You've met someone else."

She seized up in anger. "Oh shut up, Po. Shut *up*. Maybe I'm just not in the mood for your hopeless *groping*."

He came home from work one day to find the house sweltering. It hit him like a blanket the moment he walked in the door. He went to the kitchen to find Eun-young standing over the stove with the book laid open on the counter. Her face was runny with tears as she tore handfuls of pages out of the book's long spine and stuffed them into the flames that shot and flickered out of the hole.

"Eun-young, what are you doing?" he said, rushing towards her. "You're going to burn yourself."

She jabbed a hand at him. "Stay right there, Po. Don't come near me. Do you hear? I'm nearly finished. Don't touch me." He froze where he was and watched her rip the remaining pages out in generous handfuls and throw them into the ever-lengthening flames that leaped out of the stove. The heat spread through the kitchen like a disease. When she finished, Eun-young twisted the hard covers until they came free of the spine and then tried to stuff *them* in the hole. Of course they wouldn't fit. He watched as she banged the covers with great fury over and over against the iron top, trying to squeeze them in. She wailed in desperation. The covers caught fire and flames licked at her wrists. She dropped the two pieces on the floor, backed away from the stove and buried her convulsing face in her hands.

Po rushed over, stomped on the covers, picked them up in one hand and put the lid back on the stove with the other, cutting off the flames' violent reaching. "What, you're burning books now, Eun-young?" he said. He looked at the front cover and was startled to see Japanese printed there. He looked at his wife, his eyes widening. *Another* secret she kept from him. "What does it say?" he asked after a long silence. "Eun-young, what does it say?"

She just shook all over, her anguish hunching her body into a question mark.

"Eun-young, we need to talk about this. We need to get you help …"

When she pulled her face from her hands, she looked at him with a hopelessness that had no bottom. "I will *never* share this with you," she wept. "Do you hear me? I will *never* share this with you, Po. You're not allowed *in here.*"

He flinched. Those were the words she said on the first day that he had ever spoken to her.

Eun-young plodded over and yanked the covers from her husband's hands. She went to the window, pulled it open, and threw them into the alley behind their house.

In 1965, the governments of Japan and South Korea signed "The Agreement on the Settlement of Problems Concerning Property and Claims and on Economic Cooperation between Japan and the Republic of Korea." The treaty aimed at normalizing relations between the two countries for political and economic reasons. The agreement included some $500 million that Japan would pay to South Korea as reparations for the colonial period. They called it the "Independence Congratulation Fund." The treaty stressed that this recognition, strictly between governments, would be the last word — "completely and finally" — between the two nations regarding compensation for the colonial years. Most important, it would not recognize any individual claims for compensation outside the mandate of lost property or wages. Certain elements of Korea's government fought this, but Japan was adamant.

The South Korean media took the treaty to task. There was widespread unrest across the country about the deal's particulars. The money wasn't enough, people said. And who could possibly produce the extensive documentation that Japan was demanding for individual claims? Editorialists wrote about the inherent racism of the deal, pointing out that Japan had acknowledged and paid compensation for personal injury to *other* countries, Western countries — Canada and Greece and Britain — but not to Koreans? Are we simply sweeping this all away, they wrote, the very recent history of them seeing us as an inferior race of people — in the interest of *trade*?

Eun-young followed the stories every day in the newspaper and on the radio. They hardened the walls of that cavity she carried inside her. Each new revelation caused another aspect of Pusan, her life there, to slip away like morning fog. It was as if whole buildings and streets and neighbourhoods were evaporating before her eyes, one after the other — everything that Po had helped to build. What purpose did her life serve now if everything was settled — "completely and finally"? Was she to keep on as Po's wife, cooking and cleaning while he built and built and built? Is this what her life would amount to?

It was not settled. It would never be. If the Japanese wanted documentation, they could look at the cartography of scars all over her legs. They could hear about the nightmares, about the illnesses, about the ugliness that covered her, inside and out, the shame and bitterness that flowed through her like the Han River. They could hear how she could not love the man she loved.

No. They would never hear about these things. If she couldn't share them with Po, how could she possibly share them with a Japanese bureaucrat?

It was true: Pusan was vanishing from her. She needed to be in Seoul. It was for Ji-young that she felt this. If her little sister would never piece together what really had happened to her, then Eun-young would do it for her, *make* her understand. Her, and her children. And then their children after that. She would tell them all. She would tell them everything, and bear the shame of doing so. Eun-young would not let them all move on without *knowing*.

And when the streets and buildings had all disappeared, when Pusan's harbour had slipped into the sea and its mountains had floated off like clouds, Eun-young could do nothing except show the most exquisite kindness to the man she was about to betray. Gone were the evenings ruined by inexplicable anger and sadness; gone were the abrupt arguments over domestic trifles. When Po came home from construction sites, Eun-young would already have a hot bath waiting for him, would already have the kitchen teeming with a sumptuous meal she'd been preparing all afternoon. He was a little disarmed by this return to wifely devotion, and silently mistrusted it.

Eun-young assuaged her guilt by convincing herself that Po would claim another wife in no time at all. How could he not?

He was such a gentle, devoted man. Had a kindness that moved inside him like tendons. He would not be alone for long. She was certain of that.

She thought at first about leaving during the day, while he was at work. Have him come home to find her clothes gone, her books gone. But that wouldn't do. He could easily get in contact with Ji-young and Chung Hee, track Eun-young down, confront her for answers. She thought about writing him a long letter instead and leaving it on the kitchen table before she left. But what would the letter say? How could she put into print all the things she couldn't say out loud to him? No. She would need to sit on the floor at their kitchen table, her head down in the pose of a submissive Korean wife, and wait until he came home. Wait, and then face him. Confront this one difficult moment before even more difficult moments, in both their lives, would begin.

He was late getting back. When he came in, she saw him before he saw her. As he closed the door behind him, Po's eyes fell to the rubber mat in the entryway where they stacked their spare shoes, and noticed that hers were all gone. He turned then to face the sitting room and spotted the bookshelf he had nailed to the wall for her, empty now of the few texts she had splurged on and bought for herself. His face crumpled in confusion. And that's when he looked down at the alcove by the door and saw two large canvas bags stacked one on top of the other.

Eun-young had stood without realizing it. Po looked up then. Drifted into the kitchen to stand before her, his face full of stupefaction.

"You going on a trip, Eun-young?" he asked.

Her hair fell in her face. "I'm going to Seoul, Po."

"To see Ji-young?" He waited, but she didn't answer. "When will you be back?"

She licked lightly at the scar over her lip. "I won't be back. Po, I'm leaving. I'm going to *live* in Seoul."

His expression would not process what he was hearing. His mouth was open a little, his teeth gleaming between his lips.

"We both knew this day was coming," she went on. "I think you'd agree. I'm sorry, Po. I'm so sorry."

"What's his name?" he asked gently.

"Ah, Po …"

"What's his name?" he asked again, a bit more forcefully. "I have a right to know. What's his name, Eun-young? What does he do for a living? Does he care for you? Is he faithful to you? Will he *love* you, in that way I can't?"

She just trembled all over. "Po, there is nobody else. You don't understand. You will never understand."

Then she saw it, the body language that showed him trying so hard to get angry, to *be* genuinely angry. And failing at it.

"Eleven years ago, you made a vow to me," he said.

"Po, I know —"

"Eleven years ago, you stood up in front of my family and friends, and your sister, and God Himself, and you proclaimed to us all — I choose *him*."

"I know," she said. "I should have never done that."

His face was rushing downward, like a waterfall. He looked like he might collapse under its weight.

"I'm sorry, Po," she wept again. "But I have to leave. I have to leave you. I have to live in Seoul. I have to live alone."

"Eun-young …"

"I'm sorry, Po."

"I'm a good man," he muttered. "Eun-young, I'm a *good man!*"

"*Po* — I know that!"

"Then *why are you doing this?*"

Tell him. Go ahead. Tell him the truth. Do you think it will make him love you less, to know what the Japanese did to your body? Do you think he can't handle it? He murdered women and children. He was ordered *to murder. So tell him. Swallow your shame and just tell him the truth.*

She couldn't bear to tell him the truth. So she told him something less than true, something that would remarkably, and in the long run, cause him less pain.

"I'm leaving," she said, stepping up to him, "because I don't love you." She swallowed. "I don't love you, Po. And I *never* did."

And so he did collapse then. Just sort of floated down the kitchen wall, like one of the ashes from the book she had burned in the stove. Floated down and sat there on the floor.

She practically had to walk over him to get at her bags by the door.

CHAPTER 17

Summer winds down and I've been summoned to Rob Cruise's apartment in Itaewon. The order came earlier this week in an email tinged with desperation. *Get your asses over here, Saturday, 11 a.m.* 11 a.m.? Does Rob even caress the lips of consciousness that early on a weekend morning? In half-mad paragraphs I learn that his summer camp, The Queen's English, didn't go, didn't quite *catch on*. He's a touch belligerent over what he sees as the pigheadedness of Seoul's wealthy elite. Never occurred to him that rich families would want more than fancy brochures and a Westernized curriculum before releasing their children to his charge. They did, and he's stung by their lack of naïveté. So he's emailed me, Greg Carey, and Jon Hung with a brazen, near-panicked demand.

Rob didn't include Justin on the email. That's because Justin's current contract with ABC English Planet is wrapping up and he's moving back to Halifax. He has some supply teaching lined up at his old school, and come the new year he'll resume his full-time job. I have mixed emotions about Justin's departure. It's always exciting to hear when somebody, anybody, re-establishes a life back home. When you've been teaching in Korea long enough, such a thing seems impossible, or at least unlikely. I'm happy for him. But I'm also concerned about not having him as my roommate anymore. Without his steadfast interest in my own plans, that near-parental probing, I worry that I'll waver from my ambitions, slide back into a kind of expat apathy. I imagine emails from Justin arriving months from now, asking *What, you're still there? Still slinging English like hamburgers? Still tramping around Itaewon? Still coming whenever Rob Cruise beckons?*

Yes. Once again, I come when Rob Cruise beckons. Don't ask me why. Christ. I'd like to think that this time it's *not* to listen to another of his crackpot schemes, but to *help* him, to show him what can happen — to any of us — if we just pull ourselves together a little. But who am I kidding? There's something so *seductive* about the way Rob lures a person in. Guilts you into feeling that if you don't join him in his insane adventurism, you're somehow numb to the sensuality of the world, that you're missing out, that you're letting *yourself* down. No wonder so many women fall into his traps.

So I make the trip on the subway. Itaewon on a Saturday morning is like a lolling lion after a frenzied feast. The streets are quiet but pockmarked with cow patties of vomit; the night-clubs' neon is off and dulled by the sunshine; empty beer bottles line up on ledges and curbs. I head south on foot, navigating through the foreign ghetto and counting streets along the hill until I find the one that leads to Rob's building. He's got a sweet deal: a proper one-bedroom apartment and access to a rooftop patio. I have on occasion sat up there with him among the kim-chi drums and pigeon shit to watch the sun come up after a night at the bars. The apartment next door also has a rooftop patio and is occupied by a couple of Korean "juicy girls": not prostitutes, but girls paid by bars to hit on Korean businessmen and keep them drinking. I've watched Rob stand on his roof and flirt with these impossibly gorgeous women across the alleyway on their days off.

I double-time up the iron stairway to his landing and find the apartment door already ajar. I push it open to discover Jon

Hung and Greg Carey sitting at the table in Rob's small kitchen, their faces full of mirth. "Hey, you actually beat me here —" I say as I begin peeling off my sandals, but they put hasty fingers over their lips — *shh-shh!* Another second and I can tell why. I turn to face Rob's closed bedroom door. Oh, I see — that is, I *hear*. Last night's fun has not quite wrapped up. Holy *shit*. The boys motion to an empty chair at the table and I come and sit, cringing a little. Oh my *God*. The muffled noise behind the door is an utter *pornophony*. The girl, whoever she is, sounds like she's having the time of her life, panting, screaming, admonishing, and pleading into the cosmos as if something were profoundly unfair — *ah-hh?, ah-hhh??, ah-hhhh???*

I press the balls of my hands into my brow. "We shouldn't be here," I say, wincing.

"Hey, the door was unlocked," Greg Carey whispers. "Those are her *shoes* over there."

The racket subsides for a moment and we hear the shuffle of bodies changing position. There is a mutter we don't catch, but then another one we do. "Robbie ... Robbie, no ... *no*, Robbie ..." The boys and I look at each other quizzically, our mouths gaping. The pleasing groans resume but then once again cease. "Robbie, no! ... Not there ... Not *there* ..." The boys have burst into silent hysterics. And me — I'm gripping the top of my head with both hands. The air is shattered then by an eardrum-piercing castigation. "Unnatural! Unnatuuurraaal!" The boys have practically fallen off their chairs. There is a bang and a thump, bedsprings relaxing, a quick whoosh of clothes being yanked back on, and then the bedroom door sails open. The girl staggers out. Her face, smeared in last night's make-up, looks old and clownish. She sees us sitting at the table, enthralled. "Ack!" she exclaims. She rushes over to her little open-toed shoes, steps into them clumsily and then flies out the door like a startled crow.

A moment later Rob swaggers out, doing up the front of his cargo pants. His expression alters just slightly when he sees us — *Oh, you're here already*. He drops himself into the last empty chair and pulls cigarettes from the pocket on his leg. "Some women are just so out of touch with their own pleasure," he sighs, lighting up.

We're frozen in our shock, but Rob just shrugs it off. Switches gears instantly, ready to talk business. He addresses me over his cigarette. "So Michael, tell me something — what do you know about writing for the Web?"

"Uh, very little," I stammer. "Why, why do you ask?"

His head is bobbing already. "Okay, okay, so here's my idea."

Jon and Greg groan. "Rob, dude, we've been here before," Jon says.

"I know, but just hear me out." He puffs his cigarette as if desperate to shorten his lifespan. "I want to start an online magazine for foreigners in Korea."

"Really?" I ask. "Do you know anything about publishing?"

"No, but you do. I'm going to make you my editor-in-chief."

"So you *don't* know anything about publishing."

"Look, I know what this town *needs*. Just listen to my idea. Does it make sense that expats have to go to one website to find jobs, another to get the news, another to find out which DJs are playing in which clubs? *It doesn't make sense.* There should be one place where all that stuff gets, you know, coagulated."

"You mean aggregated? Collated?"

"Congealed, perhaps," Jon joins in.

"Look, whatever. Shut *up*. It's a good idea!"

"Oh, it's a great idea." I smirk. "I can see the tagline now: *Waegookin Daily: Your source for news, views, and malapropism.*"

"Mala-*what*? Look, Michael, don't mock me. This is a solid idea."

Greg Carey scratches his unfortunate mustache. "I'm not giving you any more of my money, Rob."

"I know. You won't have to. I already owe you two-and-half mill for your investment in The Queen's English."

"You owe me three mill, Rob."

"Fine. Three million won. Listen to me." He leans in and speaks to us as if conveying a secret. "You three are my *guys*. Do you understand? I consider you, like, my brothers. When I get these ideas, I already have roles picked out for each of you. That's how brilliant I think you all are. Michael, you're gonna run editorial; Jon, you're gonna sell ads and keep the books; Greg, you're gonna run the technical end."

"I don't know anything about computers," Greg says.

"I'm a disgraced journalist," I add.

"I already have a good-paying job with the KOSPI." Jon shrugs.

Rob looks at us, collapses against his chair, and takes on a rare posture: deflated. He seems desperate and on the cusp of a difficult realization. He presses his lips together and blows smoke out his nostrils.

"I'm also thinking of opening a Tim Hortons franchise in Seoul," he says finally.

"Oh, Jesus Christ," I reply.

"Look, I want to do *something*." Then, a quick slip into honesty. "I haven't made any real money in a while."

A short, brutal silence hangs there for a bit.

"Maybe you could become a gigolo," Jon jokes. "I'm sure there are lots of lonely Korean housewives who could use your … services."

Rob looks at the ceiling.

"Rob, he's kidding," I say.

Rob's eyebrows do a little two-step.

"I'm kidding," Jon reiterates.

Rob just shakes his head and comes back to Earth. "I mean, am I wrong? There are tons of Canadians in Seoul, and they all love coffee. I think a Tim Hortons would really fly here. And expats need their own publication. They do. Am I right or am I wrong?"

"Rob, you need to find something that you can actually pull off," I say. "Something you're good at."

"Besides shagging chicks of course," Greg beams.

Rob straightens up in his chair, confident again. "Bah. It doesn't matter. I've got tons of privates lined up. I'll be fine for now. I'll figure out something to do."

He switches gears again and asks the boys about their plans for the evening. Greg Carey, with wormy exuberance, suggests a trip to Hooker Hill. Rob agrees, saying he doesn't feel like "playing" the bars tonight. Jon acquiesces with his cold, corporate indifference. Naturally, they exclude me from these discussions.

The boys eventually leave, but Rob asks me to stay behind for a bit. He makes us coffee and then we head up into the hot August air of his rooftop patio. The city is glazed in a meringue of smog. Namsan Tower stands bland in the distance.

"So if I ask you something," Rob says as we plunk down in his lawn chairs, "will you be honest with me?"

"Sure."

"If I ask nicely, do you think Ms. Kim would hire me back — just for a few months until I get my shit together?"

"Oh my God, Rob," I laugh, "are you kidding? She'd never welcome you back. There are *still* stories of your antics roaming the halls of that school."

"*Fack*," he exclaims. "That twat — she always could hold a grudge. Shouldn't have burned a bridge with her. *Man.* I'll have to come up with something else." He sips his coffee and then looks at me. "What are *your* long-term plans?"

"I'm thinking about going back to school next year," I tell him. "Getting a teaching degree."

"Fuck, man, good for you. You're a great teacher."

"Thanks. And I'm also thinking of ..." And here I pause. I've not mentioned this other thing to a soul, but it feels strangely apt to reveal it to Rob, to make him the first person I expose to these ambitions. "I'm also thinking of writing something. A book, maybe. Partly about some of my experiences here but ..." And I pause again. "But partly about some other stuff I've been learning ... about Korea."

He sniffs at the sky. "Fuck, I could write a book about this place. I mean, you don't even know *half* the shit I've done. It would be bloody bestseller, let me tell you."

"I don't think you're entirely literate, Rob."

"Sorry?"

"Literary. I said you're not exactly literary."

"Oh yeah." He crinkles his face. "I suppose you need to be, to write books."

"I suppose."

He looks at me. "And what about Jin? Will she follow you back to Canada?"

"That's the plan, as far as I know."

"She's a good chick. Crazy as a bag of hammers. Lots of skeletons in that closet. But she's — well, *you* know. I'm impressed you've been able to hold on to her this long."

"Surprised, even?" I ask.

"Hey, you're a very intense guy, Michael. Very focused. She'd dig shit like that. See, that's my problem." He sets his coffee mug down on the stone floor of the patio. "I got the same issues with women as I do with jobs. I get bored very easily.

Especially with women." He nods to himself, growing serious. "*Especially* with women."

"I'll never understand your sexual addiction, Rob."

"You *can't* understand it," he says to me. "I'm all about the *next thing*, you know. I get this crazy buzz whenever I'm with a new chick. It hits me in every molecule. I mean, I just can't get enough. I come to every new sexual partner with a ... what's the word? Ferret?"

"*Feral.* Jesus, Rob. It means wild, untamed."

"Yeah, feral. A *feral* excitement. I keep thinking, *Yeah this is it, this chick is exactly what I want.* But every time I try to stick it out with someone for a while — meaning more than a couple of weekends — it fades away. I lose interest in a girl once the sex becomes as ordinary as going to the toilet."

I must be making a face as images pass through my mind, of women lying down for men and being treated like latrines, because Rob says to me:

"I know, it's appalling. I'm appalling. But this is what I feel. I'll be in the middle of sex with someone I've been with for a couple of weeks, and I'll think, *this is no more interesting than takin' a piss.*"

"You're right, Rob. I can't understand it." I rub the back of my neck. "Look man, you seem like you want some advice. So here it is. I think Korea is very bad for you. It brings out the worst in who you are; it smothers your better self, the little bit that does exist under all that shagging and self-deception. I think you should leave. You do have a teaching degree, right? You taught at a middle school in Ontario for a while, didn't you? You should start thinking about moving home and doing something like that again."

He hangs his chin over his shoulder, blows smoke. "I can't ever teach in Canada again," he says.

"Why?"

"Because ... because I did something really stupid at the middle school where I taught."

"Rob?"

"The kind of stupid thing where they don't let you teach again. Ever."

"Rob, what are you telling me?" I try to catch his eyes. "What, did you fucking ..."

He looks at me hard. "What I'm telling you, Michael, is that you think *you* know what a ruined life is. Why? Because you fucking fabricated a bunch of stories in a newspaper? Well I say bullshit to that. Small potatoes, man. You have no clue." He shrugs at me. "Why would I ever leave this place? A country where schools can't be bothered to do background checks, and on weekends I get all the hot- and cold-running sex I want."

He flings his cigarette butt over the rail. I can't say anything to him. My tongue is dead at the bottom of my mouth.

He turns back to me. "But I'm happy for you, dude. It sounds like you got a plan. And if Jin follows you back to Canada next year, then all the better. And I'm happy for Justin, too. I genuinely am. I'm glad to hear he's leaving. He deserves better than this place. But me? *Fack*. I'm not exactly oblivious to the oblivion that awaits me."

He gets up and collects our empty coffee mugs.

"I'm gonna go," I tell him.

"Yeah, I should get my day started. I'm gonna go jerk off — whatshername left me in the lurch. And then —"he nods over the rail at that big, mad megalopolis "— find a way to make me some money today ..."

I confront my future by marking milestones in the rice-paper calendar that hangs on my bedroom wall. You need to do this sort of thing when you're planning to re-enter academia. By X date, I will need to have acquired my old transcripts; by Y date, have sent off my applications. And by Z date — sometime early next spring — I will know where I've been accepted, if anywhere. I mark the dates because if I don't I might miss them, distracted as I am by all that Seoul has to offer. And if I miss them, I'll lose another year of my life to this place.

And yet — there is more going on with me than these shallow plans to seize a new career. My research continues unabated. Jin's great-aunt stands like a hunched, angry pillar in the middle of my mind. Eun-young's story has seeped into my DNA. My research leaves me baffled and I long to question Jin about its accuracy. Thirty-five times a day? Really? Soldiers line up outside cubicles, erections already tenting their loincloths? Really? Did that happen? Could that *really* have happened?

This is not my story, but I'm going to tell it. I'm going to try.

The apartment won't be the same after Justin leaves. The school will assign me another roommate in no time; probably a twenty-two-year-old naïf fresh out of a B.A. Justin and I joke about that as we sit in his bedroom among the boxed-up books and open suitcases of clothes. It's strange to see his headboard wiped clean of the photos of Cody; it looks brand new. Justin's just three days away from flying out to Halifax.

"Probably be a punk," he says of this hypothetical new roommate.

"Ill-read," I reply.

"He'll probably go to Itaewon and get laid his first weekend here."

"Another Rob Cruise in the making."

We laugh.

"So how are you feeling about everything?"

He shrugs. "It is what it is. I *am* anxious to get back to a proper school. Back to where I belong."

"You're lucky to be escaping now," I tell him. "Rob Cruise is on a bloody warpath."

Justin just snorts. "A news site for waegookins? That guy has no clue."

"You know, I once asked him if he knew why you had come to Korea, and he told me to fuck off. But I'll ask you — do you know why *he* came to Korea?"

"Yeah. Because he was teaching at a school in Ontario and got fired."

"But do you know why he got fired?"

"Rob was always vague on the details. What I know is that he followed some girl to Guelph after he got his teaching degree. I know — hard to imagine him ensconced in monogamy. He said he was there for a while, living with this girl, but then *some shit went down*. You know how he talks. He got fired from the school and, for whatever reason, had to get out of Dodge in a hurry. I assumed his story was similar to mine." He pauses. "Why? What did he tell you?"

"Not much more than that. Except — I don't think his story is anything like yours. Maybe I'm just projecting here, but —" I look at him. "Do you think he … *you know*."

"I had my suspicions."

"So then why were you friends with him?"

"Hey, what can I tell you? His generosity can be hypnotizing. When I arrived in Seoul I was flat broke, cleaned out by my divorce. And you know what the school's like — it takes two months before you see a full paycheque. So Rob swooped in and lined me up with all these great privates right off the bat. And he took me out with him, showed me around Itaewon and Hongdae, introduced me to pretty girls. He taught me the Korean I needed to get around. You know what he's like, Michael — you've felt this yourself. We've all gone through these phases with Rob. You, me, Jon …"

"Jin," I frown.

"Yeah, Jin. But in the end, you *have* to stay clear of him. If you're going to be here for another whole year, Michael, you need to know that."

"Yeah, I do know that. But still. There's a part of me that wants to help him. That feels like I *should* help him."

"I don't think he wants help," Justin shrugs. "I mean, Rob just isn't the type who would —"

The phone on the floor, our landline, rings.

"Hang on a sec." Justin scoots off his bed and picks it up. "Hello? … No, this is Justin. Do you want to speak to him? … Hello? … Hello?" He hands me the phone. "It's for you, I guess."

I take it from him. "Hello?"

"Michael."

"Jin? Hey, what's going on?" There's dead silence on the line. "Hello? Hello?" I roll my eyes at Justin. "Fucking cellphones," I say.

"Michael."

"Jin, I'm here. What's going on?"

She bumbles through some Korean, either to me or someone standing there in the background with her.

"You know, you may want to try speaking to me in English," I laugh.

"Mi'chael." It's only when she says my name like it's two words that I realize she's crying. "Michael, my *umma* died."

"What?" I'm sure I've misheard her, that she's mangled her English. "Your great aunt? Eun-young? Your *eemo halmoney*?" All the hope plunges out of me.

"No, Michael. My *mother*. Tae." I hear her swallow a throat-ful of snot. "My mother died this morning."

"Oh my God. Are you at home?"

A little sparrow's chirp: "Yes."

"I'm on my way."

I cover the phone and speak to Justin. "When you go to work, tell Ms. Kim I won't be in today. Jin's had a death in the family." Then back on the line: "Jin? Jin, I'm on my way."

Barely audible: "Okay."

I hang up, hurry out of Justin's room. I strap on my sandals and grab my keys and wallet. "Shit," I mutter. "Shit. *Shit.*"

"Who died?" he asks, leaning against his doorway.

"Her *mom.*"

"Shit."

"Shit. *Shit.*" I open the apartment door and fly out onto the landing. Descend the stairs two at a time. Then outside to the street and off toward the subway.

PART 3

. . . .

EXACTLY ONE THOUSAND DAYS

CHAPTER 18

Jin's brother, Carl, is rushed home from Los Angeles for the funeral, which will occur over three days. As the eldest son, the only son, he is to act as the *sangju*, the master of ceremonies.

On the evening of the second day, I arrive at the funeral home encased in my only suit, appropriately dark. I'm awash in butterflies as I walk up the stone steps to the embossed double doors. I've been reading about Korean funeral rites on the Web and am worried about my etiquette. I called Jin earlier in the day: "Should I bring money? It says guests bring envelopes with cash in them."

"No Michael," she said. "As a friend of the daughter you don't need to bring money."

A friend of the daughter? I asked Jin, "How do I say 'I'm a friend of the daughter' in Korean?"

The funeral parlour is not much different than ones back home — sombre and austere, the floor thickly carpeted, pillars and arches everywhere, walls sporting anodyne landscape paintings. I wait in a short lineup that leads into the main chamber. Everyone here is in black — the men in dark suits, the women in either Western-style dresses or full *hanbok*. The air is brush-strokes of whispers and weeping as I move into the main room. Here, I see that the women stand together on the left side, the men on the right. I look over to the far side to see a dark curtain pulled across the front to hide the casket. A table is set up to the side of the partition and has a framed photo of Tae on it. Even from this distance I can see the severity of her features. Next to the table is a small wooden box where family members and close friends can discreetly drop their envelopes of cash. At the front of the room stands an exhausted but stoic-looking Carl. He would have come straight here after his flight landed from L.A. He is wearing the customary accoutrements of a *sangju*: a tall hemp hat on his head and a hemp armband — thick and white with two dark stripes. Carl is three years younger than Jin and looks boyish. Yet I can sense the deep commitment he has made to suppressing his grief until he has completed this most traditional of tasks. I will have to wait until the end of tomorrow's graveside service to be introduced to him: As the ceremony's *sangju*, he is not to speak at this point in the proceedings.

I feel a hand touch mine.

"Hi."

"Oh, hey."

"Thanks for coming."

"You kidding? I wouldn't have missed it." I jostle her grip. "How are you holding up?"

"'Mokay." Jin's eyes are all puffy, as if she's been in a minor fight, but that's not what I'm looking at. I find myself staring at her hair: she has tied dark, elaborate ribbons all through it. They look so alien there.

She leads me up to the front, where I catch the sharp, ancient odour of incense. As we approach the table, I see why: little sticks of it are burning on sandalwood trays all around the framed photo of Tae. Jin's hand parts from mine and she passes me one of the sticks, then motions to a lit candle on the table. "Go ahead and light the incense," she says. "It's tradition." I do what I'm told, hovering it over the candle's flame. The tip glows orange and a silvery snake of smoke joins the others in the air.

"Now bow," Jin says. "Bow to my mother's photo."

I look at her. Realize now why the ribbons seem so out of place in her hair. It's not just because I've never seen Jin wear them, or *anything* distinctly Korean. It's because they clash somewhat with the slinky black dress, Western-style, that she has also chosen to wear.

I turn to the photo, to Tae's cold stare, and I bow. She just stares back. She just stares through me.

This is how it happened: It started with what she assumed was simply bad heartburn after dinner. It was severe enough to complain about it, severe enough for Minsu and Jin to offer to fetch her an anti-dyspeptic from the *yakguk* across the street. Tae said not to bother, that she would just go lie down. Minsu and Jin went about their business for the rest of the evening — he watching a Korean singing show on TV, she repairing to her room to read. Hours later, in the middle of the night, Tae shook Minsu awake. The heartburn had turned to a constricting force: She couldn't catch her breath and her fingers had begun tingling in frightening ways. Minsu got up and helped her put on some clothes so he could load her into the car. He woke Jin and told her he was taking Tae to the emergency room. *For what, indigestion?* Jin first thought, but then got dressed to join them. Their wait in the ER lounge was over an hour. Tae sat hunched in her chair, clutching herself inwardly as if freezing to death. She eventually got in to see someone, and Minsu and Jin waited. An hour passed, then two, then three. The late August dawn began creeping up on the emergency room windows. And then the doctor came out, his face ashen. He took them aside, to a little room. They had lost her, he told them. She had passed away on the examination table.

· · · · · · · · · · · · · ·

The chamber is packed now with mourners — women on the left, men on the right, and Carl standing silently before us. As quiet, sombre conversatons swirl around me, my mind and eyes begin to wander. The dark partition that separates Tae's casket from the mourners strikes me as odd. It's not acceptable to see the coffin during this portion of the ceremony; her framed photo on its table is meant to stand in for it. The burning incense swirls and churns around the picture in thin, diaphanous plumes. The whole presentation creates a mystic sense of Tae's spirit rising and saying goodbye. I look at Tae's family and friends all around me. Some faces are stoic; some are leaking tears.

Yet, there is only one person here in the full paroxysm of grief. She is engaging in what Koreans call *kok* — a wail of unfathomable anguish for the departed, a howl not just of sadness, but of deep guilt for allowing a loved one to die. Her moaning nearly drowns people out. She stands across from me, here at the front of the room. At first I mistake her for Eun-young. How could I not? Her body is hooked over on itself, her elderly face pustular with mucus and fiery tears. She is inconsolable. But it isn't Eun-young. It's her sister, Ji-young. Of course it is. She stands there with her husband, Chung Hee, his face like trembling granite. They are here to bury their fifty-one-year-old daughter.

So then, where *is* Eun-young? Surely she would have come, too. I turn tactfully around to scan the crowd behind us. So many raven-haired heads bowed out of respect. But then I do spot her, far off in the corner. She is wearing a simple black frock buttoned to the neck, her thin grey hair pulled tight against her scalp.

I look closely. She is standing back there by herself. Utterly alone. Of course she is. I look again, and notice that her face is stone dry.

The next morning, I travel out by subway to the burial plot. The cemetery is a wide park of flowing hills adorned with short shrubby bushes and gingko trees. The headstones here are soft-edged stumps, stone cylinders jutting out of the ground. I find it remarkable how tightly packed the markers all are — barely enough room for a small child to move between them. The graveyard looks like a metropolis in miniature.

The casket has been moved onto the bands over the grave and Carl assumes his position at the head of it. Staying at Jin's side, I watch as one of the funeral attendants turns the crank and the casket completes its final ritual: it lowers and then raises three times, as if bowing to the audience, then sinks slowly into the ground. Once this happens, Carl is finally allowed to speak. He gives a short speech. There is a slight trembling at the corner of his mouth: He's held up so well in this sacred role of *sangju*, but as he nears the end of his responsibilities he's ready to have his own moment of grief. Finally he finishes. Bows deeply in his hemp hat to his mother's casket in its grave.

People mill around after the service is over. Jin asks whether I'll be okay by myself if she goes and talks to people for a while. I nod: of course. I watch as she slinks around the headstones and makes a beeline to Eun-young, who is once again standing alone. Jin takes the old woman's hands in her own, bows as she greets her. They talk for a bit, and Eun-young reaches up to caress the ribbons that Jin has tied in her hair. I wait to see if Jin will eventually go over to her grandmother, too. But she doesn't. She leaves Ji-young to the comforts of others.

"Hello there, chief."

I turn to see Jin's father approaching me from behind with Carl. I reach out and take Minsu's hand, squeeze it and bow to him as deeply as I can.

Carl shakes my hand when I finish. "It's wonderful to finally meet you, Michael," he says. I'm surprised: There is no whiff of a Korean accent to his English. Three years in Los Angeles have done him well.

"You have my deepest condolences, Carl," I say to him. "You did a fantastic job today."

"Did you understand any of it?"

"Not a bit. But I could tell you were being very brave for your mom."

"Thank you."

"Tell me, Carl: What is your Korean name?"

His lips pull away from his teeth as he smiles. "Don't laugh," he laughs, "but my Korean name is Bum Suk."

I press my own lips together. "It's very nice to meet you, Carl."

Minsu smiles, too, but looks a bit left out of the conversation. His English isn't nearly as good as his children's. He turns to Carl suddenly, then seizes him by the arm in a manly way, jiggles it, and points at me. "This is the man who's going to *marry* Jin," he bursts out, apropos of nothing.

Carl's eyebrows fly upwards. "Does *she* know this?" he smiles at me.

"I, I don't think she does, no."

Minsu looks proud of himself, like he's pulled off a very good joke. A moment later Jin spots us standing together. She bows to Eun-young, raises a finger, as if to say she'll be right back, and then comes over, steering through the headstones. She puts an arm around her brother's waist, but addresses me. "What are the three of you talking about?"

"Nothing," I say.

"Nothing," Carl adds.

And Minsu just gives one of his cryptic thumbs-up.

Jin speaks to Carl in Korean, then says something to her father. He says something back, Jin interrupts him, but then Carl interrupts her. They laugh a little, together. I stand on the outskirts of their conversation waiting for either Jin or Carl to start translating. But they don't. I half expect this to end much like *my* mother's funeral ended. I anticipate Jin asking if she can follow me home — weary now of all this family sadness and needing the kind of solace that only I, as her boyfriend, can give. We've had no alone time in four days.

She looks over at me, stony-faced. "Michael, I've agreed to accompany Eun-young home on the subway. I trust you can find your own way back to Deachi from here."

My eyes widen. "Yeah," I stumble in a welter of disappointment. "Yeah, yeah, that's fine."

She gives Carl one last squeeze and he kisses the top of her head. Then she hurries back over to Eun-young. I watch them. I watch them as they leave. I watch as something confusing, horrendously confusing, happens. They leave without saying to goodbye to anyone.

What? Did Eun-young not say a word of condolence to her own sister, Ji-young, for the entire funeral?

It takes the school less than two weeks to find me a new roommate. I'm disappointed; I was so looking forward to being by myself in this apartment for a while — or more accurately, being alone with Jin. But it wasn't meant to be. Any concerns I had about the new guy being another Rob Cruise are completely unfounded. His name is Paul. He is from New Zealand. And he is a born-again Christian. On the night he arrives, he moves uncomplainingly into the smaller bedroom and welcomes me in as he unpacks his suitcases. He even has gift for me: a T-shirt printed with the silver-fern logo of his nation's beloved All Blacks rugby team. "I hope it fits," he says as I examine it through its crinkling cellophane package. I watch Paul pull a floppy, leather-bound Bible and books by Rick Warren out of his suitcase and set them up on the small plastic bookshelf I left in the room for him. I feel compelled to mention then that I have a girlfriend, a *Korean* girlfriend, and that she sometimes spends the night.

He shrugs. "Makes no difference to me."

Paul has never been to Korea before, so over the next while I show him the ropes. I take him to get his immigration papers stamped, explaining how the subway works on the way. I show him where the post office is, where the pharmacy is, how to order his dinner from the front-counter staff at the school when we're on break. We find him an English-language church in the next neighbourhood over, Dogok, and we sign him up for Bible studies. He asks if I want to sign up, too. I mumble a no, and expect him to push me a little. Oddly, he doesn't.

And yet. I notice things about Paul during those first couple of weeks. He's often uninterested in chatting about mundane, everyday things — anything neutral that he can't filter through the prism of Christ. He is also mistrustful of the word "luck" and makes a point of correcting me whenever I use it: there is no such thing as *being lucky*, he says, only *being blessed*. And when I let him in on my plans for going back to school, he gets excited and uses his favourite word: *purpose*. "It's so awesome that you've been given a purpose for next year, Michael." (I catch the passive verb, but don't need to ask, *given by whom?*) Paul is all about purpose. "What is the purpose of your life, Michael?" he asks me, *challenges* me in a variety of clandestine ways.

· · · · · · · · · · · · · ·

Jin and Carl invite me out to a bar. This *hof* is a gritty basement grotto off the main drag of Itaewon. There are U.S. soldiers here, boisterous in the corners, and the sound system plays an album by the Red Hot Chili Peppers. I'm pleased that Jin picked this spot. She's come wearing a brainy French beret and tight blue jeans, so much more like her usual self than the ribbons she had worn at the funeral. Carl, meanwhile, is in a pink golf shirt. It would look ridiculous on me, but as a Korean male he somehow pulls it off. This is our first time hanging out, just the three of us. Our chance to bond.

"That's one thing I'll never get about Western culture," Carl is saying over the din. "Is it true — you actually *see* the corpse at the funeral?"

"Not at the funeral," I tell him. "At the wake. It's called 'open casket.'"

"That's disgusting," Jin says.

"No, it's not."

"It *is*. What, people just line up to see the body?"

"Something like that."

"Did you have an 'open casket' when *your* mother died?"

"We did."

She crinkles her brow. "For what purpose?"

"It's all about closure, I guess. It's one last chance to say goodbye before the person's sealed up for good."

She gives a little shiver of revulsion. "Ugh. Such a morbid superstition."

"What superstition?" I say. "Jin, you believe in *fan death*."

It's true. We've been together two summers now, and each time she sleeps over she insists that I not set up the fan in my room next to the bed to keep the summer heat and mosquitoes off our bodies. Many Koreans believe that you should never sleep with a running fan next to your bed. The idea is that, as you exhale carbon dioxide, the fan will blow it back in your face and you'll suffocate in your sleep.

"Hey, fan death is real. It's *science*. I have a coworker who lost a grandparent to fan death."

Carl is chuckling. "I must admit, after three years in the States, I realize we Koreans pretty much take the cake on superstition. Especially when it comes to death. You know, in olden times when a Korean passed away, the family would treat the body immediately afterwards. They'd trim its fingernails and place uncooked rice in its mouth to ward off evil spirits."

I turn to Jin. "And what, that's not morbid?"

She sucks her teeth and wants to change the subject.

I ask Carl about Los Angeles, about chef school. He's loving it despite all the trials of being a rookie — the constant burn marks up his arms, the minimum wage and surly head chefs at the restaurants where he apprentices. It'll be all worth it when he moves home to Seoul, he says, and gets his pick of upscale restaurants to work at. In the meantime, he's soaking up as much of America as he can. His English wasn't great when he moved there — "Worse than Jin's," he jokes, giving her shoulder a loving bump with his own — but now considers himself fluent. He lives in an apartment outside Hollywood with a couple of other immigrants — a guy from Pakistan and another from Belarus — but they hardly speak at all. Carl's main friends are white guys he's met at the school. I ask if he's ever encountered racism in the States. He says of course he has, but he takes it all with a sense of irony. He even owns a chef's apron that reads: KISS THE GOOK.

"So when do you go back to L.A.?"

"Well, Chuseok is just around the corner, so I'm definitely sticking around for that." The Korean Thanksgiving is the nation's biggest holiday. It's ancestral in nature and encompasses three full days. Carl goes on: "I'll have to see how well my father holds up before I decide to leave. But I can't afford to miss much more of school."

I turn to Jin. "So about Chuseok," I ask. "Did you want me to …"

"Michael, I've been meaning to talk to you about that," she says. "Listen. Chuseok is very sacred, very big for Korean families. And for our family, more so this year than ever. I don't want to offend you. I mean, you can come if you really want to. But I was thinking, maybe this year … especially if we do go to Canada next year, and I miss Chuseok altogether … that maybe, you know …"

"I understand," I say.

"Are you sure?"

"Yes." But Carl gives her a look like *he* doesn't understand.

"I'll take lots of pictures. I promise!"

"Oh, speaking of which," I say, and reach down to pull my digital camera out of my satchel. "Do you mind if I get a shot of you guys?"

"Not at all," Carl says, and the two of them scoot in together.

I turn on the camera and aim. Jin and Carl appear in the centre of the viewfinder. I adjust the zoom and hold the camera a few inches from my nose. I'm just about to press the button when Jin does something I've never seen her do — not once, in all of the photos I've taken of her.

She flashes the "kimchi" *V*, her spread fingers popping up at her chin.

I look up from the camera, a bit shocked. She just looks back with a blank stare, her eyes a straight line below her French beret. I return to the viewfinder and snap the photo. She holds the *V* even after the flash has come and gone.

You did the whole "kimchi" V, Jin, I think. *You always felt that was a bit daft. So what's next? Are you going to start wearing* hanbok *now?*

CHAPTER 19

Eun-young and her grandniece did not speak much on the trip back from the funeral. It was like the two of them, arm and arm, had slipped through time itself, fallen out of sequence with the ruckus of life around them — the crowded subway ride back, the walk up the main drag of Eun-young's midtown neighbourhood, the turning down to her narrow side street. This little boulevard, with its orange bins of rotting kimchi and bleak 7-Eleven, held an aura of decay, of solitude, of people who minded their own business. Eun-young's building was at the very end, small and squat with a dragon-scale roof and short wrought-iron gate. She lived in the basement suite by herself.

The two paused on the sidewalk out front and Eun-young hung her cane over her wrist. "Thank you for escorting me home, Jin-su," she said. "You didn't have to do that."

"I wanted to do that," Jin-su replied. The fleshy mounds around her eyes were still swollen and red. "Here," she said, "let me come in. I'll make you some tea and help you get changed."

Eun-young shook her head. "No. I'll be fine. You should be with your family."

"*You* are my family," her grandniece snapped. The anger, the vehemence, with which she spoke, was bottomless. "Eemo-halmoney, you are *our* family."

Eun-young turned her liquid eyes up to her. *Your* mother *never really thought so, did she. We've been through this so many times before, Jin-su. Her death this week alters nothing for me, even if it alters everything for you.*

She ran her tongue over the scar above her lip, and looked to change the subject. "And what about your *waegookin* friend?" she asked. "Is he family now, too?"

Jin-su blinked at her, then looked away.

"He was staring at us at the graveside," Eun-young went on. "He's always staring at me, Jin-su. It's like he's got a throat full of questions he'd like to ask."

Her grandniece said nothing.

"Tell me, Jin-su — is he a decent man?"

"Very much so."

"Are you going to marry him?"

"*Eemo-halmoney.*"

"Come now, you can tell me. One woman to another."

Jin-su lowered her gaze. "He wants me to follow him back to Canada next year."

"*Canada*?" Eun-young could not imagine such a place. "Are you going to do it?"

Jin-su tilted her head back and looked at the sky, her face scorched by sudden tears.

"I have so many things to think about," she replied. "I believe I could live for a thousand years and still not have enough time to think about everything I need to think about."

"I know exactly how that feels."

Her grandniece looked at her once more. "Eemo-halmoney, please let me come in."

"No. It's okay. Your father needs you, and so does your brother, and your grandparents. You should be with them. It's been a very hard day."

Jin-su at last conceded with a nod. "I love you very much," she said. "Call me if you need anything. Or if you just want some company."

Eun-young patted her hands, but then turned away toward the gate. She didn't look back as she climbed her way up to the building.

Inside and down the stairs — one-two, one-two-and-three — and Eun-young was at her door. Turned the key in the deadbolt and hobbled in. When she popped on the light, her dank basement apartment fluttered to life in fluorescent grimness. Eun-young began pottering about, changing her clothes and going into the bathroom to take her medication, two pink pills from a bottle in her medicine cabinet. She downed them with a glass of water at the rusted sink. They would settle the ache that ricocheted through her hips.

She went back out to sit in the wicker chair she kept near the door. She remembered her father having this exact kind of chair in this exact place in her childhood home. She had come to understand why he had kept such a thing there: it provided a bird's-eye view of his domain, such as it was. Hers was even less — just two rooms in the basement of a decrepit building. Eun-young settled into the chair and cast her eyes up at the *real* reason she had not allowed Jin-su to accompany her inside. There, at the place where the upper wall of her bedroom met the apartment's low ceiling, grew a long dark-green cartography of mould. It spread like faded tattoos all the way from her front door to the top of the wall at her bathroom. The unsightly mildew had cropped up clandestinely over the last several weeks, starting as small dark patches in the corners but then extending outward along the length of the apartment, getting out of hand before Eun-young realized how bad it was. What would Jin-su say if she saw it there now? *Eun-young, your walls are* rotting. *You need to move out. Why won't you move?* She knew exactly where Jin-su thought she should move to — the spare bedroom in the Park apartment that Bum Suk had left behind when he went to America. But Eun-young would never entertain such an idea — even now, with Tae dead and buried. She looked up at the mould again. It was bad but, perhaps, manageable. A bucket of bleach would do it. She'd need to find a brush with a long handle with which to scrub the walls; she would not risk standing on a chair. Or maybe the landlord, if she mustered the courage to speak to him, would come and do it for her. He was a feckless twit, but if she asked him he would probably —

She stopped herself. Ran a finger along the sinewy treads of her wicker chair. *Why are you pondering such mundane things? You don't care about the mould on your walls. You have just watched your family bury your sister's daughter. Poor Ji-young, who has never known a fraction of the anguish you have, wailed out the kok with complete abandonment. It alarmed you, the groan that rose from her throat, the tears that bled across her wrinkled face. Admit it, Eun-young,* she thought. *After all you have witnessed, all you have suffered, you still couldn't grasp the pristine failure one feels over burying a child. That was Ji-young's han — the sadness that will constrict her heart for the rest of her days. And what did you do? You, so knowledgeable in the ways of pain and grief? You stood at the service alone, away from her, from the family. Staying at the very edge of their lives, as you have done for decades.*

She looked up again at the mildewy rot on her wall. *No, Jin-su,* she thought. *I will* never *leave this apartment.*

. . . .

Except the mould really did have to go. So the next day Eun-young went out and bought bleach and a scrub brush with a long handle. At home in her bathroom, she filled a plastic bucket with hot water and mixed in the powdery blue crystals, then lugged the concoction out to the main room and got to work. As she reached up and stroked the brush along the length of her upper wall, Eun-young found her thoughts falling absently, inexplicably, onto Jin-su's *waegookin* friend. Or perhaps it wasn't so inexplicable: hadn't this mildew, she thought, begun to crop up around the night of the birthday party when Jin-su first introduced him — the night he took that photograph of her, and she had surreptitiously removed it from his camera when he left it behind? *He knows*, Eun-young thought. *Jin-su has told him. Such is her love for him, I suppose — and her love for me.* Eun-young wondered if the *waegookin* knew the privilege that he'd been given. *Even my own husband didn't know what you know,* waegookin. *Imagine that. A man who loved me, who loved me more than anything, wasn't privy to what Jin-su has shared with you.*

As she re-doused the brush and edged it along the wall again, Eun-young wondered what *Tae* had made of the *waegookin*. Actually, she didn't have to wonder — of course her niece would have disapproved of him, and expressed that to Jin-su in various subtle and unsubtle ways. But had Tae known that her daughter let the *waegookin* in on their little family secret? Tae was all about keeping Eun-young's past in the closet, and the fact that Jin-su would share it with someone else — a *non Korean*, no less — would have infuriated her. Eun-young had become adept over the years at ignoring Tae's endless displeasures, her need for secrets. Tae saw Eun-young's history as a threat to the family's reputation, and argued that it should never be discussed with people outside of their kin.

Which was fine by Eun-young. Her shame had not diminished over the years, and her need for solitude, to live on the very periphery of her family's lives, grew only stronger. But then, in 1991, the first of the comfort women, Kim Hak Soon, came forward to tell her story. The family was instantly in disarray. They insisted that it was Eun-young's choice whether she wanted to join the growing armada of old women who were coming forward. But it was *clear* where Tae stood on the matter. Oddly enough, Jin-su — then in her mid teens — was just learning about the family secret, and she immediately embraced it as a way of rebelling against her mother. *No*, Eun-young thought as she scrubbed the wall harder, *it was more than that*. Jin-su embraced her *eemo halmoney* as a way of rebelling against the whole family, maybe even the whole country itself. As awareness of comfort women grew, Jin-su became *enraged* to think that Korean society — not to mention her own family — had helped to suppress such traumas for decades. She expressed her rebellion by trying to become Eun-young's best friend — visiting her often, showing her more kindness than anyone in the family, even drawing that creepy charcoal sketch of her. Jin-su also expressed that rebellion by doing some patently un-Korean things, things Eun-young really couldn't imagine, in the foreign quarter of Itaewon when she got a little older. The *waegookin* boyfriend was the culmination of that.

In the end, Eun-young had decided that nothing would change. She was still just so horribly ashamed, and no matter how much the world learned about comfort women — the books, the news reports, the radio documentaries — she would not come forward. This meant, for example, that she didn't head over to the Japanese Embassy for the weekly protests — where comfort women, the ones who *had* spoken out, descended onto the sidewalk out front with their placards and their banners, chanting and singing and demanding recognition from the Japanese government. It happened every Wednesday afternoon, without fail. Eun-young had never participated, had never taken up one of their placards and pumped it up and down and shouted at the Embassy windows to say, unequivocally: *I was one of these women, too.* Not once, in the twelve years since the gatherings had started.

It also meant that she had never travelled down to Kwangju to visit the "House of Sharing" — the place where many of the comfort women now lived together. It was a kind of commune, a living museum to what they all went through. Eun-young refused to go there, to set foot in a place that had built replicas of the stalls where they had been raped. *What, am I to stand in one of them and marvel at it like a tourist? Am I to listen to these women share with strangers, on a daily basis, ordeals that I couldn't ever speak of to my own husband?*

She scrubbed at the wall furiously, and let her mind fall once more on Jin-su's boyfriend. *Don't stare at me with your curiosity, waegookin,* she thought. *I am not like those other women. I am a coward one thousand times over. I cannot move beyond the disgrace that weighs me down like sandbags, that threatens to drag me into the centre of the earth. Look at me — I couldn't grieve with my own sister this week when she buried her child. I could not mourn the loss of her first-born because I am too selfish, mourning the loss of my never-born, the children I couldn't have had because the Japanese ransacked my womb.*

Eun-young reached the end of the wall, scrubbing hard into the corner by the bathroom, and then lowered the brush. She looked back across the length of her apartment. The mould had faded but was not yet gone.

. . . .

On the Sunday after Tae's funeral, Eun-young went to church for the first time in weeks. Manoeuvering up the concrete steps under the steeple and pulling open the lobby door, she felt a mild guilt for being absent. It wasn't something the rest of the congregation foisted consciously: their nods at the sight of her weren't laced with malice, just a pleasant *Oh, you came back. It's nice to see you again.* But there was also a prying curiosity behind their gazes: *Was there a reason you stayed away?* One of the ushers, a girl of about seventeen, offered to take Eun-young's arm and help her to a pew. But Eun-young raise a palm and shook it at her: *No, leave me be.* This was her reputation among the other churchgoers, to be tetchy and unwilling to accept help. Eun-young found a place near the back, eased her bones into the pew's wooden grip, and lowered her head to pray.

She had been coming to this church, off and on, for sixteen years. The sermons struck a chord with her, she had to admit. Sins washing away in the blood of Christ; giving your burdens over to God to carry; knowing that you could be loved no matter what you did. Inside the church, she felt a serenity within herself that she hadn't believed possible.

And yet. Certain sermons infuriated her. The idea, for example, that Christ suffered more on the cross than any human could imagine. *Really? Does Christ know what it's like to be raped thirty-five times a day for two years? To have one's legs burned by hot pokers, to be urinated on, to be penetrated by two men at once?* She would leave the church steaming under these blasphemous thoughts and not come back for weeks. But then she *would* return, in need of the calm that she'd found under this roof. And each time she did, she'd lower her head to pray just as soon as she found a pew to sit in. Which was what she was doing now: beseeching God to forgive her absences and fill her mind with all the reasons why this was where she belonged.

Today the sermon was about the war in Iraq, and the power of prayer. The minister — just a young fellow really, about thirty years old — was telling a story he had learned over the email from a colleague in America. It involved a family in the colleague's congregation who had a son stationed in Baghdad. The young man had given up a comfortable job as an accountant shortly after 9/11 and enlisted in the army, a decision his family supported because they believed it came from God. But now, with their boy posted right in the heart of a worsening situation — suicide bombers and I.E.D.s, sectarian slaughter and those atrocities at Abu Ghraib — the family began questioning whether this was what the Lord wanted for their son. They began questioning whether the *war itself* was what He wanted. "And these are God-fearing Republicans, my colleague tells me," the minister said. "This family came to him for advice because they knew the questions they were raising were a slippery slope. Before long, they might have begun questioning God's benevolence, or even His very existence. And so what did my friend tell this family to do? To pray. Simply to pray. We can only know a small part of God's intentions for us. But if we choose, we can be in God's presence whenever we wish — simply through the power of prayer. So pray, he told them. Pray every day; soak up the love and light of God. It will provide you with something far greater than mere answers to earthly questions. Use your prayers not to interrogate God, but only to be with Him."

The minister ended his sermon by telling the congregation to pray there in their pews, and Eun-young did as she was told. She thought she felt it then, the presence that the minister had promised. It *was* God, wasn't it — touching her shoulders and calming that cacophony in her mind, thoughts about Tae's death, about Ji-young's grief, about the *waegookin* and his stares, and that terrible trip to Pusan sixteen years ago? *Is He here?* she asked. *Is God really with me in this place?*

After the service, Eun-young hobbled into the lineup in the aisle and waited her turn to shake the minister's hand, nodding at the people who smiled at her and wished her good morning. When she approached the young minister, he reached out and touched her elbow.

"Eun-young, it's so good to see you," he said. "You've been away for a while."

"I have, but I'm back," she replied, and then frowned. "Young man, my niece passed away last week."

"Oh Eun-young, I'm sorry to hear that. Was she very old?"

"No, just fifty-one. Her mother, my sister, is devastated. She's just — devastated."

The minister nodded solemnly. "Of course she would be."

"I've been at a loss since it happened," Eun-young mumbled. "I've been feeling … feeling …" The minister tilted his head, waiting for her to finish, but Eun-young changed gears suddenly. "Young man, I have a question … I have a question about sin."

"Yes?"

"It's not about whether God can wash away sin. I already know your answer to that. But I want to ask you what counts as a sin."

The minster's eyes flickered for a moment over Eun-young's shoulder at the people behind her waiting patiently for their turn with him. They were used to this, the old woman with the scar over her lip who often sought spiritual guidance at inappropriate moments.

"Go ahead, Eun-young," he smiled, his eyes falling back to her.

"Is happiness a sin?" she asked.

"Generally no — unless its source contradicts how God would like us to treat each other."

"Is anger a sin?"

"Generally yes — unless it eventually leads us to seek out God's word and follow it."

"Is solitude a sin? Being alone? Cutting yourself off from other people?"

"You and I have discussed this one already," he smiled. "Eun-young, God wants us to have community. He wants *you* to have community."

She found herself weeping, lightly. She pulled at her cheeks with the heel of her hand. "I'm sorry. My niece, my niece died last week. I'm sorry. I'm sorry."

"It's okay. Hey, it's okay."

"One last question," she said, and then paused. "Could forgiveness ever be a sin?"

The minister's face nearly cracked in two from his smile. "*Never*," he said joyously. "True forgiveness could never be a sin."

But her frown just deepened. *I don't believe you.* She hobbled off curtly, stabbing at the lobby floor with her cane. One-two, one-two-and-three, and she was back on the sidewalk and heading home.

By the time Eun-young returned to her basement apartment, the minister's words had fluttered out of her mind like birds. When she unlocked the door and stepped inside her mildewy hovel, the certitude and tranquility of church was gone, replaced by a tumult that began brewing inside her. She shuffled over to her little kitchen to begin her lunch, took down a bag of rice from the cupboard and tried to measure some for the rice cooker on the floor. But stopped before the first grains came out. She set the bag back down, began to tremble. Closing her eyes, Eun-young tried to pray once more, tried to find God's presence as she had in the church. It wasn't there. She prayed as hard as she could, but it was like her low ceiling and mouldy walls had sealed Him out. *Even God is not allowed in here*, she thought. *It's a crock — all of it. What I feel is not peace. I feel alone. I should have told the minister that — I feel so alone. If forgiveness is not a sin, then why does it seem so wrong? Maybe if I had known God when I was younger, knew His purpose for me before I was taken to the camps and made into a whore, I would be capable of compassion. But I'm not. I am not capable. I'm sorry, Ji-young. I cannot understand your grief. It's not that I hated Tae, even though she gladly abetted my isolation with her disapproval. It's not that. I cannot help you in your mourning because I cannot understand what it means to love a daughter. And it's because I don't love anyone, or anything. I am like an island floating in the sea, without even a sliver of soil touching the mainland. I have no path to cross over to you.*

God is not here. He has never touched my heart. Not once.

But then nights later, weeks later really, the phone rang. The sound was like an intruder, so rare that it was for the phone to ring at all. Eun-young sat up in bed, the sheets crinkling around her. It was the middle of the night.

She didn't get up right away to answer it. But when it didn't stop, she swung her brittle legs around and touched the floor with her feet. The phone rang and rang as she raised herself from bed and limped out into the main room, where the phone sat on a low table next to her wicker chair. She stood before it in her nightgown. There was only one person it could be at this hour.

She answered it.

"Hello."

"Eun-young …"

"Hello, my sister."

"I'm sorry to call so late. I've gotten you out of bed, haven't I?" She was speaking in a low voice. Perhaps trying not to wake Chung Hee.

"It's alright."

"Eun-young … Eun-young …"

"Speak to me, my sister."

"Why haven't you come? It's been weeks now. Why haven't you come to see me?"

"I'm sorry, Ji-young."

"I don't want an apology. I want a reason. Why haven't you come to see your sister?"

Eun-young licked her lips, but Ji-young cut her off before she could speak. "I haven't been able to sleep. My doctor warned me about this. He said the sudden death of a loved one can cause insomnia. It can last for months. Did you know that, Eun-young?"

"I did, yes."

"Of course you did. You know so many things."

"Ji-young, please …"

"I can't stop thinking about Tae," Ji-young went on after a moment. "I mean, I realize her soul has crossed over, that she has taken her place among our ancestors. I *know* that. But I can't stop thinking about *her* — her body. I can't stop thinking about my little girl in her *box*. Do you know what I mean? Eun-young, do you know what I mean?"

"I know exactly what you mean."

"You know so much," Ji-young repeated. "You are so wise. Why have you kept your wisdom from me? Why, Eun-young? Why haven't you come to see your little sister in her grief?"

Eun-young lowered her head, felt a flush appear around her neck like a wreath. She scoured her brain for all the rationales for staying away. *They are there*, she thought. *Your justifications are there, aren't they? No. No, they are not. They are not there. You speak of God not being in this place, but it is your* reasons, *not God, that have abandoned you. They are not here. You cannot speak your reasons aloud because they are not really here.*

"I'll come, Ji-young," she said.

"Eun-young ..."

"I'll come."

"You promise?"

"I do. I'll come. I'll be there tomorrow."

CHAPTER 20

Jin is wearing *hanbok*.

    Jin is wearing *hanbok* in some of the photos she's showing me on her camera. She races through them to get to other pictures, from her recent trip to Paris.

"Wait, go back," I tell her.

"What?"

"Go back for a sec."

We're on my bed, huddled over the viewfinder. We haven't seen each other in more than a month: After the extended break with her family at Chuseok, Jin went to France for three weeks on business. It's great having her in the apartment again, but also a little weird. Awkward. We're waiting for Paul to leave for the day. He's off to Suwon to hike the fortress there with friends he's made at Bible study.

Jin scrolls back a few pictures. And then there she is, under that tent-like dress in its layers of pastel.

"You're wearing *hanbok* in these ones," I say.

"Well, it *was* Chuseok."

"Jin, you never wear *hanbok*. You always said it looks unflattering."

"Michael, Chuseok was different this year. I told you that. It had to be, coming so close after my mother's death. I felt, how you say, *obligated* to be a bit more traditional."

"But I've never seen you wear it. You look different. You look ..."

"Michael, do you have a problem with me wearing hanbok?"

I bristle. "Of course not. I don't. It's just that ..."

A knock rattles my door.

"Come on in," I sigh.

Paul peeps his head in bashfully, like he's worried we won't be decent. "Hey, you two."

"Hey, man."

"Hi, Purposeful Paul."

His smile curdles a little, like he's not sure if Jin is mocking him. "I'm off to Suwon," he says. "I won't be back until late. Have a great day, you guys."

"You too, man. Enjoy the hike. It's fantastic."

"Yes, have fun down there."

After he's gone, I turn back to Jin. I want to talk to her about the things I've been noticing, these little slippages in her personality. But I don't get the chance. As soon she hears Paul close and lock the apartment door behind him, she sets her camera on my nightstand and then moves in on me. Her palms run over my thighs, and she kisses my throat.

"Hello there, stranger," she croons.

Within a minute, our clothes are on the floor. It's been so long since we've had sex, so long since I've had her undivided attention for any stretch of time. It's nice; but again, weird. Passionate, but in the tawdry way of a one-night stand.

After we're done, she throws on one of my T-shirts and goes to use the bathroom; and when she returns, spots something on my floor near the bookshelf. It's the 2004 academic calendar from the University of Ottawa. Tucked in its pages is my application form. She brings them over to the bed and climbs in with me. Hikes up her naked legs and rests the book on them.

"So are we really going to do this?" she asks, flipping.

She said *we*. I cling to the fact that she said *we*.

"I would certainly like to."

Her expression is an eddy of indecision, so many thoughts swirling around her head.

"So tell me how it would work."

"Well, it's a two-year program. I'd have a B.Ed at the end. I could probably find some freelance editing during the summers to help keep us afloat."

"And what would I do?"

"I'm thinking you could apply for a job at the Korean Consulate. Or maybe do some freelance translating. You *are* fluent in French, after all."

"And how often would we come back to Korea?"

"As often as we can afford. If I'm going to be a school teacher for the rest of my life, I'll have two months off every year. We could spend entire summers back here in big smoggy Seoul."

She doesn't smile at that. She just sticks out her bottom lip and thinks hard.

"Jin, we'll come back as often as we can."

"But is that what *you* want?" she asks suddenly. "I mean really, Michael. Are you willing to spend every summer vacation commuting between our two countries?"

"If it means being with you."

"But wouldn't it be simpler to take Korea — to take *me* — out of the equation completely?"

"That doesn't make any sense," I tell her. "You're the reason we're even having this conversation."

"But maybe you'd be happier with a Canadian girl. Did you consider that? Why be chained to Korea for the rest of your life just because you think you're in love with me?"

"*Hey*. I don't *think* I'm in love with you."

But she turns away then, away from the severity in my tone. "Maybe it would be better if you weren't in love with a Korean.

Then you could move home next year with no complications. Did you ever think of that?"

"I don't know what to tell you, Jin. You're the one I want to be with. I have nothing else to say."

Thankfully, she smiles a little. "Even if you don't like me wearing *hanbok*?"

"I told you — I don't have a problem with you wearing *hanbok*."

"You think it makes me look ugly."

"It doesn't make you look ugly," I say. "It makes you look pregnant."

She huffs. "Well, I'm not *pregnant*."

She kisses me between the eyes and then slides out of my sheets to go take a shower.

Another month and another month, and I'll still be on this assembly line of English. My classes at the *hagwon* grow more predictable with each new batch of kids. There's the princess in the first row, there's the thug in the back. There's the kid too smart for his own good, sarcastic and demanding linguistic explanations. *Why not "gooder"? Why not caught "blue-handed" when doing something wrong? Why is "losing your temper" bad when "having a temper" is also bad? Why, MichaelTeacher, why?* His essays teem with personality, but I still need to scribble corrections in the margins. No, Louis Armstrong was not the first man on the moon. No, Jesus was not betrayed by Judas Asparagus. He means well. At least he doesn't write ad nauseam about the World of Warcraft or Pokémon. The older kids want to talk about America. They can't believe Kerry lost the election. How could so many people be so stupid? "Bush is crazy man! Crazzzy man!" the kids scream at me, as if I had something to do with his victory.

My life is bifurcated now, between the grind of today and my plans for next year. The application to Ottawa is in the mail and I'm imbued with optimism. I've already begun researching the city, thinking about neighbourhoods to live in and commutes to campus. Does Ottawa have a Korean community? Will Jin be able to get a job? What sort of visa will she need? I plan and I plan. You might say I overplan. I take ideas to Jin looking for clear-cut approval: Let's spend the summer in Halifax: JazzFest and the buskers and day trips down to the South Shore; let's go to Ottawa a couple of weeks before classes start and be tourists, walking the ByWard Market and exploring Parliament Hill. She nods with acquiescence, but there is no commitment behind her eyes. Only distraction. She is deeply distracted. I mention my worries to Paul, but his advice is just a thin gruel of determinism. *Have* faith *that she'll follow you to Canada, Michael. If it's meant to be, it'll be.* I don't want to have faith. I want to fucking kidnap her. I want to make things *happen*. It's no use talking to Paul about this. He doesn't believe that we're in control of our own lives. I wish Rob Cruise were around for me to seek his counsel. He'd know what I should say to Jin to extinguish these reservations, to take charge of our relationship. But I haven't seen Rob since the summer. I don't even know what he's doing for a living this year. I don't even know if *he* took *my* advice, and fled the country.

And let's not forget about my *other* little project. I feel like I've done all the research on the Web that I can. I've read every article, testimonial, bit of history out there for public consumption. The time has come to take this obsession to the next level.

I ask Ms. Kim for a Wednesday off. Any Wednesday, it doesn't matter. I realize that beseeching her for this favour is risky business: my absence from the school, even for a day, could put me on her "bad teacher" radar. She'll have to ask one of the Korean front-counter staff — all of whom are bilingual, more or less — to teach my classes. She'll hate doing this because Koreans aren't supposed to teach Koreans at an English *hagwon*. It goes against the advertising, against what the school has promised all the mothers: Our teachers are the real deal — Western, almost always white, and *native speakers*. Still, it's only for one day. I ask Ms. Kim for this during our prep period in the most diffident voice possible. I have to be careful. She is forever on the look-out for ways that her foreign teaching staff might be ripping her off, always one beat from flying off the handle. Still, she likes me. Considers me obedient and reliable. We negotiate the terms: I won't be paid for the day, and if I'm back in time I should come in and teach my evening classes — for free, as a gesture of thanks. I have no choice but to agree. Why do you need a Wednesday off, anyway? she asks. Personal business, I tell her. Something I can only do on a Wednesday. Thankfully, she doesn't ask for details. What would I say if she did? *Tell me, Ms. Kim, do you have a grandmother?*

Wednesday is when Seoul's comfort women gather outside the Japanese Embassy for their noontime protest. This has happened every week, without fail, for the last twelve years. I am off to observe it in the name of research, bringing along a big spiralled notepad like the kind I used when I was a middling journalist. As the subway rumbles me northward, I feel that old hollow sensation in my stomach. These blank pages speak of obligations I've never been comfortable with: to be assertive, to ask tough questions, to bother people, to insist they share their stories, to get it down, to get it right, to get it lucid. I'm determined to lift what I want from these women in the name of telling a good story.

But my visit to the Embassy is an absolute bust. The atmosphere of the gathering is nothing like I had imagined. I expected there to be speeches I could understand, angry chants thrown like stones at the Embassy windows, elderly ladies pounding their chests in anguish as they demand justice. It is nothing like that. There is a perfunctory air to this assembly, a well-entrenched routine. I watch these women sitting behind their long banners and waving their ping pong racket-like signs in the air. The songs they sing are almost cheerful; a few of these ladies are actually smiling. Someone does make a speech, a university-aged girl who has come out to show her support, but it's entirely in Korean and garbled through a megaphone. I roam the small crowd, jotting observations and posing a few limp questions to a handful of people. Hardly anyone speaks English, and the ones who do can tell me nothing beyond what I've already learned on the Web.

I should have brought Jin. She could have been my translator, giving me the confidence to come right up to these old women and put better questions, harder questions to them — to make them reveal the little details about their experience that I can't learn from books or articles. But I haven't even told Jin about this project. I suspect she'd be furious if she knew I was even up here.

I return to Daechi at the end of the afternoon, thoroughly dejected. The apartment is empty: Paul has already left for the *hagwon*. I go into my bedroom and sit at the little wooden desk I scavenged off the street, and slap my notebook on it. I open the ancient laptop I brought over from Canada and turn it on, launching a new document. I look down at the few, scant notes I had taken. I look up at the computer's blank page, all its possibilities.

What the hell, Michael? I think. *Are you going to be a coward for the rest of your life? Are you going to do nothing, be nothing?*

You know *that there is a different route into this. You know there is another way.*

And in that instant, I feel like I hold the entire thing — every last word of what I want to write — in my mind at once. It's there, as real as anything that has ever happened to me. Real because it is so *unreal. Please forgive me.* I beseech this to Jin, to Eun-young, to myself, even to Paul's big benevolent God. *Please forgive what I'm about to do.*

And then I begin typing.

CHAPTER 21

Eun-young rode the subway across Seoul, heading east. Today was not the tomorrow that she had promised to Ji-young. It had been more than a week since her sister's late-night call — time that Eun-young had taken to perform this inner alchemy, to turn the dull metal of her fear into a golden bravery. But now, sitting in the toss and pitch of her subway seat next to a teenager reading a violent comic book, Eun-young didn't feel brave. Cowardice slumped her shoulders and one thought kept caroming through her mind: *Have I waited too long to come? Have I just waited too long?* It wasn't simply that Ji-young might be hurt or even angry that Eun-young had taken a week to keep her promise. Eun-young was worried that the tides of her sister's grief might have receded since her call and this visit would be all for nothing, another opportunity squandered.

Have I waited too long to come? This reoccurring mantra reminded Eun-young of something else — a single, disastrous return she had made to Pusan so long ago. The memory of it seeped into her mind then. It may have taken her a week to face Ji-young, but it had taken twenty-three years to face what she had done to Po. This act felt exactly like that one — the same sense that she had allowed her fear to fritter away a chance to set something right. That she had let her cowardice get the better of her.

· · · · · · · · · · · · · · ·

The year had been 1988. Seoul's great coming-out party, the eyes of the world beaming onto the culture of Korea. Eun-young had been dreading the Olympics. She'd grown accustomed to her country's global irrelevance, to its placidly controlled society and closed doors, intended (as every Korean knew) to give the wounds of the past time to heal. And heal they had. The country had changed so much in the years leading up to the Games — the collapse of the police state, the rise of real democracy, a freer press, more liberties, more *growth*. And now, in hosting the XXIV Olympiad, Koreans were saying to the world: "Come to us. Line up at our door. We have spread ourselves open for you."

It all made Eun-young nervous.

She was working as a cleaner in a downtown hotel at the time, long days of pushing her cart of disinfectants and toilet paper rolls anonymously through the hotel halls. Foreigners had begun descending in swarms; she had never seen so many unfamiliar skin tones, had never heard so many strange tongues. The dark Africans with their colourful flags embroidered on their luggage; the brash Americans in their nylon track suits; the icy Scandinavians with their earnest attempts at the language. And, of course, the ever-polite Japanese — so many Japanese journalists with their notepads and cameras and microphones. Fascinated, they were, by all the quaint minutiae of her country's customs, everything their parents and grandparents had tried to wipe out.

It was two days before the opening ceremonies. She was dusting coffee tables with a feathered wand in the little lounge off the hotel lobby. On the couch just beyond where she worked, a radio journalist from Japan, no more than thirty years old, was interviewing an Olympic organizer. Another young Japanese man, a translator, sat next to them, converting the journalist's questions into Korean as he asked them. Eun-young discreetly feathered her way over, catching snippets of their banter. When the interview finished, the organizer got up to leave; and when he was out of earshot, the two Japanese boys leaned in and exchanged a callous, sarcastic quip about the man's answers. Eun-young missed most of it, but she caught one word that ripped her stomach clean out of her body. The word flew from the journalist's lips in a spray of cruel laughter.

Chosunjin.

Chosunjin!

It had been nearly forty-five years since that racial slur, the embodiment of old Japanese bigotry against Koreans, had scorched her ears. But the journalist, born after the occupation, born even after the Korean War, had uttered it with such nonchalance. Eun-young stopped and stared at them, but they didn't even see her. She slapped her duster down on an end table and marched over to a vase of orange roses standing on a pillar by the doors. Yanked the flowers out and smacked them to the floor, then carried the vase over to where the men were sitting, winding her way around the couch. Eun-young didn't hesitate as she decanted the perfumed water over the journalist's head. She slammed the empty vase at his feet, and it broke on the thin carpet. "Your grandfather probably *raped* me!" she said in perfect Japanese, shocking the young man as rivers ran down his sport coat. Then she spat in his face.

The hotel manager rushed over from behind the front desk. He began apologizing frantically to the boys, bowing and bowing and bowing again. Then he turned to Eun-young, to where she stood quavering before them, and fired her on the spot.

Days later in her basement apartment, freshly terminated and navigating the rapids of her rage, she could barely bring herself to watch the opening ceremonies on her little TV. What a grotesque pantomime of harmony and peace, she thought: thousands of Korean dancers undulating on the stadium floor with great synchronized rotations; the parade of drums; the jets streaking a rainbow across the sky; the mass displays of taekwondo. It sickened her. It looked whorish. And for the first time since returning to Seoul in 1965, since uttering the truth about her past to Ji-young and Chung Hee in a cloud of disgrace, she felt an overwhelming compulsion to speak her history to the greater world. She imagined herself storming into the stadium, seizing the microphones, turning to the cameras of the world and screaming, *Stop this! They raped us! Don't you know? They raped us and raped us and raped us again!* But who would listen to her, this embittered sixty-year-old woman, divorced and poor and living on the margins of this colourful culture now mincing around in front of everyone? Five billion people in the world and who would want to face such an ugly truth at a time like this? Who among them would look past what she was and see the person she could have been, the person that the Japanese had so heartlessly stolen?

The answer came to her like a knife in the back. Five billion people didn't need to know the truth, but one did. One man could learn about everything that happened, and *understand*. Understand, and still love.

The next morning, she packed a small bag and rode the subway to Express Bus Terminal. Bought her ticket and climbed aboard the shuttle that would take her to Pusan. The bus was nearly empty; hardly anyone was *leaving* Seoul. Eun-young felt a flush of excitement course through her as the shuttle weaved its way out of the city through rugged mountains and flat rice fields of green. She could hardly believe what she was doing. For years she had fantasized about breaking down and visiting Po. What would he look like now, after twenty-three years? Old and withered, like her — or distinguished and handsome? She always assumed that he had remarried after she left him, and now wondered what his wife would be like. Younger than he, most likely, and pretty. How many children would they have? They'd be almost adults themselves by now, if they existed. How would his family react to her presence on their doorstep? What was the plan, anyway? She decided on it in an instant. If she found him, Eun-young would insist that they go down to the seaside park where he had asked her to marry him. There they would sit on a bench to talk, and she would tell him *everything* — the complete, undistorted truth about what her life had been, all that she should've told him when he confessed his desire to marry her.

The shuttle rolled into a Pusan she hardly recognized. How the city had changed in the intervening decades, growing wide and expansive around the mountains in an insane array of highways and skyscrapers. At the bus terminal, trying to get her bearings, Eun-young had no choice but approach a tourism kiosk and ask for help reaching the neighbourhood where she had once lived. The city's network of buses confounded her, but she eventually worked out the right line to take. She sat up front near the driver as the bus lumbered through main drags and side streets, many of which Eun-young could not place. Out the windows, she saw that Pusan was not immune to Olympic mania: banners and five-ringed flags were strung up on every light pole; the sidewalks were full of young people with their faces painted thickly in the national colours; every storefront displayed large TVs that aired the Games on endless loops. Every now and then the bus passed a locale that Eun-young *was* familiar with — a street market she had shopped in as a young wife, or a cinema that she and Po had attended as a childless couple. Her heart burst at the sight of them, a fast rush of nostalgia injected into her veins like a drug.

The bus finally deposited her onto a corner outside her old neighbourhood. After a moment's hesitation, she shuffled down

Po's street and was pleased to see their little house still standing. Pleased even more that it was in good shape, its iron roof gleaming, its walls brightly painted, even a couple of flowerboxes beneath its shuttered windows. A woman's touch. Eun-young nearly smiled, but then grew sombre. She mounted the stoop and knocked on the door. Heard the faint whir of bodies moving through rooms and halls that she had known so intimately. The door opened and a young woman appeared at the threshold. She was maybe in her late twenties. Pretty, but with her hair already cut short, to the length of a housewife's. Her face was neutral as her eyes fell on Eun-young, flickered a little when they passed over the scar that ran beneath her nose.

"Yes?" the woman asked, wiping her hands on the apron tied across her hips.

"I'm sorry, I'm —" Eun-young stammered. "I'm sorry, do you live here?"

"Yes," the woman replied, a little alarmed now.

"I'm sorry," Eun-young repeated. "I'm looking for someone. Does, does Po still live here?"

"Who?"

"Po. Kim Po Hun. Does he still live here?"

The woman shrugged. "No. There's no one by that name here."

"I'm looking for someone," Eun-young repeated aimlessly. "His name is Kim Po Hun. He used to live in this house. Can you help me?"

Just then a young boy, about five years old, scurried up behind the woman and poked around her side. He had a small South Korean flag tied bandana-style around his head and his face was painted in Olympic rings. His eyes were huge as he stared up at Eun-young. Behind him, a TV blared the Games somewhere deep in the house; Eun-young could hear the warning whistle of a boxing match.

"You say he used to live here?" the woman asked, hoisting the child onto her hip. "Perhaps he was the previous owner."

"Yes, maybe. When did you buy this house?"

"Four years ago." The girl marvelled at her own words. "We bought this house, oh my, four years ago now."

"And you know nothing of the previous owner?"

"We didn't learn his name, but we knew …" and the woman half smiled, half frowned. "We knew he was a *noh chong gak* who had lived here for many years. Sadly, he died in this house. His family was anxious to sell. It was how we got the place so cheaply."

The muscles of Eun-young's face slackened and her heart sank a thousand miles. A *noh chong gak*? It couldn't have been Po. It made no sense. He would have remarried. Another woman would have scooped him up in no time at all. There was no way he would have lived out his days as a confirmed bachelor. And he would not have died in this house, alone.

The woman could see that Eun-young was distressed. "Did you want to come in? I've just finished making some walnut cakes."

Eun-young ignored her. It *could not have been Po*. She was convinced of it. He would have sold this house after she had left him — sold it because it was full of too many memories, memories of her, of them together, and sold it so he could move on with his life. And the man that this woman spoke of was somebody else, another man who had owned this house in the years in between. *He* would have been the *no chong gak*, not Po.

"I've upset you," the woman said. "Did you want to come in?"

Eun-young waved her hand. "No." She couldn't bear the thought of stepping inside to see the home she had shared with her husband, to see its recognizable nooks and alcoves, and also how much it would have changed. "I've disturbed you enough as it is. Thank you."

"Are we talking about the same man?" the woman asked, concerned.

"No," Eun-young replied, stepping down off the stoop. "The man I'm talking about is married. He is *married*."

"Well, I hope you find him."

Eun-young nodded weakly, then turned away from the house and began walking back up the street, leaving the woman and her son to stare at her in mild confusion before closing the door.

Her subsequent wander was not directionless. The pathways of familiarity were reborn in her brain, the streets no longer foreign but tapping into a disquieting muscle memory. She knew exactly how to find her way to the neighbourhood where Po's family had lived. It was within walking distance, if she felt strong. There was no guarantee that any of them were still living there, but she had to see for herself. Eun-young began to choke up again as she made the trek, her head full of so many rancid anxieties. It was as if they aged her a decade as she walked.

She arrived in their neighbourhood half an hour later — and discovered that the cluster of small Korean homes where Po's parents and siblings had lived were gone, torn down and replaced by an office building that housed a Department of Motor Vehicles and an English *hagwon*. Eun-young's heart sank. Po's family had most likely scattered and moved to other districts in the growing metropolis of Pusan. She stood on the corner in front of the office building, shaking her head. She now had to find her way to the bus terminal to catch the late afternoon shuttle back to Seoul. Why had she even bothered to come? What had she hoped to —

Across the street, she saw a storefront that she recognized. It was a small dry cleaners that Po's sister Pan-im and her husband had owned. It still had the overhead sign that Eun-young remembered from those years ago, with its bright yellow background and black Hangul lettering. She stood staring at it for a moment, then crossed the street toward it. As she did, a woman came out toting a long plastic bag of jackets over her shoulder, their hangers clasped in her palm. Another woman came out behind her, waved and wished her a good day. The second woman was Pan-im. Fiftyish now, in a gray work shirt and slacks.

She turned then, casually, and saw Eun-young standing on the sidewalk. At first the smile stayed on her lips, but then her eyes found the telltale scar over Eun-young's mouth. Eun-young watched as recognition flooded the woman's face, a face that suddenly stiffened, brow tightening and eyes like hot stones in their sockets.

"Hello, Pan-im," Eun-young said shyly.

Her former sister-in-law just stood there with her lips packed tightly together.

"I said hello, Pan-im."

Po's sister bared her teeth. "Hello, you little whore."

The word knocked the wind from Eun-young's lungs, much like the journalist's use of *Chosunjin* had done days earlier. She couldn't seize enough breath to form words.

"What are you *doing* here?" Pan-im spat.

"I'm looking for Po," she finally muttered. "I came down from Seoul today. The Olympics … the Olympics drove me out of the city … I couldn't watch them … I needed to see Po … I needed to tell him …"

"Po is dead," Pan-im said, in a tone that was almost proud. Proud at how those words cut off Eun-young's rambling with such force.

"Wh-when?" she quaked, and already knew the answer.

"Four years ago."

Eun-young brought a hand to her mouth.

Pan-im's smile was nothing but pure hatred. "Look at you," she said. "Look at you, Eun-young, standing on the street outside my store after all these years, and *weeping*." She let out a laugh. "You, the little woman of mysteries. You, who left my brother with no explanation, abandoned your marriage for no reason. You, who arrived in our lives like a ghost out of some oblivion, then vanished back into it as quickly as you came. And leaving my brother *destroyed* in your wake. And now here you are, not a ghost at all but a woman of flesh and blood — and *weeping*, weeping in front of me and my little store!"

Eun-young felt as if she had been stripped naked and put on display.

"Do you wish to know what happened to him? Hmm? Yes? No? Speak, woman."

Eun-young could not. She clenched her chin in her clavicles and stared at the sidewalk.

"Nineteen years, Eun-young. Nineteen years of unwavering solitude. We tried to reason with him, to talk him out of it. But he was adamant — and he held his ground until the day he died. Oh, he still showed up for work every day. He still came out for Chuseok, for birthday parties, for other family things. But he was *never* really with us. He stayed entirely locked up within himself, and no matter how much we pleaded with him to come out, he never relented. He never stopped mourning the loss of his little woman of mysteries."

"I didn't know …"

"You didn't know? Who cares! Listen to me, Eun-young. My brother was never a strong man — he was a bit of a wimp his whole life. But he deserved better than to grieve over you for so long, and to die in that house by himself. That's right. One day four years ago, his heart just gave out. It just stopped beating, Eun-young. It just didn't want to go on. We found him *face down in the cat food by the door!*"

Pan-im took a step closer to her. Eun-young flinched, certain that her sister-in-law would strike her. Passersby on both sides of the street had paused to stare at them.

"You, a little woman of mysteries?" Pan-im went on. "Ha! Well, you're no mystery to me. I think I know what you were before you came into our lives. A *prostitute*, that's what I think. A whore, Eun-young. I think you sold your body to American soldiers while they were carving up our country with the Russians, and then fled down here out of shame — looking for a life of solitude and never expecting a good man to fall in love with a dirty rag like you."

"Not true … it's not true …" She could feel the neighbourhood's gaze all over her.

"Look me in the eye, Eun-young, and tell me you never had a man before Po. Look into my face and say you were a virgin on your wedding night. Can you do that?"

Eun-young stepped back, began to turn.

"You can't, can you? Because you're a whore. I'm right, aren't I? You're a whore! You're a horrible, horrible whore! That's it, Eun-young, walk away. Go on. Turn your back on me, just like you turned your back on Po. Walk away, you prostitute. Go back to Seoul, you harpy. Look everyone. Look at the whore from Seoul! Look at her as she walks away from the family she ruined. Look at the woman who killed my brother! Look at her! Look! Look before she vanishes again!"

The kid with the violent comic book got up to get off the subway. Eun-young had been watching him out of the corner of her eye for countless stops as he sat in the seat beside hers. A teenager, maybe sixteen, his pure-black hair foisted off his scalp in every which direction and held in place by some foul-smelling spray. The only interruption to his reading was a quick call on his hand-phone. Discussion of a video game, mostly — and the mention of a girl. Now, the boy stood at the doors, grasping the hand strap as he waited for the subway to pull up to the platform. Flipped open his handphone once, probably to check the time. The doors opened and he slipped out coolly to go meet up with his friends.

That is youth, Eun-young thought. *That is what youth is* supposed *to be*.

Her thoughts lingered on her botched trip to Pusan during the Olympics as she closed in on her visit to Ji-young. Why did that hateful voyage stay in her mind now? It had to be more than this familiar feeling of arriving somewhere too late for her presence to have any impact. Why did this trouble her so much now?

Because Po had died of a broken heart.

That's right. His heart had just stopped beating. The same thing had happened to Eun-young's mother. She had been waiting, with a useless hope, for Eun-young to come back from wherever the Japanese had taken her — and knowing deep down that she wouldn't. Not ever. And her heart, shattered and weak, just gave up in the face of such horror and sadness. And the same thing had happened to Po. Waiting — and then just giving up.

And now here Eun-young was, so many years removed from those days, but facing it all over again. And it was Ji-young who was overwhelmed by that unshakeable sense of *han*, all that accumulated sadness strangling her. And waiting for the one person who could come and help her, who possessed the wisdom to ease that sorrow.

Her station came and Eun-young hobbled toward the doors. The subway stopped and she stepped out onto the platform. Walked through the turnstiles, then up the escalators that led to Ji-young's neighbourhood. A short walk down the main drag and she was at her apartment building, a low brown structure with old Hanja lettering over the door. Eun-young stepped into the lobby and made her rickety climb up to the second floor. On the landing, she paused before Ji-young and Chung Hee's embossed steel door. And then knocked. A moment of excruciating silence, and then the deadbolt turned. The door opened. And Ji-young appeared before her, wearing a black linen dress with matching kerchief tied over her hair. Her face looked utterly ancient in its sadness as it stared for a moment at her older sister standing at the threshold. Eun-young felt shame wash over her, felt like every stained cell of her body wanted to flake away, felt that every violation she had endured was now visible on her skin and that she could never —

"You came!" Ji-young said, and threw her arms around her sister.

"I'm so sorry," Eun-young wept. "I meant to come sooner. I did. It's just taken me a while. You know? It's taken me a while. I'm so sorry, Ji-young."

"Don't be foolish, don't be foolish, I understand, you're here now, please come in, come on in, my sister ..."

The apartment that Ji-young and Chung Hee shared was small but brightly lit, with real hardwood floors, Korean scroll paintings on the walls and a venerable jungle of houseplants — ferns and cacti and African violets — lined up on the rock ledge leading to the frosted door of the sunroom. On shelves everywhere were framed pictures of children and grandchildren.

"I'll make some tea," Ji-young said, squeezing her sister's hand. "Go sit in the sunroom and I'll bring it in to you."

Eun-young did what she was told. She slid open the frosted door and sat on one of the mats by the low cherry-wood table, tucking her legs under her and setting her cane against the wall.

Ji-young soon came in with a teapot and small ceramic cups arranged on a tray. She set them down on the table, positioning herself on the mat across from Eun-young's, and began to pour.

Eun-young reached out for her hands. "Perhaps under the circumstances, I should be serving you."

"Don't be silly. Here." And she handed her one of the steaming cups.

The two old women sat in silence for a moment, sipping their tea.

"Is Chung Hee home?"

"No. He went to the park to play *changgi* with some friends. He should be back soon."

"How is he?"

"Better than last week," Ji-young said with a nod. Sipped her tea and lowered her eyes. "Last week was very hard."

"And how are *you*, my sister?" Eun-young asked, trying to pry Ji-young's gaze back up. "You mentioned insomnia on the phone. Has it improved at all?"

"A little." Ji-young frowned, lowered her stare even more. Then she said: "I have been a fool."

"Oh Ji-young, why do you say such a thing?"

"I shouldn't have called you so late at night — and in the *state* I was in."

"No, it's fine. I shouldn't have stayed away for so long. I have been struggling, Ji-young, to know how to handle all of this. I'm not sure what you need, what any of the family needs from me, or where I fit in. I spoke to Jin-su after the funeral and she said —"

Ji-young turned her face up suddenly. "Eun-young, I need to *speak*."

Eun-young fell silent, and Ji-young went on.

"I know there are aspects of your life that I will never know about. You have endured things that I can't even comprehend.

All my life, I have looked up to you. I *know* how lucky I was, not to have gone through what you did. Everything I've been blessed with is a result of me being born five years after you. I *know* that. I know that whatever strife I have had in my life pales in comparison to yours. But Eun-young, I have lost my *daughter*. And I will not measure my pain against yours. It is not something one can measure. But it is *my* pain, Eun-young. And I need to speak it — to you."

"Speak," Eun-young said.

And so Ji-young did. She sipped her tea and spoke of Tae. Spoke of the enriching childhood she had tried to give her despite their joyless poverty throughout the fifties and sixties. Spoke of the reflection back to Ji-young of what Tae became as she grew older — suddenly obsessed with marriage and bearing children, the stones of obligations she would need to carry as a Korean woman. "I told her stories of my own desires for a family," Ji-young said. "I told her: 'Here I was, a girl of seventeen or eighteen, and my country was being ripped apart by war — and all I could think about was finding a man to marry and having his children.' Do you remember, Eun-young? Of course you do. I was *obnoxious*!" She spoke of how Tae had taken those same ambitions and warped them into something Ji-young could not approve of: a fixation on status, on what the neighbours thought, on her obsessions with social climbing and how Jin-su and Bum Suk were to be educated. It all seemed out of touch with everything Ji-young knew about how the world really worked. She had tried to steer Tae away from those hollow pits of materialism, the wealth she demanded of Minsu, the gadgetry she was always accumulating, the immense pressure she put on her children, to say to her: *Look at what your aunt went through — do you honestly think any of* this *matters so much?* But there were disappointments in Tae's life that Ji-young just couldn't get her to shake: the constant fights with Jin-su about how she should live *her* life; the stress she put on Minsu to climb the corporate ladder; the initial displeasure she showed (later reversed) when Bum Suk asked to study culinary arts in America. By the end, their house seemed saturated in conflict, to the point where Ji-young could hardly bear to visit. It was like Tae had a perpetual scowl branded onto her face. "I know her childhood had been hard. We had been so poor for so long. And I know that it bred these fears, these horribly shallow fixations of hers. But what? *What?* I wanted to scream at her. We all suffer hardships in our lives. I came to learn that my sister — you, dear Eun-young — was a *sex slave for the Japanese.* I watched our mother die of a heart attack when she was just thirty-nine. I watched our country torn apart and its fate decided by foreigners. It happened before my eyes. I always wanted to say to her: What is it in you, Tae, that makes you the way you are? We *all* suffer hardships. But eventually we learn a terrible truth about our lives. We learn that soon, the source of our unhappiness stops being about the traumatic things that happened, and *starts* being about how we've failed to deal with them. That's what I should have told her, but I never did. It was really the only wisdom I could give her. But she died before I thought enough to speak it."

Her sister's words left Eun-young shaking. A spasm she struggled to contain, to hide. She set her teacup down on the table but it upended with a rattle from her quavering. The spilt tea rushed to the raised edge of the cherry wood and spread like fingers. Reflexively, Ji-young reached out for the mess but Eun-young seized her by the hand. Her grip was fierce, the fist it made convulsing.

"Say it again."

"What?"

"Your wisdom — your wisdom to Tae. Say it again."

Ji-young rolled her eyes upward, as if trying to remember exactly what she had said. "How did it go? Oh yes. The source of our unhappiness stops being about the terrible things that happened to us and starts being about our failures to deal with them. The wrong choices we make to get beyond our traumas — *that* is what really makes us sad." She chuckled a little. "I should put it in a fortune cookie."

"Say it again."

"Eun-young, please. I should go get a cloth to clean this up."

Eun-young let her go and Ji-young climbed to her feet to go to the kitchen. While she was gone, Eun-young pulled herself completely inside her own mind. A mind that was suddenly hemorrhaging. She thought of Po, rotting away in that house in Pusan for nineteen years, pining for the wife who abandoned him. She thought of herself, living in stubborn solitude in her basement apartment with mould growing on the walls. And then she thought of Kim Hak Soon, the very first comfort woman to come forward, and the bravery she showed to tell her story in the hopes that it would change everything.

Ji-young came back with a cloth and began dabbing away at the spilt tea until it was gone. Just as she finished, they heard the apartment door open and Chung Hee come in. He set his keys down noisily on the chest of drawers in the living room and then called out for his wife.

"We're in here," Ji-young yelled back.

"We?" he asked as he came in to the sunroom, and saw Eun-young sitting on his floor. He stared at her blandly, his cheeks sinking a little.

"Hello, Chung Hee," she said.

"So you finally decided to pay us a visit, did you?"

"Yes, finally." She looked up at him in his tweed cap and collared shirt, his Confucius beard gray with age. Very much the Korean gentleman.

Ji-young, sensing this brief tension, tugged at her husband's pant leg. "How was the park?" she asked.

And then Chung Hee did a strange thing. He laughed a little, his shoulders heaving.

"What's so funny?" Ji-young asked.

"Oh, I really do need to tell you this," he said, sitting himself down next to them. "Ji-young, do you remember that young guy I was telling you about, the one the boys and I met at the park that time? Ho Su is his name." He turned to Eun-young. "He's maybe forty years old. A decent enough man. He works for government, and I must tell you he speaks and reads English *perfectly*. Anyway, he was there again today. And he told us all the most hilarious story. He got it from an American novel he had just finished reading. He's always reading American novels."

"What's the story?" Ji-young asked, curious.

"It was about this young couple on their wedding night," he replied. He turned to Eun-young again. "I hope you won't mind me telling this. It's a bit racy. Stop me if you think I'm going to offend you. But it was about these young newlyweds, very much in love, who both came to their wedding night as virgins. After their wedding, which was in New York City, they got a room in one of the best hotels in town. A honeymoon suite way up on the thirtieth floor or something, with a great view of Manhattan. It was a stifling summer night, so they opened the room's big windows to let some cool air in. After they did, the young bride went into the bathroom and closed the door to prepare herself for, you know …" He chuckled. "Oh, it *is* rather morbid. I don't know if I should tell you."

"Go on." Ji-young smiled.

"So while his new wife is in the bathroom, the young man gets very excited, dancing around the room and throwing his arms in the air. He is, after all, about to lose his virginity to the woman he loves. In his enthusiasm, he climbs onto the hotel bed and begins jumping up and down on it. Imagine this: a young guy, maybe twenty-three, and he knows he's about to make love for the first time. He's so excited, and he's jumping up and down on the bed, higher and higher, as if it were a trampoline — so excited, so *excited*! He's jumping higher and higher, like a little boy. And then he jumps so high that he loses control of his jumping, and he leaps clean out of the open windows and falls —" Chung Hee's eyes were watering now. "— and falls thirty stories to his *death*!"

Eun-young watched her sister. Ji-young had placed a hand over her mouth.

"So of course," Chung Hee said, barely able to continue, "a few minutes later the blushing bride comes out of the bathroom, wearing some kind of gaudy lingerie, looks around the empty room, and thinks, *Where* the hell *did my husband go?*" Chung Hee had nearly keeled over now.

Eun-young was still staring at her sister, waiting for her to move her hand away, waiting to see the reaction underneath. Her eyes gave away no clues. When Ji-young did lower her hand, Eun-young saw a mouth shaped into a little *O* of joy. The way her brow had loosened, the way her shoulders moved, she could tell that Ji-young had, for just that instant, forgotten her grief. Had allowed herself to partake in this brief moment of silliness.

"Oh Chung Hee, that's a *terrible* story," Ji-young laughed. "It's a terribly hilarious story."

They both turned to look at Eun-young. A little worried that this talk of sex and death and a ruined opportunity had upset her.

She surprised them both. She surprised herself. "That *is* an amusing story," she said, feeling her lips curl upward into a smile.

CHAPTER 22

This is how I'm dealing with the past. By putting one word in front of the other, this thing I once tried so hard to do, this act of aggression against the page, vandalizing it with my thoughts, my voice, my words, my *perspective*. It's indecent, it's arrogant, it's an act of thievery and narcissism. That's why I was so terrible at it. I couldn't muster enough egotism to do it properly. I balked under the responsibility of stealing stories and claiming them as my own. I did not inherit my mother's pristine self-absorption the way my sister did. I was always the quiet, rumpled guy in the corner who spoke little and was afraid to ask the tough questions. It all seemed like robbery to me. I failed at it; I failed spectacularly. But now, here, on the other side of the world, I'm putting one word in front of the other. I'm crafting a story that doesn't belong to me. I'm taking these horrific leaps of faith, extrapolating on things I barely understand, filling in the blanks with my imagination, everything I was taught not to do.

And I'm loving every minute of it.

Paul sees me in the grip of my little project and thoroughly approves. He's convinced that this book, or whatever it is, has been given to me by divine intervention. He lives vicariously through my enthusiasm. I get up and work in my room with the door closed in those slow morning hours before we need to report to the *hagwon* in the early afternoon. Paul's role, which he embraces happily, is to pass by my room at that precise moment when, if I don't stop I'll make us both late, and knock on my door, once, a single thump of his knuckle that yanks me out of my head and tells me it's time to go. I sign off and go shower, get dressed and gather up my lesson plans and half-marked essays, and then we're off, out into the grey winter streets of Daechi with its Hangul signage and red crosses. On those walks to the school, Paul puts me at ease to share with him what I'm working on, and I do, telling him things that I don't even tell Jin. The reason I'm so open with Paul is because he's so open with me. I learn it's been five years since he was "saved" and he hasn't looked back. Every thought, every plan, everything he does now is varnished in the gleam of Christ, and he sees his new life, everything that he's been given, as "awesome" — awesome in the truest sense of the word. He is struck with awe. "God's love and purpose is so *awesome*," he says. He's not trying to evangelize my soul, at least not intentionally. He's just so excited by his life's new course. And I find that, on our walks to school, I can tell him about myself and my project: what I'm learning about the Korean identity, the rape camps in China, what Eun-young would have gone through, all the things that the Japanese did. Paul can relate to how a newfound obsession can bring desperately needed focus.

Christmas comes and goes, New Years comes and goes, and on a smoggy-grey day in late January, a package arrives from Canada. The University of Ottawa. I am *in*! I had no doubts at all. With this news, my days of slinging English at the *hagwon* already begin to feel like the past, like they belong to somebody else. I talk to Ms. Kim about my contract. She asks if I'll stay on until May. I agree. I email Justin in Halifax and tell him the good news. He emails me back, excited for me, and offers what I had hoped he'd offer: to put Jin and me up for the summer until we move to Ottawa. Justin has some news of his own: he has resumed his full-time teaching job at his old high school, and he has also begun dating somebody. Has fallen in love for the first time in forever. His emails radiate a kind of excitement and hope that I didn't think possible of him. He's turned a corner. He writes and says as much. "Life isn't perfect, but it's good," he writes.

I couldn't agree more. I imagine my life nine months from now and grow lightheaded. I will be a student for the first time in ten years, studying to be a proper teacher. I will also be spending my free time working on a book about the comfort women of Korea. And I will be living with Jin, and we'll begin planning our lives together. Of course she will be lonely at times and long for Seoul. We will squabble. There will be days when I'm frustrated with being a student again — studying, being *theoretical* about everything, not earning money, surrounded by people younger and less experienced than me. And there will be days when I doubt that I can even write a book, when putting one word after the other seems so hard, so impossible, the most impossible thing in the world to do. Life will not be perfect. But it will be good. It will be better than good. It will be — what's the word?

It will be *awesome*.

"May seems a bit early," Jin says when I tell her about my contract talks with Ms. Kim. We're having lunch together at a diner near the school. I was late arriving to meet her, couldn't yank myself out of the book in time, and she stood out in the February cold waiting for me. Now, even with our food here, she still seems cold. She shivers each time the diner door opens as another group of patrons come in.

"What do you mean?" I ask, chopsticking some bean sprout into my mouth.

"Michael, my father's birthday is in June," she replies. "I'd really like to be around for that." She's barely touched her own lunch, a dish of kimchi *bokembop*. It sits on its oval plate in a greasy mass of orange that she moves listlessly around with her spoon.

"I don't have to go in May," I say. "I mean, my job will wrap up then, but I could stick around Seoul for a month or two after that."

"And do *what*? Michael, where would you live?"

"I don't know," I say honestly. "Maybe a love motel. I could —"

"For two months?" She shakes her head. "You're crazy. Every day you stay in Seoul without work will cost you thousands of won that you should be saving for school. No, you should definitely go home in May. Especially if Justin has offered to put you up for the summer."

He's offered to put us *up for the summer*. "All right," I sigh. "So what, then? Tell me how it's going to work, Jin."

Her bottom lip comes out and I watch her downcast eyes. She's thinking hard. "Maybe I'll fly to Canada later, by myself. I could come in July."

"So we'd be apart for two months."

"I don't know what else to do. Michael, you have to understand how big this is for me. I talked to my managers about working remotely from Canada. They said absolutely not. And now that I've brought up the idea of quitting on them, they've put me in their — how you say — *bad radar*."

"What difference does it make?" I ask. "Jin, if five months from now you're going to be living with me in Canada, who cares what they think of you now?"

"You don't understand. You've been through this before, but I haven't. I don't know what it's like to let go of one life and completely embrace another. My future has *never* been open-ended, Michael. Not once. You have to know how hard it'll be for me to buy a one-way plane ticket to some place called *Halifax*."

"Look, if this is about work, don't worry. I have savings, you have savings. We're going to be fine."

"It's not about work," she mumbles.

"And it's not about your father's birthday, is it?"

"No."

"Then what is it, Jin?"

She says nothing. Scoops a little *bokembop* into her mouth. Shivers again as the diner door opens for another group of hungry Koreans.

"Jin, do you *want* to come to Canada?" I ask for the thousandth time.

"I'm scared to come to Canada."

"That doesn't answer my question."

She glances over to another table, where two middle-aged Korean women are sitting by the window overlooking the street. Their faces are old and harsh-looking. They're leaning in to each other.

"You see those two *a'jumah* over there?" Jin says *sotto voce*. "They've been staring at us since we sat down."

"Really?" I say, turning.

"Don't *look*." She licks her lips. "They're talking about us under their breath. They don't like us. They don't like me sitting here having lunch with a foreign man."

"That's ridiculous," I say. "Jin, this is Daechi. There are English *hagwons* on every corner. They probably see mixed couples sitting together all the time."

"Doesn't mean they *like* it," she says.

"Can we stay on topic, please?"

"No. They're making me uncomfortable. Can we leave?"

"Fine."

I pay our bill and then we get up to go, leaving our half-finished lunches behind. On the way, Jin halts at the women's table. They stop talking and look at her, a little bashful, unaware that she had caught snippets of their conversation. I double back and take her by the wrist.

"C'mon, Jin."

But before I can pull her away, she manages to snarl one sentence at them. The only word I catch that I know for sure is *Hangukin*. Meaning: a Korean person. As opposed to *Hangul*: the Korean language. So she said something like: I am a Korean. Or: I am still a Korean, you know.

Out on the chilly February sidewalk, Jin and I stand staring at each other. Eventually, I glance at my watch. "I should get to the school," I say.

"Yeah, I need to go, too." She sees the worry that has suddenly slumped my shoulders. She touches my fingers with her own, gives them a jiggle, in reassurance. "Michael, I'll look into a plane ticket for July. We can fly to Canada separately. I know it's not ideal, but it's the best I can offer."

"Jin, I won't make you do anything you don't want to do."

"Yes, you will. Either way, Michael, you will."

Either way? What the hell does that *mean?*

I move in to kiss her goodbye, but she pulls away from me — exactly like she did on our first date.

Her eyes flicker to the women in the window. I turn. They *are* staring at us.

"Jin, we've been dating for *two years*."

"I have to go."

"Jin —"

"No. I have to go. I'll call you later."

And she leaves me there on the sidewalk.

. . . .

The traffic of Seoul is no longer alien to me. This pulse, this pound, this rush of streets and buildings, these buses and subways, these *soju* tents and street markets, the road-side bins of rotten kimchi, the iron gates, the palaces, the pagodas, the bland government buildings, the litter, the convenience stores, the lugubrious Han River holding its ancient secrets to its breast — I know it all. How far I have come in these two short years. There are 11 million people here, spread out in this breathtaking megalopolis, and yet I feel in complete command of its geography. There is no neighbourhood I couldn't find. No moment when I feel that expat's fear of being lost and in free fall. I sense that gravitational pull that ensnares so many of my fellow teachers — to stay, to stay indefinitely no matter what your plans were when you came, no matter the status of your student loans or who is waiting for you on the other side of the world. To stay. To live this life of zero expectation, zero pressure to do anything more, to *be* anything more. I wonder if other expats feel this way in the last couple of months before they leave. This sense of a great interregnum. This time in between, the accomplishment of living in Seoul and knowing you could thrive there, but knowing also that you'll leave it behind. I feel a sense of privilege knowing that I get to leave.

And in these last couple of months, I want to soak up as much as I can. I head off one night to Myeung-dong to meet up with Jon Hung at an upscale cocktail bar. He has given up his corporate gig at the KOSPI and returned to teaching — this time at one of the universities. Like Rob Cruise before him, he finds it doesn't pay enough, and so he's constantly on the hustle for privates on the side, commuting around the city like a madman to sling English at Korean housewives. He looks worn down by this grind, unable to see much beyond the tip of his nose. He also moved in with a new girl a couple months ago — trying this "monogamy thing," as he calls it — but is considering breaking it off, hates the way she "bosses him." He asks less about my plans for the spring and more about my life right now. He is baffled, but oddly envious that I have stayed at ABC English Planet this entire time, and that I'm still with Jin. He wants to know what it's like, that *constancy*. I tell him how it's helped me find my focus, locate my place back in the world, and my way out of Korea. He doesn't quite believe me. "I can't ever see leaving. I think I'm going to be here forever." He says this in a neutral way, like it's neither good nor bad. "And you'll be back," he sniffs. "If you're staying with Jin, you'll be back."

I shrug. "Of course, to visit."

And here he grumbles about there being nothing for guys like us back in North America. Nothing this good, nothing this *easy*. "I think you'll come back here to work. I've seen it a thousand times. Guys like us say we'll leave Korea, but we always come back. After a while, you realize there's nothing left for you anywhere else."

I smile at how wrong he is. And I feel sorry for him. He asks about Justin. I tell him he's back in Halifax, and that Jin and I will be staying with him for the summer.

"What's he doing?" Jon asks.

"He's teaching," I reply.

"You mean *teaching* teaching?"

"Yeah, teaching teaching." Again, Jon is perplexed. He can't fathom how one lets go of Seoul and all its stimuli, and moves back, *settles* back to a small city on the periphery of Canada. It breaks his brain to think of it.

If Jon Hung represents the old guard in this interregnum, then Purposeful Paul represents the new. He may not have tried to indoctrinate me into his born-again beliefs, but he has succeeded in indoctrinating me into his other passion — international rugby. It's the remaining holdout, the sole vestige from his previously un-Christian life. On weekends, we ride the subway into Itaewon to watch his beloved All Blacks on the big screen TV at Gecko's. I wear the T-shirt that Paul gave me when we first became roommates. The atmosphere at Gecko's is electric on these Saturday afternoons, powered by beer and global camaraderie. The place teems with Brits and Kiwis and Aussies and Koreans. Even the bombastic GIs pay deference to the manly ultra-violence radiating from the screen. On the first Saturday that Paul and I come here, he takes the time to explain the rules of rugby to me, and also the history of the All Blacks' signature custom at the beginning of a game: the hauka, a traditional Maori war dance. He even demonstrates it for me, there in the crowded bar. Imagine: this a geeky, born-again New Zealand Christian with his face now contorted by intense guttural rumblings, his arms swinging and chopping, his hips and knees pumping stiffly. *"Kam'atay! Kam'atay!"* he barks and sways, while the drinkers around us watch on awkwardly. This is what I love about Paul: he is so completely unselfconscious, so happily ensconced in his true nerdy self here in the madness of Itaewon's sleaze. He smiles at me when he finishes. "Now you try it, Michael."

I raise my stein to him. "I'm good. I think you nailed it, Paul."

I have to admit, I'm not here in Itaewon strictly for the rugby. I am also searching for rumours of Rob Cruise. I can't help it. I have not seen nor heard from him since last summer. In this bar, on these streets, his presence floats through the wreckage of weekends. Here in Itaewon I run into people

I know or know of: former teachers at ABC English Planet or other teachers who know or knew him. They all have stories to tell when I posit, "So has anyone heard from Rob?" There are tales of fistfights with U.S. marines, reports of a run-in with Korean police and threats of deportation. Someone says: Did you know he slept with my director's sister? Or: He slept with my director's wife. He slept with my roommate. He slept with my best friend. He slept with this chick I'm tutoring. Me, I want to say: He slept with my girlfriend, but that was before I met her. The consensus is clear: He's a pig; he's a charlatan; he's larger than life; don't trust him around your woman; but man, he's so well-connected — if you need a job in Seoul, he's the guy to talk to. Through it all, Rob's whereabouts become apocryphal:

I heard he got cancer.

I heard he got *married.*

He must have moved away by now. He still can't be teaching here, can he?

Purposeful Paul is aghast and mildly intrigued. "Who *is* this guy?" he asks me. And I think of degrees of separation. This expat community really is a queer family tree, a microcosm of generations. Teachers who knew teachers who knew teachers who …

I give Paul's shoulder a friendly shake. "You don't want to know," I tell him. Meaning: If you met Rob, you'd want to do what I wanted to do — try and *save* him.

Somehow Jin and I make it through my last eight weeks in the country, this dance to the end. We survive the ambiguous airstreams surrounding our noncommittal conversations, and the concomitant results: the listless, half-hearted lovemaking that now soils my bed. An unsatisfying union of bodies divorced from their preoccupied minds. Jin clings to me afterwards, there in the mess of sheets, but in a way that makes me feel unsafe, unsettled, like I'm fading uncontrollably into death and she's just a loved one at my side, saying goodbye.

We make it through these last eight weeks and I find myself at the comical end of my *hagwon* tenure. In the final few nights, the kids get wind that I won't be back after Friday, that I'm going home to Canada. *"Really?"* groans John, groans Jenny, groans Sue. "F minus!" someone exclaims from the back row. I'm touched. I had no idea.

On my penultimate shift, one of my youngest students, Jennifer, makes a shy approach to my desk after class to give me a homemade card. Hands it over in the respectful Korean way — both thumbs clamping it as she extends her arms toward me and bows her head. But as soon as I've taken it she scurries off, embarrassed, out the door to join her friends before I can read it. I look down at its yellow construction paper. Taped to the front is a photo of us taken about a month ago by one of the front-counter staff on the day that Jennifer finished Basic 5 and moved up to Junior 1. I'm standing tall behind her, mentor-like as she beams proudly into the camera. The inside of the card is adorned with girlish stickers of stars and Asian cartoon characters. In green pencil crayon, she has written:

> Dear Mikal teacher,
>   This is Jennifer. I will miss you. Thank you so much for teaching me Engrish. You are a very kind man, even though you are balding. Good luck in Canada.

God, I *will* miss their backhanded compliments, their lopsided logic.

On my last day, I go through Ms. Kim's insistent ritual — the other teachers gathered around as she makes a big presentation of giving me a gift for my two-and-a-half years of service. I know not to open it in front of her, so instead I put it in my satchel and bow deeply to her. As I'm about to leave for the night, leave the *hagwon* forever, she comes over and touches my arm. I've never seen her touch anyone before. "You are a good teacher, Michael," is all she says, then returns to her desk, to the piles of paperwork overflowing on it.

Back at the apartment, amidst my packed-up luggage and bare walls, I open what Ms. Kim gave me. Fittingly, it's a pen. A very good pen. One to write things with.

Work backwards to a 5:10 flight and you'll learn the absurdity of the modern condition. Two hours for the commute out to Incheon (just to be safe), two hours for security (just to be safe), and we're left with barely enough time for a hasty goodbye lunch with Paul before we scuttle off with my bags in tow to the bus station near the COEX. Yes, I say *we*. Jin is joining me on the trek out to the airport, has eschewed another Saturday shift (risking a deeper foray into her boss's "bad radar") so she can see me off. Airport goodbye, kiss-kiss, hug-hug, that romantic-comedy classic. Seems appropriate and worth the risk to her career, considering what's about to happen to me.

The three of us go for lunch at a seafood joint near Seoulleung Station, a place with huge bubbling aquaria out front housing crabs the size of monsters. I stack my suitcases near the door, much to the chagrin of the wait staff, and then we park ourselves on the floor around a low ornate table. Jin orders our lunches with icy Korean efficiency, and then says nothing, or almost nothing, for the duration of the meal. Paul fills in the blanks, warms our chilly awkwardness with jokes and high praise for me as a roommate. A great guy to live with, wink-wink. The food takes forever to come. I'm glancing at my watch, cognizant of the hour, cognizant of the modern condition. I think: two hours' commute to Incheon Airport, two hours' grace for security. I think: 10.5 to Vancouver, 4.5 to Toronto, and two to Halifax. Plus layovers. What's that? A late-night touchdown, Justin bleary-eyed at Arrivals but happy to see me. Twelve hours after that, he and I will be sitting at a patio bar in downtown Halifax, bottles of Alexander Keith's stuffed in our fists.

I look at Jin, next to me here on the floor. So distracted, so anxious to get going. I think: where's our damn food?

It comes, finally, and we eat and chat and toast to my good health. Paul's a bit overboard by the end. Speaks of my kindness, my generous soul. When we finish eating, he pays the whole bill for us, won't take a single won from me. Outside on the sidewalk, he's fully aware now of his status as a third wheel. Maybe he knows what's coming. He gives me a hug as I stand there with my bags and whispers in my ear, "May God keep you, Michael. May God keep you, no matter what." He says goodbye to Jin; he'll never lay eyes on her again. Then he's off, down this neon-choked street back to the apartment I no longer live in to get ready for his day. He's got a private at 2:30.

We cab it to the bus station and then stand in the wicket line for tickets. I pay for us both, my wallet fat with both Korean and Canadian bills. Jin says nothing, won't even look at me, as I hand over her printed slip.

Naturally, I overestimated things: The commute to Incheon Airport does not take two hours. Jin *knew* that I had overestimated. Sitting there in our raised leather bus seats, staring out the tinted window, I find myself cursing this traffic-less highway that loops and churns past high-rise condo buildings and office towers, carting along the Han River and then up and up and out of the city. The mudflats of Incheon appear all around us in less than an hour. My stomach does a horrible roll. We're going to have an embarrassment of time together at the airport. I touch Jin's fingers, there on the armrest. They're cold.

"You're so quiet today," I tell her.

Her chin is buried between her clavicles. "This is very hard," she says, almost childlike.

"I know."

Inside the massive terminal, one gets a whiff in the air that this is a place in between, a nexus, an embassy, a consulate. You stack your bags on one of those L-shaped carts and push the short end around, looking for direction, to be taken in, to be adopted, to become ensconced into the protocols of your chosen airline. Jin knows this airport like a second home and leads me exactly where I need to go. The Air Canada counter is only modestly busy, the line snaking through a couple of turns in that rat maze they make you walk through. I imagine us late instead of ridiculously early: We'd get me checked in and then rush off to the security gates; a quick, efficient goodbye, lacking in melodrama — *have a safe flight, call me when you land, no problem, and Jin would you book that ticket for July already* — and I wouldn't have to stew in my anxieties for another hour or two. Jin stays with me in this line while I climb the ranks, my bags piled onto the cart in front of us, and before long I'm at the front and then waved over to check in. The woman at the counter is crisply official, her face painted in just the right amount of makeup. She is Korean, but addresses me in flawless, unaccented English. I half expect a minor interrogation: *How long have you been in Korea? Why are you leaving? What are you going to do back in Canada?* But nothing of the sort. Just takes my name and the name of my destination. Checks her computer. Asks to see my ticket. Asks to see my passport. Glances at the picture and then flips through the glossy pages, perhaps checking for a visa violation. Asks how many bags. *Lift them up here, please.* Weighs each one; they're a bit on the heavy side; perhaps considers charging me extra; decides against it. Prints off the tags, those long strips of barcode-covered stickers. Peels them back and loops them around the handles of my bags, seals them shut. Presses a button and off my bags go, clomping onto the conveyor belt like a line of lazy horses. See you in Halifax, Michael. All that I'm left with is my carry-on bag weighed down by books and slung over my neck and shoulder. The woman prints my boarding pass, circles the gate, circles the time, then gestures in the general direction of security. *Have a great flight. Next please.*

Funny how she didn't need to ask whether Jin was coming with me.

So here we are in this enormous edifice with nothing left to do but say goodbye. We wordlessly agree to drag out our suffering and wander off towards the brightly lit shops that surround the security gates. The stores here display all manner of overpriced mementos and touristy knick knacks. "My God," I say as we meander, "this isn't an airport; this is a mall where planes just happen to land."

"That's funny," Jin says without laughing.

We hold hands as we browse around the displays and shelves. One shop sells little wooden boxes of ginseng wrapped in cellophane. Another sells porcelain dolls of Korean girls decked out in the pastel blooms of *hanbok*. I pick one up, run my finger over its braided hair and down the silky material of its dress. The face is so tight, so virginal. *I can be yours for the right price*, it says. I wave the doll at Jin, touch its nose to hers. *"Hanbok,"* I say, and she nods solemnly. "Should I buy one?" She just shakes her head.

Out of the tense boredom of this wait, we decide to take the escalators up to the second floor in an exploratory wander. Up here, we discover an unwelcoming corporate utopia: expensive cocktail lounges and upscale restaurants with track lighting and angular mobiles dangling from the ceiling. We stroll past their heavy black doors and velvet ropes. "Are you hungry?" I ask Jin.

"Not at all," she replies.

Still, I check the menus posted outside out of curiosity. "Good lord," I whistle, "12,000 won for a *bibimbap*? This really is a place for people who know nothing of Korea." I look at her. "Am I right?" She agrees, but then looks off vaguely down the hall. *Jesus, Jin*, I think. *Jesus Christ. I'm trying here. Can you at least acknowledge that I'm trying?*

Back down to the main level, we decide to settle into the chairs on the opposite side from the security gates. It's quiet over here, away from the line-ups and storefronts. Jin takes my hand after we sit, laces her fingers into mine, and rests her head on my shoulder. Stays like that for a long time. I think: *this is so nice*. She wants to feel my skin on hers, wants to rest her head in the groove of my neck. This is perfect. No plane trip and two months apart could sunder this moment of tenderness.

We stay like that for a long time. Maybe we even fall asleep a bit, there in our chairs. Time seems to liquefy, streak away like wax off a burning candle. I eventually look at my watch.

"Shit, I should probably go through."

We stand in unison; and as I turn, I see that Jin has begun to weep.

"Why are you crying?" I ask.

She wipes the tears away, clinically, little tugs with the heel of her hand. She returns to me then, in full force.

"Michael, I'm not coming with you to Canada," she says.

I swallow. Stand there, silent. I know exactly what she means, but decide to play dumb. "Of course you aren't. You don't even have a plane ticket. Jin, we've talked about this so many times. You're coming in July instead."

She shakes her head. "You know that's not true. Michael, we both need to admit, here and now, that that's not true."

I try to laugh. "C'mon, you have no idea how nice Halifax is in the summer. You'll miss the buskers if you wait until the fall and meet me in Ottawa."

"Don't joke. Don't torture me."

Stay ignorant. No matter what, stay ignorant. "Jin, I know this is an emotional day for you."

"Michael, stop it. I'm not going to join you in Canada. You know that I can't. This has to end. Today."

"What, at Incheon fucking Airport? Oh come *on*." I reach out for her hand but she steps back from me, out of reach, as if I've already become a stranger to her. I press my lips together. Grit my teeth. "What is this about? Are you worried about your dad? He'll be fine. Carl comes home next month and can look after him. Are you thinking you'll be left out, that you'll miss things? Jin, it doesn't matter. I promise you, we'll come back here as often as we can. Three times a year, four times a year, ten times a year if need be. I don't give a *shit*."

"Michael, you're being ridiculous."

Despite my best effort to fend it off, I feel a hollow resignation come over me. It seeps into my bloodstream like lead. She has been waiting all day to spring this trap on me. No. She's been waiting weeks, months. Ever since her mother died, really. Nine months of corroding cowardice, of self deception, of procrastination. Waiting until I'm standing right at the gates to my future before she musters the courage to carve herself out of it.

"So, what?" I say. "We split now, here at the airport? You couldn't do this sooner?"

"I'm sorry," she says. "This is the hardest thing I've ever had to do."

"And so what's next, Jin? You get back on the bus to Seoul? Go back to your job, back to your father's home? Wear *hanbok* on holidays and wait for a nice Korean man to marry you? Is that what you're telling me? Is that what you want?"

Her accent seems so thick now when she speaks. "If it's any consolation to you, no Korean will want to marry me. I carry the stink of other men's pleasure on my body."

"How can you fucking *say* that?" I'm just about ready to vomit. "What would your *eemo halmoney* think if she heard you talk like that? Eun-young would know, Jin. It's disgraceful that you'd say that. About *us*. You don't know what you're talking about."

She looks not at me nor beyond me, not at the floor in shame. She just sort of floats there in her thoughts, a dark searching stare.

"Look, let's give this a week," I say. "I'll call you from Halifax next weekend. We'll talk it over, and if you still feel —"

"No. I've made up my mind. I'm sorry, Michael. I'm so *sorry*. I will never forgive myself. I know I should have done this sooner, and that I'm a coward for waiting until now. But that's the way it is. I'm sorry. But I've had to make some hard decisions in my life, about what I really need to be. I am transforming into someone you won't recognize. The old Jin is gone. She's *been* gone for a long while now."

"Jin, you don't need to do this. I will follow you wherever you need to go."

"You can't follow me, Michael."

"I can. Please. You don't need to do this."

"I do. I have to do this."

"But *why*?"

"Because I need to be Korean."

She quakes there under the weight of that declaration. So alone, so fragile, and yet so determined. Resolved to leap off the ledge that I can't talk her down from.

She wipes the snot from her nose. "I will never forget you. You are such a good man. You are. *Believe* that you are, Michael. And there is a part of my heart that will always —"

But I turn on my heels; a swing of my carry-on, and I am fucking out of there — off toward the security gates. I will not allow her to finish me off. I don't even look back. Not once. It's true. I leave her standing there in mid-sentence. Let her quaver under the destruction she has wrought. I don't look back. Not once.

I get in line at the gate, surrounded now by strangers. There is a glass case to our right displaying the array of personal items we're no longer allowed to take on board, like a police line-up of brands and logos: canisters of shaving cream, tubes of liquids and gels and sprays. And next to the display, big garbage bins in which to dump your belongings if necessary. I march through the frosted partition and the line bifurcates. Soon someone in an airport uniform waves me forward toward the long metal table. Makes me go through the security rituals. And what rituals they've become. Dump keys and watch and pens and coins into this little plastic tub, their collection plate. Off it goes on their conveyor belt toward the X-ray machine. (I worry vaguely about someone on the other side nabbing my stuff.) Now take off your shoes, put them up here. Really? Yes, take off your shoes, sir. Got a laptop? Take it out, please. Open it up. Turn it on for us. (They swipe it down with this oversized Q-tip.) Okay. Turn it off, close it up. You can go through now. (I stroll over the metal detector's threshold with civilian innocence.) Beep beep. Okay, stand here, sir. Sweep sweep with the wand, and they find the culprit. Undo your belt, sir. Hold it open, nice and wide. Sweep

sweep with the wand. Turn around. Lift your arms up, please. Sweep sweep with the wand. Okay, you can put your arms down. Move back to the table. I do to discover them checking my bag with their rubber-gloved hands, rooting and rooting. Behind them, supervisors watch to make sure everything is done right, the sacraments of this near-religious ceremony. Finally they say: you can go now. And I'm left to pack up everything, my whole life, all that they've disassembled and left strewn here. I do up my belt, reload my pockets, put on my shoes, strap down my laptop, fasten up my satchel, and sling it back over my shoulder, check for my boarding pass, and then I'm in one piece again and finally free to go.

And do you want to know the funny thing? I barely make it to my gate on time. They've already started pre-boarding the plane when I get there.

There is something about the airport in Halifax. It's on the outskirts of the city, way out there, really, and its runways are surrounded by deep, thick forest. It makes for a strange land-ing experience. Your plane will glide over trees for the longest time, hovering above the unforgiving wilderness as you make your long descent toward the ground. It seems to take forever. You can't see the airport from where you sit. You'll stare out your window, down at the spruce racing toward the belly of your ship, and there will come a point at the end when you're sure that the runway's not even there, that the forest is truly endless, and that your plane has no choice but land on top of it. You will doubt the sound of the landing gear coming down. You'll doubt the sense of slowness coming over the cabin, the gradual lunge for-ward. You will hover over the trees; you can almost smell the sap in their branches. But then the runway does appear in a flash, coming out of nowhere, its long strip of pavement ready to embrace you. And you feel that godless bump of tires touching tarmac and hear the roar of your engines as they negotiate the newfound earth. And you will be home.

It is late at night when my plane begins its descent into Halifax. Up here, I can see the lights of the far-off city hugging the harbour as I press my face against the window. Even in the pitch blackness beyond those lights, I sense the shape of a peninsula. It is the city. It is the land. This is not an island, floating alone in the sea. There is that sliver of ground that connects this shape to something larger. Connects it to everything. I watch that land, its trees, rise up to meet me. I brace myself for its touch.

To believe in a peninsula is to believe that you are not alone. That there is something there connecting you, plugging you in to something bigger. I swallow to keep my ears from popping as we make that last turn toward home. I ready myself for the scream of engines. The tires float over the top of trees, impossibly close, impossibly close. And then there it is: the runway. And when we finally touch down, I feel myself yanked forward with a great surge.

CHAPTER 23

She knew the directions for getting there by heart, had committed them to memory years ago even though she had never gone, not once in the decade since the House of Sharing had opened. Eun-young knew that this was a bizarre sort of reasoning: to want to know exactly how to find this place without ever feeling, until now, the gravitational pull to go there. It surprised her how easy it was to implement the directions that she had engraved into her brain. She took the 1113 bus to Kwangju and then a taxi from Twaechon terminal right to the House's front courtyard, which overlooked six acres of property and the serene permanence of mountains in the distance.

She watched it all materialize in the cab's windows as they pulled up. When they did, she paid her driver and then clambered out on her cane. Closed the door and stood there in perfect stillness as the taxi pulled away. The air was crisp with the first hints of autumn, cooler here than in Seoul. She looked up at the six mismatched buildings of the compound. How ordinary they seemed, she thought, so different from the monolithic image she had assigned to them in her mind. Still, there was no mistaking this place: out front of the courtyard, standing on a tall plinth, was a bronze statue of a comfort woman. Eun-young shuffled over to it and craned her neck upward to look at the brown face as it gazed out stoically. The woman, frozen in her sadness and accusation, was exactly what she was meant to be — a stolid totem to the unspeakable.

As Eun-young moved up to the main building and into the museum lobby, she sensed a paralysis come over her, her shoulders tightening with unmistakable claustrophobia as she stood near the arched windows facing out to the grounds' grassy perimeter. In the foyer, a young woman manning the front desk looked up from her paperback and smiled when she saw Eun-young. "Welcome to the House of Sharing," she called over. "Come on in. We *are* open." Without waiting, the girl began to assemble an assortment of brochures by rote and then extended them to Eun-young as she took her tentative steps toward the desk. The girl watched as Eun-young didn't even look at the pamphlets after she took them; so she began explaining aloud how the House worked: there was the museum proper, she said, two dormitories that housed the grandmothers (that's how they were to be referred to — the *grandmothers*) who lived in the compound full-time, as well as a temple for praying, an educational centre, and a gallery for the paintings that the grandmothers created during their "art therapy" sessions. "There are also gardens all around the property that you're welcome to look at," she said. Eun-young knew every one of these facts already, had read about them a hundred times before coming here. The girl's face blossomed with curiosity. "And what brings you to visit us today?" But Eun-young said nothing, didn't even nod as she limped past the desk, past the girl, and deeper into the House.

She crept solemnly into the first exhibit she came across: the Room of Proof. Long hardwood floors, track lighting on the ceiling, and walls holding rows upon rows of mounted photos. They were black-and-white images, taken in and around the rape stations during the war. Eun-young paused, then stepped up to the first one by the entrance. The grainy picture showed three Japanese soldiers standing over a group of young women squatting in the mud. The men smiled gamely for the camera while the girls' faces were downcast and blankly obedient. One of them was clearly pregnant. Eun-young glanced away from the picture, from the sudden bloom of memory it caused. She moved farther along the room. The next photo showed Japanese soldiers lined up outside what was clearly a rape stall. They were laughing amongst themselves as they waited their turn. Another memory spread like ink through Eun-young's mind. The sound of: *Hayaku! Hayaku! Hurry up! Hurry up, it's my turn!* Phrases she hadn't heard, hadn't thought of, in decades.

She stepped back, and back again, nearly to the centre of the room as claustrophobia slammed into her once more. She circulated her gaze around this dimly lit space. Every one of these pictures depicted something that Eun-young identified with instantly, a memory that she had buried under the waves of her swelling *han*. A tent. A truck. A wooden building. A glimpse of the Chinese countryside. Framed displays of identification papers, yellow and faded, marked with stamps she hadn't seen in sixty years. She stood frozen there among them.

A couple of people came in through the doors on the opposite side of the room. Eun-young kept her head low as she listened to their voices echo around the walls in mid conversation. The first belonged to a young woman. The second belonged to a man. She listened intently. When she caught enough of the man's voice, Eun-young jolted under the sound of it. He clearly worked at the House as a guide, was explaining something to the girl, but his accent was all wrong. It was *wrong*. There was no mistake that he was speaking Korean — in fact, he was speaking an obscure dialect from Daegu — but his accent was *all wrong*.

His accent drove bayonets into Eun-young's ears.

She looked up. The young man was maybe in his mid-thirties, with long black hair pulled into a ponytail. He was dressed in slacks and a collared shirt with a plastic nametag fastened to his breast pocket. The girl he was speaking to looked like a university student: she had a canvas knapsack on her back and an assiduous look on her face. The man was just wrapping up an explanation of how the grandmothers went by bus to the Japanese Embassy in Seoul every Wednesday for their weekly protest. When he finished, the girl touched his arm and thanked him, and he bowed to her and waved goodbye. When she was gone, he was left alone in the room with Eun-young. He glanced over at her and bowed again, more deeply this time.

"Welcome to the House of Sharing," he called across to her.

Fury rose up in her cheeks. She shambled over and got right into his face. "You're *Japanese*," she barked.

He nodded with weary resignation. "I am, yes."

"What, what are you *doing* here?"

"I am a guide."

"*Obviously*. But, but you know what I mean. How on Earth — how do they …"

He just looked at her.

"How on Earth," she tried again, "do they allow a *Japanese man* to work in a place like this?" Her eyes dipped for a moment to his nametag. It read "Sokasu" but was spelled out in Korean characters. *So'ka'su.*

He tried to smile at her. "I get that question all the time." When she didn't reciprocate, he added, "It's a very long story."

"I want to hear it," she said. "Tell me. Tell me now. What … what are you *doing* here?"

He swallowed, pausing under the cloud of her hostility. But then began. And what amazed Eun-young was how this elucidation didn't come out by rote, even though he probably recited it several times a day. He told her that his grandfather had served in China for ten years during the war, but had never talked about his experiences. One day, when Sokasu was still quite young, he found a box of his grandfather's old army mementos, and inside was a photograph of a young Korean girl. When he asked his grandfather who she was, he replied by saying that she was a comfort woman. Sokasu didn't know what the term meant. "When I pressed Grandfather about it," he told Eun-young, "he just wanted to change the subject. He wouldn't answer any of my questions. I think he was ashamed to even —"

"Was he a *rapist*?" she barked.

"I don't know. I'll never know. He died without ever talking about it." Sokasu plugged onward. Explained how, when he was nineteen, he moved to Tokyo for university. There, he became friends with a group of Korean exchange students — and from them learned so much about his country's aggression against theirs, all the things that he had never been taught in school. "I mean, I knew nothing about Korea — other than it had been our colony. I had no idea what we had *done* here." And from these friends, Sokasu learned what the term "comfort woman" really meant. "And so I had to come," he said. "I had to see these grand-mothers for myself."

"How long have you been here?"

"Many years. I fell in love with the House immediately and started volunteering, mostly as a guide for Japanese tourists. But it took a long time for the grandmothers to accept me, to let go of their suspicions and their anger. But eventually they did. And now I work here full-time. It helps that I learned the language. I even mastered a number of Korea's rural dialects."

She felt herself soften towards him. "I noticed," she said,

nodding to the place where he had stood with the girl. "That must have been difficult. You speak very good Korean."

"Thank you. It was hard. It took me years. But worth it. It allows me to be here, in this place, fully. It lets me be a part of the House."

"Why do you do it?"

"Why do you think?" He looked so intently at her. "I am not guilty of anything; but I am still responsible." He tilted his head at her. "And what brings you here today?"

Eun-young gazed absently at all the photos mounted on the walls around them, and the wattle on her neck began to tremble. To speak these words. This admission that she could not even speak to her own husband. This confession that rang of shame throughout her family. The disgrace that she brought to everything she touched.

"I was one of these women," she creaked. When she looked back at Sokasu's face, he was nodding; but there was something else there, just the slightest hint, barely noticeable, of incredulity. A reflex, perhaps. So she repeated her sentence, this time in flawless Japanese. "I was one of these women, young man." His face grew dark. "That's right," she said to him. "You chose to learn my language. But they *forced* me to learn yours."

His disbelief fluttered away like a bird, and he raised his face to her. "What's your name?"

"Eun-young."

"It's nice to meet you, Eun-young," he said. "What was your Japanese name?"

"Meiko."

"Where did they take you?"

"To Manchuguo. I was there from early '43 until the end of the war."

He gestured to her face. "And that scar over your lip?"

"A soldier cut me with his sword when I refused him."

Sokasu moistened his own lips. "Eun-young, would you like to meet some of the other grandmothers?"

She looked at the floor, her voice tremulous again. "I don't know."

He smiled calmly. "Well, come on. Let me take you on the tour, and maybe we'll run into some of them."

She liked the art gallery best. Most of the paintings were quite crude, like children's drawings, but some did show a surprising artfulness. Eun-young moved from picture to picture with Sokasu standing behind her, letting her soak them in. A number of the paintings depicted the same concept: a young girl, often naked, cowering on the ground while Japanese soldiers leered over her. There were scenes of men pulling girls away; scenes of reunification with family; scenes of violence, a woman blindfolded and tied to a tree; scenes of countryside, rural villages in Korea or the scorched landscapes of wartime China. After examining each sketch, Eun-young let her eyes fall to the title printed on the small placard underneath. "Where did my youth go?" "Deprived purity." "Chosun Girl Dragged Away."

"We don't tell the grandmothers what to paint," Sokasu explained from behind her. "And obviously, we never judge what they do. This is all about their healing. We encourage them to express their feelings, their memories, in any way they like. And we exhibit their works here so guests can see those things in their rawest form." He waited a bit for her to respond, and when she didn't, asked: "What do you think, Eun-young?"

"I am a little surprised."

"By what?"

"I am surprised there isn't more anger here." She motioned in the general direction of the wall. "I mean, some of these are actually quite cheerful. I'm surprised that a few of the women found something nice to paint about."

"Can I ask: what would *you* paint about, if you attended one of our art therapy sessions?"

Eun-young thought about it. "I would paint a picture of my own legs."

"Really?"

She nodded and turned to him. "I am not going to *show* you, obviously, but I have scars on my legs that are far worse than the one on my face. The soldier who cut me here," and she ran a crooked finger across her lip, "was an exception. Most of the men, if I refused them, took out their frustrations on my legs. They burned me with their cigarettes or the hot poker from the fire, or they cut me with their bayonets. I thought this was ironic, since the men all agreed that I had very attractive legs; the sight of them naked always drove the soldiers wild." She turned away from him. "It struck me as such a *Japanese* thing to do: to vandalize that which they found beautiful." Sokasu said nothing, so she went on. "Each scar on my legs is a symbol of my resistance. So I would choose to paint them."

Soon they found their way outside to explore the gardens that peppered the compound's property. There were rows of cabbages and radish, bushes of carrots and bean sprout. As they walked among the leafy lines, Sokasu explained how gardening was one of the women's favourite hobbies. As they came around a corner, they saw a grandmother come down the stairs from one of the dormitories carrying a jug of water. She was a bit hunched, but her face was full of mirth. She approached her row of cabbages and began splashing their leaves with the water. She was singing, happily, an old Korean folk tune.

"Would you like to meet her?" Sokasu asked Eun-young.

She hesitated but then said: "Okay."

They went over and the old woman looked up from her work. Her face bent into a grin when she saw Sokasu, her eyes vanishing into her wrinkles.

"Good afternoon, Soon-neuh."

"Good afternoon, Sokasu," she replied, then waved at her cabbages. "I thought I'd come out and give them one last drink before we uproot them for the winter. This crop isn't nearly as good as last year's."

"Soon-neuh, I would like you to meet someone. This is Eun-young."

The old woman bowed. "It's nice to meet you."

"Likewise," Eun-young replied. "I recognize your name. I saw one of your paintings in the art gallery, didn't I?"

"You did. It's called 'Waiting for Rescue.' I'm a regular Picasso around here. That piece is Sokasu's favourite. Isn't it, boy? Don't be shy — tell her how brilliant I am."

He blushed, but then motioned to their guest. "Soon-neuh, this is Eun-young's first time to the House." He hesitated. "She's been wanting to visit us for years."

It was as if they spoke a code to one another. Soon-neuh looked Eun-young up and down, her old-woman eyes flooding with knowledge. "You're one of us, aren't you?"

"I … I am, yes."

"I can tell. Even if you didn't have this," and she tapped at her own mouth with her finger, "I could tell. You have the look. You carry the spirit of our suffering on your shoulders."

"How long have you been a resident here, Soon-neuh?"

"Six years," she said cheerily. "Six years in March."

"Do you like it?"

"I *love* my life here. It's so tranquil and full of camaraderie. Believe me when I say, there is no better place in the world for women like us to be." She set her water jug down. "Tell me, Eun-young, where did the Japanese take you?"

"Manchuguo. And you?"

"Thailand for a while, then Indonesia. I stayed there after the war, for decades. I didn't move back to Korea until the early 1990s."

"When Kim Hak Soon came forward?"

"Yes, exactly." She motioned to Sokasu. "Of course if you want my story, you're better off asking *him*. He has such a good memory for details. Some days, he tells my story better than I do." She grabbed his chin and gave it a motherly shake. "He's such a good boy."

"I still find it hard to believe," Eun-young said, "that you trust a Japanese man with your stories."

"Well, we do. Unlike the grandmothers, Sokasu never gets tired of describing what happened to us. Tour after tour, visitor after visitor, he gladly recounts our ordeals from memory. And he never makes a mistake. *Never.* So we trust our experiences to him." She paused. "And what about you, Eun-young? What are your experiences?"

"I … I don't know where to begin. I have so many memories. But they feel as stale as bread now — like I've kept them inside for so long that they've lost their flavour."

"Don't be silly," Soon-neuh said. "Just speak the first thing that comes to you. What do you remember most?"

"I remember … I remember my *unni*. I had an *unni* for a while in the camps."

Sokasu furrowed his brow. "*Unni*? You had a *sister* in the camps?"

Soon-neuh laughed and seized him again by the chin. "Ah, so

your Korean is not so perfect, after all. Of course I joke, Sokasu. You wouldn't know this. Here, we mean *unni* as an older female friend. *Like* a sister who takes care of us." She turned to Eun-young. "You were very lucky to have had an *unni* in the camps."

"I was. Natsuki helped keep me alive, and gave me hope."

"Whatever became of her?" Sokasu asked.

"They tied her upside down in a tree and dismembered her. For speaking Korean. They made us all come out into the yard to watch."

Sokasu and Soon-neuh lowered their heads.

Eun-young ran her tongue over her cleft lip. "That doesn't seem so stale after all."

Soon-neuh touched her hand. "Eun-young, have you thought about moving out here with us?"

"I don't know."

"Well think about it. Your memories are no use to anyone where they are now — languishing in your heart. If you wish to give your stories to the world, then rest assured that you can do it best here. You can trust the House with them. We all trust the House with them." She shrugged. "Who knows. This time next year, you could be out here with me scowling over another pathetic crop."

Both Sokasu and Soon-neuh stared at her, waiting for her to speak, to smile. But she didn't. She just glanced absently at the row of vegetables.

"Think about it," Soon-neuh said again. Then she turned to Sokasu. "And *you*," she said, seizing his face once more. "Don't think I've forgotten. We still need to find you a *girlfriend*, you know."

They moved back inside, Sokasu and Eun-young, standing just outside the Room of Proof. A tour bus had arrived while they were in the gardens, and the tourists were now moving around the walls of the room, looking pensively at the mounted photos there.

"I don't want to go back in," Eun-young said. "I, I don't want those people thinking I am a resident here. I'm not ready for that."

"It's okay," Sokasu said. "There is another place I want to show you, anyway, but I'm not sure if I should."

"What is it?"

"It's in the basement. It's called the Room of Experience."

"Ah yes." She raised one of the brochures in her hand. "It's listed here."

"It is. Do you wish to see it? You don't have to if you don't want."

"No, take me down there. Let's go, before these tourists find it."

So they moved down the winding staircase and into the dark, moist basement. The floor beneath their feet was stone tile over cold earth. Sokasu went first down the lit hallway with Eun-young trailing behind him on her cane. By the time he reached the doorway with the curtain over it, she was a few yards back and had paused in the hall. He turned and looked back at her.

"I'm sorry," she called out.

"It's okay. Take your time."

Finally she walked forward and he pulled the curtain back for her as she arrived at the door. Eun-young paused, then stepped over the threshold and into the room. Her eyes moved from floor to wall to ceiling.

Sokasu stood behind her. "We tried to replicate it as best we could, but it wasn't easy. They weren't all the same, of course. Some were just holes in the wall. Others were almost like proper bedrooms. But this a composite. A composite replica of what we know."

Eun-young looked around again. The room was stark, its walls a bare wood tacked against the House's cement foundation. In the far left-hand corner lay a tatami mat. It was authentic but looked too smooth, too neat. Had clearly never been used for anything. At the foot of the mat was a small chest of drawers with a stack of tickets on top. The tickets were preposterously inaccurate — the kind of stubs one might receive at an amusement park in Seoul. In the other corner was a small pile of dishes. Again, relatively authentic, but looking unused.

"What do you think, Eun-young?" Sokasu asked. "I mean, the rooms were never this large; we probably widened this to accommodate tourists. But I still think —"

"There's no detritus," she said.

"I'm sorry?"

She waved her hand vaguely at the floor. "It's too clean. The stalls had debris everywhere. Broken bowls, used condoms, cigarette butts, mud that the soldiers had tracked in on their boots. That's what I remember: the stalls were always so filthy. This, this place is far too clean."

He swallowed. "Well, it *is* for tourists."

Eun-young turned then and reached out behind Sokasu for the thick canvas curtain that hung over the door. She seized it in her wrinkled fist and gave it a quick, sturdy tug to open it. The sound filled the room. "Now *that's* what I remember," she said. "Do you hear that?" And she snapped the curtain again. "Do you hear it? That snap? That *SNAP*?" She snapped it again. "Now *that* is accurate. The noise of the curtain being *SNAPPED* open. Whenever I heard that sound, I knew I was about to be raped."

Sokasu nodded, but then took her wrist in his hand and led it away from the curtain so she wouldn't do it again.

• • • • • • • • • • • • • • • •

They were back outside, on the grounds of the compound. The wind had picked up and the temperature had dropped. Just beyond where they sat on a bench, a sculpture of an old woman, faded and green, rose out of the ground, cut off at the waist. She was naked, breasts sagging, and face marred by wrinkles. Her spindly arms were grabbing hold of the soil around her, as if she were pulling herself up from a drawn bath.

"Eun-young, you know what I'm about to ask you," Sokasu said.

"So go on and ask."

"Would you consider moving down here, to join us in the House? We do have room. One of the grandmothers passed away about two months ago. There is a space in the dormitory for you, if you want it."

She gazed out past the sculpture to the edge of forest beyond the House's property. It was a copse of gingko trees, their sturdy branches stretching to the sky.

"I don't know what kind of setup you have in Seoul," he went on, "but down here you would be —"

"I don't have much of a *setup*," she cut him off. "I've lived alone for the last forty years — in a damp basement apartment. I have family, but I'm not really a part of their lives. I live on the edge of their existence, with my memories and my shame."

"All the more reason you should be down here. There is no shame in this place, Eun-young. We *renounce* shame. And your memories would be put to good use by the House. Believe me. Your memories would not languish as they have."

"Better not to have memories at all."

"But you *do* have them," he said. "So why keep them in a basement apartment, rotting and fading away until you die and leave the world ignorant of your story?"

All I ever wanted was to die. I've been waiting to die ever since I was fifteen. I've been waiting for the spirit to come and carry me away from all this noise, to a place of perfect serenity.

It was as if he had read her mind. "There is no place as tranquil as this one," he said.

She turned on the bench and looked at him.

"Eun-young, you will find a peace here that you've never known. There is no place on Earth as peaceful as this one."

"On Earth," she said.

"I'm sorry?"

"On Earth. No place on Earth."

He stammered. "That's right. You … you shouldn't have to wait until you die to find the peace you seek."

She turned back, stared hard into the copse of trees, their branches so much like old arthritic limbs. A swallow took flight from one of them and fluttered around in the sky before landing on another.

"I'm going to leave now," Eun-young said.

"Okay. But promise me that you'll think about it, and that you'll be in touch with us."

But she didn't answer him. She rose from the bench and planted her cane firmly into the grass.

"Eun-young, shall I call you a taxi?"

She said nothing.

"Eun-young, do you want a taxi?"

But she didn't respond. Sokasu sat on the bench and watched her hobble off, past the sculpture and toward the trees — unaware of what she was doing, and what she wanted.

Eun-young didn't look back. She headed for the forest, to be there among the trees and their limbs, their birds taking flight. She went into the woods to feel the Earth stop beneath her feet.

She went into the forest to be alone with the silence.

ACKNOWLEDGEMENTS

This novel owes a huge debt to a number of books on the subject of Korean comfort women that came before it. Nonfiction titles that helped with research and inspiration include: *Comfort Women Speak: Testimony by Sex Slaves of the Japanese Military*, edited by Sangmie Choi Schellstede and contemporary photographs by Soon Mi Yu; *Silence Broken: Korean Comfort Women*, by Dai Sil Kim-Gibson; *Japan's Comfort Women: Sexual Slavery and Prostitution During World War II and the US Occupation*, by Yuki Tanaka; and *Comfort Women: Sexual Slavery in the Japanese Military during World War II*, by Yoshimi Yoshiaki. Works of fiction include: *The Tent of Orange Mist*, by Paul West; *A Gesture Life*, by Chang-rae Lee; *Comfort Woman*, by Nora Okja Keller; and *A Gift of the Emperor*, by Therese Park.

Thanks to my first readers: Nathan Dueck, Peter Saunders, Art Moore (to whom this book is dedicated) and especially my wife Rebecca, whose insights into and edits on the manuscript proved invaluable.

A special thanks to Jin Kyu (Justin) Kim, who helped me immeasurably with various aspects of Korean spelling, culture and tradition in the book.

Thanks, as always, to my family for their support over what was an extremely difficult writing process.

An excerpt of *Sad Peninsula* appeared in the Spring 2011 issue of the online literary journal *The Quint*. Thanks to editor and friend Yvonne Trainer for accepting it.

And thanks to Shannon Whibbs and everyone at Dundurn for the opportunity.